Ke 

Presents

Carnival of Horror

Story selection & formatting by Kevin J. Kennedy

Edited by Brandy Yassa

Cover art by by Bill Stewart

Full wrap cover design by Michael Bray

First Printing, 2018

Table of Contents

Wobbly Bob
By
David J. Fielding

Wobbly Bob sat on the back of the big painted wagon, all by his lonesome, gazing at the lights of the city that shone in the darkness.

The lights weren't that far off; not over four, maybe five, miles across the scrub and flat of the Texas landscape.

Even though the tiny points glinting on the horizon were only a half-hour's ride distant, right now they seemed more than a world away to Bob.

The night air was bracing. The last gasps of winter had still been leaving frost on the ground in these middle days of March, but Bob didn't mind. He had always preferred cooler weather to the blistering heat that came with the summers in this part of the country, and this chill was a welcome one. So, he sat there in the cool night air, with his plate of Ma Macabre's day-old beans on his lap and tin mug of hot black coffee in hand, and just watched the distant lights of the city twinkle and shine.

Bob had never been in a city, but he'd seen many of them from a distance, and this one, Austin, was bigger than most. He'd heard from some of the others what cities were like... a mix of excitement and noise, not unlike the carnival itself on a Saturday night, only so much bigger.

Bob let out a sigh, and his gaze shifted from the glow of the few electric and gaslight lamps of the city, as his attention turned skyward, to the flickering belts and clouds of stars splashed across the black night sky. Bob had as much a chance of visiting the pin-pricks of light swirling overhead as he did in Kansas City, New Orleans or Austin. And each time the wagons found their place on the outskirts of such a place, Bob's thoughts always seemed to turn on the same subject. Cities invariably conjured up a feeling for Bob that was a mix of both sadness and a sense of relief.

The part of him that wanted, just once, to experience what it would be like to walk a city's streets, that was the sad part. Bob knew he'd most likely never get to clomp along the boards outside a livery, or look into shop windows, or to smoke a cigar outside a saloon. Because someone like Bob just didn't belong in such an environment.

Wobbly Bob wasn't welcome there, never would be; he was just too *odd*, too misshapen.

Bob took a sip of the hot coffee, enjoying the quiet of the night and the low hubbub of the others gathered around the camp's fire forty yards behind him.

Yet even if part of him was sad at the thought of not getting to ride into Austin with Mr. Kincaid, there was that another part of him, a larger part, which was glad he couldn't go. The thought of crowds and the crush of horses and wagons would have just made Bob feel closed-in and more than a bit afraid.

Bob wasn't a sizeable creature; he was no taller than your average ten-year-old human child. And so, getting knocked to the ground and trampled by hooves had been, and always would be, a source of concern.

No, thought Bob, it was much better here, with his friends, on the outskirts; rather than amid the crush of strangers and the hustle and bustle of the city, of that he was quite sure.

Besides, Wobbly Bob had other things to worry about.

For one, all the chores that would soon need tending to... *Kincaid's Traveling Cavalcade of Phantasmical Wonders* would set up for business in the early hours tomorrow, and that meant Bob and everyone else would be pounding stakes, pitching tents, spreading hay, stringing banners and many back-breaking tasks. All of which had to be taken care of, and the exhibits and acts ready to go by the time the sun set, so they could greet and entertain the throngs they hoped would come see the bizarre oddities, exhibits, and most of all, the freaks, of Kincaid's Cavalcade.

Mr. Kincaid had been walking around earlier in the evening boasting that the crowds from Austin would be the best they'd had in months.

"Why, you wait and see, my friends! This here's the capitol of the state, ya see? Lots of folks with extra cash to spend, lots of fine ladies looking for a good scare or two, and their gents all too willing to pay for it. They may have seen some fancy opera singers, or they may have seen some dramatic acting on Millet's grand stage at the Opera House; heck, they may have even seen Lillie

Langtry herself, *Stoopin' to Conquer*, or had themselves a velocipede race or three... but in this here year of 1886, ain't none of 'em seen the likes of you!"

And even though the majority of the folks in the camp had grudgingly agreed with the hyperbolic owner, Bob wasn't so sure. He'd wanted to say as much to Mr. Kincaid, before the owner had climbed up on his horse and took off for the city and the stunning red, orange, purple and yellow light of the western horizon, but he didn't. Kincaid wouldn't have listened to him anyway—he never did.

There was something different in the air, something that Bob thought Kincaid should know about before they played this city.

But what that something was, Bob couldn't say. He couldn't put a finger on it.

Bob was also well aware that the Cavalcade – and Mr. Kincaid himself – needed this show to be a good one.

Kincaid's coffers were all but empty, and like every other one of the people that worked for him, Bob had a couple of I.O.U.'s in his back pocket that supposedly covered his last two months wages.

The key word was *supposedly*. Bob may have been small and warped in stature, but he was no dimwit. He knew the longer it took Kincaid to make up for expenses, the longer it would take before any of them saw or felt silver coins in their hands.

Why the upkeep on the horses and other animals alone was enough to eat up what little petty cash there was in the till. And replenishing that, plus payouts for paints, flyers, and six dozen other things that were needed to run the carnival, all of that would push back payment of IOU's and everything else.

Supplies and stores were running mighty low, and the last four days on the trail had been nothing but beans and coffee; which led to a lot of grumbling among the other carnies and performers.

Most were thinking about seeking work elsewhere. Becky the Selkie had even threatened to have her tank and wagon hitched to the next train to San Francisco, where she could find a spot at *Lwelleyn's Marine Marvels and Aquatic*

Oddities, that city's permanent exhibition at the pier.

"Oh, it would be so nice," she'd cooed in her lisping drawl, "to be close to the sea again."

"No more bumpy trail ruts and dust, no more tramping from town to town," she had sighed, floating in her giant glass tank, filled with 5,000 gallons of water and decorated by picturesque images of seahorses, fake sea plants and a columned archway from long-lost, sunken Atlantis.

Bob had tried to sympathize with her as he tossed the few scrawny catfish into the tank, but despondent, Becky had just wrinkled her nose at the limp and tasteless things, then snatched them between her needle-sharp teeth and swam down into the dark corner to eat in peace and silence.

Bob couldn't blame her. Lanky Pete had been disappointed with the fish, too, when he had pulled them from the muddy waters of some lake three days behind them now.

"Phhfff. These ain't fit to throw to a dog, sad to say," Lanky had rumbled in disgust.

But the drudgery of setting up for business, the nagging worries about finances and his concern for Becky weren't the thing nagging at his mind, sitting here on the back of the wagon and staring out at the lights of distant Austin.

No, it was something else. Something intangible, something Bob didn't quite understand. But it was out there; hidden in the dark places in the alleyways and side streets, where the gaslight lamps and incandescent electric bulbs of Austin couldn't penetrate, something lying in wait in the chill of this March evening.

Bob looked down at his plate of beans.

He hadn't been very hungry before and seeing the cold, dark stuff congealing on his plate, glistening in the flickering light, just drove the last of his appetite into the dirt.

Looking about, making sure that Ma couldn't see from where she was sitting with the others near the big fire, Bob got up off of his seat on the wagon steps, and, moving into the deeper shadows around the other side, dumped the beans onto the ground. Then with his giant foot, he kicked earth and sand over them, burying them so no one could see.

Bob then turned and clumped back toward the chow wagon.

He lurched from side to side, in a gait familiar to those in the Cavalcade, but if observed by a stranger or carnival visitor, would have been described as eerie, unnatural, or perhaps gut-wrenching and horrifying.

There were always those who, when catching sight of Wobbly Bob, would recoil in disgust or loathing. The majority of the folks in Kincaid's sideshow were ugly to be sure, but they also could use bits of clothing or a hat to hide what made them different. Not so with Bob. Because, compared to everyone else, Bob didn't look that human at all. At first glance, what caught everyone's eye was Bob's gigantic right foot. It dominated that side of his body, dwarfing all the other normal parts, and it was the cause of his lurching, unstable gait. The size of it would look more appropriate on some huge, sculpted statue or a Roman monument. Almost the entirety of Bob's right side of his body showed off the enormity of this grotesquery: the bulbous toes with strands of wire-hard hair and yellow and cracked nails, the blotchy skin, the rough and calloused heel.

Near the top of his chest, just below the collar bone, was where the abnormal appendage stopped and the ordinary part of Bob's right side continued. The giant foot and leg tapered to a regular (or almost regular) size at his hip. He had a hip, just like any normal person; it was just not in the right spot. Most would never see it, covered as it was it by special shirts that Bob wore, shirts made by a seamstress friend of Mr. Kincaid. What you couldn't see under those shirts was this: Bob's upper thigh and hip on his right side were fused up into his chest cavity.

A doctor had examined Bob a few years back and had marveled at how the bones had been uniquely molded and was fascinated that they didn't seem to cause Bob any discomfort. All of Bob's inner organs were squeezed over onto the left side of his chest and belly, and, as far as the doctor – and anyone else for that matter – could tell, appeared perfectly normal. He had all the regular functioning equipment and was a bright, witty and soft-hearted soul. His face wasn't unhandsome; it's just that with his deviant features, people tended not to look close enough to notice.

Wobbly Bob waddled over toward the half barrel full of suds that the chow crew had set out for the dirty dishes. His big right foot had just clomped down inside the ring of light cast by the campfire when he heard the rushing clop of hoof beats behind him.

Bob turned to see Mr. Kincaid dropping off of his blue roan, then walking her into camp and over to his personal wagon. All the other folks were still up and gathered around the fire finishing their meals. They watched, too, as the Cavalcade's owner tied his mare up, then stood stock still for a moment before turning to face them.

The man looked different from his regular boastful self; Bob thought, he seemed... smaller somehow.

Kincaid strode toward the fire, opening his mouth to speak, but the thundering of other horses charging toward the collection of wagons and tents drowned out anything he might've said to them. All eyes turned to the five men on horseback who appeared out of the dark and pulled their mounts up hard at the edge of the camp. All of them had glints of star-shaped silver on their chests, gun belts and two of them had rifles out.

Most everyone was up and on the other side of the fire now, putting something between themselves and these men from the city.

"Now, Sergeant," Mr. Kincaid said in a placating tone, walking towards the men on the horses, his hands raised. "I thought we'd agreed you'd let me talk first before barrelling in and scaring everyone half to death."

A tall man, with a dark mustache and dark eyes, urged his horse forward and then spat into the dry earth.

"Yeah, well," the man growled. "I thought it better if I just cut to the chase."

The big lawman slapped the reins on the flank of his big black mount, urging it several steps toward the fire, letting the light and heat wash over him and giving all the members of the Cavalcade a good view of his height and face. He was tall, broad shouldered and didn't look friendly at all. He had one hand on the butt of big Colt, and it was obvious he had no qualms about using it.

"My name's Chenneville," he barked across the flames. "John Chenneville. I represent the law here in Austin. And these stumblebums behind me, they do, too."

There were a few snickers from the men on the horses. But, if it was a joke, it didn't seem that funny to Bob and the other freaks. Mr. Kincaid was white as a sheet.

"Now, we're really not here to frighten any of you... uh," Chenneville allowed his eyes to flick over every one of the people standing across from him, "... folks."

Bob couldn't pick up what the other four horsemen were whispering to one another behind the big lawman, but he could imagine. Growing up as he had and traveling on the circuit had exposed him to the worst that people could say about him and his friends. He was all too familiar with the sneering laughs, the derisive looks, the hateful words.

"What I am here to say is that, we've had some real nasty business befall us of late," Chenneville continued. "And we're real suspicious of just about everyone; strangers, drifters, and especially those that frequent the dark."

"Uh, what the good sergeant is trying to say," Kincaid stepped in, "is that the city has had several gruesome deaths… ah, murders if you will…"

"Now, after the fuss you made when we rode in here, who's the one doin' the scarin', mister?" Chenneville growled.

Kincaid seemed to shrink in on himself.

"But yes, yer boss here is right. We have had several women attacked and killed during this last year of '85: first one on about New Year's twelve months past, and the last two, three months ago, this Christmas Eve. First, they was killin' servant girls, but this last time, they claimed two whites. Someone, some fiend… has been killin' in the dark. No one's seen him, no one's caught him. Those witnesses that caught glimpses of the killer all give different accounts, and we don't got a clear picture of who he is, or what he looks like. Some say he's white, some say black, some say fat, some say thin as a rail. Could be tall, short, wide; truth is, with all the infuriatin' different descriptions … well, he – or it—could be just about anyone. And, folks have been pretty much in a frenzy about it, as you can imagine."

Everyone around the campfire was silent.

"These here killings have been spread out, over the weeks and months of the year. Ain't no pattern to 'em—ain't no rhyme or reason, neither. They is just cold, brutal killin's, and the only motive we know of is bloodlust."

Chenneville glared through the flames at them and the men behind him on horseback looked grim and dangerous in the flickering orange glow.

Wobbly Bob was thinking about Becky.

She was vulnerable alone in her tank, nowhere to run to, nowhere to hide if someone with dark intentions slipped under the tent flaps late at night and then into the water with her, bearing a knife. Bob shook the ugly thought from his head.

"Are you accusin' us of something, mister?" Ma Macabre threw back at Chenneville. "'Cause, we rolled to a stop not more'n six hours ago. I bet anyone yer deputies there done seen us take the trail round from the West and South."

Ma was a grizzled old cuss, eighty if she was a day, corncob pipe clamped between her teeth and a few wisps of grey hair clinging to her knobby bald head. One of her eyes was twice the size of the other and her skin was the color of tanned leather.

She was the least odd looking of all those who performed with or who called the Cavalcade their home. Next to Flat Jack or Sammy Split-in-Three, or even Bob himself, if you saw just a glimpse of her, you would think she was just your average old, wrinkled-as-a-dried-apple grandmother. But when she got her dander up, like at this moment for instance, then she was a frightening sight, indeed.

For what gave Ma her name, what made her macabre, were the striped quills jutting out from her forearms, shoulders and the back of her neck; quills that Ma had had sewn into her skin, quills that were quivering with protective anger.

“Good thing ol’ Ben Thompson ain’t ‘round no more,” the voice of one of the deputies floated over the crowd. “He’d done most likely handled this little band of misshapen devils with a volley of hot lead and slug o’ rye.”

This horseman followed it up with a high-pitched laugh, looking at his fellows for agreement, while murmurs of fear ran through the ranks of Bob's friends.

"Lyle," growled Chenneville, glancing back over his shoulder, "we all know you was sweet on Ben, but for this once, keep yer yap shut."

At that, a loud guffawing started among the other deputies and the one called Lyle hollered at them to close their own traps or he'd see to it that their laughing would be the last thing they ever heard. He said it in a language that was a lot bluer than Bob had heard in a long while.

"Stick a cork in it, Lyle," one of the shadowy deputies barked. "You ain't shot your pistol in six months, let alone checked to see if the damn thing is even loaded."

"ALL RIGHT!" bellowed Chenneville. "All of ya! Shut yer damn mouths!"

The deputies fell silent. Chenneville hadn't taken his eyes off the crowd gathered before him. He spat into the dirt, and then answered Ma's question.

"To start with, I ain't accusin' ya of something," the big sergeant said. "Not yet."

"Now, while it might be true that one or maybe even a few of these boys here might've seen you take the south road 'round the city to this here spot," Chenneville said, leaning forward on his saddle, looking Ma right in the eyes, "and while it may be true that ain't none of ya, 'cept for Kincaid here, done set foot inside the city limits, that don't give none of ya a free pass. And even if it is true that ain't none of you here got reason to carry any guilt over the deaths of the women been murdered here, that don't mean one, if not more of ya, don't, neither."

Chenneville leaned forward in the saddle, eyes shining in the firelight.

"See, what I do know to be true, is that this here traveling freak show has been making the rounds in the central part of our good state for almost the whole year. You entered the great state of Texas on January 9th, having just left the confines of Louisiana a week before, the rodeo grounds in Alexandria to be exact. And once you crossed into Texas, y'all made your way to the city of Jasper, where you stayed four days."

Chenneville held up a familiar looking leather ledger.

"It's all here, written down, nice and legibly by Mr. Kincaid. I do like me a man who keeps a good record of his accounts. Makes me think that man is an honest man, trustworthy you might say; one who keeps things above board. Tells me they got nothing hide."

"Now, sergeant," Kincaid chuckled, "I'm just your average, normal business man. Record keeping is all part of..."

"Jury's still out on whether or not any of us consider you normal, Kincaid," Chennevville growled. "Maybe you just look that way. You own and run this band of freaks, and after the year we've had, me and my boys know how easy it is for evil to hide in plain sight."

The members of the Cavalcade murmured and sifted their feet. Chenneville's free hand was on the butt of his pistol.

The murmuring and shifting stopped.

"Let's get back to your travels," Chenneville turned a page in the ledger. "After Jasper you headed north to Paris, where you stayed another four days, made your way west to Ft. Worth, then made several other stops in your way cross the New Mexico border.

"You were five days in Lincoln then crossed back over to stay three more in Midland before making yer way down to Ft. Stockton, where it says you were ‘unfairly and unduly harassed and belittled by the soldiers there’,” Chennevile paused before adding, “No doubt with cause…”

The big lawman flipped through several more pages of Kincaid’s ledger.

“From there you stopped at Painted Spring, then Kerrville, Seguin, Le Grange, back up to Belton then Llano, Menardville and Fredricksburg… I could go on, but what this here ledger tells me is that your little band has been circling our fair city for the better part of this year.”

“And?” Ma spoke up. “What’s yer meanin’?”

“My meaning is, if there is a cold-blooded, night-prowlin’ killer among you, you weren’t more ‘n two, three days ride at anytime from the city of Austin. And see’n how’s you are always on the move, that same killer would’ve found it easy to slip away from the caravan when you are on the trail.”

“Wouldn’t have anything to do with the fact that we’re… different,” Big Billy Behemoth, the six-hundred-pound strong man interjected. “Right?”

Chenneville glared at the members of the cavalcade.

"It's got everything to do with you bein' different," he snarled.

"Now, Sergeant," Kincaid took a step toward the man's horse. "I assure you that though my friends and colleagues…"

Chenneville's gun was in his hand and pointed toward Kincaid in a flicker of light and speed. Kincaid stopped, mouth open, arms and hands flying up into the air.

All the horsemen behind Chenneville followed suit, guns cocked and aimed at the crowd on the other side of the cook fire.

"We got no proof and we got no cause to haul a single one of you to the calaboose," Chenneville's voice was ragged with meanness. "But believe me we're lookin' for one."

He walked the horse forward a few steps.

"Listen up. We don't want you here. No need for you to make camp or unpack any of your freakshow stuff here, or fifty miles from here or in this whole damn state as far as we're concerned. You just keep movin' on down the trail. As far from here as you can get and don't ever think about making a return to the city of Austin."

He let the words sink in.

"Do I make myself understood?"

Chenneville wheeled his horse round to face a frightened Kincaid.

"Come sun up, you better have this whole caravan headed east away from here. Otherwise, there will be some dark deeds done. Get gone. And don't come back."

With that, the lawman and his posse left the camp… the clattering sound of hoof beats, ugly curses and parting insults filling the late air.

Kincaid turned to the crowd of distorted and odd-looking people that made up his traveling sideshow. His face held an expression of shock and dismay, they all knew what this meant in terms of finances and this sour turn would likely mean the death of Kincaid's Cavalcade.

"My… my friends…," Kincaid stammered.

"Save it," Lanky Pete said, stepping to the forefront of his fellows. "We all know this ain't your doin', but we also know it means we are done for. Chances are the law is gonna cable all

Bob's voice sounded small and weak in the lightless confines of the tent.

"No one," a whispered voice said. "No one at all."

Bob jumped in fright as a dark shape separated itself from the deeper dark near the back of the tent. One moment the corner was just pure black, the next it became something else.

"You'll do," the voice said. It was slippery sounding, low and menacing.

The shadowy shroud of a figure had pulled away from the inky dark corner and moved up to him, sliding across the space as fast as a desert rattler, but oh-so-silent and much, much more menacing. The man was tall, rail thin, almost skeletal. A freak, like the others out by the fire.

Bob looked up into the thing's yellow eyes as it towered over him.

"You don't know me, do you?" the shape asked.

Bob tried to answer, but his tongue and throat were dry with fear.

"Oh, I'm sure you do, though. How could you not? I've been among you before, in one fashion or another. You might have a memory of the

Contortionist, or perhaps Rubber-face, or Limber Lionel, the Knuckle-Cracker, even Ripper Jack... but never the same name twice, never the same face. My talent you could say, like quills or a fish's tail, or an over developed appendage..."

"I've been living among the citizens of Austin, all year long, in one guise or another. Playing I was one of them—a cook one week, a chicken thief the next, sometimes even a lawman. Not one of them ever figured it out, not one of them ever came close to catching me, because all of them are stupid and weak. But, the time has come for me to move on. I've learned so much and have so much more work to do."

Bob tried to turn, but cold, shadowy, claw-like fingers reached out and gripped him by the shoulders.

"You are an ugly, awful looking thing," the frightening shadow said. "But then again, it'll be so much easier to twist myself into something that resembles you, to throw them off the scent. Yes, you'll do. You'll do just fine."

The shadow did something then... something Bob didn't quite understand—couldn't fathom. Bob thought he heard the cracking and snapping of bone, and another, stranger sound—not unlike the sound of a hemp rope being pulled and stretched.

A flicker of steel flashed in the dim light and Bob felt a sharp and stinging pain, once, twice, three times.

Then he felt himself slipping down toward the hay-covered ground, the shadowy thin man standing over him, changing, contorting. And Bob thought, *this is what others must feel when they looked at me.*

After that, Bob felt nothing, except, maybe, just a slight 'pop' in his ears.

And then it was all over.

*****

Out by the fire, the members of Kincaid's Cavalcade were still arguing about their circumstances, debating about what to do, where to go.

"We could head north, maybe New York, Pennsylvania. Weather's cooler. I miss me a cool glass of Cider Jack," Ollie, the Three-Armed Clown offered.

"And how are we supposed to survive the journey? We got little-to-no cash, food stores are low..." was Hank, the Dog-faced Man's reply.

"Well, we gotta do something..."

More ideas came, more shouted replies of agreement or dissent.

"What about London?" a voice called from the back.

All eyes turned to look at the familiar, misshapen form of Wobbly Bob standing in the shadows near one of the wagons.

"London?" Kincaid asked, and a few other voices echoed him as well.

Another round of raised voices, questions of concern, worried grumblings.

"Can we afford it?"

"There's just enough in the till for passage on a freighter out of Corpus." Bob's voice floated through the crowd. His tone was compelling and spoken with the hint of a smile. "We could work crew jobs, perform for the passengers... and no one in Europe knows us, has never seen the likes of us... right Mr. Kincaid?"

"London, you say?"

"Yeah, sure," replied Bob's shadow. "I think we could make a killing there."

The End

Mister Weasels and the Cosmic Carnival
By
H.R. Boldwood

Mister Weasels smiled when he saw the first bud of spring peeking through the soil of Pikeville. Then he squashed it with the toe of his big floppy shoe. Death and spring. Damned if that didn't put a song in his moldering heart.

At six-foot-five, the clown cut an imposing figure. Scraggly puffs of bright orange hair on the sides of his head framed a maniacal grease-painted face. His polka-dotted clown suit, red suspenders, and rubber chicken-catching pants would have looked benign, even beguiling on another clown. But not on Mister Weasels.

He chain-smoked Camels in the railyard, waiting for the carnies to exhume the weathered bones of the Barlowe Brothers' Carnival from their boxcar tombs. Within hours, there would be a carnival unlike any other: mystical, dreadful, and eternal. The perfect place for a demon clown to hide. And carnivals bring children—far more satisfying to squash than plants. Not to mention that eating the little shits kept him alive.

If he played his cards right, he might even get his hands on that meddlesome runt, Dewey Frick. Never had he dealt with such an irritating, persistent gnat of a child. And for Mister Weasels, who had always been, and would forever be, never was *a* very long time.

Indeed, mused the clown, *by now, Frick would be a grown man.*

"You there! *Weasels,*" called a carnie from the nearest boxcar. The roadie was short, round, and disheveled with three days' stubble and random wisps of hair jutting out from his otherwise bald head. Mister Weasels had no idea who the man was, but then, he couldn't be bothered with keeping track of the carnival's rank and file pissants.

"Madame Zelda wants to see you," the carnie said. "Stay put. She'll be out shortly."

Zelda was the carnival's fortune teller. Her psychic talents drew patsies to the midway like moths to a flame. Frozen cross-legged inside a wooden booth, she seduced the crowd with her lacquered, red come-fuck-me smile and her mysterious divinations that fluttered out on tiny scraps of paper.

Weasels turned his collar to the cool spring air and stubbed out his cigarette.

What could that bitch-in-the-box want now?

He had reason to be leery of her. He'd been the one who trapped her inside that box a few centuries earlier, give or take. But who was counting? There was room for only one Djinn in this carnival, and although her powers were strong, his were stronger. Of all the nefarious acts he'd ever committed, sealing Zelda in the box was the one that had upset Old Man Barlowe most. He'd almost exiled Weasels over the ordeal.

To her credit, Zelda had taken her confinement with dignity and refused to beg for her freedom. She was imprisoned in the box because Weasels had bested her. Proud and regal, she did her job and bided her time, prophesying that power was a crap shoot, and that someday, Weasels would roll snake-eyes.

The demon clown had laughed her off and reveled in his victory. With a tenuous truce in place and the pecking order established, Barlowe relented and allowed Weasels to stay.

Weasels thought of these things as he waited for Zelda to emerge from the boxcar, and it occurred to him that he'd made a tactical error. He should have killed the bitch when he had the chance.

The carnies wheeled Zelda, secured by a multitude of leather straps, down a ramp and dropped her in the gravel as if she were nothing more than a pinball machine. Weasels couldn't help but think of Hannibal Lector and struggled to suppress a grin.

As he reached for her power switch, the box lit up on its own. Zelda sprang to life, and her red lips curled into a snarl.

"Don't touch me."

Not wanting to antagonize her before knowing the reason for their meeting, Weasels took a step back.

"Fine, then. What do you want?"

"Love the shoes, Clown Boy. We don't go live until tomorrow." Her wooden eyes rolled. "Oh, that's right. You don't *play* Mister Weasels; you *are* Mister Weasels."

"And you're a freakin' mannequin in a box," he said with a smile that was far too wide. "What's up?"

"Dewey Frick is coming for you."

Weasels's laugh echoed through the train yard. "And how would you know that?"

"I'm in his head, Weasels—in his dreams," she whispered. "He trusts me."

"Why wouldn't he? You sided with him against me thirty years ago." Weasels cocked his head. "Why betray him now? You wouldn't shed a tear if that meddlesome brat did me in."

"You simpleton. He'll take the rest of us down with you. It would mean the end of the carnival. The end of us all."

"Only if he wins. He didn't last time." Weasels smiled, as if savoring the memory of a juicy steak. "I got his toady, Buck, didn't I?"

"But Dewey almost got *you.* He knows your weaknesses, Ezra."

Weasels flinched at the sound of his given name. "So, for the sake of the carnival, if not for me, how do we get rid of him?"

"*How,* is up to you. *Where*, I can arrange. I'll lead him to the fun house tomorrow night before the carnival begins. You can off the little shit in there."

"Let me guess. In exchange for your... assistance... you want me to set you free."

Zelda's smile was paper thin. "Once I deliver him, you let me out of this box—*before* you deal with him, or I'll whisk him away and you can watch for him over your shoulder every day for the rest of his mortal life. Agreed?"

She'd waited thirty years to play this card. That was the last time the carnival had come to Pikeville—the time he'd met Dewey Frick, the one and only bargaining chip worth her freedom.

Weasels took a bow. "Well, tou-fucking-che⍰, Zelda. Nicely played. Seems you have the leverage now. But time and tide, Zelda. The pendulum will swing this way again. You can count on it."

Zelda knew of time and tide. She'd been imprisoned in her wooden tomb for 320 years, four months, and three days. She'd taken advantage of her time in isolation by developing new and unusual talents. Talents no one else knew about. Especially Mister Weasels.

Her brain continued to evolve daily. She developed telepathy and silently communicated with the network of psychics and illusionists she called friends. She even learned how to manipulate minds. Practicing was easy, what with traveling from town to town. She picked people at random and projected the illusion of dollar bills laying at their feet. It was fun to watch the wretches scramble, only to be dismayed when the money disappeared. There were other changes, too. Her visual acuity changed hour by hour, and soon, she began to see a fourth dimension.

When the carnival pulled into Pikeville, the changes stopped. Her transmogrification—into whatever it was that she was becoming—appeared to be complete. She could see portals into the nether and beyond, and little wormholes that offered entrances to other far-away worlds.

How ironic, she thought, that she had fully *become* in Pikeville. Time and tide were about to turn.

When the time came, Zelda arrived at the fun house a little ahead of schedule and without Dewey Frick. She'd never intended for him to be there. That wasn't born of any loyalty to the kid. She'd have handed him over to Weasels in a heartbeat if it had suited her. All she needed to do was manipulate Weasels into seeing Dewey's image. Easy-peasy. Weasels would never see the rest coming.

#

Dewey Frick. Weasels licked his lips and listened to the growl in his gut. Soon. Very soon, he told himself. He arrived at the fun house a few minutes early, filled with anticipation. What would the brat look like, now? Better yet. How would he taste? Normally, a middle-aged man wouldn't provide sustenance to the demon, but Weasels had marked Dewey at the age of twelve. That made him a five-course meal, aged to perfection.

Zelda, who'd been waiting for Weasels, didn't waste time with pleasantries.

"The kid's inside the door, waiting for further instructions from me, which will of course, never arrive."

Weasels stepped around her and made for the door but was stopped in his tracks by an unseen force.

"Don't fuck with me, Zelda. You know better."

"You're not going in until you keep your part of the bargain."

"How do I know he's even in there?"

Zelda smiled. "Consider this a bonus gift." She planted a vision in Weasel's mind of a full-grown Dewey Frick standing just inside the doorway, holding a knapsack filled with hammers, stakes, and crosses.

Weasel's laughed. "What a pathetic selection of baubles and toys."

Zelda ignored him. "You have thirty seconds to get me out of this booth, or both the kid and I are gone."

"Very well," sighed Weasels. "The thrill was gone anyway." His bloodshot eyes spun round and round inside their sockets, generating beams of light that seared the hinges on Zelda's wooden booth, blasting them apart. The top to the box popped off and the sides fell to the floor. He lifted his hand, motioning for Zelda to rise. She sprang up like demented jack-in-the-box. For the first time in over 320 years, Madame Zelda was free. And Weasels couldn't have cared less. All he wanted was his pound of flesh.

"Dewey Frick. *Now.*"

"Fine," Zelda said, gazing at her arms and legs as if she'd never seen them before. "He's all yours. Just inside the door."

The loudspeakers crackled. It wouldn't be long now before the carnival opened. The song "Rocketman" blared across the midway. Weasels turned toward the fun house, then glanced back at Zelda who tossed him a wink.

"Catch you later, Ezra." She walked away, her soft soprano voice harmonizing with Elton John's. The corner of her lip curled almost imperceptibly. "Much later," she whispered. "Much, much later."

#

Weasels slipped inside the door to the fun house, hoping to take Dewey by surprise. In the dull red glow of the emergency lights, he could see Dewey far ahead, facing away from him, as if looking deeper into the darkness. Weasels had expected Dewey to look older and taller, not that he was disappointed, but in his imaginings of this long-awaited moment, he'd also expected to see Dewey's face.

And he wanted more than anything for *Dewey* to see *his* face.

Weasels tapped the bulbous toe of his shoe against the wooden floor, causing Dewey to spin around. *Was it him?* Weasels wondered. *Was it really him?* Weasels stepped forward, peering into the soft, red glow. Then the floor fell away and the unmistakable sound of Madame Zelda's laugh filled his ears.

He plummeted down through a long, narrow channel, tumbling faster and faster, until the sides of the tunnel were nothing more than a blur. His body whirled and twirled, weightless through the infinite void. At the far end of the channel he could see bits and pieces of the nether hurtling by, shapeless and gray, but as he continued to fall, the nether gave way to a spectacular array of stars.

Certain that he was about to be sucked into a bottomless black hole, he breathed a sigh of relief when the spinning stopped, and the vortex he'd been traveling through disappeared. Realizing he was no longer on planet Earth, his relief quickly faded.

The air was breathable, but he felt lightheaded, as if the oxygen level was too high. He stepped forward and found the gravitational pull was different. His feet struggled to stay on the ground.

What the fuck...

The area was cordoned off by what appeared to be a high-voltage fence. Surely, this must be some kind of intake station. A sign bolted to the fence read:

"Welcome to Bozos 4

Home of the Cosmic Carnival

Voted The Galaxy's Death Match Destination

by

Interstellar Carnival Magazine"

The conniving bitch had sent him to the Mirthoid Quadrant!!!!

Zelda would pay for this. Oh, she would pay through the nose, if she had one left by the time he was finished with her. And yet, somewhere deep inside, he was amazed. Who knew she had the stones?

His stomach rumbled. It had been over a week since he'd eaten his last meal. Children were hard to come by in the winter months. It was spring now—time for the little ones to emerge like a horde of locusts—time for him to gorge. But he didn't see any children. He shuddered to think of what could happen if he didn't feed.

People continued to arrive in much the same way he had, being spit out of wormholes. To his left, an alien creature stared at him from inside what looked like a border patrol booth.

The creature was barely five-feet tall, his flesh an arresting shade of blue. He wore a propeller beanie, a star-covered shirt, and gold lame, four-legged knickers.

His voice was small and nasally. "Welcome to The Cosmic Carnival on Bozos 4. Name?"

"Weasels."

All four of the alien's eyes swung toward him simultaneously. "That's it? No last name?"

Weasels sighed. "Oh, for god's sake." He leaned down and whispered, "Ezra Cain Weasels."

The creature nodded, four of its six claws busily stamping a multi-page, interplanetary passport. "Business or pleasure?"

"Neither. I was sent here under false pretenses." Weasels's eyes blazed. "Send me back, *now*."

The alien's snicker sounded like the call of an Aldarian loon. "Incoming clowns report to Station B." He pointed a long, blue claw toward a barbed-wire passage on his left.

Weasels didn't like the smell of things, didn't like it at all. His razor-sharp teeth descended and a growl hummed in his throat. He leaned in, nose to nose with the border agent.

"Listen, Papa Smurf. I said, send me back. *Now*."

The conversation was interrupted by two burly blue aliens. Weasels recognized them by reputation. They were members of the fabled Blue Guard, a notoriously violent security force on Bozos 4. Well over seven-feet-tall, the guards dressed in knee-length black boots and crew-necked, stretchy uniforms with insignias above the heart. Their doubled-edged Aldarian adzes had claimed many lives. They grabbed Weasels by his arms, dragged him down the barbed-wire passage, his stomach groaning loud enough to be heard.

"You wouldn't happen to have any *children* here, would you?" he whined, as they tossed him into an underground dungeon.

The dungeon was dark and dank with iridescent dirt floors and stone walls. A single torch lit a small swath of the interior. He thought he was alone, until a voice echoed in the darkness.

"Well, now. If it isn't *The* Mister Weasels. Your reputation precedes you."

A tall, goateed man emerged from the shadows from perhaps twenty feet away. He was olive skinned, with jet black hair, and sculpted arms. Naked from the waist up, he had six-pack abs and a smooth, hairless chest. He wore harem pants that tapered at the ankle, and gold pointed shoes.

Weasels' mind whirred trying to place the man, but couldn't.

"Damn straight, it does," Weasels said. "*Everyone* knows me, M.C. Hammer Daddy. Who the hell are you?"

The man bowed. "Zoltan the Magnificent, at your service."

A magician. Weasels's grease-painted lips drew into a frown. The man likely knew Zelda. Psychics, illusionists, they all hung together. An odd, chatty little group.

Zoltan continued. "My lady friend and I were on our way to Giggilon 2 yesterday from our home on Midway, and ... somehow... we arrived here. Come, come, my dear," he coaxed, waving into the darkness. "Step forward and meet Mister Weasels."

A large, hairy woman inched into the circle of light.

Zoltan swept his arm with a flourish. “Presenting, Bertha, the Bearded Lady.”

A rather large woman with a black, Duck Dynasty beard, Bertha lingered at the fringe of the light, quivering and staring at the ground.

Weasels rolled his eyes. “Imagine that. Carny freaks in jail. It’s *literally* universal.”

Zoltan’s voice took an edge. “Yuck it up, Clownie. Do you have *any* idea where we are?” Terror blazed in his eyes. “We’re on *Bozos 4*—in the *Mirthoid Quadrant.*”

The few snippets Weasels had heard about the Mirthoid Quadrant weren’t good. Stories of clowns being shanghaied to intergalactic carnivals, never to return home, and rumblings of a ruthless, interspecies slave trade. Bozos 4, a class three planet, was ruled by the Ministry of Mirth, known for their voracious thirst for blood.

But Weasels didn’t frighten easily.

"Bah! Everything I've heard about this place is rumor and speculation."

"Really? Speculate on this." Zoltan pointed to an iron gate at the far end of the dungeon. "According to the guards, that gate should be opening at any moment." His eyes grew round and wide beneath the light of the torch. "God knows what's on the other side."

The sudden screech of metal on metal brought their conversation to a close. The gate slowly rose, shuddering and groaning with every inch. The raucous chanting of a crowd bled through from the other side, growing louder and louder until the dungeon floor began to vibrate.

Despite the hunger that gnawed in Weasels's belly, he chuckled. Only one thing could frenzy a crowd like that. They wanted blood. And so, they would have it.

He glanced at the Bearded Lady, who had neither spoken nor moved since he arrived. Her lips quivered beneath her beard, causing it to twitch. A small puddle formed between her legs and began to spread. Weasels smiled. She was as good as dead. Then he turned back to Zoltan and saw the rhythmic clenching of his fists, the dead calm in his eyes, and the set of his jaw. *But this one, this one wants to live,* Weasels thought. He tightened the bulbous cherry nose prosthetic against his face and whispered, "Yeah, well. Fuck him."

Although members of the dreaded Blue Guard herded them into the stadium, Weasels needed no prodding. He sauntered into the ring and shot his middle finger high into the air, doing a 360º turn, and flipped off the entire crowd. Even as he provoked them, he was amazed at their diversity. Tartarens were socializing with Volarians, Krakenites were chatting with Gorgonians. Even the short, squat Territes with their five arms and two heads sat peacefully beside their sworn enemies, the green-skinned, twelve-eyed Dorkmongers. It wasn't their love of innocent, polka-dotted carnival clowns that united them, it was their common desire to dance with the devil—to taste of the carnage yet to come. The crowd stomped their appendages in unison, showing support for the three gladiators. And then, the dungeon gate closed behind them.

When the fight ended, only one would leave alive.

Weasels nodded to Zoltan, and held up a single finger, asking for a moment's patience. He walked to center of the arena where the sniveling Bertha had collapsed to her knees, crying, with her face buried in her hands. He reached inside her lengthy beard and tilted up her chin, then gave her the sweet, silly smile of a carnival clown and honked his big red nose. The last thing she saw was his glowing red eyes as he grasped her head between his hands and twisted it clean off her shoulders, taking her spinal column along with it. He held it high, so that the stark, white vertebrae gleamed beneath the light of the bright Mirthoid Moon. Then he threw it aside and watched it bounce willy-nilly across the ground.

The crowd leapt to its appendages and screamed for more as the rest of Bertha's body twitched and flopped on the ground like a floundering fish. Weasels took a sweeping bow, flinging her golden blood from his arms in a macabre arc. Caught up in the applause, he didn't notice Zoltan approaching from behind.

Spittle flew from Zoltan's mouth as he launched forward and tackled Weasels, pinning him on his back. Zoltan's fingers dug beneath Weasels's clown collar and squeezed his neck. Weasels's breaths came in short, ragged gasps. His eyes had begun to close, when Zoltan sneered at him and said, "I almost forget to tell you. Zelda says hello."

Fucking Zelda.

Weasels's hands sprang to life, opening and closing, his fingers clawing at the air. He forced his hand up to the chest of his clown suit and found his squirt flower. He pressed down on his suit and squeezed the flower pump, forcing the fluid to douse Zoltan's face. Weasels's eyes blazed molten red as he stared at the stream of harmless water and transformed it into sulfuric acid.

Zoltan's face began to pock, and boil, and blister. "My eyes!" he screamed. "My eyes!" He instantly released Weasels's neck, and threw himself writhing onto the floor, then scrambled blindly on all fours across the arena.

For the moment, Weasels ignored him. Turning the water into acid had used most of his energy. Eating was no longer a matter of hunger—it was a matter of survival. And not a child in sight. Desperate times called for desperate measures.

Zoltan whined, covered his face with his hands, and staggered to his feet like a drunk. He wouldn't be hard to finish off. Weasels reached down deep inside his chicken-catching pants and smiled. No one ever bothers to frisk a clown. *So many toys we carry,* he thought. Some of them meant for children. And some of them, most assuredly, *not*.

He pulled out his specially adapted rubber gun, aimed, and fired. The BANG flag, attached to the edge of a harpoon, shot through the air at Zoltan's head. But the exhausted Zoltan tripped over his own feet and fell flat on his face. The harpoon sailed harmlessly overhead.

The crowd roared and Zoltan rolled over, panicked, having no idea what caused their reaction.

Always the showman, Weasels pulled a never-ending handkerchief from his sleeve. He marched toward Zoltan, lifting his floppy clown shoes high into the air and slapping them to the ground. Then he twisted the scarf around the magician's neck and used it as a garrote to choke him. Weasels pretended to give him a big sloppy kiss on his cheek, then whispered in his ear, "Tell our good friend, Zelda, she's next." With a final twist of the scarf, came an audible *crack* as Zoltan's neck snapped.

The audience flew to its appendages, and stomped its approval, screaming, "*WEASELS! WEASELS!*"

On the verge of collapse, Weasels sank several rows of his serrated teeth into Zoltan's neck, tearing away a large chunk of flesh. Then he lifted his face, awash in blood, to the audience. He was the victor. And to the victor go the spoils. Where were the spoils? The magician had tasted like ass. Surely, this godforsaken rock must have a child on it somewhere.

He continued to gorge on Zoltan's corpse until he regained his strength, then with his head held high, he strolled to the gate and waited for it to open. He'd won the match. The ridiculous contest was over.

But the gate did not rise.

A rhythmic chant rose among the crowd, *"SPARKLES! SPARKLES! SPARKLES!"*

Weasels's eyes flung open wide. *Sparkles? Who the hell was Sparkles? And what happened to WEASESLS! WEASELS! WEASELS?"*

An announcement blared overhead. "And now, your victor, Mister Weasels, from planet... Earth, will face the reigning King of Carnival Combat, The Sovereign Sultan of Smackdown — *SPARKLES!* As a demonstration of its benevolence, The Ministry of Mirth has decreed that the winner of today's match will be set *free*!"

The screams of the crowd drowned out the sound of the gate's grinding ascent. When it reached its zenith, a moment of absolute silence descended over the arena.

Then Sparkles emerged.

Sparkles was over eight feet tall with a shiny, purple body and four hands, each sprouting six long, curved talons.

Perfect for disemboweling, thought an envious, but anxious, Weasels.

Sparkles's face was merely a fleshless skull, with two huge voids where eyes might once have been. A shock of white hair shot straight up from his skull in a snowy mohawk. His teeth, longer than Weasels's, were fixed in a ghastly grin and chattered convulsively.

Weasels gave an involuntary shudder. He'd seen these monstrous alien clowns before. They came from the planet Carnivale, the sister planet of Bozos 4. He glanced at Sparkles's pants, and his mouth went dry. Sparkles wore bottomless, chicken-catching pants—*the pants of the great ones.* A multitude of evils could hide inside those wondrous wearables of the midway.

Clearly, Sparkles was a clown to be reckoned with.

Sparkles locked eyes with Weasels, and then bowed deeply from his waist. Weasels returned the show of respect. But before either could move, two clown cars roared through the gates to the center of the arena. These were not just any clown cars. They were tricked-out, blood-letting hotrods from hell.

According to the announcer, the rules were simple. It was a race to the death. No holds barred. The clowns climbed into their respective cars; Sparkles, into a modified, purple-glittered, Novarian Gnatmobile, with the name *'Sparkles, The Corpse Collector'* painted on its side, and Weasels, into a jet black, customized 1980 Pinto with the name ***'The Other Guy'*** scratched on the driver's side door. Weasels hesitated as he climbed into the Pinto, staring at the unnerving rainbow of dried alien blood splashed across the seat.

And then, he got angry.

He was playing second banana to Barney, the purple alien, and driving a piece-of-shit Pinto with an anonymous nameplate. Sparkles was the home crowd favorite.

Sparkles must die.

A three-foot blue alien wearing a poodle skirt and lime-green pigtails stood in front of the two cars. A scarf dangled from between the claws of her upper left tentacle.

She threw it down, and the death match began.

All these buttons, thought Weasels. He pushed one marked 'rocket thruster', and his car careened head-on into the wall. He recovered quickly, but saw the glittering clown in hot pursuit. Weasels drew him in closer, then at the last minute jerked his steering wheel to the left and hit the gas. Sparkles couldn't stop and slammed into the arena wall.

While Sparkles was busy trying to right his car, Weasels studied the buttons on his control panel: *Oil Can Harry, Blazing Lasers, Cherry Nose Chainsaw,* and an intriguing button labeled, *Who the Hell Knows*?

Sparkles veered off the wall with a vengeance and chased Weasels across the arena. Sparkles pulled to within twenty feet of Weasels's car, and then pulled closer still, all the way up to his bumper. Weasels hit the *Oil Can Harry* button, blanketing the windshield of Sparkles's car with a blast of oil. The crowd booed and hissed.

Sparkles shrieked. Then his bony jaws slid back and forth as he gnashed his teeth. He reached out the driver's side window and wiped off as much oil as he could with the sleeve of his clown suit. Next, he pulled something up from the backseat of his car. A potato gun! Weasels laughed and roared past the glittering Gnatmobile, but his grease-painted mouth formed a perfect '0' when he read the words printed on the side of the gun: ACME Rocket Launcher.

Sparkles took aim and fired. An RPG screamed across the arena and skidded across the top of Weasels head, then continued its trajectory, ultimately blowing up a segment of the arena wall. Bits and pieces of the stadium blasted into the audience, decapitating some and maiming others. Mismatched body parts flew through the crowd like shrapnel and soaked the survivors in a kaleidoscopic array of alien blood.

The audience screamed for more. *"SPARKLES! SPARKLES!"*

Mister Weasels pulled a 360, then sat idling, staring into the deadlights of Sparkles's *Corpse Collector* car. Weasels's finger hovered over the *Blazing Lasers* button on his control panel. Then he gritted his teeth and pressed the button over and over. Laser beams pulsed from his radio antenna, and locked on to Sparkles's car.

Bullseye. The car burst to smithereens, launching Sparkles up through the air. But then he plummeted downward and smashed into the ground, leaving a body-shaped crater in the arena floor. The audience watched as a tiny puff of smoke rose silently from the hole.

At first, the crowd grew quiet, then murmurs and fidgeting erupted in the stands. *What of Sparkles—the King of Carnival Combat? The Sultan of Smackdown? Surely, he wasn't...*

A gasp arose from the bleachers. Then another. And another. One at a time, twelve curved talons popped into view at the top of the crater, dug into the ground, and pulled the shimmering clown out of the hole.

Mister Weasels let loose a primal scream, aimed his car at Sparkles, and tromped on the gas. Then he found the button marked *Cherry Nose Chainsaw.* He bore down on the home crowd favorite, smashed the button with his fist, and screamed, *"Die you big purple bastard!"*

A chainsaw popped out of an exterior panel in Weasels's driver's side door. The whirring blade hit Sparkles hip high, splitting his body in two.

A shower of black, Carnivalian sushi flew back at Weasels who greedily licked it from his face. He watched the halves of Sparkles's body twitch their death dance, then turned off the engine of his clown car, and crawled onto its roof. There he stood, arms raised in victory, pumping his fists in the air.

Then he remembered the *Who the Hell Knows?* button on the control panel.

Eh, what the fuck.

He reached inside and pushed the button. Fireworks soared high into the air, bursting into a thousand tendrils of brilliant light that streaked into the stratosphere. A finale for the ages.

Weasels took his bow.

The stunned crowd began to chant, quietly at first, until their unified voices gathered strength and erupted into a crescendo of, *"WEASELS! WEASELS! WEASELS! WEASELS! WEASELS!"*

*

Despite the begging of the Bozosians, Weasels refused to stay and serve as the Cosmic Carnival's Sultan of Smackdown. He wasn't worried about his ability to maintain the title. On the contrary, he'd clearly proven that no one *ever* fucks with Mister Weasels. But there wasn't a single child to be found *anywhere* on this bunghole of a rock. And there was still Zelda's betrayal to deal with, not to mention the comeuppance he owed that ankle-biting menace, Dewey Frick—all matters of grave importance.

As promised by the Ministry of Mirth, Weasels was set free, and at his request, the formidable Blue Guard escorted him back to the worm hole. He stood at the edge of the swirling vortex and stared inside. Who knew where it might take him? Worse yet, would he ever find the Barlowe Brother's Carnival again? Would he ever return to the midway that had been his home since time began?

But at the end of the day, it didn't matter. He had to try. Besides, he believed in destiny. A real clown made his own fate.

He took a deep breath and jumped into the maelstrom with a grim smile on his grease-painted face. While he tumbled and turned, traveling through space, he spent every waking moment plotting his revenge against Madame Zelda and his nemesis, Dewey Frick.

There would be no truce. There would be no mercy—there would only be the wrath of a demon clown who refused to be denied. *I'll never stop until I find you,* he mused aloud.

And for Mister Weasels, who had always been, and would forever be, never was *a* very long time.

The End

Abandonland
By
Jason M. Light

Eric looked at his friend and shook his head in disbelief. "It's bullshit. There's no fucking way he can get power to that old thing. It's been shut down for two years!"

Pat didn't seem to share his friend's concern. He was too focused on the fact he was going to ask his girlfriend, Pam, to marry him. That they were but seniors in high school didn't temper his enthusiasm. "He said he can do it. Why shouldn't I believe him?"

"Uh...because we've tortured that guy since grade school? It's a set-up."

"Oh, come on! This is Lawrence we're talking about. He isn't anywhere near that cagey."

"You think he's smart enough to jerry-rig an old Ferris wheel in an abandoned amusement park, don't you?"

"He isn't jerry-rigging shit! It all still works. It's all still there. The place hasn't been closed that long. Besides, he isn't going to try anything stupid. He knows I'd kick his fucking ass. He's wanted to be our friend since the fifth grade, right? What was that, 1981? Five, six years ago? He sees this as his chance. He isn't going to fuck that up."

"What did he say? How did he say he could do it?"

"He said there's still power to the park."

"Bullshit!"

"There's an electric fence. And safety lights. They've got to power those things somehow. You know the dude's a savant. He won every science fair we ever had. By a mile!"

"Safety lights?"

"Yeah."

"For what?"

"Insurance, dipshit. Someone breaks in, like we're gonna --"

"We?"

"Yeah. I need a wingman I can count on. Plus, you'll be my boots on the ground. Make sure that asshole doesn't try anything stupid."

"You just said he wouldn't."

Pat sighed. "Look. I want you to be there when I ask her."

"On the Ferris wheel?"

"No, dumbass, just... I don't know...there. For support, you know. Like, what if she says no and takes off? You want me walking around an abandoned amusement park by myself all depressed?"

"Lawrence will be there."

"Lawrence isn't my best friend. You are. Cool?"

"All right. Okay."

"Anyway, they've gotta have safety lights and insurance in case someone wanders in and breaks his neck. They could sue."

"Bullshit. How is someone gonna wander in if the gates are electrified?"

"All right, so they sue for getting their goose cooked. It's ridiculous, but it happens. Someone buys a cup of coffee from McDonald's, burns their mouth on it, sues for a million bucks because the coffee was too hot. Look it up."

"Those stories are made up to sell you tabloids. We're gonna get in there and he's gonna leave us stranded."

"So what if he does? We can find our own way out. I just need him to fire up the juice and get the Ferris wheel started. We'll climb down if we have to. It's not like it's a thousand feet tall, or anything. Come to think of it, that might add to the atmosphere. Might be romantic."

"Climbing down a Ferris wheel is romantic?" Ericasked, shaking his head. "Single life is vexing enough for me. I don't know how you do it."

"Do what?"

"Have a girlfriend. Something like that would drive me nuts."

"What about Katie Bovnyk?"

"Bovine? What about her?" Eric asked, guarded.

Pat pushed his nose up and started snorting and rooting around like a pig.

"Shut up!" Pat finally stopped when Eric didn't take the bait and try to engage him in a fist fight. "So, the park has power, and he can run the Ferris wheel ‘cause that used to be his job. Doesn't mean the Ferris wheel's gonna have power going to it. You know they cut it when they boarded the place up."

"There's a main disconnect switch right next to the control panel. It has to be close in case something goes wrong. He said he even had to use it a couple times."

"It's still gotta have power. No way it has power. No fucking way! Lawrence is nuts."

"He knows where the main breaker boxes are, and which ones power what."

"They'll be locked up."

"He's got the keys."

"He kept his keys?"

"Said no one ever asked for them back." Pat shrugged. "Place closed down unexpectedly during the off-season."

"That's hard to believe."

"Just so."

"You've seen them."

"I have."

"How do you know it's not just a ring of random keys?"

"I don't. So, you see, it isn't even breaking and entering if you have keys. It's just...entering."

"What about security?"

"They aren't going to pay someone to walk around an empty park. Come to the grocery store with me tonight."

"Why?"

"That's where Lawrence is working. Talk to him yourself, ask him questions. You'll see. And hey, Katie works there, too." He winked.

"Shut up."

"I know she's hot for you."

"Yeah? She tell you that on your date? Oh no, wait, you stood her up, I forgot."

"I didn't stand her up."

"Not what I heard."

"We never agreed to go out in the first place!"

"That's not what she thinks. I think you sent her into a comfort food coma after you didn't show."

"I didn't do anything to her."

"Exactly."

"You coming with me or what?"

"All right, but if this is some kind of set-up, I swear to God..."

"It isn't. I'll pick you up at eight."

#

"So you'll be there?"

"Yeah. But I want Pam to blow me first. Before she's an engaged woman."

"Blow yourself."

"I could do it."

Pat didn't answer. He just kept driving them toward the grocery store.

"I'm big enough."

"I get it. But save that kinda talk for Katie."

"Fuck you."

"That, too."

He pulled into the mostly empty grocery store lot and parked near the back, by the cars belonging to the employees. Lawrence's Mustang was there, so was Katie Bovnyk's more practical Ford Escort. They observed the store for a few moments, watching as a couple of people went in and a couple more came out hauling paper bags full of goods, but it was a relatively slow night.

"All right, let's go talk to him."

"Aren't there managers?"

"A night manager, yeah."

"Won't he overhear us? What if he tells someone?"

"He won't care. He's only a couple years older than us and all he's worried about is getting the floors swept so he can steal a sixer he's got hidden in the dairy cooler and get home. Come on."

A cold blast of conditioned air hit them as they stepped on the mat that engaged the automatic door. Katie was standing in the manager's booth, her back to the door, and she did not turn to see them come in. Another girl, which neither of them knew, was reading a paperback romance at her register station, waiting for another checkout to walk up. Lawrence was nowhere to be found. He was probably in the back smoking a cigarette with the night manager, who was always going on about fucking his girlfriend.

"I'm heading to the back room," Pat said. He was familiar with the store as he'd worked there the summer after their sophomore year.

"Can I come with you?"

Pat nodded at the manager's booth. "Why don't you go see your girlfriend?"

"No way!"

"You sure?"

Eric looked at Katie and something stirred. Something about seeing her up there in that manager's booth, her hair down for a change -- in school she'd kept it pulled back in an angry-looking ponytail -- wearing that crisp white shirt with a name tag. Had she lost weight since school let out? Was her skin clearer than it had been just a couple hours earlier, when he'd seen her in the hallway? Was she wearing honest-to-God makeup?

"All right," he said distantly, but Pat was already gone.

Eric approached the manager's booth and when Katie saw him her face lit up momentarily. She thought he was a customer at first, but when she saw it was just another of the assholes from school who would only give her the time of day long enough to tease her, her smile dropped.

"Oh," she said, "it's just you." When she moved, she made a jangling sound Eric mistook for being a Slinky of loose bracelets. But she wasn't wearing any bracelets.

"Hey! Is that any way to treat a customer?"

"You're not a customer. You don't have any money."

"I've been working at the frozen yogurt shop on the corner."

"What do you want? I'm kinda busy."

"You look great, Katie. My God, you look amazing!" He wasn't fucking with her, and Katie knew it. She knew she looked great, but it was nice to hear it from someone else, even if Eric was a dick most of the time. She would rather have heard it from Pat, who stood her up once, but hearing it from Eric was okay, too. Hearing it from anyone was okay.

"Thanks."

"What are you doing up there? Are you the manager?" They both knew he was joking, but Katie blushed.

"That'll be the day!"

"So, what, then?"

"I sell books of stamps, money orders, cash checks, make keys. Mostly I make keys." She hoisted the ring of nondescript keys hanging on a chain around her neck, which could be shaped and polished on the machine in the booth with her, and which were the source of the jangling sound she made whenever she so much as took a breath.

"Responsibility looks good on you."

She blushed again. "What are you doing here?"

Eric gestured toward the back of the store. "Pat's talking to Lawrence about helping him out with something."

"What?"

"He's going to ask Pam to marry him." As soon as he said it -- no, while he was saying it -- he regretted opening his mouth. He could see the disappointment flash in Katie's face, but it was gone as quickly as it had come. Katie still had feelings for Pat, in spite of the fact he was the cruelest kind of asshole to her and just about everyone else, too, but she also understood they were never meant to be together. News of his pending engagement to the prettiest, most popular girl in school only solidified that. It seemed to give Katie closure on the whole stupid thing, and it wasn't lost on Eric what it all meant for him. Now that Katie was no longer hung up on his friend, or at least, now that she knew she couldn't do anything about it even if she was still hung up on him, it opened up the possibility Eric himself could go out with her. The fact that it made him Katie's second choice, not to mention the fact that until today he had never once considered asking her out, even if he'd secretly wanted to, even as he and Pat rooted around like hogs with their snouts raised when making fun of her, didn't seem to bother him.

"Good for him," Katie said, then she looked confused. "But why does he need Lawrence's help?"

"He's going to ask her on the Ferris wheel at Adventureland."

"It's open again?"

"No. Lawrence used to work there. He still has his keys."

"That's crazy."

"You're preaching to the choir, sister."

Katie smiled. Eric knew she wasn't used to boys speaking to her like this, and even though he was aware he was no real catch, he was glad he was the one. He might have made fun of her when they were in school, hell, everyone did, but out in the real-world Katie was the successful one, and Eric found that intoxicating.

But the smile fell from Katie's face, revealing the insecure girl beneath, when she saw Pat and Lawrence striding toward them from the back of the store.

"Well, hello, Katie," Pat said, an evil little grin on his handsome face. Asshole he was, Katie still felt a spark of electricity race through her when she saw him. Especially his face. He had the face of a model. He leaned on the counter of the podium and smiled up at her, beaming. Forget his perfect face, it was his hair that did the trick. His hair was fucking pluperfect. He elbowed his friend out of the way. "Is this jerk bothering you?" Before she could answer he said, "I told him you didn't want to talk to him, but do you think he listened?"

She opened her mouth to say Eric hadn't been bothering her at all, that she in fact liked talking to a nice guy for a change, but nothing would come out, and by the time it did -- a small squeaking sound that embarrassed her even though there was no one left to hear it -- Pat, Lawrence, and Eric were going through the out door, back into the night from whence they came. And they were laughing and making hog sounds.

But Eric hadn't been laughing, he was just

guilty by association. He genuinely felt bad for Katie. He felt bad for her and thought there would be time to tell her that, to tell her he was embarrassed to be part of that rude clique, that he wanted to get to know her better when those assholes weren't around.

#

"There's no security," Lawrence confirmed as Pat applied the bolt cutters to the padlock. "You can make all the noise you want." He told his bully he wouldn't be the one doing the breaking-and-entering. He'd help him run the Ferris wheel, but that was it and he'd be out of there. "I don't even know why I'm doing that much," he'd said. It was probably because Pam was white-hot. Pat knew Lawrence had a thing for her since junior high, when she started getting curvy in all the right places. Everyone did. It was also the reason he trusted Lawrence not to do anything stupid. If he tried to hurt Pat, he'd be hurting Pam, too.

Pat squeezed the bolt cutters and the lock fell away in a clatter. Somewhere in the distance, a dog barked, then all was quiet again. There was a chill in the air. Halloween was a week gone. It was late. Probably closer to the end of the witching hour than the beginning. Even if someone wondered what the dog was barking at, they would wait a minute and then go back to sleep.

Pat looked at each one of them. Lawrence, who was sober for a change, Pam, who looked cold, hugging herself and shivering, looking miserable, and Eric, who was trying but failing not to ogle Pam. He knew his friend wanted to put his arms around her, warm her up, tell her it was going to be all right. Pat pushed on the gate, but it still wouldn't budge.

"Here," Lawrence said, stepping up with a key in his hands. "The padlock was extra." He unlocked the gate and swung it open. They all stepped inside the darkened park. Lawrence pushed the gate to but did not re-lock it.

Pam looked at him.

"In case you need to make a quick get-away. You can't climb these fences. They're electric. If you so much as touch it, your whole body will turn black." He snapped his fingers. "Like that."

"What if someone comes in?" Pam asked.

Lawrence chuckled. "Like who?"

It didn't take long to get to the Ferris wheel. There were no crowds to fight. No lines to wait in. They walked right up to the loading station, skipping the maze of bars and chains that made up the line queue.

"This place is creepy," Pam said, shivering. "No wonder they call it Abandonland now."

"They called it that a long time before it closed," Lawrence said. "That's why it closed. Get in and buckle up."

"We don't need to buckle up," Pat said.

"Yes, we do!" Pam said.

Lawrence shrugged.

"It's a Ferris wheel, honey, not a roller-coaster."

Pam looked at Lawrence, uneasy.

"Suit yourself," Lawrence said. "No skin off of my nose." He took a flask from an inside jacket pocket and pulled a drink out of it.

"Are you supposed to be doing that?" Pam asked.

Lawrence smiled. "What are they gonna do?" He chuckled. "Fire me?" He threw the main disconnect switch. Nothing.

"What's the matter with it?"

"Gotta hit the breaker. Be right back."

"How are you gonna get in to it?"

Lawrence held up a ring of keys. "You need these."

"Go with him," Pat told Eric, who'd been standing idly by, too shy to speak in front of Pam.

They went away. The park was black as pitch. It was so dark their eyes would not even adjust. They were gone so long that Pat and Pam ran out of things to talk about. Pat could feel the ring box bulging in his pocket. He kicked his feet a little, causing the car to rock back and forth. Its bearings were dry. It creaked and groaned.

"Cut it out!" Pam hugged herself. She wasn't having fun. Pat had second thoughts about popping the question now. He wanted everything to be perfect. "What's taking them so long?"

"Maybe they're having trouble finding it."

"I thought you said he worked here!"

"He did. But it is pretty dark. Or maybe he had the wrong set of keys. Whatever it is, I'm sure it's fine."

"I don't know."

Pat started to hop out of the Ferris wheel.

"Where are you going?"

"To see if I can help. Sit tight."

"Are you insane? You can't just leave me here!"

Pat laughed. "Baby, it's an abandoned park. There's no one else here besides me and you and Lawrence and Eric."

"Why is Eric here, anyway? He creeps me out the way he just stares at me all the time."

"You ought to be used to that by now."

"He looks at me too long."

"I'll just have to kick his ass, then. Meanwhile he's just making sure Lawrence doesn't try anything."

"Like what?"

"Like... I don't know... anything stupid."

"Stupid? Like breaking into a closed amusement park to ride a fucking Ferris wheel?"

The ring of lights around the Ferris wheel snapped on, blinding them momentarily. A couple hissed and popped in tiny balls of ozone-melting short circuit smell and smoke.

Pat laughed. He sat down hard in the plastic seat. It swung back and forth.

"See!"

"Be careful! Stop rocking it!"

"It's fine." They heard a metallic snap in the near-distance and the Ferris wheel groaned and jerked, lifting them into the air. "Oh! Here we go!"

They reached the pinnacle of the ride and it began to fall back toward the ground again, leaving their stomachs high above the darkened midway. "Isn't this great?" He lifted his hands into the air as they descended, but Pam closed her eyes and clutched the lap bar, holding on like grim death. The wheel lifted them toward the top again, and it seemed to be gaining speed. Pat told Lawrence to whisk them around a couple of times and then stop them at the top, so he could pop the question. When the wheel dropped and lifted them a third time and a fourth and fifth, Pat began to get worried. No, not worried. He was pissed.

He tried looking at the operator station as

the wheel flashed by, but it was too dark to make anything out. Finally, as his eyes continued to adjust, he saw a figure standing at the controls. The figure wore the stark white shirt all the employees of the grocery store had to wear, which he'd once worn himself when he worked there, and seeing it eased his mind a little. Either Lawrence was just fucking with them, or he was having trouble getting the wheel to stop. If it was the former, Pat planned on kicking Lawrence's ass. If it was the latter... well, he'd kick his ass for that, too. He was supposed to know what he was doing.

"Hey!" Pat called as the car swung down toward the station for the dozenth time. "Hey, stop us at the top, asshole!"

"Don't piss him off!" Pam said, her eyes still closed.

Finally, two rotations later, the wheel began to slow, and after another pass it stopped with their car near the top. Looking out over the darkened park wasn't as romantic as if the whole thing had been lit up, but it was still pretty cool. The night was clear and crisp, and enough of the moon was out to give them a dim view of all the abandoned booths and rides. It was, Pam decided when she finally opened her eyes, eerily beautiful.

They sat in silence for a little while looking out over the park, into the distance. They saw small ovals of pale light on distant streets and highways, could see the outlines of buildings on the horizon. After a while, Pat took Pam's hand in his own and looked at her, but she didn't look back at him like he thought she would, like he wanted and needed her to. Her gaze remained fixed on the skyline.

"Hey," he said, but still she did not look at him. This was not going as planned. "Hello?" he said, teasing, and she finally seemed to snap out of her wool gathering.

"Yeah?"

"You okay?"

"It's really pretty, isn't it?"

"You know what else is pretty?" He reached into his pocket for the ring box, heart pounding, but just as he did, the lights ringing the Ferris wheel snapped off. The darkness and silence which followed were deep and total. Immediately, the once-distant drone of tires on the highway was relatively loud, but just a note louder was the echo of the piped-in cackling witch laughter that had been issuing from the speakers at the haunted house on the other side of the midway. They hadn't been able to hear it over the hum of the Ferris wheel lights. The sound faded into the distance but not before covering Pam in goosebumps. Pat fumbled the ring box and heard it, and the ring once inside it, clatter to the ground, bouncing off every steel beam between them and the earth. "Shit! Fuck!"

Pam chuckled. "What is it? What was that?"

"Fuck! Fuck!"

She laughed again, and this seemed to anger her boyfriend. He turned to her, and though the sudden lack of lights made visibility poor, she could see that his face was wrinkled with stress and full of blood.

"Fuck!"

"Hey..."

Pat stood and began to climb over the bar.

"What the fuck are you do--"

He turned and backhanded her across the cheek, the sudden movement causing the car to sway violently, nearly tipping them both over the side. Pam was stunned and a million new stars were added to her field of vision, mixing with and dominating those that had been winking at her in the clear sky since they'd risen to the apex of the ride. In the seconds it took her to understand what had happened, Pat had clambered over the side and was climbing down the steel girders of the Ferris wheel.

She peeked over the edge and saw him descending expertly, dropping from one heavily-riveted crossbar to the next, until he was nearly to the ground. He might have been twenty or thirty feet short of his mark when the Ferris wheel lights flashed on again, a shower of sparks bloomed, and Pat's agonized voice rang out, echoing all over the park and beyond, rousing the dogs in the surrounding neighborhoods again. The lights flickered out immediately, the air smelled of ozone, and moments later Pam heard Pat's body land on the thin metal plates of the loading station with a sickening thud of finality.

Again, the silence was absolute, the darkness so deep she felt like she was drowning, sinking into the pits of a black ocean.

"Help," she said, though she didn't raise her voice loud enough even to anger the nearby dogs because her mouth hurt from being hit. "Help me."

She looked over the edge of the still-swinging Ferris wheel car and could just make out Pat's body, limbs pointing in different, impossible directions. He wasn't moving. Was that a pillow of blood seeping out behind his head? Or was it just a shadow?

"Pat?" Her boyfriend did not stir. "Help!"

For a moment she heard nothing but the heavy silence all around her, but then she thought she heard the rattle of chains. All she could imagine was a mummy or a Frankenstein stumbling out of what had once been the haunted house somewhere on the midway, but it was too dark to see. Whatever shapes she saw shambling through the blackness would probably be nothing more than her imagination, but she didn't think the sound of those chains, or whatever it was, was anything but real.

She sat in the car for a long time, occasionally looking over the edge, down at the loading station, where her boyfriend's electrocuted body had landed. He hadn't moved. Some kind of animal -- a dog, probably, though she couldn't tell for sure -- was rooting around, sniffing and nudging him. She tried to shoo it away, but after glancing up at her and growling, the dog went back to its business. The next time she checked, the dog was gone, but when she looked again some time later, it had returned with others, and they were all digging in.

She called for help again, louder this time. The dogs paid her no attention, and the tires on the distant highway continued to drone, oblivious to her plight. She watched those pale headlights and wondered why no one knew she was there. She wondered why none of them were coming to help her. Couldn't they see she was stranded? Didn't they know Pat had died and was being eaten by stray dogs? Why weren't they coming to help?

Eventually her tears dried up, and she began to understand. She deserved this. She was a terrible person. She'd been such a bitch to other people at school. Guys tried to be nice to her, but she wouldn't give them the time of the day. Especially if they were bold enough to flirt with her, and doubly especially if they weren't even cute. Who did they think they were? She'd been cruel to all of them except Pat, who was the biggest jerk of all and who would have deserved her poor treatment. Thinking about that, she glanced over the edge again, expecting to not feel anything for him, to at least not feel sorry for him for what happened.

But Pat was gone. There was nothing but a pool of blood where his broken body had once been. Had the dogs roused him? Was he able to somehow get up on his broken legs and limp out of there? Leaving her in the...

But no. Pat had not gotten up. He had been dragged away. She followed the streaks of his blood down the thin metal planks that made up the loading station, down the corrugated metal stairs to the cement of the midway, and watched as the dogs took him.

She thought of all the girls she'd been mean to at school. It wasn't just the boys. She was meaner to the girls who wanted to be her friends than she was to the boys who were hot for her. She thought if someone wasn't cool enough -- and no one was -- she would just be wasting her time with them, damaging her social status beyond repair. Instead, she realized now as her stomach began to rumble and her swollen mouth dried up, she'd just been wasting her time with Pat.

At some point she dozed off, waking only when the Ferris wheel car began to sway. The once-black eastern sky behind her was now a shade of gray. The sun was coming up.

She looked over the side of the slightly swaying car and saw someone scaling the dormant side of the Ferris wheel, climbing with purpose towards her car. It wasn't Pat. What was left of her boyfriend still lie a few feet away from the ride, but the dogs were gone. Maybe they found out he was sour meat, not even fit for them, or maybe whoever was climbing the Ferris wheel had chased them away. She held her breath, afraid if she so much as breathed through her nose it might whistle and give her presence away.

But as the figure came closer, she realized that wasn't necessary. It was Eric, Pat's friend with the wandering eyes. He might have leered too much, but otherwise he was harmless. Wasn't he? She couldn't puzzle it out, she just knew she was happy to see him. When he finally made it up to her, she could have cried.

"Are you okay?"

"Yes, I think so. What's going on?" She must have sounded like she'd just been to the dentist.

She couldn't really feel her mouth.

"Everyone is dead."

"What do you mean?"

"Pat is--"

"I know about Pat. I saw him. Where's Lawrence? Can he get us down?"

"No. The circuit's blown. I don't know how to fix it. We'll have to climb."

"What do you mean? Can't Lawrence fix it?"

He looked at her a long time. "He's dead, too."

"What?"

"Someone stabbed him."

She didn't believe him. Or if she did, she didn't believe he wasn't responsible. But she had no choice but to go with him. When they got to the bottom, if her legs cooperated, she would just run. But when they finally reached the bottom and she saw Lawrence lying face down in a pool of blood just outside the operator booth, a knife sticking out of his back, her legs would not move.

"Come on," Eric said, imploring her to follow him. "We've got to go."

"Who did this?"

"I don't know. That's why we've got to go."

She looked at him. She looked the other direction. The sun might have been coming up, but the park itself was still a maze of shadows.

She followed him to the front of the

park.

#

They arrived at the gate through which they entered. It was still closed, just like they'd left it, and though Pam was grateful for Lawrence's insight in leaving it unlocked in case they needed to make a quick getaway, for which she also felt bad because Lawrence would not be making any kind of getaway, quick or otherwise, when Eric reached for the handle to give them their deliverance, she knew at once he would find it locked.

"Shit," he said, shaking the gate. He shook it loud enough that the unseen dogs struck up their chorus again. "What the fuck! Someone locked us in. That fucker Lawrence, probably."

He gazed up at the top of the gate and the surrounding fence. It was at least sixteen feet high. It might as well have been a hundred. There were no footholds to be used.

"You can't climb it," Pam said.

"I know. It's too tall." He turned around and considered the darkened park before him. There were a million hidden corners and an untold number of supply sheds placed throughout. He'd seen them on his many visits to the park, gazing out over the landscape during slow climbs on roller coaster hills. He knew there would be a ladder in at least one of them, if he could just find one in the dark. And if not a ladder, maybe a pallet he could stack against the fence.

"No," Pam said, "it's electric. You'll die. Just like Pat."

He shook his head. "Circuits are blown, remember?"

"All of them? And are you sure?"

He thought for a minute, running his hand through his hair.

She bent down and picked up the discarded bolt cutters her boyfriend had used to break the chain the park used for extra security on the gate. She threw the tool at the fence and a white-hot shower of sparks exploded as it made contact. Their own personal little fireworks show. The fence hissed and popped and then all was silent again.

They tried to find another way out, running along the perimeter of the fence, but all the gates were locked, and all of them were live. They didn't even notice the jangling sound of unmade keys -- when they finally heard it, Eric remembered it from the store, when he was talking to Katie, and how every time she so much as breathed, the keychain around her neck played a metallic melody -- getting closer, circling them, until it was much too late.

The End

The Frog Prince
By
Joe X. Young

His voice was soft, almost child-like, yet cut through the air with rapier skill, rising above all other sounds. "Cans, guns, darts, ducks, and helter-skelter." A few heartbeats intervened before he repeated the phrase, his eyes scanning the approaching public. It was market day in Maeston and what was usually the town car park now teemed with the Wednesday bustle of traders at tables, all yelling the virtues of their wares. Market day was a nightmare for some, but for the folk at Funland it meant more buses heading into town and more potential punters at the fairground, all eager to soak up the supposed 'Carnival atmosphere' and be relieved of their cash in exchange for a good time.

"Cans, guns, darts, ducks, and helter-skelter."

A weaselly looking figure stood at the booth of the Dodgems, watching as Harry strolled along his domain, Harry's battle cry so annoying that it made Tony want to ram one of the plastic ducks from the 'hook-a-duck' so far down Harry's throat that he would be shitting plastic for a week.

"Tony, Oi, Tony, what's wrong with you now, got magnets in your boots?" Said Carl as he leaned out of the Dodgems booth and tapped Tony on the shoulder.

"Nothing that a fifty calibre round wouldn't sort out." Tony replied as he stepped from the siding onto the iron plates of the Dodgems track and headed for the cars to pull them into position before the punters gathered.

"Cans, guns, darts, ducks, and helter-skelter," Harry called out then smiled, his row of teeth not perfectly straight but all present and clean. It was a smile of innocence and good intention. Today he wore his special jacket, a shiny Bomber-Jacket festooned with studs, enamelled badges, sew-on-patches, and button badges of all descriptions, far too many to count, some of which had been given to him by happy members of the public. The jacket must have weighed fifty pounds, yet that didn't bother Harry at all as he wore it as a beacon to attract the attention of the bemused public who wanted to check out the 'crazy badge guy'.

One thing Harry understood was how to attract attention, and for some reason nobody could fathom, it was as if everything that Harry did actually worked like a charm. He always amassed a good crowd and had a way of making them spend their hidden money. The cash they didn't intend to use, as it wasn't a rainy day, flowed like it was Monsoon weather once Harry got going. Some days he took almost everything they had.

"Cans, guns, darts, ducks and helter-skelter."

The first trickle of punters came through into the yard, looking around, unimpressed by the dated look of the amusements on offer. No amount of freshen-up paint jobs could help the generally dilapidated stalls and rides to rise above their murderous assault on nostalgia.

Tony stood astride the steps of the dodgems, legs splayed and hands on hips like M.C. Hammer in camouflaged combat pants, but coming across more like a poor-man's version of a Bollywood dancer. It was his usual stance, try to appear bigger than his five-foot-six frame allowed, try to be the one the girls see first. Be the one on the most popular ride. Be bigger and more important. King of the Dodgems. Take the attention before people notice the boyish nutcase with the badges, or worse still, before they get halfway through the concourse and see Glen. If they get that far, it's all over. Glen was an anachronism. Even though it was the eighties, he looked as if he had stepped out of any 1950s American town in which he was the cool guy, the six foot tall one with the jet black D.A. hairstyle, white t-shirt accenting his tanned and muscular physique, Ray-Bans from behind which he could eye-up the talent without them catching him, cigarette seemingly defying gravity at the corner of his mouth, and all of the confidence which goes along with knowing that you're the most handsome guy in a thirty mile radius. All he needed was the Harley Panhead Hydra-Glide and he'd be good to go. The girls didn't care about the lack of motorbike though, they took him anyway.

"Erm, wanna go on the Dodgems then?" Tony called out, feebly, to a small group of teenagers.

"Just lookin' thanks" said one of the girls before they all ignored him and quickened their pace.

"Cans, guns, darts, ducks, and helter-skelter." Harry's tone remained the same as usual, and the teenagers looked across and turned toward him as if transfixed. Tony jumped onto the iron plates, ran across to the Dodgems booth, leaned in past Carl, and turned up the music so loud that all heads cranked in his direction. 'Wood Beez': (Pray like Aretha Franklin) filled the air. Carl grabbed the knob and turned Scritti Politti back down to regular levels.

"What the hell Tony, are you trying to get us kicked off here?" Carl glared as Tony slunk back a little.

"No, I'm just sick of that bastard getting the punters. If they can't hear him they won't notice him." Tony cocked a thumb in Harry's direction, noting that Harry was already taking money and positioning people in front of the various side-shows he controlled.

"I tell you what Tony, it's near the end of the season, we have a few more days and the weekend left. On Sunday you can play the music so loud it'll make his ears bleed, but until then, we have to keep it legal, ok? Look, I know Harry's a bit odd, but he's harmless enough. I don't see what your problem is... Oop!... Look lively." Carl pointed behind Tony at the teenagers getting into the Dodgem cars. Tony put on his best fake smile and headed toward them.

"Cans, guns, darts, ducks, and helter-skelter." Heartbeat "C'mon you lot, it's all good fun, and if you don't win a prize I'll make you feel like you have," With the Dodgems having popped its cherry for the day, other people started to ascend the steps to the platform. Harry had a few punters on the helter-skelter, one on the ducks, and he was personally attending one of the gun stalls for health and safety reasons. The guy shooting was attempting to blow a red star out of the centre of a card. It was possible, had to be possible by law, but with the way those guns sprayed the lead/antimony shot, it was hardly likely to result in a win. The warning horn blared and the Dodgems started up. Tony was in full swing now, running from one Dodgem car to another, checking that the girls had their seatbelts correctly positioned across their chests (something he never did for the guys), helping them to steer their way out of collisions, and generally chatting them up. The guy on the machine guns failed to remove all traces of the red star from the card; it was a great effort, but there was still enough red there as to be clearly visible.

"Thank you, sir, it was a good effort," Harry said as the punter walked away. "Cans, guns, darts, ducks, and helter-skelter," he called out as he headed for the girl who was playing on the 'hook-a-duck'. "Hello Trudy, I was wondering when you'd show up. Don't tell me you're still trying to win the big Kermit?" He looked up at a large floppy plush frog, three feet tall if it was an inch, arms almost as long as its legs, and bearing only the slightest resemblance to the Muppet. Trudy was a local, a regular there, seventeen but with the dress sense and bearing of a much younger girl. Plump and plain, her NHS bespectacled face, round and pale freckled, lit up at the sight of Harry walking toward her.

"Yeah, me again, sorry," she said, casting her gaze down. "I've almost given up hope of winning him now. It's not long before you close for the season either, so the odds aren't good."

Harry reached forward and took the hook-ended pole away from her. "Look up at me," he said. She did. "You've been coming here for three seasons trying to win that frog and have spent so much money trying that I'm going to make a deal with you, okay?" He smiled and reached behind the stall, retrieving a large wicker basket full of small sealed packets. "This is the 'Pick-a-pack'. It's an instant win thing, though the odds of winning are pretty slim. You get three for a quid, but if you buy a fiver's worth, I will guarantee you that you'll go home with that frog."

Her face lit up. "Guarantee it? How come?"

"Dead simple, if you try the pick-a-pack, win-or-lose I'll give you the frog just for being my best customer."

She pulled coins from her purse and handed five pounds worth to Harry. He dumped them into his apron without counting and stirred the contents of the basket.

"Right, you have fifteen chances here, not as though it matters because win or lose you're going home with Kermit, so dig in and good luck." The girl reached in, her broad smile counteracting any lack of hope of winning. She pulled out the fifteen tickets. Harry replaced the basket and reached up, unhooking the frog from an overhead beam. "I'll just sit him here ready for when you are done, would you like me to hold the packets while you open them?" He held his hands out, palms upward together, and she placed the packs on his palms. He deftly pushed them into a stack and held them in one hand. Nervously she tore open the packets; all she needed was a palindromic number, anything where the first and last figures matched.

371. 892. 110. 467. 903. She passed the dead ones to Harry who tossed them on the ground over the stall rail.

446. 978. 338. 759. 201. Trudy didn't care; she was getting her frog regardless but kept opening them anyway.

884. 368. 921. 628. Harry held out the final packet, she took it and ripped the perforated seams open, unfolding the little square of stiff brown paper.

404.

"Is this it? Is this a winning ticket?" she said, holding up the 404.

"Sure looks like one to me," Harry replied.

"Looks as if this is your lucky day!"

Trudy jumped around as if she were standing barefoot on a hotplate. “I can’t believe it! I’ve won him at last. I’m going home with a Kermit!” Tears welled up in her eyes.

“Well, not quite, no” said Harry.

Trudy stopped bouncing and looked serious. “But I won! I had 404! You said I’d get Kermit even if I lost, but I won” she looked close to tears.

“Trudy, you’re wrong, you’re not going from here with a Kermit... You’re going with two.” Harry smiled and took another Kermit from the beam.

“Omigod, omigod, omigod! But I thought...” Trudy grabbed the first Kermit, hugging him tight as Harry passed her the second one.

“Hey, a promise is a promise. I said I would give you a Kermit for being my best customer, so that stands. You just got lucky today. Oh, and as another loyalty bonus...” he unpinned a badge from his jacket, it was a brightly enamelled frog wearing a crown. “Here’s the Frog Prince. Hopefully it’ll remind you that not everything you hear is a fairy story. May I?” He gestured to her lapel, she nodded, and he pinned it to her. She draped both Kermits down over the rail and gave

Harry a hug and a kiss on the cheek while he stood awkwardly, not knowing what to do.

"Will you be getting different frogs next Season?" she asked.

"I have no idea, I may not even be here next Season. A lot can happen, but if I am here again, I'll see if they have better ones we can get. No guarantees though as it's up to the boss, and he's tight as a duck's arse".

She finished the hug and picked up her Kermits, hoisting them to her shoulders and becoming almost invisible sandwiched between the two large plush toys.

Harry laughed. "I tell you something for nothing, Trudy, it's worth it just to see you carrying those! Can you do me a favour before you leave though and just walk around the grounds one time so people can see it's possible to win stuff?" She nodded with a knowing wink, said goodbye, and left in the direction of the Amusements Arcade at the far end of the strip. Harry dashed behind the darts stall to the storage shed and grabbed another couple of Kermits from a storage cage. He returned to the hook-a-duck and hung them up just in time as the siren signalled the end of the Dodgems and the cars slowed to a halt, the mass of teenagers watching as Trudy carried her spoils away. Within minutes Harry was swamped with customers all wanting to win a big plush frog.

Things quietened down by lunchtime as those people who didn't much fancy the available hot dogs or tinned burgers left in search of proper food. The whole of the grounds buzzed like slumbering bees, and the workers made the most of the lull before the afternoon when everything got hectic again. Harry's boss came over to relieve Harry so he could go on a lunch break. It didn't happen often, but when it did, Harry was happy for the change of scenery.

"Before you go, I want a word," said Rob, looking stern. "What the fuck was that with that girl leaving here with two of the big Kermits? I saw her on the high street with them. Those fuckers are three quid each and I know she didn't 'win' them." He asked.

"It's simple Rob; you saw how many people there were here, all part of the plan. That poor kid has spent three seasons and easily over a hundred quid trying to win a three quid frog, she was getting depressed over losing all the time."

"So, what do you think we're running here, a charity? I'm supposed to be making a profit on this crap and you're giving it away."

"Actually, I made a deal with her. I told her to spend a fiver and win or lose I'd give her the Kermit, so you're two quid up on the deal. I also asked her to walk around the grounds with it so people can see that they can be won. It's great PR as she's a local, a regular who'll be back next season. And it's great for you right now as there's probably going to be hundreds of people seeing her going home with those frogs, which makes it look as if they are easy to win. I gave her one frog and she won the other one legitimately."

"Legitimately my arse, I know your tricks, but if you reckon it's going to make more money I'll take your word for it."

"You don't have to take my word for anything Rob, I've made the daily target, and it's only just lunchtime, so today I'm having a Chinese for lunch instead of a bag of chips, and yes, you're paying for that." Harry undid the straps off his apron and passed it to Rob, who felt the weight of the coins in the cash-bag as he jiggled it up and down a couple of times. "I'm off to stretch my legs and get my grub; I'll be back as soon as possible."

"Nice one." Rob took a wad of cash from one of the pockets on the apron and peeled off a ten pound note, passing it to Harry. "Try not to be too long, I'm on a promise this afternoon and said I'd be back by one."

"I'm going across town to 'The Golden Dragon'; a bit farther to walk but it's off the main drag so less likely to have a queue. I'll be as fast as I can." Harry walked under the entrance arches and away, passing through the market.

Tony got down from the sidings and approached Rob. "You having him back next Season?"

"The kid's a good worker; my takings have trebled since he started here, so it's a no-brainer."

"He's the no-brainer. I mean, look at his jacket, what the fuck is that all about!"

"Showmanship. I'm from three generations of this and people like him don't come along all that often. He's a natural."

"He's a dick," Tony replied as he walked off seething.

Within the hour Harry returned, carrying a white plastic bag with his lunch inside.

"You can bugger off now Rob, I'll sit in the pay-box with this." He raised the bag slightly and headed to the narrow Helter-Skelter booth.

"You sure? I still have a little time."

"Nah man, you head off. Have a good whatever and I'll drop the bag around tonight."

"Don't worry about that, I've taken most of it, left a twenty float." He pointed toward the Helter-Skelter. "The cash-bag's in the drawer. Don't bother tonight, just bring it in the morning."

"Right you are," Harry shouted from the booth whilst opening a plastic tub of chicken fried rice. Rob crossed the concourse without looking back, got into his van, and left. There was a slight trickle of punters, most of whom were happy to be spectators, casually strolling around and randomly commenting on the generally poor state of the sideshows. Every so often one or two would appear interested in one of Harry's stalls, so he abandoned his food to go serve the people.

By mid-afternoon the market traders started to pack everything up and gaps began to appear across the car park. It usually signalled the slowing of trade for the fairground, but with this being the final week it would be different. All of the people who wanted to go there but didn't get around to it during the season proper would be making the most of the final throes. It would be worse on the weekend, jam packed, and Harry would be lucky to get home before 1am. As it was, only Wednesday could he reliably be home by 11pm. It was long hours and quite often hard ones, but he loved it all the same. He had not long finished his lunch when a familiar face turned up. It was Trudy, standing at the hook-a-duck, hand clasped behind her back, swaying slightly, nervously, from side to side.

"Oi, knobhead. Your girlfriend's back," yelled Tony, pointing over at Trudy. Harry looked first at Trudy and then at Tony, giving him a middle-finger salute before leaving the booth and heading for the hook-a-duck.

"What's this? Two frogs not enough for you?" he asked with a grin.

"I'm not here for more frogs. I love them, but two's enough unless you get different ones. I just came back to tell you that I walked all around town with them so everyone could see them and I told a lot of people where they could win one before taking my froggies home."

"That's, erm, nice of you I guess, thanks for that. Weren't you embarrassed though? They're a bit big."

"That doesn't embarrass me at all. I'm more embarrassed about what rat-face over there said when I came back here."

"Oh, you heard that!"

"What did he mean by that? Have you told him I'm your girlfriend or something?"

"Hell no. Sorry, I mean I don't tell him anything at all if I can help it. The guy's always being a bit of an asshole, making comments and giving me the evil eye, shit like that. He's just best avoided."

"I wouldn't mind though, if you told him that. I'd mind it even less if it were true."

"Ah, you just want to kiss me to see if I'll turn into a frog." Harry joked.

Trudy laughed and nodded. "That would be so cool, but I'd be happy with you as you are too."

"Is this your way of actually asking me out?"

"Yes, I have to. I've been trying to pluck up the courage for ages and it's the end of the season. After this weekend, you'll vanish into the ether like you usually do. I don't want to have to wait until next Season. It's taken me all of this time to get brave enough, so if you're going to reject me please don't make a big thing of it, especially not in front of rat-face."

"I'm sorry Trudy, I had no idea. I don't know what to say, I mean, I like you, you're a nice girl, but don't you think your parents might have something to say about it?"

"Do you think I'm a child? I'm eighteen soon and you're probably around my age so it'll have nothing to do with them anyway."

"No, I meant that they'll object to you dating someone who works at a fairground."

"Like I said, none of their business, besides which, after this weekend you're unemployed aren't you?"

"I guess that somehow makes it better. Being a dosser is always better than being 'Carny folk', we tend to have a bad reputation because of the likes of Tony. Look, I have to get back to work, but I tell you what, I do odd hours and it'll be about 11ish when I'm done here so I'll be knackered, but how about you swing by sometime soon and we'll make plans for when I'm free?"

"You mean that's a yes? Like you'll go out with me?"

"Absolutely. I'll be working my butt off for the next few days, but from Monday on I'm all yours, here... Give me your number and I'll call you." He grabbed a piece of paper and a pen from behind the counter and handed it to her. She wrote her number down and passed it to him. He carefully folded the piece of paper, put it in his jeans pocket, then leaned forward open armed to hug her. Trudy seized the opportunity and threw her arms around him, hugging him tight and kissing him so hard he felt his lips mash against his teeth. She stood back, gave a huge smile, and walked away, somehow looking taller, prettier and more like a grown-up than she ever had. Tony seized the opportunity and leaped from the dodgem tracks, missing all of the steps and kicking up dust and grit as he landed, before skipping merrily over to Harry.

"I saw that, so she IS your girlfriend after all, you fucking cradle snatcher!"

"She wasn't, but she is now, and for your information she's almost eighteen, so a two year difference hardly makes me a cradle snatcher."

"Wait 'til I tell Rob that the one you gave the Kermits to is your girlfriend. He'll pop an artery."

"He won't give a shit. When he made me Manager he said I can do whatever I want as long as it makes more money, and he certainly can't complain about the takings."

"So, is she coming back later or does her mommy want her in bed by seven?"

"Y'know something Tony, you should be on the stage... Sweeping it. Haven't you got shit to do instead of harassing me?"

"Nothing that's as much fun," he replied.

Behind him a huge figure loomed. "Guess again fuckwit. Someone's just threw up in seven, so you'll have to get it sorted," said Carl. "Grab a bucket from stores. The ride stops in a minute and we can't start again until seven's clear."

Harry smiled. Tony glowered and went off in search of a bucket and cloths.

"Giving you a hard time again, was he?" Carl asked.

"The usual. I should thank him really; she heard what he said earlier and asked me out."

"Good for you, I hope she makes you happy. Don't mind him, he's just pissed off that you do better than he does."

"At what?"

"Everything," Carl said as he went back to his booth to sound the end of the ride.

Tony returned, dawdling into action steering seven back to the running boards before assisting a young girl in getting the safety belt off her vomit covered chest and clearing the puke from the car. There was a slight delay and they were a car down as it had to dry off, but it wasn't long before the dodgems were going full belt again.

The early evening drew in and a pair of coaches settled in the car park. Within minutes the bad news circulated, they were coach parties of disabled people, mostly Downs Syndrome, and destined to head for the Funfair. Normally coach parties were sought after as they are always full of eager punters who attack everything like mosquitos, but as the Fairground policy was that those with severe disabilities could use the rides for free, the general atmosphere was low.

Whenever they turned up, there was no getting rid of them until closing time.

At the far end of the Midway, Glen rapidly corralled the mini-rides, chaining them together and dropping canvases across them before locking his booth and heading for the Arcade. The Ghost Train slapped up a board on the booth and locked the doors. The disabled folk drew closer.

"They're all yours" Tony shouted to Harry and headed for the Dodgems booth to shut everything down.

"Only if you want to lose a day's wages," Carl shouted. "And be nice, they can't help being how they are."

The first of the coach party had split into three small groups; one headed for the front Arcade and the other two entered under the arches, some zeroing in on the Dodgems and the others headed to the hook-a-duck. Harry sprang into action.

"Cans, guns, darts, ducks, and Helter-Skelter!" he yelled as he straddled the hook-a-duck and grabbed the hooked poles. The no-fee policy only extended to the rides, but Harry made sure that everyone only paid once and got their money's worth.

Over in the car park two static figures watched from the shadows.

For three hours straight, the coach parties commandeered the Dodgems, all cars stayed full of the non-payers, who remained seated except for the occasional ones who'd had enough and abandoned the Dodgem cars allowing others from their party to get in there. Carl lowered the music, 'Stars on 45' softened away to a screech of microphone.

"Last ride," Carl said over the Tannoy. It was still an hour before usual closing time but he knew from experience that it would probably take best part of an hour to convince the punters to leave. The carers gathered those not on the Dodgems into a group by the arches, getting them to stay put whilst searching for stragglers and doing a head-count. Harry headed over to the Dodgems and stepped up the running board, swinging casually in front of the booth.

"Hey Carl, whose turn is it to do the bins today?"

"Ours... why?"

"Because one of the coach party is having a piss in one."

"Fuck off," he said, flashing a grin.

"I shit you not. She's right behind your booth with her knickers at half-mast, straddling the bin. It's dripping out of the base, see for yourself. I'll go alert the carers," Harry said, pointing at the window behind Carl.

Carl stood up, turned, and looked down out of the window. Sure enough, he could see a grey-haired woman sitting on the bin. Harry jumped down and walked over to the assembled guests in search of a carer. He found one and pointed out the situation. The carer, suitably horrified and apologetic, went to take care of the woman on the bin. As Harry walked back toward the hook-a-duck, Tony came bounding up like a Tigger on acid.

"Look at that fucker over there," he said, pointing at the woman who was no longer perched on the bin. "And it's your turn on the bins tonight... enjoy!" he laughed.

"You might want to look at the roster. Carl says it's a Dodgems day, and I'm pretty sure he's not going to be emptying it. I mean, why have a dog and bark yourself?"

The carer approached with the woman in question.

"I'm so sorry about this, but I don't suppose you have a toilet we can use... She's quite a mess back there and I can't take her to the coach like this," the carer stated.

"There's a public one across the car park, only a staff one here, but I think under the circumstances..." Harry knocked on the door of the Dodgem booth, explained the situation and asked for the key, which he took over to the carer before leading the women to the staff toilet. Carl pointed at Tony and then at the bin.

"I ain't touching it. She's done a shit in it; anyway, it's a stalls day so Harry has to do it."

"He did it yesterday. It's us today, which means it's YOU today. Get cracking, it's stinking the fucking grounds out."

Harry waited at the end of the corridor until the carer re-appeared.

"Thank you for this. I'm so sorry, we try to make sure that everyone uses the loos on the coach before they leave, but..."

"No worries, when you gotta go you gotta go."

"I'm afraid I have to get Helen back to the coach, but I'll come back and clean the mess up."

"There's no need for that, it's all under control. We empty and jet-wash them nightly anyway."

"Are you sure?"

"Positive, as long as you and… Helen… are ok that's all I care about." Harry locked the loos and led the women back out of the building. When he was outside, he saw Tony was removing the plastic sack from the bin, liquid excrement oozing from the perforations usually meant for draining dumped drinks. He was doing his best to keep his head turned away from the sight and smell but had to keep peeking to make sure he wasn't spilling any. He dumped the sack into an open wheelie bin, slammed the lid down, and returned the bin out of public view to the waste area. When he returned, the coaches had left and regular public were riding the Dodgems. He walked straight past them to Harry.

"I don't know what you said to Carl, but it should have been your night on the bins. Yuk it up fucker, I'll wipe that smug grin of your face." Tony issued the warning even though Harry wasn't grinning. Harry ignored him.

"Cans, guns, darts, ducks, and Helter-Skelter"

"You want 'Helter-Skelter' I'll give you 'Helter-fucking-Skelter'! I'll go all Charles Manson on you, wait and see." He headed back to the Dodgems.

From across the car park, two figures watched.

It wasn't long before the music lowered; Billy Joel left a Tender Moment Alone and was segueing into Paul Young's 'Every Time You Go Away' to get the ladies in the right mood for a night of Romance with the Carny boys. Glen loitered on the Dodgem rails, singling out his prizes for the evening. Tony pulled abandoned cars to the end of the track, checking the seats for lost cash or jewellery and the foot wells for handbags and cameras. Harry had already pulled canvases across his stands and was walking the runner of the Helter-Skelter, checking for dropped items stuck in the runners and making sure everything was structurally sound. By the time he'd come down from there, Tony and Glen had left and much of the grounds had fallen into darkness. It only remained for Harry to go to the generator shed and turn off the juice before locking up and heading home.

Harry crossed the car park, not a soul in sight. He checked his watch, 11:20 p.m., too late to stop for more Chinese food. The town was deserted save for the occasional vehicle passing through, and Harry took advantage of that. Not bothering with crossings as he headed for home, he took the most direct route down the steps and followed the canal's dimly-lit towpath. Across the canal he could see the silhouette of the back of the fairground, the Helter-Skelter rising above everything else, looking like some skeletal turret of a ruined castle. Two thirds of the way along the towpath he saw a figure step out of the shadows and stand still in the middle. He felt a chill, that primitive early warning system that something wasn't right here. No exit, he couldn't turn back, too far, could run but so very tired. He had little choice but to walk ahead. The figure was probably just a wayward drunk, or maybe one of the local kids, spray-can at the ready, tagging the wall to mark his posse's territory. Maybe.

Maybe.

As he drew closer, what passed for light glinting from the murky canal water helped to illuminate the stranger, casting his shape in a soft glow. It was a shape Harry recognised, he'd know those M.C. Hammer pants anywhere. Tony.

"Took your fucking time didn't you!" Tony said calmly.

"Had a lot to do. Never mind though, come Monday we can all relax," Harry replied, relieved that it was only Tony.

Tony leapt forward, punching Harry in the face, knocking him to the ground. He straddled Harry, pinning his arms down, and started slamming his fists down repeatedly on Harry's nose and mouth, ignoring the spraying blood from the mess he was making.

"Oh I'll relax all right, no more of you shouting about the fucking cans, the fucking guns, the fucking ducks and the fucking Helter-fucking-Skelter."

"You forgot... The fucking... darts," Harry spluttered through the blows.

Tony stopped, leaned back, spat in Harry's face, and then jerked forwards, slamming his elbow into Harry, shattering his nose and cheekbones, smashing his teeth back into his mouth and rendering Harry unconscious in a brutal flailing finale. He rolled Harry into the canal and headed off home, pleased with himself that it had all gone so quickly, so effortlessly.

Harry sank, disappearing beyond the reeds and into the murky water.

Thursday morning brought with it the usual routine of everyone setting up: shutters opening at ten o'clock sharp, tarps pulled away, boards removed, walkways swept. Except for Harry's section. Tony turned up for work a little earlier than usual, eager to see what was being said about Harry, but there was nothing much. Someone suggested someone else should go around to Harry's flat, see if he'd overslept or was ill, but nobody was free to do it. The power was off, but Tony went and got the master key to the generator shed and soon everything was coming to life as coloured bulbs flickered out of sequence and machines began to growl. Carl turned up and phoned Rob to tell him Harry wasn't there. Rob was furious, but said he'd be at the fairground in ten minutes, which turned into forty, not as though it mattered, mornings were always slow. It wasn't like Harry to not show up, he was usually the first on the grounds. There had to be good reason. Nobody thought anything much of it until the afternoon when a local kid said Harry's body had been fished from the canal. Several hours later, a couple of Police officers turned up. Tony made himself scarce, but Carl called for him over the Tannoy. He took a few deep breaths and headed for the Dodgems booth.

"Yep?" He ignored the Policemen who were talking to Rob and shied away from their view.

"It looks like it was true about Harry being pulled out of the canal. I know you both go the same way home so the coppers are wondering if you might have seen anything suspicious. They want to talk to you when they've finished with Rob."

"Not that I can think of..."

"Don't tell me, tell them," said Carl, pointing to the Officers who were heading toward them. One of them spoke directly to Tony.

"I suppose you know by now that your colleague Harry was found across the back there in the canal last night."

"Yeah, heard about that, poor little sod. I didn't think he was the type."

"The type?"

"Suicide. You don't suppose he chucked himself off the Helter-Skelter, do you?"

"Wrong side of the canal, and we're ruling out suicide as a possibility. He has all of the hallmarks of having the shit beaten out of him. I know you live near him so we're wondering if you saw anything suspicious on your way home."

"Not that I can think of, no. Oh, hang on, there was a couple of people hanging around on the car park last night. A bit strange actually, they weren't moving, just standing there looking over here. They were still standing there when I left; maybe they had something to do with his murder."

"Murder? You've been misinformed, he's not dead, he's up at the General, doing well all things considered."

"Did he tell you what happened?"

"He can't speak yet, face too badly damaged, and he's pretty out of it on tranquilisers, but if he does try to speak there'll no doubt be someone there to hear him or hand him a pen and paper."

"You don't suppose those guys in the car park did it, do you?"

"Well we won't know that unless you can give us more to go on. Can you remember anything else about them?"

"No, other than that they were there. You could ask around though, I'm pretty sure I wasn't the only one to see them. They were there for ages just standing in the shadows."

"I saw them too, well, I mean I saw a couple of people just standing there, other than that it's just like Tony said, it's too dark to be able to identify anyone. Even on a fairly bright night we have the lamps over the arches which cast a glare, so everything beyond that looks dark."

"Fair enough," said the senior Officer. "Thanks for your help gents, if you can think of anything else you know where to find us." With that, they turned and walked in the direction of the ghost train to continue their investigation. Rob headed over to Carl.

"Can you believe this shit? There I was ready to tell him I don't want him back next season if he's going to be this unreliable only to find some fucker tried to kill him. Who the fuck would want to do that to him? He wouldn't harm a fly."

"There's always someone. I mean, he's an annoying fucker sometimes, but Jesus Christ you wouldn't expect that sort of thing around here. Maybe it's a holidaymaker who lost too much money on the stalls!" Tony offered.

"It's possible I suppose, but it'd be a first. I know people get mouthy, but to try and kill someone over a few quid? Anyway, I hope they catch the fucker and string him up," said Carl.

"I'll get someone to cover for me and go to the General later, see if I can see him. He has no family, so I'm probably the closest person to him apart from his girlfriend" said Rob.

"How the hell do you know about her? He only got with her after you left here yesterday." Tony looked spooked.

"The Coppers told me he had her phone number in his pocket. She's with him right now, won't leave his side. Poor kid."

"Yeah, such a shame for both of them. If you do get to see him and he's lucid, give him my best," said Carl.

"Will do," said Rob before he headed into the main Arcade to use the phone.

As the day progressed, the talk of Harry subsided only to get jump-started again when Wilton turned up. He was not long out of school and eager to find work. He'd helped Harry out before so knew the ropes, but at sixteen he wasn't allowed to operate the two-gun stalls. Carl said he'd keep an eye on those until another recruit, 'Disco Dave,' turned up at 7:00 p.m. and the conversation started up again. The evening continued in a semi-typical routine, loads of punters, no coach parties, and a smattering of locals asking where Harry was or trying to get gossip if they'd already heard. The latest word on which, courtesy of Rob, was that Harry was still unconscious and likely to stay that way for the foreseeable future. Evening transitioned to night and the Fairground calmed down, a blessing in disguise for those who were not used to the shifts on Harry's stall. At 9:30, Disco Dave gave Wilton ten quid and sent him home, telling him he'd get another fifteen if he did all day Friday.

From the car park two figures watched Wilton leave, and waited.

10:00 p.m., time to start wrapping the whole thing up for the day. Disco Dave pulled the tarps and put the shutters up. He checked the runners on the Helter-Skelter and put a new padlock on it. Harry had left with the keys as usual, but they were not amongst his personal effects at the hospital, so the old padlock had to be chopped off. Dave pocketed the keys and gave Carl a nod before leaving. Without Harry to lock everything up, that task now fell to Carl and Tony as they had the only other set of keys. Carl gave them to Tony and left him to shut the electrics down and lock everything up.

From the car park two figures watched Dave leave and Carl drive off soon after. When all of the lights were out, they advanced.

Tony powered down the generator and was locking the main door when they attacked.

Something like a strap, strong, thick and padded, slipped around his neck, and he was dragged over backwards. He hit the ground hard, his head smacking gritty tarmac with enough force to make him scream if the ligature hadn't been too tight to allow it. His assailants dragged him backward, pulling him to the Dodgems. He could hear the sound of breaking wood, strained to see the cause, hoping for help as the main door to the storage area cracked and splintered. He was struggling for breath, losing the fight for consciousness. His head raised, bumping repeatedly as he was dragged backward up the wooden steps to the Dodgem tracks. The ligature loosened just enough so he wasn't garrotted and he grabbed at it, forcing his fingers under the velvety textured cloth. He pulled in precious breaths, his lungs aching with the effort, his bulging and bloodshot eyes attempted to focus, to see his assailants, but all was a blur against the darkness of the night and the canopy of metal mesh and wood above him.

Suddenly, a sound. One of the generators spluttered into life and the gentle hum of power coursed through the plates. The lights stayed off. He felt himself being pulled across the plates into the centre of the Dodgems track and then came lights as each of the cars took power, their headlamps waving beams which criss-crossed in the darkness. He heard a crash as the door to the storage area gave way and a host of figures burst forth, heading his way. He saw them, illuminated by the headlamps, recognised them, tried to make sense of what he was looking at but couldn't. All he could do was lay there wide-eyed, terrified, gasping for breath as the Dodgem cars slammed into him, ramming his torso, crushing his arms and legs, slapping his bloodied and broken carcass around.

The generator stopped, headlamps diminished to darkness. And then...

Silence.

Except for Tony, who lay there panting, his torn and broken ribcage making breathing almost impossible to achieve. His eyes tried adjusting back to the darkness. He could make out a shadow as one of his assailants leaned over him for one final gesture before they left him alone. He felt it, that final assault, but couldn't scream. He could only lay there.

The next morning the fairground was closed to the public. Police were questioning staff as forensics officers busied themselves putting white canvases around the crime scene and taping off the trail from the storage room doors. It was a crime scene unlike anything they had ever encountered. Tony, his corpse a twisted mess of bloodied cloth and bone, lay in the centre of the tracks, surrounded by blood-spattered Dodgem cars. Within each of the cars sat a three-foot-tall plush frog.

D.I. Warren leaned over Tony's corpse.

"What's that? It looks as if something has been rammed into his eye socket."

A forensics guy leaned over, reached into Tony's ocular cavity with tweezers, and carefully extracted a gore-smeared enamel badge of the Frog Prince.

The End

Zoltara
By
Christina Bergling

"Why in the hell would we want to go to a carnival?" Matt groaned.

"Because it will be fun," Hannah replied.

"Will it?" Matt cocked his head to the side. "There's no way carnivals have anything cool anymore. Everything good would be politically incorrect."

"It's supposed to be a modern carnival."

"A modern carnival? What would that possibly include? No freaks because that's exploitation. No rickety rides because lawsuits. No animals because PETA. No rigged games because no one can handle losing now. So, popcorn and funnel cake is what you're offering me. Basically, let's go to some food trucks."

Hannah rolled her eyes exasperated. "You are such a condescending ass. Just look at this."

Hannah turned her phone toward her brother so her could read the event page. He pulled the screen toward his face and began scrolling with his fingertip.

"The rides are all virtual reality," Hannah summarized. "The animal show is all robotic animals. You freaking love robots, Matt."

"I do love robots," he replied, still sliding his finger up the screen. "A farmer's market with the most impressive genetically enhanced produce? That sounds like a bunch of cancer."

"You don't have to eat it. You can stick to the popcorn and funnel cakes."

"Funnel cakes are damn delicious."

"So yes?" Hannah snatched the phone back and pressed it between her palms.

"Ugh, fine. Yes. But if it's lame, like I know it will be, we're out in less than an hour. Deal?" Matt extended his pinky finger toward her.

"Deal!" Hannah wrapped her pinky around his, then aligned their knuckles so their thumbs touched.

"So where is this monstrosity anyway?" he asked.

"In the old mall."

"What? Are you fucking kidding? This bullshit is inside too?"

"It's all electronics. Where did you expect it to be? In a parking lot like the ones when we were kids?"

"Now, those were the shit," Matt mused.

"Those death traps?"

"Yes!" Matt smacked his hands on the kitchen table. "Where's the thrill if you aren't a little bit worried the Ferris wheel is going to collapse at any moment?"

"I hated the Ferris wheel."

"I know. So, we'll go to your boring, indoor, kid- glove carnival. Pussy."

The door to the mall whooshed as Matt pulled it open for his sister. She tapped her cheek on her shoulder and smiled at him as she walked in. He rolled his eyes in return. The stores were all dark. A few had dormant wares crouched in the shadows, but many stood as empty shells of shopping since past. The hall lights dimmed from their expected fluorescence to allow the twinkling lights of the carnival to paint the tile in strange patterns.

"Lighted for ambiance," Matt mumbled. "Just pretending they're outside at night, like a carnival should be."

"Stop being such a fucking snob," Hannah replied. "You said you would give this a chance."

"I said we would go. I never said I would give it a chance. I feel it needs to be said that this is stupid."

"So noted."

As they walked down the shadowed hall, the carnival music grew, rolling out in the traditional, hopping rhythm. Strings of large LED Edison bulbs hung suspended between red and white striped tents erected in the former food court. The tents looked awkward and monstrous standing unnaturally within the building.

"This is just ridiculous," Matt huffed.

"Matt, knock it off."

"Tell me it's not ridiculous."

"OK, it looks stupid, but we're here. We're trying it out."

Matt rolled his eyes again, as if that was all he could do with them.

Hannah tossed her long hair over her shoulder defiantly at him and hustled a few steps in front of him so she could not register the disdain on his features. Despite the tragic juxtaposition of whimsical carnival tents and music against the hollow corpse of the shopping mall, Hannah still felt a subtle thrill humming on her nerves. She skipped into the aisle between tents as Matt trailed behind her, smartphone in his palm.

Hannah peered through the flaps of the first large, striped tent. A massive pumpkin occupied the center of the floor. The bottom compacted flat under the weight, but the ridges rounded up to at least Hannah's chest. A stem the size of a small tree trunk sprouted from the center. Beside it, ears of corn the size of Hannah's entire leg stacked in dry husks. Long tables held up grand and deformed shapes resembling grocery produce.

"You hungry?" Hannah said back over her shoulder.

Matt lifted his eyes from his phone screen to scan the tent unenthusiastically.

"That is not food," he declared. "That is cancer."

"Oh, I think the robots are next."

Matt perked up at the mention of robots and slipped his phone back into his pocket. A blend of children laughing, subtle gasps of the crowd, and a mechanical shifting floated out from the next, larger tent. Matt caught up to Hannah and pressed through the doorway before her.

As Hannah made it past the edge of the flap, she nearly collided with her brother's back. He stood frozen in the entryway, his eyes locked upward and his jaw hanging. Above him, a giant mechanical elephant swung its trunk in gentle figure eights through the air. Its huge metallic ears rolled stiffly in segmented panels of metal. Between each hinge and segment of the creature, colored wires wove like veins and small lights flashed.

"Holy shit," Matt breathed.

"Now, what's stupid?" Hannah teased, checking her shoulder gently against her brother's. He wavered at the push but did not take his eyes from the massive robotic elephant.

"You're still stupid," he replied.

Matt regained his composure and allowed his eyes to wander the tent. Beside the elephant, a shining silver tiger paraded around before regally mounting a platform and perching atop it. Its mechanical eyes flickered bright red and its tail clicked as the metal segments swished back and forth fluidly along the platform.

Their eyes snapped up as a flock of glinting metal birds flapped and soared overhead, weaving through the air around the elephant. The mechanical wings whined as they shoved the tiny robots into flight in expertly programmed patterns.

"This is amazing!" Hannah exclaimed as they moved among the robotic beasts.

Finally, she had to reach out and drag her brother away from the hypnotic gaze of the mechanical tiger's eyes. Even as she tugged him from the tent, his gaze lingered on the majestic robotic beasts.

"Those were amazing," he breathed as they stepped back out onto the tiled floor below an artificial sky.

"I told you this would be cool," Hannah mocked.

"I didn't say this was cool." Matt gestured at the entire sad display in the vacant mall food court. "I said that those robots were amazing. The articulation they achieved. The amount of engineering that must have gone into recreating such lifelike mannerisms."

"Yeah, yeah." Hannah waved her hand to brush aside his words. "Oh, look! Rides."

"Those are not rides."

"You can get a hard- on for metal animals and yet have no interest in virtual reality rides?"

"Not 'no interest'. Just appropriate expectations. We're at a carnival in a mall. I'm not setting the bar high."

"Well, let's go objectively evaluate the data then."

"You be objective. I'll be judgy."

"You are always judgy."

Hannah laughed and bounced toward the next tent. Even though the opening was high enough, she ducked her head below the large, colored blocked letters spelling Virtual Carnival Rides. Four lines snaked from each corner of the tent to converge in the center. A silent string of standing patrons, faces illuminated by their phone screens, waited to stare into another digital reality.

"Gross," Matt mumbled as they queued into line.

"See, judgy. You were just on your phone in the food tent. You stare into a computer for hours on end."

"That is not the same as this."

"How is it not?" Hannah propped her hand on her hip and tipped her head.

"This is supposed to be a carnival. Outside, under the stars. The smell of elephant shit, the crunch of dropped popcorn. The thrill of rides that might kill you. This is just—I don't know—neutered."

"This seems right up your alley. What is with you and the old school carnival?"

"Grandpa," Matt said.

"Grandpa?" Hannah furrowed her brow.

"Yeah, he took me to the carnival the summer before he died. We went in every tent. He took me on every ride. He told me all about how carnivals were so much better and more dangerous when he was a kid. How they still had some actual magic in them."

"Where was I?"

"That was the summer you were at Girl Scout camp or band camp or whatever the hell."

"Dance camp," Hannah corrected.

"Yeah, whatever."

The line shuffled forward until Hannah stood before the vacant chair for the virtual rollercoaster.

"Wait, you're going first?" Matt asked.

"Yeah, I'm going first. This was my idea after all."

Hannah plopped down into the large, molded black chair. The headrest wrapped around her ears with speakers on each side. As she settled in and buckled the seatbelt, the chair shifted side to side subtly. The carnival tech stepped forward. He did not look like a carnie. He could have stepped out of any office building or been knocking on the front door with pamphlets about Jesus. He looked so clean and ordinary that she would not even remember his face when she left the tent.

Without a word, the tech handed her the glasses, and she seated them over her eyes. The lenses illuminated a vision that turned night into day, changed the interior of the sad mall tent to a dazzling sunny day. She turned her head from side to side to see herself seated in a traditional rollercoaster as it climbed steadily above the wooden boards suspending it. She could hear the clicking of the tracks and a steady chatter of theme park attendees in her ears.

Her pulse quickened as the coaster climbed higher into the bright sky she saw around her. She forgot about the carnival and felt the rumble of the tracks against the base of her legs. A scream escaped her throat as the car plunged over the crest of the first hill, rattling violently along the tracks.

"That was so awesome!" Hannah beamed as they pressed back out of the tent.

"It was OK," Matt replied.

"You're just disappointed you didn't fear for your life."

"Exactly. It's just not the same. I heard you scream like a bitch though."

"Shut up!" Hannah slapped at her brother. "Looks like there is one tent left."

Hannah extended her finger down the row of tents and pointed to the last on the end. The tent hunched smaller than its siblings, shrouded in shadows from the distant bulbs. It glowed from inside, and the word “Fortune” flickered in neon lights above the entry.

“No,” Matt said, firmly. “I draw the line at bullshit fortune telling.”

“We’re going. It’s part of the full experience.”

“Fortune telling is bullshit, Hannah,” Matt insisted. “They are all just vague statements that could easily be interpreted to apply to any person or situation. Then the optimistic dummies have that seed in their head and create all sorts of illusory correlations to make them true. It is nothing but a hustle and not even a good hustle at that.”

“See, judgy. Did you see the fortune teller with Grandpa?”

“No.”

“You said you did EVERY thing.”

“We paid the little machine with the mannequin in it.”

“So, you still got a fortune. What did it say?”

“Grandpa’s said, ‘All good things must come to an end.’”

Hannah stopped for a breath.

“You don’t have to do it, but I’m going to do it. Come with me?” she finally asked.

"Fine. I'll come watch you get played."

Hannah's pace slowed as she approached the Fortune tent. Something about the way it hunched glowing in the shadows quickened her pace and set the nerves along her skin on edge. She thought it felt like excitement with a thickened lump in her throat. With the virtual rides and the robotic animal show behind them, Matt extracted his phone and showed his disapproval for her indulgence by losing himself in the light of its screen.

Hannah edged through the entry, allowing the thick canvas to ripple across her bare shoulder. As the tent swallowed her, its eerie glow enveloped her, and the anxiety in her chest dissipated into a strange calm. She vaguely heard Matt enter behind her but had nearly forgotten he was tailing her.

"Good evening, my dear," the fortune teller tech smiled, seeming to materialize in the odd light.

The man looked near identical to the carnival tech in the virtual rides tent. He donned the same crisp white shirt, black pants, and thin black tie. The same square black glasses perched on his nose. A quirky smile snaked over his lips, but his eyes did not participate. Instead, his eyes were wide and somewhat blank. Hannah found herself staring at him without a word in her head.

"Are you here to have your fortunes told?" he continued.

"She is," Matt replied, stepping up beside Hannah. "I'm just here to watch."

"One cannot simply be a voyeur to another person's future," the man stated, expressionless.

"He doesn't believe in fortune telling." Hannah finally found her voice. "He thinks it's all a clever hustle. Maybe you could prove him wrong with my reading?"

"Your brother?" the tech said.

"Yes." Hannah turned to give Matt a knowing glance.

"Come on," Matt huffed. "Anyone could tell I was your brother. We're of comparable age and have the same basic aesthetic features."

"You do look alike," the tech smirked.

"So, what is a fortune telling in this 'modern carnival'?" Matt waggled his fingers in air quotes.

"Step this way, my good sir, and I will show you," the tech said.

He stepped forward and outstretched his hand into the ominous light around them. In the thin air, his fingertips found the edge of a curtain and parted it to reveal a large, black screen.

"What is that?" Matt laughed. "It looks like a giant iPad."

The man smiled again, in the twisted shadows carved in his face. This time, his eyes twinkled softly.

"Your reading, my dear?" the tech asked Hannah.

Hannah stared at the black screen, entranced. She nodded gently and stepped forward.

"Simply touch the screen to awaken her." The tech bowed and gestured to the screen.

Hannah raised her index finger slowly in front of her, looking over her shoulder at her brother. He had sheathed his phone back in his pocket and watched her with a strange interest. They locked eyes, and he pressed his chin forward to encourage her. The digit trembled slightly as she jammed it into the screen.

A ripple swept over the screen from her impact. Light spawned from her fingertip, spreading until the entire screen glowed. A woman appeared in the center in the stereotypical gypsy attire and turban, a recreation of the mannequins in old fortune telling machines. Her eyes throbbed in a fierce and unnerving green, and a sly smile curved her beautiful face. She towered as a head and shoulders consuming the screen then eased backward to life-sized.

"Good evening, my child," the woman on the screen said in a thick, cliché accent. "My name is Zoltara. Tonight, I will be your guide into your past, your present, or your future. You make the choice, but beware, you cannot unknow what I will tell you."

Zoltara waved her hand across the screen, coin bracelets softly tinkling, and three words appeared in shadowed gold below her: Past, Present, and Future.

"Choose one below," she directed, with a smile.

Hannah looked over her shoulder at her brother.

"Present," he blurted.

"Someone is more curious than only watching," the tech observed, softly.

Matt glared at him from the side of his eyes. Hannah stepped forward and tapped the Present button. The word exploded into a shower of sparks, and Zoltara emerged from the blast with her green eyes gleaming.

"At this present moment…" Zoltara paused for a dramatic breath. She looked down then flicked her eyes up. Hannah flinched as it seemed like she was looking at her. "Your brother thinks fortune telling is a scam."

Zoltara seemed to flit her glance over Hannah's shoulder at Matt. Matt charged forward to stand beside his sister. His mouth groped at words for a moment before he spoke.

"That doesn't prove anything," Matt insisted. "This thing probably listened to the whole conversation we had right here and adjusted its reading to match."

Zoltara leaned her face closer to the glass and slyly lifted one eyebrow.

"See?" she said.

Matt and Hannah instinctively took a step backward and a step closer together.

"OK, that was creepy," Matt said.

"Still so skeptical," the tech murmured, forgotten beside them.

"Yeah. Yeah," Matt stuttered. "I still think it's a hoax. Creepy and well executed but still a—"

"Scam," the tech echoed Zoltara.

Matt nodded. Hannah looked between the two, chewing her bottom lip.

"Try again," the tech offered, simply.

"What?" Hannah asked.

"Try again. On the house. To dissuade the skeptic."

Hannah looked up into her brother's eyes. He reflected her tentative confusion rather than providing an answer.

"Might as well," she said.

She shrugged awkwardly and stepped forward toward Zoltara again. Zoltara seemed to grin slightly at her and eased back to a life-sized distance again. The initial moment replayed. Zoltara waved her hand across the screen, coin bracelets jingling. The three words reappeared in shadowed gold below her: Past, Present, and Future.

"Choose one below," she instructed, with the same smile.

Hannah looked back at Matt once more. She still found no direction swimming in his eyes.

"Past," she said to herself as she tapped the screen.

Zoltara stepped through the shower of sparks and set her eyes seemingly on Hannah once more.

"Your past," she began then paused. "When you were nine years old, you borrowed your father's scientific calculator. It was in your room for two days. When you returned it to your father, it was broken, the screen cracked and one of the buttons missing. Your father was furious. Your brother never told you that he broke the calculator and said nothing."

A clever and defiant look settled on Zoltara's digital features, managing to make her look more realistic. Hannah's jaw dropped, and her mouth hung agape. She whipped around to glare at her brother. His wide eyes and twitching lips gave her all the confirmation she needed.

"You asshole!" she cried. "He grounded me for weeks! And you said nothing."

"I know. I'm sorry. But I was seven. I just panicked," Matt pleaded.

"I can't believe you never said anything. You are such a piece of shit." Hannah pursed her lips hard and paced in a small circle. Then she turned and looked at her brother. "Now, say it."

"Say what?"

"Say. It."

"Fine. It's true," he grumbled

"So, this fortune telling is not bullshit?" Hannah planted her hands on her hips.

Matt bit at his lip and shifted his weight between his feet. He fidgeted subtly, shifting his arms up and to his sides.

"This doesn't prove it's not," he finally said.

"Doesn't it? Zoltara told me something you've kept a secret for almost a decade. How would she know that? It's probably not even on a computer for her to magically hack to over the internet, is it?"

"No," he mumbled. "I never told anyone. Once you weren't grounded anymore, I just forgot about it."

"So, it's not bullshit, is it? It's not a hustle."

Matt pressed his lips and crossed his arms but did not argue.

"I think we can agree that this was a successful reading," the tech stated, stepping forward and tugging the near invisible curtain back over the screen. "I would like to invite you to download the Zoltara app to continue your fortune experience on your mobile device."

The tech slipped his fingertips into his pocket and held out a card to Hannah. Defiantly, she glared at her brother and took the card in her hand. Zoltara's face graced the majority of the card, along with her name in the same golden text as the fortune teller program. When Hannah flipped the card over, she saw app store logos and a QR code.

"Thank you," Hannah smiled.

She turned from the man and the woman behind the curtain and left the tent, Matt chasing behind her.

"You're not really going to download that thing," Matt remarked from his couch cushion.

Hannah held her phone to her face, navigating through the app store with her fingertip.

"Of course I am," she replied.

"Don't do that. Zoltara was creepy."

"You are just mad that she snitched on you. And that you were wrong about it being a scam."

"Hold on. Hold on. Let's break this down." Matt turned on his seat to face his sister. "If it is a scam, you do not want to download that app. It would definitely be malware. And if it's not a hustle, and I'm not saying it isn't, do you really want an app that can accurately read your past, present, and future on your phone? Enough apps read your contacts and messages to try and sell you shit. What do you think Zoltara is going to do?"

"You are so paranoid."

"I am not paranoid. I am informed. And smart."

"And conceded."

"It's not conceded if it's accurate."

"Um, yes it is." Hannah glared at him playfully. "I'm downloading her."

Hannah tapped the buttons and brought Zoltara onto her phone.

"This is going to go so wrong," Matt said.

Hawkins, their dopey brown mutt, wound himself between Matt's legs until Matt relented and pet him firmly on the head. Hawkins's tongue tumbled from his mouth and dangled between his teeth as he panted. Matt tried not to smile but could not resist.

"Well, then you'll get to gloat about being right again," Hannah replied.

"I do love being right. It just happens so often."

"That's why you don't want me to download her. Because you were WRONG about her."

"Shut up." Matt swiveled back around to face the TV.

Hannah rolled her eyes to herself and turned her attention to Zoltara. She launched the application and tapped her finger in the center of the screen to summon the fortune teller. The app mimicked the original program perfectly. Zoltara's face greeted her as a miniature of the digital fortune teller she had met the night before.

"Good morning, my child," Zoltara said in her accent. "My name is Zoltara. Today, I will be your guide into your past, your present, or your future. You make the choice, but beware, you cannot unknow what I will tell you."

Zoltara waved her hand and conjured Hannah's choices.

"Choose one below."

Hannah shot a glance at her brother.

"Don't look at me," he said, refusing to return her gaze.

"I obviously need to try future this time," she decided.

"I said, don't do it. I don't want to know."

Hannah gnawed on her lip briefly before bringing her finger down on Future. The sparks sizzled across her phone screen until they revealed Zoltara's bright eyes. Her digital stare seemed even more piercing from the small, restricted screen. She seemed to peer right into Hannah, as if Hannah could feel Zoltara's gaze caress her mind.

"Today," Zoltara began before hesitating. "On her way home from work, your mother will be in a car accident. A blue SUV will run a red light and sideswipe her on the passenger side. The car will be totaled, and your mother will go the hospital, but she will be fine."

"Holy shit," Hannah breathed.

"Don't tell me," Matt said. "I told you I didn't want to know."

"What time does Mom leave work?"

"What? Why?"

"What time?" Hannah reached over and snatched her brother's arm.

"Like an hour ago. What did it say?" Matt stiffened and perked on the edge of the couch cushion.

"Zoltara said Mom will get into a car accident on her way home."

"What?" Matt leaped to his feet in one rapid motion.

"She said a blue SUV is going to hit her on the passenger side and the car will be totaled and Mom will go to the hospital."

"Shit! I told you not to download that!"

Matt pushed his fingers into his hair and tangled them in the strands as he started pacing around in front of the couch. Hannah crossed her arms and leaned on her knees as she anxiously chewed on her lip. Then Hannah's phone rang, and they both froze.

Hannah still had the device dangling from her hand, but she stared down at it perplexed, as if she didn't know what to do with it. She looked into her brother's eyes, to see her own fear staring back at her, as she swiped to answer and brought the phone to her ear. Her eyes only continued to widen as her father's voice dumped the news into her head.

"Yeah, Dad," she responded. "Yeah, I understand. Is she going to be OK?" She chomped on her lip as she listened. "Yeah, OK. I'll see you when you get home."

She tapped her screen to hang up. Matt practically vibrated in front of her.

"Well?" he asked.

"Zoltara was right," she said, softly.

"How right? What did Dad say?"

"That Mom was in an accident, got sideswiped. The car is a loss, but Mom is fine. He's bringing her home in about an hour."

"Holy shit," he breathed.

"I have to see what she says next."

Hannah moved to lift her phone to her face. Matt slapped her arm down.

"Are you crazy? Mom just got in a car accident. What do you think Zoltara will do next?" Matt gaped.

“Zoltara didn’t do it. Any more than she broke Dad’s calculator when I was nine.”

Matt huffed and rolled his eyes.

“How can you still doubt it?”

“Well, of course you’re going to believe it now. That’s part of the scam. It probably accessed your phone’s GPS then cross referenced the vehicles registered at this address against police reports, which would have included the cars involved and Mom’s condition.”

“You are such a conspiracy theorist!” Hannah threw up her hands.

“Just because it is a conspiracy doesn’t make it wrong.”

“And how did it know about the calculator? Was that available anywhere digitally? Any chat? Any text? Ever?”

“No,” Matt pouted.

“Then how do you explain that?”

“I don’t know. I must have told someone online, but I thought I never told anyone. Not even in the three-dimensional life. I just wouldn’t mess with it. You don’t know what it will do next.”

"You cannot think the entire thing is a hustle and think a fortune telling app makes things happen. It can't be both," Hannah said.

"I don't think it's legit, but do you seriously want to even mess with it? After this?"

"She told me the future. Of course I want to know! Think of all the things I could know."

"And never unknow," Matt said, quietly. "This is a stupid idea, Hannah."

"Well, you don't have to do it. It's all bullshit, remember? Call me down when Mom gets home."

Hannah clutched her phone to her chest and hurried out of the room. She scurried up the stairs and closed Matt's judgment on the other side of her bedroom door. Zoltara already waited for her behind her lock screen. Her eyes burned brighter as the screen illuminated fully. Hannah did not hesitate to tap on Future once more.

"Back so soon, my child," Zoltara grinned. "Your subscription includes one future reading per day. However, on your first day, you can purchase an addition future reading for just one dollar. Press the Buy button below to charge your app store credit card."

Zoltara winked through the screen. Without a thought, Hannah tapped on the Buy button. The screen erupted in its customary sparks, and Zoltara emerged again from the glimmer.

"Tomorrow," she said thickly. "Your brother will be in a physical altercation after school. Intervention will spare him from serious harm."

With the last word, the app closed itself and returned to her home screen. Hannah lay back on her mattress, dropping her phone on her chest and drumming on the case with her fingertips.

The next day, the students spilled out of the high school in the echo of the final bell. Teenagers congregated in small circles on the grass, showing their phone screens to each other and laughing. Hannah bounced down the concrete stairs toward the student parking lot, where she met Matt every day after to class to drive him and his friend Danny home.

As she approached the edge of the blacktop, Hannah could make out Matt and Danny in the center of a group of bystanders. Brandon, an asshole from Hannah's class, stood menacingly in front of them, shouting unintelligibly. Hannah's pace quickened as Brandon lunged forward, shoving Danny aside and grabbing Matt by the shirt.

By the time Hannah jogged over to the swelling crowd, Brandon threw Matt backwards into the pavement. Hannah heard the crack and thud of the impact and felt a hot rage blaze under her skin.

Your brother will be in a physical altercation. Hannah heard Zoltara's voice echo in her head and felt a strange detachment wash over her. Her rage dissipated into observant focus. She watched herself march up to Brandon and shove him in the back.

"Brandon!" she heard herself shout. "What the fuck is your problem?"

Brandon whirled around with clenched fists until his eyes bugged out at the sight of her snarling at him. Hannah felt the harshness in her face and her stance, yet she executed no control over it. It just happened.

"This don't have anything to do with you, Hannah," Brandon barked.

"Get away from my brother." Hannah heard her own words separate from her mind again.

"Nah, this little bitch—"

"Well, you're going to have to fight a fucking girl if you want at him."

Hannah heard the collective gasp then hush ripple through the observers. She felt her fingernails digging into her palms and arms trembling rigid beside her. Brandon glared between her and her brother on the ground. Then he rolled his eyes and stormed back toward the school. As the crowd began to scatter, Hannah moved over to Matt to help him off the ground. He shrugged her off and hurried with Danny to her car.

"Um, you're welcome?" Hannah said, catching up to them and dropping herself into the driver seat.

"You're welcome for what?" Matt asked. "You just made me look like a bitch."

"Yeah, but I kept you from getting your ass kicked in front of half the school."

"I don't know that being saved by your big sister is better."

"Zoltara told me it was going to happen," Hannah stated.

"Who the hell is Zoltara?" Danny chimed in from the backseat.

"Some bullshit fortune telling app my dumbass sister downloaded after the lame modern carnival I told you about," Matt told him.

"I bet you didn't mention the sweet robot animals and virtual rides you loved. Or that Zoltara snitched on you from when you were seven," Hannah remarked.

"He did mention the robots," Danny responded.

"What did Zoltara say about this?" Matt asked.

"She said you would be in a physical altercation and that intervention would keep you from getting hurt," Hannah answered.

"That's vague and specific at the same time," Danny mused.

"She didn't say you would intervene?" Matt said. "She didn't tell you to?"

"No," Hannah replied.

"Well, the mere suggestion of intervention could have been the inspiration for it," Danny said.

"So, Zoltara made me do it?" Hannah laughed.

"Yeah, kind of," Matt agreed. "You need to stop messing with that app."

"Saved your ass," Hannah said.

"Show me," Danny said, leaning forward against the back of Hannah's seat.

Matt whirled around to glare at him. Hannah pulled her phone from her back pocket and summoned Zoltara. She tapped through the prompts until Zoltara's green eyes smiled up at them from the glass.

"Tonight," Zoltara disclosed "You will suffer an unfortunate accident with a sharp instrument. Part of you will never be the same, but rest assured the bleeding will stop."

"Well, that's ominous," Danny said.

"Guess I'm not the only one who needs my ass saved," Matt muttered, clicking his seatbelt.

Hannah navigated their slice of suburbia to drop Danny off and get them home. When they dropped their backpacks in the entry, Matt instantly vanished up the stairs to his computer. Hawkins chased clumsily after him. Hannah wandered into the kitchen to root out a snack and found a scrawled note waiting for her.

"Han, please chop up the vegetables for dinner. They are in the drawer in the fridge. Help your mom out. Dad," the note read.

Hannah rolled her eyes and fetched the groceries from the fridge, popping an apple into her mouth. She sunk her teeth into the flesh and let the fruit dangle in her jaws as she found the cutting board and pulled a knife from the block.

An unfortunate accident with a sharp instrument. Hannah heard Zoltara's fortune reverberate again then laughed it off. She could cut up some carrots safely.

She pulled a carrot from the grocery bag and set it across the cutting board. She held the carrot down with one hand and gathered the knife in the other. The handle felt at home in her palm, and again, she felt that strangely comforting separation happen between herself and her skin. She pressed the blade methodically through the carrot, hearing the snap each time it separated the segment, and fell into a light trance. The carrot could have been cutting itself.

The knife moved into slow steps toward her hand, one chunk at a time. Her heart tried to pound as it got closer, yet the sedation pressed down on top of her, made her feel farther from herself. Her hands seemed to stretch away into the distance until she could barely see their movements.

The cuts approached the stem of the carrot. Her fingers gathered tightly on the remaining nub. When there was nothing left to slice, she lifted the blade very slowly and watched herself bring it through her own finger. She sliced the tip of her finger at the same angle as the carrot, separating the tip from the full digit. Blood welled from the cut and pooled until the removed portion floated on the cutting board.

Even as the calm detachment waned and Hannah swelled back into control of her skin, she could only stare in shock, still clutching the knife.

The stitches irritated Hannah as she lay not sleeping on her bed in the dark with morning looming. She had not slept in any of the hours pushing her towards dawn since the emergency room. Her reattached fingertip felt numb and foreign. She dragged the bandage methodically along her collarbone, staring into the ceiling she couldn't yet see. Her eyes and fingers seemed to twitch together. Until she reached over and grabbed her phone.

"Good morning, child," Zoltara said in the same inviting yet mocking tone.

Anxiety tickled the edge of Hannah's brain and a doubt that sounded alarmingly like Matt sang in her ears. An instinct to uninstall Zoltara surfaced only to be drowned below the unnerving thrill of knowing, of glimpsing the future, of releasing herself into that weightless trance.

She touched Future and waited.

"Today." Dramatic pause. "Man's best friend meets an untimely end. Tears are coming, but they won't be yours."

Zoltara folded into the closing app, and Hannah was left perplexed with her home wallpaper illuminating her face. Finally, her screen went dark, and she lay there immobile and awake until morning broke across her bedroom.

Once the sun had fully taken over the sky, Hannah dragged herself from her sheets, and she shambled through her morning routine. When she stood in front of the mirror, she scarcely recognized the sunken eyes and sallow pallor of her own face.

"Hannah," her mother shouted from some obscure corner of the house. "Don't forget to feed Hawkins."

Hannah's eyelids draped heavily over her vision as she dragged herself into the kitchen. She flipped on the coffee maker before snatching Hawkins's empty dish from the floor. At the scrape of metal against the hardwood, Hawkins stampeded into the kitchen. His tail whipped violently enough to topple him as he sat excitedly in the doorway. Hannah smiled at him as she leaned into the pantry and scooped dry dog food into the dish.

As she stood back up, the detachment swelled over her again. She nearly tumbled out of herself as her body shifted across the kitchen and reached under the sink. From some imperceptible distance, she saw herself add extra flavor to Hawkins's breakfast.

Hannah's tears did not come, but Matt's did. His tears did not stop since they left the vet with an empty collar and leash. He held the two, tags clanking together softly, as he sobbed in the backseat beside her. Hannah reached out for his shoulder, but he curled away from her. She felt her heart breaking for him somewhere beneath the thickening distance growing between her and the world.

An untimely end.

Alone in her room, Hannah could still hear Matt sobbing through their shared wall. A ragged, retching rhythm she had heard in the worst times of their conjoined life. She wanted to cry with him. She wanted to share those tears. Yet the space inside her only widened. Instead, she felt an itching need to hold her phone, a twitching desire to query Zoltara again. She craved another seed embedded deep inside her brain.

She managed to bite at her lip and pick at her fingernails until the clock rolled past midnight. When the day reset and she could access her new fortune.

"Today," Zoltara paused, and her eyes sparkled. "Your brother's best friend won't know what hit him. But you will."

Zoltara smirked, and Hannah felt a flinch somewhere she still felt. Then the app retreated, and the screen went dark.

Hannah drifted through the day, tethered to her body by an unraveling string. Her flesh moved through the halls, sat through the classes, and brought Matt and Danny home afterward.

"What's with you today, Hannah?" Danny asked as they walked into her house.

"What do you mean?" Hannah managed to force out the words.

"I don't know. I mean one day you're throwing down with Brandon, and today, you haven't said a thing. It's like you're not there. Is it Hawkins?" he asked.

"Yeah," Hannah lied, "I'm pretty heartbroken over Hawkins."

"I'm sorry." He smiled at her gently out of the side of his mouth.

Hannah smiled back but felt something different. Where she should have felt kindness and affection, she felt something more like opportunity, something more like destiny.

Danny dropped his backpack beside the others on the floor and pulled himself onto a stool at the kitchen counter. Hannah heard Matt moving on the floor above them, searching his room for the game on which they were going to waste the afternoon. As Hannah moved behind Danny, the infectious calm throbbed over her. It pounded in such a seductive rhythm that she could not hear anything else.

Hannah's body walked deliberately across the kitchen as her awareness dribbled behind. She marched directly to the cabinets and extracted a large pan. Like the knife, it felt right in her grip, necessary. The weight of it seemed like foreshadowing, her own little fortune reading.

"I remember when Hawkins was a puppy and he would run so fast he skidded out across the kitchen," Danny was saying, looking down at the counter awkwardly.

Matt's footsteps padded across the ceiling above as Hannah's arm heaved the pan high and brought it cracking across Danny's back. She heard all the wind explode out of his lungs and go sputtering all over the counter where he was staring. The impact reverberated through his torso like a drum and echoed up Hannah's arm.

Danny groped weakly at the edge of the countertop before wilting and collapsing to the floor. His limbs slapped against the hardwood loudly. Hannah's legs stepped to straddle his crumpled body, and she wielded the pan again, heaving it high and bringing it down on his head. The metal rang out in a terrible chime at the impact. Danny's voice broke as he cried out in pain.

"Hannah!" Matt shrieked as he walked into the kitchen.

Hannah froze with the pan above her head again, trapped somewhere bewildered between prophecy fulfillment and her brother's terrified voice.

"What the fuck are you doing?" Matt yelled. "Get off of him! Get away from him!"

Matt charged across the room and violently shoved Hannah backward, almost hard enough to knock her back into herself. She felt a moment of clarity break painfully upon her mind before it was swallowed by the stretching fog again.

"He didn't know what hit him," Hannah said flatly, "but I did."

Matt never came back from the hospital. Hannah sat mutely on the couch waiting for him as the sun died in the sky and the light drained from the windows around her. Matt had made up some story about how Danny had fallen, but he could not look at Hannah. She could feel the rage and disgust radiating off him, and it penetrated her detachment until it burned. Somewhere beneath it all, she felt her anguish building.

She could hear her parents moving around the house, but she felt like they were on another planet. She couldn't think of anything but her brother. Not Danny, not Hawkins, not her 'frankenfinger'. Only Matt. She had to know where he was, and she knew who would be able to tell her.

"Right now," Zoltara said, somehow deeper and more dramatically, "your brother has gone back to the source. He is headed back to me to pull back the curtain and show you what a scam looks like."

Hannah should have known where he would go. She should have known what he would blame. She could almost see him back in the mall, through Zoltara's eyes. She snatched her keys and sprinted to her car.

The mall parking lot was near abandoned with only a few wayward cars parked between the faded lines. The dented streetlights barely lit the blacktop. Hannah hurried through the shadows and pulled open the mall doors.

The corridor managed to be darker than her last visit to the carnival. No traditional music babbled down the hall. No strings of light illuminated the empty stores. Somehow, Hannah felt comfortable, at home. Her detached body felt natural in this darkness. She sauntered across the tiles to where the carnival once stood as the shadows cradled her.

The large, colorful tents had been packed up and removed. The only evidence of the concessions was the remaining popcorn that crunched under her steps. The Fortune tent stood alone in the darkened hallway, a single sliver of light pouring out from its parted flap. Hannah knew Matt was under the tent. She could feel it at her core where her consciousness was still tethered to her flesh. Hannah reached out to push the flap aside and stepped back into Zoltara's strange light. The light felt the same as the detachment in her mind—unnerving and consuming.

"Good evening, my dear," the fortune teller tech said. "Welcome back. We have been waiting for you."

The tech stepped aside to reveal Matt behind him. Matt clawed frantically through the air, searching desperately for the seam in the curtain.

"Where is she?" Matt cried. "I know it's her fault. I know this is still some bullshit game. What did you do to my sister?"

His voice cracked again in that terrible sound Hannah knew so well. A flare of emotion blazed over her eyes as she cupped her hand over her mouth to stifle her cry.

"Matt," she finally said.

Matt spun around to face her. The anger on his face dissolved into an awkward blur of sadness, affection, hate. His eyebrows quivered at the contradiction, and his eyes swam.

"Danny is still in the hospital," Matt screamed. "You could have really hurt him. What the fuck, Hannah?"

"Your brother's best friend won't know what hit him. But you will." Hannah only had Zoltara's words.

"Hannah, that's not you." Matt eyes threatened to betray him. "Hawkins. Did you kill Hawkins too? I know you chopped off your own fucking finger."

"Man's best friend meets an untimely end. Tears are coming, but they won't be yours," Hannah replied. "You will suffer an unfortunate accident with a sharp instrument. Part of you will never be the same, but rest assured the bleeding will stop."

"Hannah, stop!" Matt cried. He turned to the tech. "Stop this. Make her stop."

"There's only one thing you can do," the tech replied.

"What is it?"

"Ask Zoltara." The tech's lips curled up as he answered her.

The tech stepped in front of Matt and effortlessly grabbed the edge of the unseen curtain. He pulled it aside to reveal Zoltara's screen. He fully exposed the glass, tucked the curtain out of the way, and stepped back. The screen reflected the dazed shock on Matt's face as Hannah moved up beside him. Before Matt could stop her, Hannah pressed her finger into the center of the glass.

The screen rippled then lit up. Zoltara materialized before them, appearing more enlivened, more lifelike than before. She stared directly into Matt and smiled before turning her attention to Hannah and waving her hand to present her options. Hannah did not hesitate to press Future once more.

Zoltara's eyes burned as she appeared from the sparks. Her smile snaked devilish and mischievously.

"All good things come to an end," Zoltara said.

At the words, Hannah's face went completely slack and blank. She turned slowly towards her brother and reached for him. The tech gently moved around them to replace Zoltara's curtains. As Matt sputtered and cursed against his sister, the tech sauntered away, drawing the flap closed behind him. As Matt's screams echoed through the empty shopping mall, the eerie light in the Fortune tent went dark.

The End

In a Hand or Face
By
Gary A. Braunbeck

A weary remnant of the young woman she once was, Fran McLachlan stood in the center of the midway holding her five-year-old son's hand and trying not to think about the way her life had gone wrong.

"Mommy," Eric implored, "what's wrong?"

Fran was glad that the massive bruises on his cheek and jaw looked far less discolored and painful today. If only she could say the same for her own abrasions--but, after all, wasn't that why God created makeup and Tylenol?

"Mommy?"

"Wha--? Oh, I'm sorry, hon. What did you say?"

"Did that lady say something bad to you?"

"No, hon, she didn't."

"Then how come you look so sad?" He

clutched his balloon-doll as if his very life depended on it.

Oh, Christ! How could she answer that question honestly *now,* after what Madame Ariadne had shown her? How could she tell her son--the only good thing she had--that she was thinking about abandoning him on a fairgrounds nearly a hundred miles from home because of a palm-reading?

You didn't give her a definite answer, she thought. *The group's not going to head back to the shelter for another hour--you can* at least *make this time count. You can make sure he has so much fun that nothing will ever taint the memory for him, ever.*

God, Eric, do you know how much I love you?

"Hey, you," she said, tugging on his hand and smiling.

"Hey, *you!*" he replied, grinning.

"We'll have to...to be leaving soon, so what say until then we do whatever you want?"

"Really?"

"Uh-huh. You pick."

"Then I wanna go on the merry-go-round."

This surprised her. "Why? We've been on it three times today."

"'Cause you laughed when the tiger started bouncing and it wasn't a pretend-laugh like all the other ladies. I liked it."

Oh for the love of God, kiddo--why'd you have to go and say something like that?

Fran kissed her son's cheek and told herself she would. Not... Start... Crying.

"Okay," she whispered. "The merry-go-round and then... then m-maybe we'll meet your new friend and get some hot dogs."

"Hot dogs!" shouted Eric, dragging her down the midway, his balloon-doll thrust in front of him as if it were flying.

For a moment there, Fran could've sworn that her son's face actually *shone* with happiness.

And not pretend-happiness, either.

#

It began three hours earlier. Fran and Eric were having lunch at a long picnic table with several other women from the Cedar Hill Women's Shelter and their children. The kids were occupying themselves by pointing out all the sights to one another while the mothers took the time to regroup and count the money they had (or, in most cases, *didn't* have) left.

"You look a lot better today, Fran," remarked one of the women. "So does Eric."

"Yeah," Fran acknowledged. "We're both feeling better."

"Have you thought about, well... about Ted?"

Fran shook her head. "No--I mean, yes, I have, but Eric hasn't mentioned him and I'd appreciate it if none of you would bring up his father today, okay? I don't want anything to spoil the day for him."

Eric and most of the other children wandered

over to watch a group of balloon-toting clowns breeze by. One of the clowns stopped to make balloon-dolls for several of the children. Fran saw this and smiled. "Just... *look* at them will you? Everything's still *new* to them. Even with what's happened to them, they still laugh and giggle and... I don't know... *hope*, I guess. Remember when you were that young? How nothing bad ever followed you to the next morning? Moment to moment, with a new excitement each time; that's what I think 'childhood innocence' is. Maybe something bad happened *this morning*, but *now*... now's fun, you've got a ball to bounce or a model plane to fly or a doll to pretend with, and the day's full of mystery and wonder and things to look forward to and... and..."

You're babbling. Shut up.

They scattered shortly thereafter, with instructions to meet back at the south entrance at six p.m.

Fran and Eric rode the merry-go-round for the third time that day, but from the way Eric acted you'd have sworn this was the first time he'd ever been on it. Fran envied him his joy, but was at the same time aware of how precious it was. She knew by the wide smile on his face and the gleeful shimmer of his eyes that she'd made the right decision to leave Ted and take Eric to the shelter. There he wouldn't have to worry about Daddy coming at him with the belt or his fists, or be forced to cower upstairs in his room while Daddy thrashed Mommy into a whimpering, broken, swollen zombie who shuffled around, whispering, never looking up, afraid of what the next five minutes might or might not bring.

Since they'd moved to the shelter two weeks ago, Eric--who before had been a good fifteen pounds underweight--had begun eating again and laughing again and was able to sleep soundly for the first time in his short life. God, how she cursed herself for having waited so long—for having kept Eric in such a brutal, hateful, terrifying environment.

At first it was just a couple of slaps every now and then, and Ted was always sorry afterward, so Fran allowed herself to believe that he really *was* going to get better about things, that he was going to get some counseling. Then he went on the graveyard shift at the plant, sleeping during the day, and refusing to see a counselor on the weekends. As Eric grew older, Ted's violent outbursts grew, not only in number, but in brutality. A couple of slaps turned into a bunch of slaps, a bunch of slaps turned into fists to the chest, stomach, and face, which evolved into slamming her against walls and choking her, sometimes knocking her down to the floor where, until the night she'd sneaked out of the house with Eric, he'd begun to give her a couple of kicks to the side.

She was, for a moment, so numb with the weight of her thoughts that she didn't even realize the merry-go-round had stopped. Then she noticed that Eric was standing outside the circular gate of the ride, talking to a little girl who looked to be around seven or eight.

"Eric!" she called to him. "You stay right there."

Better watch it, you, she thought. *That's how kids wind up with their pictures on the sides of milk cartons. "I only turned away for a minute," says the parent.*

She quickly exited through the gate, sprinting to where Eric and the little girl--who looked vaguely familiar to Fran -- were still standing.

"Hey, you," she teased, taking Eric's hand in hers.

"Hey, *you!*" he replied, giggling.

The little girl seemed to hear someone calling her, said a quick good-bye to Eric, then turned and ran--but not before shoving a piece of paper into Eric's hand.

"Who's your friend?"

"I dunno," Eric shrugged. "She was telling me 'bout her hand." He offered the piece of paper to Fran.

It was some kind of special fair pass. On the front were the words: **Good For Two Free Readings!** The back read:

Each line, be it in a hand or face, masks another; lines hidden within lines, a secret Hand beneath the surface of the one with which you touch the world and those you love. It is only in the secret lines on the hidden hand that your true destiny can be mapped, and only one who possesses Certain Sight can make an accurate reading. If you're content with mere showmen, then please take your business to any of the fortune-teller tents--but if you want the truth, see Madame Ariadne.

"So, kiddo... wanna get your palm read?"

"Wha's that?"

Fran turned over Eric's hand, sticking the tip of her finger into the middle of his palm. "A lady looks at your hand and tells you what's gonna happen to you."

"*Aw,*" he grinned. "I saw that on a TV show. It was *neat*."

"Does that mean 'yes'?" She couldn't resist tickling his palm.

"Stop!"

She did. "Wanna go?"

"Sure. It'll be like on TV."

#

The interior of Madame Ariadne's tent was not what Fran expected--no crystal ball or beaded curtains, no candles or spicy incense or stuffed ram's head or shelves overflowing with philtres and potions.If anything, the interior more resembled the white sterilized rooms where a veterinarian might examine a family pet: white rolled-tile floor, white partition walls, chairs, and a table upon which sat--most surprising of all--a computer. Next to the computer was something Fran assumed was a flatbed scanner.

"This is Weird City, kiddo."

"Like on *X-Files*!"

"That doesn't make me feel any better."

Eric laughed, then a door opened in one of the back partitions and Madame Ariadne entered.

you to take your--are you left-handed?"

"Uh-huh."

"I thought so. Take your left hand and press it down on the glass right there."

"On the box?"

"Mmm-hmm. Don't worry, it won't hurt. It's just going to take a picture of your hand."

"Promise?"

Ariadne's smile was spring itself. "Promise."

Eric pressed his palm onto the scanner. Ariadne took a plastic-covered device and placed it on top of Eric's hand, which now was completely hidden from sight.

"Arm's in a box," he announced to Fran, grinning.

"Oh, boy."

"Hey, Eric," began Ariadne cheerfully, "did you know that each part of your hand was given to you by an angel?"

"Nuh-uh!"

"Uh-huh. As a reward for their love and friendship, God allowed each angel to add one small part to the hand of every human being; thumbs, lines, bumps, every part of your hand's a gift from an angel." She winked at him. "I read that in a book when I was a little girl. I don't know if it's true, but I think it's kinda neat, don't you?"

"Uh-huh."

There was a slight hum, a slow roll of blue light from under the cover, and it was over.

By now Fran was standing behind Ariadne, staring at the computer screen as a holographic copy of Eric's hand--composed mostly of grid lines--appeared on the monitor.

Ariadne playfully poked Eric with her elbow. "Now watch this--it's so *cool!*" She hit a key and a dark blue line rolled down from the top of the screen, passing over the grid-hand and changing it to a three-dimensional, flesh-colored hand that looked so real Fran almost expected it to reach out and tweak her nose (a favorite past-time of Eric's).

Eric squealed with delight. “Izzat mine? Izzat *my hand?*”

“It sure is,” chuckled Ariadne. “And it’s a good, strong hand, with strong lines. See that line right there? That means you’re a good boy, and this line means you’ve got lots of imagination--I’ll bet you like to make things, don’t you? Like models, and draw, and build things with clay.”

“Oh, yeah!”

“I knew it! The lines never lie. This line right here--ah, this one’s very special, because it means that you’re going to grow up”--she gave Fran a quick, secretive look--“to be someone really special--even more special than you are right now. Oh, you’ve got a good life ahead of you, Eric. You should be so happy!”

“Oh, boy!”

This went on for a few more moments, until the little girl from the merry-go-round came out of the same door from which Ariadne had entered and asked Eric, “You want to come and watch a video with me? I got *The Great Mouse Detective.*”

"*Mouse Detective!*" shouted Eric. He turned to Fran. "Can I, Mommy? Can I go watch *Mouse Detective*?"

Fran was once again struck by the notion that she knew this little girl from somewhere. "I don't...I don't know, hon--"

"That's one of my daughters, Sarah," Ariadne reassured her. "I've got a little play room set up for her right back there. Toys, books, a TV/VCR unit, and--God!--*tons* of Disney videos... I swear she'll bankrupt me with those things. I'll have them leave the door open so you can keep an eye on them. "He'll not be out of your sight for one second, Fran. I swear it."

Fran looked down at Eric. "You really want to watch the movie?"

"Yeah!"

"Okay, then. But be polite."

The only things faster than light is the speed at which some children rush to watch a Disney video--a principle that Eric and Sarah proved a second later: *Whoosh-Bang!*--Disney rules.

Fran stood in silence for a moment, watching the two children through the door as they took their seats in front of the television.

"That's quite a collection of bruises on his face, Fran" the fortune-teller commented softly. "Ted must've really clobbered him."

A breath in, a breath out; one, two, three; then Fran whirled toward Ariadne and said, "How the hell did you know my name?"

"The same way I know that you've been at the Cedar Hill Women's Shelter for the last fifteen days. The same way I know that both you and Eric were in Licking Memorial's ER *sixteen* days ago because the two of you 'fell while taking in the groceries.' The same way I know that Ted spotted you at the free clinic five days ago and followed you back to the shelter."

"He *what?*"

"You heard me. He--don't get panicky, he didn't follow the group here today. He's on swing until the first of next week, but you have to believe me when I tell you that he *is* going to be waiting for you outside the shelter sometime in the next eight days, resplendent in his remorse."

"You can't possibly know that!" spat Fran, angered more from the fear of everything falling apart than at the fortune-teller.

"Do you think I'm trying to scare you? You're damned right I am!" responded Adriadne, gently, but forcefully.

"How did you...?"

Ariadne hit a key, and Eric's hand disappeared, replaced by scrolling records: Fran's birth certificate; the date of her high school graduation; a copy of her marriage license; Eric's birth certificate (complete with foot- and hand-prints made at the hospital); her student loan application for college tuition (check returned, full amount, student withdrew from school before deadline, no money owed); copies of police reports (three domestic calls, no charges filed); and several hospital records detailing treatments given to one Francine Alicia McLachlan and Eric Carl McLachlan, some together, most separate -- including at least two doctors' handwritten notations, nearly indecipherable except for "abuse?" and "possible mistreatment."

"So?" snapped Fran, trying to keep the anxiety from her voice. "You or someone who works with you is a hacker, so what? Anyone with a computer could get this information these days."

"True enough," agreed Ariadne. "But would they also know that you once came very close to killing Ted while he was asleep?"

Fran blanched, shocked into silence.

"December 22, two years ago," continued Ariadne. "He'd lost his temper and started pounding on you and Eric came running downstairs and put himself between you and Ted--something he does quite a bit, doesn't he? --and Ted pushed him down. Eric fell against a coffee table and the corner missed his left eye by less than half an inch. Five stitches in the ER took care of the gash, and in the cab on the way home Eric said he wanted to go away because Daddy scared him. Ted was already asleep when you got home, so you put Eric to bed, waited until he was asleep, went to the downstairs hall closet and took out Ted's .357 Magnum, put in one bullet, then wrapped the muzzle in an old towel to muffle the sound of the shot --"

"Stop it!"

"You never told anyone about that, did you, Fran?"

"No... I mean, I don't *think* I..."

"So I couldn't have very well hacked that information from any computer, could I?"

"No..."

Ariadne placed a warm, tender hand against Fran's cheek. "Listen to me very carefully. I don't want to frighten you, but I have to. Eric's in danger."

Fran's legs suddenly felt like rubber, and she just barely made it into the chair facing the computer. "...someone..." she whispered. "I... I must have told someone about... about wanting to kill Ted, and you... you..."

Ariadne placed a finger against Fran's lips, silencing her, and in a soft voice—the whisper of leaves caught in the wind brushing across an autumn sidewalk—spoke of other things that *only* Fran knew… intimate details of solitary experiences, hopes, desires, petty jealousies and silly girlhood fantasies extending back through nearly three decades, and when she'd finished (by describing in detail Fran's first childhood memory of getting her arm caught in the toilet when she was ten months old because she wanted to see where the water went after you flushed), Fran--confused, frightened, and feeling so godawful helpless--was certain of one thing:

Madame Ariadne had... *powers* of some kind, incomprehensible, unknowable.

"What... what *are* you?"

Ariadne leaned over Fran's shoulder and typed a command. "First you need to see something."

The screen blinked, displaying Eric's hand once again.

"Both you and Eric have Conic hands. See the shape of his fingers? Just like yours--they're very smooth and taper from the base, gradually lessening toward the rounded tip. The Conic Hand is the Hand of Imagination. Just from the shape of Eric's hand any fortune-teller would know that he's very sensitive, often highly emotional, but not emotionally unstable. He's like you in that way, isn't he?"

Fran nodded. "He's pretty anxious a lot of the time, but he tries to hide it because he doesn't want to upset me."

"Not surprising." The image of Eric's hand turned slightly to the left, displaying the height of the mounts on the surface of the palm. "See this rise here at the base of the middle finger? This is called the 'Mount of Saturn', also known as 'The Mount Which Brings Sadness.' If you've got a Conic hand with a pronounced Mount of Saturn, you constantly worry about the safety of the ones you love, even above your own well-being. This would explain why Eric always tries to get between you and Ted when..."

"He wants to protect me," whispered Fran.

"Of course he does; he loves you very, very

much."

"I know."

"Good."

Eric's hand turned toward them, palm facing outward.

"Why do you use a computer and scanner?" asked Fran. "I mean, most fortune-tellers..."

"...would whip out the candles and crystal balls and hold your hand in theirs as they made the reading, yeah, yeah, yeah. Believe me, I know this is a bit weird. I use this because the naked eye--even mine--cannot clearly see the lines within the lines, the--"

"--hidden hand within the hand?"

"Yes. This equipment was designed specifically to reveal those hidden lines, the secret hand."

Fran looked at the image on the screen. "Okay...?"

"Can you recognize any of the lines?"

Fran leaned in, squinting. "I can see that his life line is really long." Her mood brightened. "He'll have a long life."

Ariadne shook her head. "A long life line doesn't necessarily mean a person will live to be very old. I mean, sure, in places where it weakens or breaks you can expect some health problems, but a lot of people have life lines that are incredibly short and some fade entirely, but they still live to piss on their enemies' graves. No, we're interested in one of the Fate Lines, Saturn--right here, starting at the base of the wrist and going straight up to intersect with its sister mount." She altered the image so that it now displayed only a flat red outline of Eric's hand, with the Fate Line of Saturn enhanced in bright blue, the Mount of Saturn in bright green, and at the point where the two intersected, a cluster of small markings in jaundiced yellow.

"What are those?" asked Fran.

Ariadne magnified the cluster.

Fran puzzled at the sight. "They look... almost like stars."

"They are. On the Mount of Jupiter or Apollo, they mean great success and wealth; on Mercury they mean a glorious, happy marriage."

Fran faced Ariadne. "What aren't you telling me?"

The fortune-teller looked back at the children happily watching their video and singing along with the voice of Vincent Price, then pulled in a deep breath and released it in a series of staggered bursts.

"Jesus," exclaimed Fran. "If you want my attention, you got it."

"Have you talked to your husband since moving to the shelter?"

"What's that got to do with...?"

"Have you?"

"Once--okay, twice. The psychologist says it's good for us to call our husbands or boyfriends, let them know we're all right--if they care--and to get things off our chests. The shelter gets part of its funding from Catholic Services, so they're kind of big on aiming for reconciliation, if it's possible."

"Do you think there's any chance you and Ted will get back together?"

Fran shrugged. "I don't know. Maybe. If he gets his ass into counselling and does something about his temper, and *if* he admits that there're emotional problems he's been carrying around and stops treating me like--okay, okay... please don't look at me like that.

"Maybe. *Maybe* we'll get back together."

Ariadne took Fran's hand in hers, examining it. "You still love him?"

"Y-yes," Fran hesitated, looking into her hand as if hoping to find an answer there.

"Sounds like you wish you didn't."

"Sometimes I do wish that, but..." She pulled her hand away and looked at Madame Ariadne. "Why do you need to know?"

Ariadne pointed at the screen. "When a Conic hand has a direct intersecting of the Line and

Mount of Saturn, and when that intersection is marked by stars, it has only one meaning, and it's never, *never* wrong: death by violence."

Deep within Fran McLachlan's core, at the center of her interior world where all hopes, regrets, dreams, emotions, experiences, and sensations coalesced into something beyond articulation, a crack spread across the base, threatening to bring it all crashing down.

Very quietly, words carefully measured, heart trip-hammering against her chest, she managed to get it out: "Say it."

"Ted's going to kill Eric," Ariadne stated unequivocally "I knew it the moment I held his hand."

"He w-w-wouldn't do something like... like that..."

"On purpose, no, probably not. But you know what happens when he loses his temper."

"He doesn't... he doesn't *think*, he just--"

"Lashes out at what-or whomever happens

to be in his path, which is you and Eric."

"I don't know how many times I've told him that he should just stay in his room when Daddy gets that way, but he won't. He doesn't like it when Ted gets like that..."

Ariadne cupped Fran's face in her hands. "Fran? Look at me. Look at... there you go. Take a deep breath, hold it, hold it, now let it out. Good. Do you trust me?"

"I... I d-don't know..." Fran trailed off, shrugging.

"Yes, you do," insisted Ariadne.

Fran looked into the face of the woman before her, and saw there nothing but concern, kindness, and deep, abiding compassion. "Yes. Yes, I guess I do," she sighed.

"Then you believe what I'm telling you?" Ariadne looked deep into Fran's eyes.

"Oh, God, I don't know... Fran covered her face with her hands.

The fortune-teller looked over her shoulder and called, “Sarah? Honey, would you come here for a minute?”

“Aw, they’re just getting to the part with the clock!” Sarah complained in true seven-year-old fashion.

“You’ve seen it a dozen times before, the clock will still be there when you re-wind. Just come here for a second, okay?” Ariadne looked at Fran and winked.

“‘Kay,” the child called back.

She appeared a few seconds later.

“Sarah, I’d like you to meet Eric’s mother.”

The little girl held out her hand. “Pleased to meet you, ma’am.”

Fran noticed the little girl’s hand, saw the scar that ran from between her index and middle finger all the way down to her wrist (from when her father had gone at her with a pair of scissors), then looked up into her eyes and thought, *Please, don’t let them be two different colors*, but they were--the left gray, the right soft blue--and she tried to get her mouth to form words, but everything was clogged in the bottom of her throat.

"You okay, ma'am?" asked Sarah.

"I'm fine," Fran managed to say, shaking her hand. "Do you like Bobby Sherman records, Sarah?"

The little girl's face brightened. "Oh, yes! My favorite song is--"

"'Julie, Julie,'" answered Fran.

"How'd you know?" Sarah's eyes widened in surprise.

"Lucky guess," Fran smiled.

Ariadne touched her daughter's face. "Sorry that I interrupted your movie. Just for that, I'm buying pizza tonight."

"Pizza! Oh, boy!" And Sarah surpassed the speed of light once again to bring the news to Eric.

"Don't bother trying to tell yourself that you

didn't see her," advised Ariadne. "In her way, she's as real as you or I."

Fran was shaking. "That w-was *Connie Jacks!* She was my best friend when I was a little girl. Her father used to hit her all the time, knock her around, but she never told anyone but me. She died when I was seven. Everyone thought that she'd fallen down the stairs and hit her head on the r-r-radiator, but I always thought that--"

"He did," said Ariadne. "He beat her to death. If it's any consolation, he blew his brains out about ten years ago. Guilt usually catches up with you, eventually."

Fran looked at Ariadne--having now decided that the woman couldn't be human--and said: *"What are you?"*

"I am a Hallower: a half-human descendant of the *Grigori,* who were among the Fallen Angels. In retaliation for God's not having shared all Knowledge with them, the Fallen Angels stole the Book of Forbidden Wisdom and came down to Earth and gave countless Secrets to Man. Most of the *Grigori* coupled with human women during their time on Earth, and my race was the issue of that coupling. I am a direct descendant of the Fallen Angel Kokabel. He gave mankind the Forbidden Knowledge of Time and Science and assisted the *Grigori* Penemue in giving children the Knowledge of the lonely, bitter, and painful." She lifted her left hand, palm facing outward. "He also tainted the Mark of the Archangel Iofiel, who holds dominion over the planet Saturn." She placed the tip of her right index finger at the base of her left middle finger. "It's because of Kokabel that the Mount of Saturn brings such deep sadness with it."

"That's why I do what I do–why *we* do it. There aren't many of us, I'm afraid, but that's neither here nor there. In a hand or a face, Fran, the mark of my ancestor's sin can be found; I am the only being who can read the signs, and I will spend eternity trying to ease what sadness and pain I can."

"Maybe you won't ever reconcile with Ted, I can't say, but what I *do* know is that there are six stars on Eric's hand--one for each year that he will live—and the stars are in the Patriarchal Configuration... meaning the danger will come from Eric's father. Maybe he'll do it after you guys get back together, maybe he'll do it after your divorce when it's his turn to have Eric for the weekend--who knows? He might come by Eric's school and take him, or he might snatch him from your backyard when you get your own place. All this is secondary to the fact that somehow *he will kill Eric* and you can't prevent it. But I can...

which is why you have to leave him with me. Take Eric with you, and he won't live to see his seventh birthday."

Fran laughed. She couldn't help it it's how she fought back panic. Rising from the chair, she felt light-headed. "You know, you really... really don't give a person a chance to catch her breath."

"There's not much time. What can I do to convince you? And don't ask me to sprout wings or perform some tacky parlor trick, though I can do either as a last resort."

Fran glared at her. "Tell me how Connie Jacks can still be alive, how she can still be a little girl after all this time?"

Ariadne rubbed her eyes. "I suppose the simplest explanation is to say that she's a ghost who doesn't *know* she's a ghost."

"But you said she was as real as--"

"And she is. She can bruise, throw a temper tantrum, break a bone, muddy her good shoes, get a stomach-ache and throw up if she eats too much cotton candy. Sometime in the next eight months she's going to need to have her appendix removed, and in a year or so, she's going to have to get braces on her front teeth and she's *not* going to be happy about it."

"When a child--*any* child--perishes at someone else's hand, their body dies, yes, but their *promise* lives on. What they *should have* grown up to be doesn't cease to exist because the child is dead; it simply wanders alone on a different, more abstract plane that ours. Because I am what I am, I have the ability to... for lack of a better word, *guide* that potential into a new corporeality. Do you understand?"

"You can bring them back to life?" Fran asked incredulously.

"Not in the way you're thinking, no hocus-pocus or *Frankenstein* stuff. I give their displaced potential a new home–flesh--so that it can take up at the point where everything was snuffed. That girl in there, Sarah, is the girl Connie Jacks *should have* lived to become. The only thing different is her name and her memories, because as far as she knows *I'm* her mother. She has no memory of being beaten to death, of whimpering in lonely agony for someone to come help her because it never happened to her. To Sarah, the world is a new and wondrous place, filled with fairs and pizzas and mouse detectives, and she'll never have to be afraid."

Fran tried to catch her breath. "I still don't understand how--"

Ariadne put a finger to her lips. "Shhh, not so loud. I don't want them to hear you."

"There are two kinds of time, Fran: *chronos* and *kairos*. Kairos is not measurable. In kairos, you simply *are*, from the moment of your birth on. You *are*, wholly and positively. Kairos is especially strong in children, because they haven't learned to understand, let alone accept, concepts such as time and age and death. In children, kairos can break through chronos: when they're playing safely, drawing a picture for Mommy or Daddy, taking the first taste of the first icecream cone of summer, when they sing along to songs in a Disney cartoon, there is only kairos. As long as a child thinks it's immortal, it is."

"Think of every living child as being the burning bush that Moses saw; surrounded by the flames of chronos, but untouched by the fire. In chronos you're nothing more than a set of records, fingerprints, your social security number. You're always watching the clock, aware of time passing, but in kairos, you are *Francine*."

"Children don't know about chronos, and in my care, that's how it remains."

"Sarah's not my only child, Fran. I've got hundreds more just like her, too many of whom died at the hands of a parent who was supposed to love them, care for them, protect them from harm. Some died at the hands of family friends, or suffered unspeakable deaths inflicted on them by people who stole them away for their twisted pleasures. I have *babies*, some who lived less than a month because they were starved or beaten or dumped in trash cans or left out in the cold to freeze to death or locked in cars on summer days to slowly suffocate. But that can't touch them now because in my care they live only in kairos. Chronos isn't part of them any longer."

"I will save as many living children as I can from having to die at abusive, neglectful, violent hands." She entered a series of commands, and the flesh-colored, holographic copy of Eric's hand was restored to the screen. The image magnified to focus on the stars, then focused deeper, to a series of markings beneath the stars.

"Look closely, Fran. Do you see them?"

"They look like... like squares." Fran looked up at Madame Ariadne for confirmation.

"Those are the mark of kairos. They're called the 'Walls of Redress.' They're very faint on Eric's hand, but you can see that there are six of them, one for each of the stars, and that if they were more solid, each would hold a star inside of it. The

Walls of Redress are the promise of protection. No matter what danger is marked on the hand, if there is a square near or around it, the person can escape the danger *if* the signs are read in time."

"Why are they so faint?"

"Because the part of the world in which they might or might not exist in still in flux; they can fully form in kairos or they can fade away in chronos. It depends on the decision you make."

Fran's eyes began to tear. "*Oh, God*!"

Ariadne grabbed Fran's shoulders. "It's all been arranged. When you leave here, take him around the fair once more, do whatever you want, but make certain that the last thing you do is ride the merry-go-round, and that you get off the ride before he does--who'll notice? A tired mother walking a few steps ahead of her kid when the ride's done?"

"Who will...?"

"Sarah will be there with some of her brothers or sisters and they'll bring him back to me."

"But... *Christ!*... how do I explain... what do I say to--?"

"There are over six thousand people here today. Countless children disappear each year on fairgrounds, at carnivals or amusement parks. He won't be living among only children like Sarah, there are hundreds of other children just like Eric in our care— children we got to *before* violence claimed them."

"Can I... can come with you?"

Slowly, sadly, Ariadne shook her head.

Something inside Fran crumpled. *"Why not?"*

"Because the place we're going is only for Hallowers and the children in their care." A small, melancholy grin. "Think of it as the ultimate kids' clubhouse: No Grownups Allowed."

"Will I ever see him again? I don't know if... if I could live without --"

"Yes. It won't be soon, but you'll see him again. He'll--and I know this isn't much comfort--

but he'll write to you. A letter a month, a videotaped message four times a year; that's my rule. Don't worry if you move because his letters will arrive wherever you are every third Friday, even if it's a national holiday." A short, wind-chime-sounding laugh. "We sort of have our own private delivery service."

She touched Fran's cheek lovingly. "I promise you, Fran, *I swear* he won't forget about you, and he won't feel angry for your leaving him with me. He'll miss you, because he loves you so much, but it will get easier as time goes on. He'll never lose his love for you, and he'll grow up to be everything you hoped and more. You will have your son back, one day, and there will be no love lost."

"Don't say anything right now. You've got a little while, so go on, take your son to the fair and make him laugh, make him smile, and be certain that you miss nothing--not a word, not a look, a touch, a whisper, nose-tweak, or kiss. The next few hours will have to last you for a good while. Waste no moment."

"Go on. I'll know your decision soon enough."

Fran called for Eric, then wiped her eyes and stared at Ariadne. "I don't really believe in God, you know?"

Ariadne shrugged. "Not a prerequisite for the service."

"Good-bye, Ariadne."

"So long, Fran. Catch you on the flip side."

As they were leaving the tent, Eric turned back to Madame Ariadne and flashed his palm. "I got a angel hand."

The fortune-teller smiled. "You are a strange and goofy kid, Eric McLachlan."

"Yes, I am!" Eric enthusiastically agreed.

They stopped to play a few games (Eric won a small toy fire truck at the ring-toss booth), watched some clowns parade around, shared a soft pretzel, and then, suddenly, feeling as if she were a weary remnant of the young woman she once was, Fran McLachlan stood in the center of the midway holding her five-year-old son's hand and trying not to think about the way her life had gone wrong.

"Mommy," inquired Eric, "what's wrong? Did that lady say something bad to you?"

She told him no, and asked him what he wanted to do, and he chose the merry-go-round.

This time both of them rode on the tiger, and Eric's laughter, in his mother's ears, during those final moments of the ride, was the voice of forgiveness itself.

"Can I go again?" he asked as Fran climbed down.

"Sure, honey. Of course you can." The attendant was walking by at that moment, so Fran gave him the last ticket.

"You have fun," she said to Eric.

A happy bounce. "'Kay. You stand out there and watch me, okay?"

"Okay!"

Steady.

"I'll wave at you when I go by."

Hang on.

"Have you had a... a good time today, honey?"

"*Yeah!* This was the best fun ever!" the youngster declared.

Oh shit, don't let him see it.

"I'm glad." She leaned in and kissed his cheek. "I love you so much, Eric."

"Love you, too–better get off now, Mommy, so they can start the ride."

Not daring to look at her son's face, Fran McLachlan turned around and left, catching a peripheral glimpse of Sarah getting onto the ride with two younger children whose hands she was holding—the protective big sister.

Fran looked down at her hand and wondered

what secrets were hidden there in the lines within the lines, the hand beneath the hand.

Walking away from the merry-go-round, she was startled when a sudden, strong breeze whipped past, pulling the balloon-doll from her grip, sending it upward, soaring, free, rising on the wind toward a place where chronos had no place, where the children were safe and never wept or knew fear.

Good-bye, she thought. *Be happy.*

And was surprised to feel a smile on her face.

The End

Blood Show at the Carnival

By

Guy N. Smith

"How d'you fancy going to the carnival?" Carl Johnson folded the newspaper which he had been reading and dropped it on to the floor beside the armchair. His very posture, his expression, was one of boredom. Tall and lithe with a shock of blonde hair, he hated these annual seaside holidays which his wife, Lucy, insisted upon. From his point of view they were a necessary duty, something which they could not deny their 6 year old daughter, Emma. All kids had seaside holidays. He recalled his own, resisted a wince. Bloody boring. Nevertheless, he made an effort to appear to be enjoying it. It was a parental duty which he would have to endure until Emma reached her teenage years. Then, hopefully, she would holiday with her friends. Lucy would, in all probability, go abroad with her best mate, Sandra, and leave him in peace to enjoy his own hobbies. In the meantime...

"Sounds like a great idea," Lucy was somewhat surprised by her husband's seemingly enthusiastic suggestion. "Emma will enjoy a carnival, she's never seen one before. But we need to be back by nine o'clock. I'm determined to keep her to her regular bedtime, on holiday or at home. There couldn't be anything more boring than spending the evening in these drab holiday lodgings."

"That's fine," he breathed a sigh of relief. There was a movie on TV which he planned to watch that evening. Staying in a B&B was somewhat restrictive.

"And tomorrow were going on that coach trip to Aberdovey, don't forget. It's a lovely place and Emma will enjoy making sand castles on the beach. You'll have to help her, though." A sly dig at her husband. She didn't want him going off into town and browsing second hand shops and the like.

"Sounds great," he tried to sound enthusiastic. "We'd better get ready to go to the carnival, the parade starts at 1.30." Roll on this evening and the day after tomorrow when we'll be going home.

"We're going to the carnival," Lucy gave her daughter a hug and kiss. "You'll really enjoy it and we can also go round the fairground at the other end of the promenade."

Emma gave a squeal of delight at the prospect. Carl lit a cigarette. He was bored, just like he was in his everyday job as a window cleaner. Life was sheer drudgery these days.

.....

The carnival procession had started from the far end of the small seaside town, a convoy of decorated lorries with stage settings, children dressed as fairies and gnomes, coins tossed by the crowds which lined the pavements. Shouting, cheering. At its head, perched on a raiseddais, the carnival queen was dressed in colourful finery, an exceedingly attractive young lady, smiling and waving.

Carl yawned, thought that the long convoy was never going to end. Finally, though, a somewhat dilapidated tractor brought up the rear.

"Well, that's that," he turned to Lucy and Emma, the latter tugging at her mother's skirt, eager to see the funfair. She recalled one from the previous year in their home town. Doubtless it would again be a stick of candy floss and a demand for coins to partake in a variety of games of skittles and quoits.

“Look there’s a Punch and Judy show over there,” Lucy had to shout in her husband's ear to make herself heard. “Emma really liked the one at Weston Park last year.”

The show in question had a packed and noisy audience crowded around it. The theme on the miniature stage was an all-too familiar one, Punch wielding a cudgel, his wife with a baby clasped in her arms trying to defend it from a rain of blows, a helmeted policeman attempting to intervene.

“Ugh, there’s violence everywhere these days,” Lucy muttered.

The policeman left the stage but would doubtless be reappearing. Somebody in the audience screamed.

"It's obscene," Lucy lifted up her daughter, let the child bury her face against her. "They complain about violence on TV, but here they can get away with anything. The one at Weston was much less violent. It makes me sick. Come on Carl, I think we've seen enough."

"Hang on," Carl's eyes narrowed; he would not have admitted that he needed glasses, but from ten yards he was having difficulty in discerning details. Those figures on stage were slightly blurred. There was something strange about the Punch puppet. The features were almost lifelike rather than just a carved wooden face. As if...*It was alive*!

Carl edged his way closer through the crowd, resisting his wife's attempts to pull him back. Now Judy was sprawled on the stage, Punch's blows raining upon her and her baby.

And that was when Carl saw the scarlet pool around her and knew only too well that it was not tomato ketchup or similar. *It was real blood!*

His stomach knotted, and for one awful moment he thought that he was going to vomit. The prostrate puppet's skull was split, a wide crack below the dislodged bonnet from which flowed a stream of thick red fluid. Maybe it was a hinged skull that opened up on impact and released the fluid. Maybe it was blood acquired from a butcher for that purpose. This whole performance was sick, too close to reality for his liking. Screams came from the terrified onlookers, jostling and pushing in their efforts to get away from the horrific scene.

Carl found himself mesmerised, unable to remove his gaze from Punch's face. There was no doubt that something dreadful was happening, something that had no place in a Punch and Judy show. This performance was unreal. Now the puppet's eyes were meeting his own, staring balefully, seeing him and hating him. The mouth moved, cursing him. A crude caricature had become a living entity, taken on a malevolent personality of its own. It was alive!

The facial carving reminded Carl of an Indian totem-pole embodying an evil spirit. He wanted to leave, forget the whole business; dismiss it as a figment of his imagination. Yet he could not. It was akin to being hypnotised, forced to stay and watch.

Punch turned his attention to the prostrate baby puppet, a helpless victim that screamed in pain and terror. Punch raised his cudgel, delivered a crushing blow to the tiny cranium. Then came a frenzied battering that pulped the infant to a scarlet mulch and splattered the stage until it resembled an abattoir.

The policeman puppet returned to the stage and attempted to restrain Punch. An angry confrontation followed between the figure in blue and his scarlet robed adversary, a show of hatred between good and evil that went deeper than the clash of wooden truncheons. The sparring blows no longer sounded hollow but fleshy and solid. Blood trickled from the officer's ear. He fell. Blows rained upon him, and his uniform was a sodden crimson mess.

Punch turned to his audience of one and gave a mocking bow. His hateful gaze fixed on Carl Johnson, and then the curtain was falling, hiding that bloody, inexplicable finale.

.....

Whilst Carl had stayed watching the grisly finale to that puppet show, Lucy had departed, clutching her frightened daughter in her arms. On a raised stage nearby, the Carnival Queen was being presented with a tribute amidst clapping and cheering. Lucy hurried past, all she wanted was to return to their B&B and attempt to comfort her daughter. Would they ever forget the grisly scene which had been enacted on the tiny stage?

"A doll for your child, madam? Only a pound".

Lucy checked her hurried step, turned to see an attractive girl of Indian origin sitting cross-legged on the pavement, an array of paper mache dolls spread beside her. Although crude, the dolls were dressed in bright coloured clothes making them look very attractive.

"Please, Mummy, I'd like a doll".

"Two for a pound then," came the instant reply from the seller.

"Oh, all right then." Lucy jangled some coins in her pocket, supporting Emma with the other arm.

"Any particular pair?"

"Any two will do." Lucy would probably tire of them; she had some lovely china dolls of her own, and this latest double purchase would probably end up at the local charity shop. "If you wouldn't mind putting them in a bag for me, I'd be grateful. As you can see, my hands are full".

Emma had fallen asleep by the time they arrived at the B&B. Lucy carried her upstairs to their rooms and laid her on her bed. She stirred but did not open her eyes. Lucy laid her favourite doll, Daisy, beside her but placed the two latest acquisitions on the bedside chair, still enclosed in the carrier bag. Emma could have them when she woke up.

Lucy tip-toed from the small bedroom adjoining theirs and closed the door quietly behind her. She glanced at her watch – 6.30, God time had flown. Carl had probably gone to the pub, but he would surely be back before long as he wanted to watch that movie on TV.

She sprawled in the armchair by the window, attempting to forget that dreadful Punch and Judy show. It had been horrific but was probably all faked. It couldn't have been real blood, probably tomato ketchup or similar, superbly well done but sickening all the same. What were they thinking? Those kids who had seen it would probably have nightmares, their parents too. Bloody disgusting!

Exhausted, Lucy dozed.

Suddenly she was rudely awakened by screams from the adjoining bedroom, shrieks of sheer terror and inarticulate cries coming from her daughter.

“What on earth...Emma, I’m coming!” She leapt up, thrust the bedroom door open, then stared in horror and disbelief at the scene which greeted her.

“Emma, what...oh, my poor darling!”

The child was sitting up on the bed and there was no mistaking the expression of shock and horror on her sweet features as she stared at the scene on the floor below.

The carrier bag which had contained the two puppets was lying open. Daisy the china doll was smashed into fragments and covered in a thick scarlet fluid which had splashed all around.

Lying beside her was the larger of the two new dolls. It was clutching the hairbrush from the dressing table, which it had clearly been using as a club to bash her. Next to it was the other doll, much smaller, dressed in baby's clothes. It, too, was crimson-soaked, the skull crushed and oozing that same fluid.

Lucy froze in disbelief. The upturned features of the larger doll bore an uncanny likeness to that of the homicidal Punch down at the carnival. The mouth was wide in an unmistakable snarl and the deep-set eyes were focused on Lucy as though it saw her, hating her for her interference in this terrible bloodbath.

The innocent purchase from the street seller held a dark purpose, sold to spread the evil of the on-stage Punch.

Lucy carried Emma from the room and tried in vain to comfort her. She hastily packed their belongings, with the exception of Emma's. She could not go back into that room and the terror it contained. Oh, God, as soon as Carl returns we're leaving this place to that which had been spawned here, figurines created and carved by the devil's own disciples.

The carnival had become an exhibition of blood and death, inexplicable evil had infiltrated it.

The End

For One Night Only
By
Lex H Jones 2018

Dennis wasn't entirely sure if he was asleep or awake the first time he heard the music. Whether in dreams or reality, the melody had raised him from his bed as it passed by his window. Assuming it was a real sound and not the product of his mind, Dennis wiped the frost from the inside of his bedroom window and looked out. He squinted into the darkness, trying as best he could to see beyond the empty farm fields at the back of his small home. Nothing moved, nothing made a sound. Even the wind was still.

Resigning himself to the fact that he'd dreamt the music, Dennis lay back down and closed his eyes. He knew that if he opened them he'd see the breath leaving his mouth, which would only make him feel colder. Wrapping the thin sheet as tightly around himself as he could, he kept his eyes firmly closed in the hope that sleep would come again quickly. And then the music returned. Louder this time, definitely not the product of his imagination.

Dennis sat up and looked out of the window once more, this time seeing a procession of lights off in the distance. A moving line of glowing yellow orbs, accompanied by music and cheering and laughter. He could see smaller vehicles and larger ones, some with trailers carrying heavy loads. He couldn't quite make out any figures, but that was largely due to the mist which seemed to be following and surrounding the joyful convoy as it travelled. Dennis watched as they travelled up the hill and over the brow, after which he could no longer see them. The darkness and quiet resumed in their wake, but Dennis was now filled with a curious excitement.

"It'll have been a carnival," Dennis' father, Simon, suggested as they sat around the kitchen table the next morning. "Not had one here since the war."

"Can we go?" Dennis asked.

"I'll be working too late for that. If you can get a friend to go with you, that's fine. Don't go alone, though; some weird folk at those carnivals."

"I'll ask Wilf; he's always wanting adventures."

"Good lad. I like Wild, just make sure he eats something because his Mum certainly won't bother. And don't be adventuring too far, either. Stay in the crowds, don't wander off. And come straight back home when you're done."

"Thanks, Dad."

The level of autonomy given to Dennis by his father was perhaps unusual for a ten year- old, but since his mother had died, it had been just the two of them. The meagre wage that Simon earned meant he took all the hours he could just to keep the banks away from the house, which often left Dennis alone or with his friends. He didn't mind though, and he understood enough of the situation to recognise that his father was doing his best for him. Dennis often felt sorry for his father. He'd returned from the war, married his girl and had a child, just as he'd dreamed of in those awful years of fighting the Nazis. Then his girl had fallen ill, and nobody could do anything but watch as she slowly faded away. It had been the two of them, alone, for three years now, but Dennis didn't like to say how much he missed her. He knew it would make his father think longingly of her even more than he already did.

*****

Wilf was what Dennis would probably describe as his best friend, if he was asked to choose. He'd known him the longest, and they did the most together. Some friends were right for particular activities; the crafty, careful ones were perfect for sneaking into the cinema without paying. The energetic, aggressive ones were perfect for a kick-around with the football. But Wilf was the kind who was perfect for anything. He was a bit like a gentle sheep, in that he would just follow what everyone else was doing. That's not to say he wasn't fun. Whatever activity was going on, he'd be right at the heart of it, enjoying every moment. It was simply that the initial idea for the activity would never spring from Wilf himself.

When Dennis told Wilf about the carnival at school, he immediately decided that he would keep half his dinner money for the day to have more to spend. Dennis silently thought that Wilf could safely stand to eat a few half-portions at dinner, but then immediately felt bad for it. There was something slightly wrong with Wilf, even if Dennis didn't know a medical name for it. All he knew is that Wilf's weight would go up and down rather drastically without him really having made any change to what he was eating, or how much of it. Something inside Wilf didn't work as well as it should, that was as much as Dennis could understand. That, and the fact that Wilf's mother didn't care about him half as much as she should. Whenever Dennis went to call for him, Wilf always seemed to be alone in the house. Having a mother who didn't care, and a father who left, seemed even sadder to Dennis than having once had a mother who loved you very much, but was taken away.

The boys met at Dennis' house that evening after school, and agreed to walk to the carnival from there. Neither of them were entirely sure where it had decided to set up, but Dennis could make an educated guess based on the direction he'd seen the trailers heading the night before. And besides, the sounds and smells of such a place would surely lead to its location once they got anywhere near. It was already growing dark when the boys left the house, with a low-lying mist making it difficult to see too far ahead along the road.

"Don't worry, I know the way," Dennis assured his friend as they walked along the uneven road that led up the hill. "This was where the convoy went. There's a wide open field just at the top of this hill, that's got to be where they've set up the carnival."

"I haven't seen any posters or anything." Wilf pointed out.

"Maybe they're not here for very long? Or just passing through." Dennis suggested, then grabbed Wilf by the shoulder and pointed ahead. "Look!"

The boys had reached the brow of the hill, and sure enough, a carnival was set up in the fields to the right-hand side of the road. There were a series of large tents, stalls full of games, food, and prizes. Faded yellow lightbulbs hung on strings of wires criss-crossing between one stall and the next. Oddly-dressed people moved about riding unicycles, or juggling, walking on stilts or fire eating. A carousel lay in the middle of the carnival, full of laughing children and adults as it spun around in a blur of lights, colour and music. There was other music too, which Wilf and Dennis couldn't quite determine the source of. There must be speakers hidden somewhere, they assumed. Surrounding the whole affair in a perfect circle, breaking only to form a gap at the entrance, was a line of tall flaming torches made of iron. Surrounding the carnival that way in metal and fire gave it a slightly less-welcoming look than the soft yellow bulbs did.

"Come on, let's go!" Dennis kept hold of Wilf's arm and led them both quickly to the entrance.

A clown dressed in black and white with matching makeup stood at the entrance handing out tickets. The boys approached him and reached into their pockets, but he raised a hand shook his head, then pointed at a sign to his left. "Children enter free", it read. The boys smiled, the clown smiled back, and he stepped aside and waved them in.

"Wonder why he didn't speak." said Wilf.

"Probably a mime or something." Dennis suggested.

Now that they were in the middle of it all, the boys stood still and took the carnival in. The sights, the sounds, the smells. It was another world, so colourful and cheerful and loud, with a slight air of unease that such places always brought when placed in contrast with the sleepy, quiet villages around them. It was the feeling of awe, of mystery and anticipation, of not quite knowing what you could expect.

Dennis and Wilf went to the candyfloss stand first of all, watching in eager anticipation as the stall-tender deftly turned his wooden sticks around the tumbler until they were coated in thick masses of pink. He handed one each to the boys and took their payment, then turned to his next customer. Munching on the candyfloss, the boys looked around to see what would be their next thing to take in. Dennis noticed that the fog was still visible around the carnival, not quite driven away by the lights and the people. It was thicker beyond the boundary of flaming iron torches, as though the light and heat held it back.

"Who are all these people?" Wilf asked suddenly, speaking through the mouth full of candyfloss.

"I don't know, people from the village?" said Dennis.

"Do you recognise any of them?"

"A few, I think." Dennis replied, squinting as he looked at the throng of people moving this way and that through the carnival stalls and sideshows. He wasn't lying... he genuinely did recognise a few neighbours, and some other children from school. But for the most part, he had idea who these people were, where they'd come from, or why they were dressed in such an old-fashioned manner. His concern about this didn't last long, however, when a man dressed in a pinstripe suit walked by them on stilts.

"Fancy seeing something strange, boys? Museum of Oddities, just over there! Tickets still available!"

The man kept on walking, never looking back, as though he knew that his work was done. No further enticement was needed. He was right, of course, for no sooner had the boys spotted the striped, green and white tent than they immediately ran towards it. The opening to the tent was covered with a black curtain, adding to the mystery of what lay inside. A dwarf sat on a stool beside the curtain, smoking a cigar and not looking even remotely interested.

"Two tickets?" he asked without looking up.

The boys handed over their money and took the small pink tickets that the dwarf handed to them. Dennis looked down at the ticket as though he'd been handed something precious. As he cradled the ticket in his hand, something caught his eye to his right. Something had changed… there was a spot of darkness where there had previously been light. Dennis turned to see that one of the torches had gone out, leaving a gap between the otherwise unbroken line of roaring fire. The fog seemed to immediately grow thicker in that gap—that sudden narrow expanse of darkness. Dennis's eyes widened as he stared into it. Something was moving there, in the pitch-black gap between the flames.

The pinstriped man on the stilts suddenly appeared holding a flaming torch, and re-lit the one that had gone out. He caught sight of Dennis watching and gave him a big smile and wave, then carried on going about his business. Before the smile, though, Dennis had seen the stilt-man's face. It was been filled with absolute panic at the sight of the unlit torch.

"Dennis, you coming in?" asked Wilf, standing beside the black curtain that he'd pulled back halfway.

"Sorry, I got distracted." Dennis replied, joining Wilf at the tent. He wondered if Wilf's waiting for him was due to politeness or the boy's trepidation at entering the museum of oddities alone.

Once through the black curtain, the boys found themselves inside a small, but well-stocked museum display. There were deformed babies in pickle jars, small stuffed animals with two heads, and even monstrous body parts with signs next to them proclaiming them to having once belonged to some mystical creature or other. Next to each exhibit was a large painted poster explaining what it was the viewer was looking at. The posters were faded and worn, displaying beautiful images that might have once been vibrant, but had now lost their vigour through the passage of time.

"I bet you've never seen wonders like this before, have you?" came a voice from behind the boys. They'd thought they were in the tent alone, but now it appeared that somebody had joined them in there. That, or more likely he was already inside, hidden in the shadows.

He was a tall man, wearing a black top hat and a dark purple tailcoat atop a white ruffled shirt and pinstriped trousers. His boots were shiny and pointed and his hands were covered by white gloves, in one of which was grasped a black metallic cane.

"My name is Theodore Royle, I own this circus. And this tent of wonders is my favourite part. I still love to see it after all these years," the man explained, moving a strand of his long black hair from his face to better reveal his shining eyes and broad grin.

"Aren't you bored of it?" asked Wilf.

"Oh no, how can one become bored of such wonders?" he exclaimed, turning Wilf around with a gentle hand on his back and pointing to each exhibition with the handle of his cane. "These are the things that remain hidden from the world. So many, so very many, will go through their lives seeing none of these things. And yet you, special and wonderful you, are right here seeing them with your own two eyes. Isn't that magical?"

"I suppose it is, actually." Wilf beamed.

"Are they real?" Dennis enquired, staring closely as a two-headed baby floating in formaldehyde.

"Of course they're real. You see them, don't you?"

"That doesn't mean they're real," said Dennis. "Sometimes we see things that aren't really there."

"And sometimes we don't see things that are," Royle said with a smile. "Such is the curse of our humanity."

As the man spoke, Wilf wandered over to the corner of the tent where a large box or cage was covered with a thick, black sheet. He took the corner of the sheet between his thumb and forefinger and started to lift, at which point Royle slammed the end of his cane down on top of it to hold it in place.

"I am afraid that is a secret," he explained.

"Why is it in here then? Where anyone could see it?" asked Wilf.

"It's the best place to hide it. Which is why I am often to be found in this tent. Keeping it safe."

Wilf looked back at the covered box, Royle's cane still keeping the black sheet firmly over it, then shrugged and walked away.

"Take your time enjoying the rest of the exhibits, ask me any questions that you will, but do not remove that sheet," Royle insisted, before finally releasing his hold on the black cloth and walking backwards into the shadowed corner.

Dennis and Wilf felt a little unnerved by the fact that they were now being observed, but carried on looking through the museum with as much disregard as they could muster. Once they'd finished reading each poster, carefully studying the exhibits to see whether they could see any obvious signs of fakery, the boys left the tent behind them and returned to the carnival. Wilf could barely take his eyes from the black sheet-covered box as they left, but he managed to tear himself away from it. As they left, they could see the stilt-walker quickly re-lighting another torch across the other side of the carnival. Dennis wondered if that might actually be his real job, but couldn't fathom why it might be so important.

******

Dennis was comfortably asleep in his own bed that night when Wilf had9 snuck out to go back to the carnival. His home life wasn't well known to the school playground, for which he was grateful. Boys could be cruel, and if they knew his father had long since left and his mother was rarely at home (or sober on the nights that she was), Wilf might have come under more ridicule than was normal within a group of boys. All of that said, the unfortunate familial situation made it easier for Wilf to leave the house as he wanted than it would for other boys. Not that he usually did such a thing, of course. If another boy had organised a trip,1 then he'd always be a part of it, but to decide for himself that he would leave in the middle of the night to go on an adventure? That wasn't like him at all. But that box, covered by the thick black sheet, was luring him in. It spoke to him. He had to know what was under it, he just had to.

"Don't be scared, I know why you're here. And I understand," said Royle, removing his top hat and placing a reassuring hand on Wilf's shoulder.

"Wh...why aren't you asleep?" was all the boy could think of to say.

"I never sleep. I can't," Royle replied. "They don't let me."

"Who doesn't?"

"Enough about me, you want to see what I hide under that tarp, don't you? Well, you've come this far, I might as well not keep you waiting."

Royle grabbed the black sheet and swept it away with one fluid motion, like an expert magician unveiling some magical trick. Wilf found himself staring at an iron cage, but could see nothing inside it, the darkness was too thick. He leaned closer, and at that point Royle lit an oil lantern and leaned over the cage with it. The contents were suddenly illuminated so well that Wilf screamed out loud and fell backwards once again, this time landing on his backside on the ground.

"What is that?" asked the boy.

"Oh it's quite dead, don't worry." Royle assured him, resting the lantern next to the cage. The orange illuminated a small, twisted black shape lying on its side within. It was vaguely humanoid, or at least more so than anything else Wilf could think of, but if it had been human then there must have been something seriously wrong with it. "That, my boy, is called a Changeling."

"What's one of those?" Wilf asked, feeling braver now that he was sure the thing was dead.

"We don't occupy this world alone, young fellow. There are other things out there. Some of them used to have a pact with humanity. When one of their young died, they would leave its tiny form in a human family's cot, and take away the human baby that slept there. That baby they'd raise as one of their own, changing it so that it was more them than us."

"How is that a pact? What did the human family get out of it?"

"They weren't slaughtered in their sleep," Royle grinned, his lips revealing far more teeth than Wilf was comfortable with. It was not a warm smile.

"How did you get it?"

"We once settled somewhere that we shouldn't have. Many, many years ago now. The locals told us, but we didn't listen. Thought it was all nonsense, of course. Who wouldn't? But, sure enough, they came, and took the baby of one of our performers. Left that little thing in it's place."

"And then they left you alone?" asked Wilf, halfway between enjoying what he assumed was a made-up story and being terrified of the implications if, in fact, it was real.

"Sadly, not. The child they took was ill. And they knew it. They thought we had tricked them into taking damaged goods. So they cursed us. We cannot rest, cannot stop moving, and always they follow us now. Demanding a new payment each time we dare to stop, however briefly. The iron torches keep them at bay, but they're always there. Always waiting."

"What do you pay them with?"

"I'll show you," Royle replied with a grin, leading Wilf from the tent.

Royle placed his top hat back on his head and raised the lantern before him, leading Wilf to the line of torches at the back of the green and white tent. As they got closer, Wilf was sure he could see grey shapes moving in the fog behind the line of torches, just visible in the darkness between the flames. No clear shapes could be made out, but there was a definite blur of movement. Wilf thought that there must be a large number of them, or that they moved so fast that it wasn't possible to clearly see them. Or perhaps both? Whatever they were, he didn't want to get any closer and dug his heels into the dirt.

"I believe your story, Mr. Royle. I don't want to see what you pay them," said Wilf, a quiver in his voice.

"But surely you must want the end to the story? What is a story without an ending, dear child?" Royle insisted, pushing Wilf closer.

When Wilf was standing less than a foot away from the iron torches, his gaze fixed on the fog and shadow between them, Royle stepped by him and took a comforter from his pocket. It was the king one might use to douse a candle, but large enough to instead cover the mouth of the torches. Royle leaned over and doused one of the flames, then the one next to it, and stepped back. He quickly moved behind Wilf and placed his hands on the boys shoulders.

"Mr. Royle, I want to go home," said Wilf, crying now and with a growing trail of urine running involuntarily down his leg.

"You'll have a new home soon, don't worry. That's a nicer fate than I have to endure, I promise you that."

As Royle said this, Wilf turned to look at him and saw that his face was now rotting and decayed, with patches where the bone was completely visible beneath. He looked down at

Wilf and grinned, only one of his eye sockets now possessing an eye and the other being filled by a millipede which chose this moment to crawl out and then back into the skull via a nostril.

"They won't let us rest," Royle said again, as if to explain his countenance. "And if we fail them again, their vengeance will be worse even than this. So you see, we must continue to pay."

"Please let me go home," Wilf sobbed.

"Be brave, my boy." Royle patted Wilf firmly on the shoulder, then shoved him forwards into the gap he'd created in the line of torches.

Wilf stood swallowed by the fog and darkness, frozen so firmly with fear that he couldn't even move to run back. There was a sound like a high-pitched record being played backwards a thousand t over, with voices that weren't voices screeching over one another. This sound was followed by a dozen pairs of greyish, clawed hands reaching out for him from the fog, each attached to arms that were impossibly thin and long. Wilf was able to move just enough to turn back to the carnival, where the last thing he saw was Theodore Royle re-lighting the torches and backing away.

*****

Dennis and his father ran up the hill towards the site of the carnival as fast as they could. Simon was due to be at work, but a missing boy took precedent. When Dennis had told him that Wilf had never turned up to school, and that his drunken mother had no idea where he might be when he'd gone to call for him afterwards, he'd immediately spoken to his father. It was well known in the village exactly what kind of mother Wilf had to endure, so the possibility of her child being snatched right under her nose was a surprise to nobody. Dennis couldn't be sure that Wilf had gone back to the carnival, but it seemed like the logical place to start. The sight that greeted Dennis and his father, however, was not what they had been expecting.

The tents that had formed the outer rim of the carnival were all burned and torn apart, their frames buckled and broken as if by some extreme force. The red and white sheets of the tent that were still visible beneath the ash looked to have claw marks all over them, as though hundreds of wild and angry animals had furiously assaulted them en-masse. The flaming torches were all blown out and toppled. Not a single one remained standing. The game and food stalls were shattered and collapsed in heaps among the floor. Alongside the human footprints pressed into the mud were those belonging to something...many, many somethings... that were not identifiable. None of this, however, was as shocking as the sight of the bodies.

As they entered the carnival, stepping through a gap in the carnage to gain access, Simon saw that the ground was littered with bodies. He stared at them in horror, and by the time it occurred to him to cover his son's eyes, Dennis had seen them to. Corpses littered the ground, torn and mangled, twisted into positions of horror and agony, some reaching out desperately, others curled up in a foetal ball. Whatever had set upon them had done so with such fury and power that they had no hope to defend them. Some had tried to run, some had fallen to the ground and sobbed. None had escaped. Stranger than all of this, was the fact that the corpses themselves were not fresh. The rotten, decayed state of them suggested these bodies had been here in this state for decades, if not longer. The still-smouldering ruins of the carnival around them, however, suggested otherwise.

In the middle of the carnival, half-covered by a fallen string of broken yellow light-bulbs, was a corpse that was somewhat smaller than the rest. It was also fresh, being the only one present that actually appeared to have died the night before. At the sight of this one, Simon did cover his son's eyes, not wishing him to see the Sorry remains of his friend Wilf. The rotund boy's remains were in a worse state than all of the others, his body torn apart like a pig in the back room of a butcher's shop. Simon was overcome with the feeling that whatever had done all of this, Wilf had somehow been the source of their anger. That something about Wilf was what had set them off, causing them to butcher him first and then move on to the rest of the carnival. How a small, affable child with a thyroid problem could cause such hatred, and what had been the bearers of it, were questions that Simon would never be able to answer.

The End

The Last Freakshow on Earth
By
David Owain Hughes

The year is 2081, the not so distant future, and Chinatown is a prison. One hundred years ago—between 1980 and 1990–hardcore arcade gamers, cinemagoers, TV freaks and comic book nerds took over the large oriental area and turned it into a no-go zone. The streets became violent, corrupt and the powers that be lost control. The innocent were evacuated, a bomb to be dropped, but the plan was seen as too *rad*, and so a large wall and river were constructed around the city. The waters were filled with sharks and patrolled by the government's secret police, who had more artillery than Rambo.

There is no escape from Chinatown, not that the residents want it, as they are content living out their sadistic, perverse fantasies of being their favourite character from their beloved games, movies and/or shows from a decade long extinct (but not in Chinatown, for it's *always* the '80s).

The streets are teeming with the likes of Snake Plisskin, Jack Burton, the Mad Gear Gang, Wing Gong hoods, thugs from *Class of 1984*, men and women who think they're Alex Foley, Tank Girl, Judge Dredd, Frank Castle, OCP cops, Officer Murphy and cybernetic robots, Rick Deckard, the A-Team, WWF superstars, Lt. Marion "Cobra" Cobretti... the list is inexhaustible.

Not a day goes by that doesn't see someone get body-slammed through a table or vaporised by a proton gun, and eruptions of all-out gang warfare are commonplace. Six days ago, Killer Klowns from Outer Space wannabes were seen having a ray gun battle with a Ripley look-alike and her unit of space marines.

No, that's not the *real* Bill Paxton you see, reader.

However, there are those who dedicate their time in keeping the violent ones off the streets, the vampires at bay during near-dark and the drugs from children... those who fight for truth, justice and the ~~American~~ Chinatown way...

But a new threat has arisen within the compound walls.

Enter The Last Freakshow on Earth, a horrific travelling circus that blends old-school fairgrounds, '80s arcades and traditional viewing pleasures brought into fashion by carnivals of a forgotten era for an almighty spectacle for punters of all ages brave enough to set foot beyond the morbid-looking ticket booths...

****

First evening.

Lorries, vans, trucks and cars belonging to The Last Freakshow on Earth powered over a semi-permanent bridge—to be removed once the circus finished its stint in Chinatown—and rumbled into the city-cum-prison.

Once the convoy was clear of the overpass and through a section of wall purposely opened for them (which was immediately sealed at their tail ends), the lead truck made its way to the place where they were allowed to pitch their circus.

"*Ha*! Did you see that sign, Mr Tickles?" asked Deadly Diablo, the Knife-Throwing Dynamo—Daggers for short—as he slipped the lorry into fifth gear. He glanced over at his macabre friend, who sat shrouded in darkness, and smiled. Only the glowing red end to Mr Tickles' cigar could be seen.

"No," the clown growled, removing the stogie from his mouth and blowing smoke at Daggers. "What it say?"

Daggers, who, with his one glowing red eye, ninja suit and leather jacket, looked a mixture of Kano from *Mortal Kombat 2, The Terminator* and DC Comics' Deadshot, belly-laughed as he answered. "It read, 'Welcome to Chinatown. Population: 525,050' with a line crossing it out, and someone wrote 'Who Gives a Fuck!' beneath it. Shit, I'm creased." He slapped his thigh as he doubled over in his giggling fit. "I'm glad this old cyborg can't cry, otherwise I'd have tears running down my face, blinding me."

"Someone soon *will,*" Mr Tickles chuckled, popping the cigar back in his gob. He chewed on it as he continued to laugh, his needle-like teeth almost cutting through the fat Cuban.

"Ha! That damned laugh of yours is beyond creepy, not to mention infectious, my funny friend. Think the kiddies will piss their pants over the new attraction?"

"They have been doing so thus far, no? The little shits in that last town we were at—"

"Fucking *Grimes*ville!"

"*Haha*!" Mr Tickles bellowed psychotically, filling the cab with cheer and smoke. "That place *did* fucking stink, I agree. But yeah, the kiddos there shit their pants—the adults, too—as they have in many of the other cities, boroughs and counties we've visited in the past few years."

"Hell yeah! But these eighties weirdos might be a different kettle of fish, man—we were told they're violent as fuck. They might not take too kindly to us at all."

"They'll be fine, you'll see. Trust ol' Tickles."

"Huh. Hey, our new ringmaster has his shit together."

Mr Tickles fell silent, his hand going to the collar around his neck. *Hasn't he just, Daggers? And one day, when he isn't looking, I'll snap his fucking neck and run for it, taking the others with me.*

The gigantic clown, who filled the double-passenger seat, looked in the rear-view mirror and narrowed his eyes. His morbid-coloured grease paint, which had been freshly applied before last night's final performance at Stinksville, was now peeling off in great big chunks. This was due to the heat, sweat and amount of time he'd been on the road with his new family, which was close to seventy-two hours and counting.

He was tired and irritated. His face was itchy, but he refused to scratch or remove the stale make-up.

A professional clown always *remains in character.*

"He's a good 'ideas' man, but not much of a ringmaster," Mr Tickles offered.

"Agreed, but I'm sure he'll get there. He treats us fair, don't you think?"

"Why don't you shut your yap, Daggers, and get us to location. My arse has taken about as much sitting as it can."

"Ooh, *meow*, look at you. Yes, sir!" the showman said, putting his foot down whilst laughing.

When it fell quiet within the cab, Mr Tickles let his mind wander. *How in the hell did I manage to get caught up in the mess I'm in? I never should have returned to the circus with them,* he thought, looking in the wing mirror and spotting the brightly-coloured lettering on the trailer they were pulling. Only the word *Freakshow* could be seen due to the darkness of night.

His insides went cold.

I was fucking bushwhacked by that bastard. He stroked the steel collar as if it were a loved one. *He threatened me with death like I'm some kind of fucking mortal.* And *he thinks he can keep me here forever? Pfft.* He bit through his cigar and nipped his finger, but didn't flinch. His eyes remained on the trailer. *It's as much their fault, too. Riding in there like cattle is too good for them damn freakos.*

The lorry drove over a rock, the cab and trailer hitched, and Mr Tickles hit his head against the window, bringing him out of his thoughts. "Hey! Why don't you watch where you're going, Daggers? And don't give me that bullshit about poor eyesight—you could take a gnat's cock off at six hundred paces with one of them knives of yours."

"Sorry, man, but these roads aren't the best—they don't have a council around here who re-tars the highways every twelve months or so. We're inside a prison. Do you know how much the boss had to pay to get a three-week pitch here for us?"

Can't say I give a fuck about that worthless piece of shit, and you wouldn't either, if you knew the full story about him. “No, but I’m sure you’re going to fucking—”

“Half a million world pieces, man.”

Mr Tickles turned in his seat. “Are you serious?”

“Yep.”

“That’s a lot of currency.”

The lorry hit a pothole, jiggling its passengers, followed by a second, third and fourth.

“Fuck! This stretch is as rough as the bearded lady’s arse, Daggers!”

“Yeah, we’re coming up to where we need to be, fella. Look.”

Mr Tickles gazed through the windshield and spotted a dozen spotlights in the near distance. They illuminated a large field that looked as though it was used for football and/or rugby games.

"Is that thing going to be big enough?" Mr Tickles asked.

"Apparently it's the largest spot they have available for us."

"How do you know all this? You sucking the boss' cock?"

Daggers went quiet and shrank away.

Oh, my fucking God—he is *blowing him!* Mr Tickles thought, laughing and slapping his thigh. He turned to stare out the passenger window and muttered, "Wait until I tell Custard."

As their lorry drew closer, the clown could see the turf was in disrepair. There were chunks missing here, there and everywhere, and molehills were spotted in places amongst the almost knee-high grass. "Doesn't look like they use this field anymore, Daggers," Mr Tickles concluded.

A lacklustre sign jutted from the ground on a metal pole close to the entry. There were bullet holes in it, but Mr Tickles could clearly read what it said. "Welcome to the home of Chinatown's Cheetahs. Go, Big Cats, go!"

"I guess somebody put the cats down, Mr Tickles."

Both men laughed.

Mr Tickles huffed as he opened his door, groaned and threw his legs out of the cab, ready to hop down.

"Feeling it, mate?" Daggers asked.

"Yeah, and you just know that fuckhead is going to make us start setting up."

"I would have thought so—he's looking to open doors tomorrow morning."

"What? Why?!"

"Says the arcades will be full from sunup to sundown."

"Goddamn come-sucking eighties freaks. Put 'em against a wall and shoot the lot, I say."

As Mr Tickles jumped out of the lorry, all the other vehicles in the convoy came to a halt. Engines were turned off, hissing and crackling as they started to cool.

"Get the doors opened," someone yelled.

"We'll stick the tents up first," another responded.

"Me and my boys will start unloading the big stuff—the floodlights will give us enough light," a man said.

A crane started moving.

Metal groaned as if disturbed from sleep.

Within ten minutes, the entire area was a hive of activity as The Last Freakshow on Earth began setting up.

In the midst of the chaos and noise, the residents of Chinatown slumbered on.

A few hours later, Mr Tickles applied fresh make-up inside his pitched tent with his trusty crow Custard on his shoulder. His Sideshows, Miss Necrotic and Miss Nightshade, were chained and curled at his feet, kissing and fondling each other's naked bodies. Like Mr Tickles, they were in full costume, their colours made up of deep purples, unsettling blacks and virginity-popped reds.

Outside, the clatter of heavy machinery, excited voices and the continued sound of the circus being set up chugged on, even though it was close to midnight.

“That master of ours is a fucking idiot.” Mr Tickles continued to colour his face as he spoke, his razor-sharp teeth clenched, his lips pulled back. “He’s in for a big shock once he gets that fuckin’ freezer of his open this week—”

“No longer shall we be his slaves,” Sideshow Necrotic interjected, pulling her lips away from Sideshow Nightshade’s.

Mr Tickles pulled on her chain, and a choking sound ensued from the woman. “Did I tell you to speak? Did I ask for your opinion?”

Nightshade giggled and twiddled a couple of the steel links between her fingers.

“Do you want some, too?” He slammed his fist down on his table, making his make-up skip, dance and jump. Some of it toppled and rolled onto the hay-scattered floor, and a bulb winked out.

Both Sideshows shrugged and went back to kissing and tracing each other's body with their hands.

Whores, he thought, smiling, his gaze lingering on their roaming, sliding, tweaking fingers. He licked his lips before turning back to the mirror. *Once the freakshow's up and running, I'll let the fucker's prisoners free, allowing them to cause as much death and mayhem as possible—and I'll escape in the process. Hopefully his 'freaks' will kill him during the melee.*

"We'll have to take Crys—" Nightshade started, but loud yells, whoops and cheers from outside their tent stopped her.

"The *fuck*?!" Mr Tickles got up from his chair and moved towards the exit. Before stepping outside, he turned back to Sideshow Nightshade. "I've told you to *stop* reading my mind!"

"Yes, Master."

Mr Tickles snarled at her, wrapped her chain around his fist, about to yank on it, when a commotion from beyond the tent's flaps distracted him.

"Boss! Boss! They're about to throw the switches. Come. Quick!" someone yelled.

"She's all ready to go?!" another person asked.

"Yes!" confirmed a female.

"I didn't think we'd be ready to roll so soon!"

Mr Tickles walked outside and looked all around. Most of the circus' macabre stalls, tents and rides had been erected. From where he stood, he could see the fortune teller Madam Mellontikós' booth was set up. The artwork on the boards that helped make up her stand featured crystal balls, skulls, snakes and wizards, witches, ghosts and things that looked otherworldly.

Goddamn hoodoo-voodoo bitch gives me the creeps.

The hall of mirrors had been put in place, along with the ticket kiosks. So too had the dunk tank and food courts, along with the strongman's section and the bearded lady's area. This year, Beardy Bernadette was featuring a sidekick: 'Gator Boy. Nobody knew where the ringmaster had found the half-man, half-alligator, and nobody but Beardy went near it. "It eats small children and men's dicks!" she'd rambled to Tickles one night, drunk off her face.

The big tops for the indoor arcade and main circus itself had both been set in place. The Last Freakshow on Earth boasted the finest collection of animals and performers in the world. Mr Tickles had never seen tightrope walkers, illusionists, contortionists or trapeze artists like those in The Last Freakshow. There were also the oddities who liked to perform: men and women who could lift weights by using the hoops that pierced their lips and ears, those who could swallow multiple items and regurgitate them in order, sword swallowers, human pincushions and men who liked sticking their cocks in Hoovers.

There was something for every man, woman and child who liked the odd, bizarre, dark things in life. The show came with an age restriction warning but nobody stuck to care. After all, Chinatown was a prison.

"I see the popcorn and hotdog stands are up," he muttered, sniffing the air. "They're prepping the grills, ovens and machines for the morning." *And you know how crazy Cannonball Cochise gets if his bangers ain't getting the heat they should.*

"Long hauls cross-country fuck with my machines, clown," he would grumble.

Mr Tickles gave the morbid setup before him a final visual sweep, taking in all the horror art, dark colours and deformed performers that walked among the circus' worker bees.

Before he could turn to the source of the noise, floodlights lit up the surrounding area, blinding him. Everything was drenched in bright, neon white.

"Ugh! *Fuck*!" Mr Tickles shielded his eyes and turned his head back the other way.

"It's *breath*taking!" said his ringmaster, former writer (creator of *White Walls and Straitjackets*) and inmate of Castell Hirwaun, home for the criminally insane.

My old padded cell amigo, Mr Tickles thought. The big clown turned, shielded his eyes and looked at the monstrous trailer that was a huge part of the circus. He gritted his teeth. Written along its side, in large, colourful and arched lettering was *Hughes' House of Horrors—Welcome to the Last Freakshow on Earth*! A thin mist emitted from it, encircling Mr Tickles, his carnie colleagues and the worker bees, who stood in awe (and shadow) of the impressive interactive, walkthrough attraction.

Generators grumbled into the night as more smoke burped and hissed out of them.

"And I thought *I* was an abomination..." he uttered, picking out Ringmaster Hughes, who hid in the shadows, his top hat and cane standing out against the glow of the moon and thrown shadows. And, even though the man was shrouded in darkness and a great distance parted them, Mr Tickles knew Hughes was staring at him. A shiver cut its way down his back, shrivelling his ball bag. "Welcome to your Freakshow? It's going to be a case of Welcome to my Nightmare, pal.

Your power and dominance over me will soon end…"

****

The streets of Chinatown were rambunctious.

More so tonight than any other night, or so it seemed. Maybe it was the arrival of the circus? Whatever it was, tensions in town were running at new highs. Broken, twisted and injured bodies littered the roads and pavements, and fires had been burning for hours. Many houses, tower blocks and other buildings, along with cars, trucks, vans and buses, lay in ruined heaps, the vehicles mere husks.

The seven friends, all in their late thirties, were comprised of five men and two women who lived out their fantasies in Chinatown as The Goonies: Axel (Mikey), Max (Data), Skates (Brand), Zen (Mouth), Adam (Chunk), Blaze (Andy) and Shiva (Stef – the wild one of the bunch).

"Where the fuck is Sloth?" Mikey asked.

"Jake Fratelli got him, guys. Put four bullets in the back of his head," Data, who wasn't Asian but Scottish, stated. "Fucking scumbag."

"Poor Sloth…" Chunk was close to tears. "He only wanted to see the freakshow." He held up a poster depicting the out-of-town attraction. "Think the rest of us will make it there?"

"Goonies *never* say die!" Mouth declared. "And I ain't dying before I see a bearded woman!"

"Shut up, Mouth. Loser," Brand interjected.

****

"Come out, ya little fucks!" Jake roared. The fires threw his shadows on the walls and bins around The Goonies. Jake, who looked disturbingly similar to Robert Davi and sometimes hung out with the Manic Cop, Matt Cordell, hunkered down and looked this way and that.

"How far to the edge of Chinatown?" Brand asked.

"Roughly five miles," Data declared.

"Then let's get moving." Andy stood and walked into the street.

"Yeah, come on. I think we're safe." Stef joined her girlfriend, their hands locking as they skipped down the street.

"Babes," Mouth muttered, earning a slap across the back of his head from Brand. "*Ow*!"

"More where that came from, dipshit."

"Come on, guys! Let's go have some fun!" Mikey interjected.

"Oh boy, oh boy!" Data said. "This is going to be such an epic night. Not often does the warder put on entertainment for us—"

"Not since Lord Humongous and his crew burned the cinemas down," Chunk interjected morosely, his face as long as a horse's. "Sloth..."

he muttered, wiping a tear from his cheek and then stuffing his hands in his pockets.

"Hey, don't worry, my husky friend. I'm sure we can find another Sloth running around Chinatown," Mikey reassured his friend, putting an arm around him.

"I guess, but he'd been with us years… Remember how he killed the last lot of Fratellis?" A brief smile flickered across Chunk's face.

"I do, buddy. Come on, this is our time now."

The rest of the gang moved out of the shadows and down Chinatown in hot pursuit of Andy and Stef. Carnage and destruction raged all around them, but nobody interfered with the One-Eyed Willy, gold-seeking wannabes, for they all had their own foes to deal with.

"Come on, keep moving," Brand instructed.

"Why are the streets so heavy? You'd think everyone would want to go to the circus," Mouth wondered aloud.

"They can't all be as sophisticated as us, Mouth," Chunk chuckled.

Mikey was glad to see his friend in higher spirits. *We've lost a few Sloths, Andys, Stefs and the rest, but you and I are the original members, buddy.* Mikey shook his head and checked over his shoulder—there was no sign of the Fratellis. *Pretty sure we've lost them,* he huffed. *All this way—all this danger—for a night of fun and games.* Mikey chuckled, but the others didn't hear him over the spontaneous bursts of gunfire and cracks of bone. *Been years since we've acted like children. It'll be worth it. We're normally either searching for Willy's gold or running and hiding from the Frat—*

"*—ellis*!" someone yelled, breaking Mikey's chain of thought.

"Going to get you pesky kids now!" Francis bellowed, aiming his revolver, and then he was hit off-balance when a shitty-looking Kit powered past, the car's door opened, and sent him crashing against a wall. Francis' nose shattered. Blood pissed down his face.

"*Run*!" Mikey yelled.

The group took off down the street and had to avoid a gang fight between the Cobra Kai and bunch of heavy-weight WWF stars.

"Was that Big Boss—?"

"Shut the fuck up and move, *Mouth*." Brand gave his friend a shove in the small of his back, and then a bullet whizzed past his ear. "*Shit*!" Another whined and pinged off a car door to his left.

A second and third gun started spitting lead. The bullets chased the gang farther down the road, until they cut to the right, split down an alley, hopped three fences and dodged into a secluded spot.

They were panting. Hard.

"Stop looking at my tits, Mouth!" Andy smoothed her hard nipples.

"Sorry. Danger... It gets me horny."

"Ugh! Pig... me too," Stef admitted, putting a hand on Mouth's shoulder. They looked at each other, smiled and then laughed.

"Fuck sake." Brand shook his head, smiling.

"How far to the circus?" Mikey wanted to know.

"A few miles," Data answered.

"Next time, we stay in and watch a fucking movie," Chunk grumbled, shaking his head, and then giggled. "I take that back. This has been pretty ace so far."

The others nodded and laughed.

"The Goonies love danger and adventure."

They all agreed with Mikey, feeling alive for the first time in months.

"They cut down there!" Mother Fratelli called somewhere in the distance. "Get after them, or I'll replace your arses with better brothers."

"Yes, Mama," the gang heard Jake and Francis say in unison.

"Let's get to that circus," Mikey urged.

It took the gang the best part of two hours to finally shake the Fratellis, and even then they weren't one hundred percent sure they'd completely lost them. Also, this was a big night for Chinatown, what with the circus in town, so there was a strong chance their enemies knew where they were headed for the evening.

As the sun started to set, the gang made it to the old sports field, not wasting a second in crossing the last bit of distance between them and fun.

"Look at all 'em lights!" Mikey squealed.

"Wow..." Mouth's mouth formed a perfect O shape as they stood before the circus.

Eerie music played – not just loud, but near-deafening.

Huge balloons, a hundred times bigger than hot-air balloons, floated a few hundred feet up in the air and had *The Last Freakshow on Earth* written all over them. The purple floats also had creepy clown faces and Jolly Rogers painted on them, with freakish expressions and what looked like oddities of all kinds eating babies and small animals.

A foul stench clung to the air all around them.

“Smells like death and horseshit,” Mouth declared.

“Look at those old wooden gates—is that real blood dripping down them?” Mikey pointed.

Massive wood gates, which helped support a steel fence encircling the circus, stood ajar. Torches had been erected on either side, their fires illuminating the stains on the entrance and a path leading into the ‘fun zone’.

“N-no, it can’t be....” Andy wavered.

“This ain’t like any kind of circus I’ve ever heard about,” Brand admitted.

"Come on, guys. It said on one of the posters..." Mouth started rooting through his pockets for the flyer he'd ripped from a lamppost two days earlier. "'Come see the circus of wonder, terror and *horror*.'"

"Yeah, it's all an act," Stef said, smiling. She clapped her hands together and bobbed on her tiptoes. "I can't wait to get in there."

"Care if I buy you a candyfloss, ma'am?" Mouth nudged Stef's elbow with his and winked at her.

"Maybe," she coyly winked back.

Mouth snapped his chewing gum and locked hands with her, leading Stef towards the place that looked treacherous. "Come on, guys," he called back.

Brand and Andy followed, along with Mikey and the rest of the boys.

"Things that go bump in the night," Chunk muttered, giggling to himself like a schoolgirl.

****

The Fratellis watched on from a nearby bush, the mother flanked by her boys, their pistol barrels pointed skyward.

"So, the wee babies want to see the clowns," she said in a sing-song voice.

"Aww, diddums." Francis poked his bottom lip out, eliciting a snigger from Jake.

"*Quiet*!" Mama Fratelli commanded, slapping Francis across the face. "You two grown men—and I use that term loosely—have been outdone by these punk kids on dozens of occasions. This crap ends tonight. You hear me?"

"Tonight, Ma," the boys said in unison.

"They won't see us coming." A grin pulled her mouth wide, revealing stained teeth. She drew a cutlass from her belt. The word *Willy* was etched into the steel of the curved, wicked-looking blade. "Me little hearties will be begging fer their lives after tonight's escapades."

The trio moved out of hiding and headed around the side of the circus. There was no way they were paying to get in…

****

Second evening.

Mr Tickles stood up from an upturned crate he used to sit in front of his make-up mirror and growled at his reflection. His blood-stained, needle-like teeth were on full display. He ran his pink, plump tongue over them as he savoured his last meal.

"That was some delicious *rat*tata." He held his bulging stomach as he belly-laughed, prompting his Sideshows to join in until he yanked on their chains, bringing them to a choking, spluttering stop. "*Silence*!"

Rodents scurried over his clown shoes. Some stopped and licked at the blood spatters and spilled guts; others scurried off in fear of being dined on.

"Sorry, Master," Sideshow Necrotic spluttered.

"My apologies, sir," Sideshow Nightshade muttered, pulling at the chain around her throat. A steel link was pressing painfully against her collar bone.

"That's better, ladies. Now, how do I look?"

"Devilishly divine, Master." Sideshow Necrotic's hands slid up Mr Tickles' legs, her fingertips brushing against his crotch. She licked her lips.

"Yesss, I agree… *Divine*." Sideshow Nightshade blew him a kiss before wrapping her arms around his leg and rubbing her body against his tree-trunk-like limb.

"At ease, bitches." He whipped the chains, which thrashed the floor and gave off a sound like cracks of thunder. "Save it for the crowd." Slowly, he walked to the tent exit flaps and poked his head out. From there, he looked into the big top, which stood opposite his 'home', and spied a huge crowd gathered within. The lights hadn't yet been dimmed.

Another five, maybe ten minutes, max.

He took another look in the mirror, giving himself a final check before inspecting his Sideshows and their macabre make-up and dress.

His wide-eyed smile reappeared. He loved performing more than anything, even though he was being held at this job against his will.

Not after tonight...

"Ladies and gentleman, boys and girls, and ghost and ghouls of all ages—Welcome to the Last Freakshow on Earth! This *could* be the final thing you witness before your life ends this evening... It is advised you keep your arms, hands, legs and feet as far away from the performers as possible, in here and all around my world of fun, games, and horror," Ringmaster Hughes announced before bellowing with laughter.

A hush fell over the crowd, with some playing along by 'Ooh'ing' and 'Ahh'ing' with mock fright as they lapped up the ringmaster's over-zealous speech

The lights dimmed to a disturbingly creepy red glow.

Someone shrieked.

"My freaks and children walk among you this evening. Be warned, but be unsafe, he smiled, "for you're cheap meat for my extended family and feeding them can be expensive, not to mention a bind. But, without further ado, allow me to introduce the main attraction here at the big top: Mr Tickles and his Sideshows, Miss Necrotic and Miss Nightshade!" Hughes screeched into his microphone, triggering a hearty applause, raucous whistles and rowdy calls from the audience, who weren't the least bit disturbed by his speech.

"We'll soon alter that," Mr Tickles uttered, stepping from his tent, his Sideshows in metallic tow. He crossed the short distance to the big top. When he entered the arena, the rowdiness intensified.

The giant clown held his hands out and took a bow.

This will be my last performance in a while, so I better make it a good one.

****

"Holy *shit*! Did you see the way Mr Tickles ripped that kid's arm off and drank the blood erupting from the stump?!" Mouth asked, practically jumping through the big top's exit as he flailed his arms and laughed. "It was spurting everywhere!"

"Calm down, man." Mikey smiled. "It was fake. You do know that, right?"

"Yeah, course, but still—it was cool as ice!"

"Agreed," Chunk chimed in. He had a stupid grin plastered all over his fat face. "Pew-pew-pew," he said, mocking spurting blood with his hands and fingers. "Boom, splat, *pow*!"

“Ha-ha, you guys are gross!” Andy scrunched up her nose in disgust..

“Splash went the gore!” Brand joined in, rubbing Andy’s face with his hands, causing her to shriek in surprise and terror.

“Ew, ew, *ew*!” Andy slapped at her face and jogged on the spot. Her little white skirt rode up her thighs, giving the boys an eyeful of her knickers.

Zombie clowns rode past them on unicycles and snarled at them. Their costumes, injuries, make-up, dead eyes and everything else made them look too real for comfort, and had the gang skirting them.

More of the undead loitered the parkway. Some swallowed swords; others breathed fire.

“Look, that one’s trying to juggle,” Stef said, pointing at a zombie in front of them. They stood around and laughed...until the thing’s arm dropped off. It sent them running, shrieking and laughing throughout the circus.

They regrouped by a hotdog stand and ordered food and bottles of fizzy pop. The friends ate slowly, conversing in between mouthfuls and marvelling at all the rides and attractions around them.

"Let's go in there," Data suggested, his eyes bugging.

When Mikey and the rest turned to see what Data was pointing at—Eighties Land—there were nods and whoops of approval.

"We've never been inside a retro arcade," Brand stated.

"They're things we've only seen, heard or read about," Mouth chirped.

The flickering lights and sounds emitting from the arcade's tent was hypnotising, calling and drawing them.

"It's not mine or Stef's thing, so why don't you guys go along and we'll meet you back here in a couple of hours?" Andy suggested.

"Sounds good. Let's go, Mikey," Mouth said, pulling on his friend's denim jacket.

"Hold your horses, dude. Where are you girls going?" Mikey asked.

"I want to see the fortune teller," Stef spoke.

Andy nodded. "Me too."

"Okay." Brand looked at his watch. "Here by midnight?"

The girls nodded.

"And then we can check out that place," Chunk said, pointing.

Mouth gawked. "Wow! What is it?"

"A freakshow?" Data suggested.

"Something like that, I bet," Brand added.

Chunk licked his lips. "Can we go there first?"

"No—arcade first," Mouth whined.

"Yeah, and we want to see the fortune teller," Stef pointed out.

"Okay then. As planned, back here by midnight."

They all nodded in agreement before splitting off and heading in opposite directions.

****

The Fratellis stood hiding behind ghostly stilt-walkers and ghoulish hula-hoopers as they spied their targets and licked their ice-creams.

"*Fuck*! They've split up." Francis slapped his thigh.

"Pipe down, brother. Didn't you hear what they said? They're meeting back by here at midnight to check out the freakshow."

"That'll be too late—the place closes at twelve-thirty."

"Well, maybe we can get locked in there with them and finish it!" Mama interrupted. "Come on, let's get inside and make ourselves comfortable. We're in for a wait."

****

Mr Tickles hid beneath the big top via trapdoor with his Sideshows, where they feasted on the bodies, innards, limbs and blood of a dozen or so victims from their show. A show, Mr Tickles thought, that had gone splendidly. And for this, Miss Necrotic and Miss Nightshade were allowed off their leashes to eat, a privilege they were not granted often.

"Make sure you fill your bellies until they hurt, ladies."

"Why?" Miss Necrotic asked with a full mouth.

Even though this disgusted him, he dignified her with a response. "We've been through this a thousand times since last night! Once we've finished eating, you pair will go to Hughes' House of Horrors and wait for me. In the meantime, I'll go to Ringmaster Hughes' trailer and retrieve the keys for our neck braces and the ones belonging to the locks and fridges in the House of Horrors. By the time Hughes wakes up, we'll have caused enough trouble to have covered our escape."

"What makes you sure you'll be able to retrieve the keys? He keeps them close to his person," Miss Nightshade asked.

"Right around now I'd say he's crashed. Hard."

"Huh?" she pushed.

"Just before he gave his little speech earlier, I went to his trailer and laced his chocolate drink."

"You've lost us," Miss Necrotic complained.

"Lost you, yes, but not Nightshade—keep up, Necrotic. For the past few months, I've been watching our master, making notes of his routine. Every night, at around eleven, once he's finished at the big top, he retires to his caravan and unwinds with a chocolate drink before settling down for the night."

"And?" Necrotic pushed.

"I've laced it with sleeping pills and ground glass."

"Clever. So you'll have knocked him out for tonight, but then he'll die slowly with the poison?" Nightshade surmised.

Mr Tickles nodded.

"Why not something more lethal, faster acting?" Necrotic wanted to know.

"Because I want him to suffer for all the things he's done to us."

The girls laughed before stuffing more gore into their face.

"That's right, ladies, eat up—it could be a long time before we do so again, once we've escaped. Who knows how far we'll have to travel beyond the walls of Chinatown."

Ten minutes later, with their bellies to the point of bursting, Mr Tickles led his Sideshows out from under the big top and took them to Hughes' House of Horrors, where he unchained them and told them to go inside.

"Mix with the crowds and partake in scaring them with the other acts mingling amongst them."

"Yes, Master," the women said in unison, and then crawled up the steel ramp leading to the House of Horrors' entrance.

When they disappeared through the fog, Mr Tickles turned and walked towards the rear of the circus, noting how much the crowds had thinned out. *I need to get my arse in gear—I need as many people left on the grounds as possible if my plan is to work.*

As he walked, he shoulder-charged people out of his way and grunted. Some people went to the ground whilst others called after him, but none challenged his actions.

When he got to where all the caravans, tents, cars, jeeps and other living quarters and vehicles were kept out of sight from the public, Mr Tickles marched over to his ringmaster's and peeped through the window. Luckily for him, there was a crack in the curtain.

In front of him, beyond the glass and slumped in his chair, was Ringmaster Hughes. His chin was touching his chest and his empty mug rested on the floor, the handle broken off.

The clown laughed, misting the window. He put a huge hand out and rested it on the door handle. When he depressed it, he found it locked.

"Such a wise, cautious fellow." Mr Tickles' smile grew wider, and then he yanked on the door, ripping it off its hinges and discarding it like a rag doll. Before entering, he poked his head inside to check on his boss, who hadn't moved. "Excellent."

His heavy footfalls echoed off the caravan's thin walls as he made his way towards Hughes. Once he stood over his hapless master, Mr Tickles ripped the man's shirt open and yanked the keys from around his neck, leaving behind a red mark.

"How the fuck do you walk around with all these damn keys on one chain?" Mr Tickles held the bunch up, which had close to fifty small keys with tags on it, and sifted through them until he found the one labelled 'Mr Tickles'. "Aren't I lucky you're an organised man, sir?" The clown laughed again as he jammed the required key into the lock belonging to the harnessed bomb around his neck and disengaged the bolt.

When he was certain it was unlocked, he carefully opened it and pulled it away from his body. With it clear of his person, he placed it down by his boss' side and walked towards a rack that held many other keys. He rooted through them until he found a bunch marked 'House of Horrors'.

He closed his fist around them, exited the home on wheels, and stalked towards his destination.

****

The seven friends regrouped outside Hughes' House of Horrors, their bodies slowly being engulfed by the smoke being pumped from inside the attraction. Two guards dressed in imperial clothing stood to the side of the entrance, their spears blocking the way in.

"They look like a friendly pair," Mouth observed.

"I don't recall seeing them here earlier." Brand stepped forward, and the guards parted their spears.

"Enter at your own peril," one of the masked sentries announced.

"This is going to be boss, guys!" Mikey skipped forward and up the ramp.

"Agreed." Chunk followed behind his friend with a hand on his shoulder.

The rest of the gang shuffled in behind, and the seven of them pushed through the smoke, spluttering and coughing as they did so.

"Can't see a damned thing!" one of the girls called.

"Mikey?" Data asked, putting his hand out. "You guys close by?"

When the dense fog cleared, a long trailer with built-in prisons was revealed. There was ice and icicles everywhere, bringing to mind a walk-in freezer. Somewhere close by, generators chugged away and an azure light drenched them.

"W-what the hell?" Andy's teeth chattered.

"It's not that cold," Mouth told her.

"Cold enough." Stef crossed her arms and rubbed at her gooseflesh.

"Shit, there are *actual* people in those rooms..." Data pointed out, walking over to one of the cells that had Perspex instead of bars. "They must be freezing!" He looked at a buxom woman who carried a wooden doll around with her. She scowled at Data, her miniature friend giving him the middle finger. "How rude," he said, laughing. Upon looking at a plaque affixed to the side of her cell, Data read aloud what was written there. "Allow me, Ringmaster Hughes, to introduce you to the most evil, sadistic killers to ever walk the earth: Crystal and Harry. She's a ventriloquist, and he's a doll with his own life..."

"This young rocker-type chick over here goes by the name of Punk," Mikey told them, causing Data to turn and look at the woman who looked like a child. "Says she's a blood-sucking monster with the ability to morph into something otherworldly."

"Yeah, yeah—just like this doll has a life of its own."

The friends laughed and moved on, reeling off names as they went: Man-Eating Fucks, Simone, Mr Tickles, Francesca, Storm, Porky, Baby, Doctor... The cells seemed endless.

"Hey, this guy went berserk and built a mobile fortress out of his car!" Chunk laughed.

"Most of these people are psycho killers," Brand stated.

"They don't look that dangerous," Mikey scoffed.

"Odd Owen," Data remarked. "Says he built the fort to kill all the zombies?"

"Yeah, I read about that—it was an apocalypse that happened beyond the walls of Chinatown in the early 2000s," Chunk joined in.

"Norm and Angharad. Norm rebuilt his sister, Angharad, after she died during a rock-climbing accident," Andy read as she passed a cell holding a man pushing a woman around in a wheelchair. "Now that is *freaky*!"

"You really think these Man-Eating Fucks are cannibals?" Mouth wanted to know.

"So it says on their plaque. Look at their deformities. Fuck!" Mouth pressed his face to the glass and almost pissed himself when the biggest of the flesh-eaters shoulder-barged the glass. "Settle down, big guy. I can smell wet earth coming out of their vent."

"Come on, let's keep going." Mikey grabbed Mouth by his jacket.

"Santa Klaws..."

"He looks disturbed, Chunk." Data stood next to his rotund friend as they stared at the man dressed entirely in black Santa clothing. He didn't move, just watched them. Darkness shrouded him. One of the girls continued to reel off names.

"Dacchas, Raj the Sun God—"

"Is that a fucking mummy?!" someone asked.

"—Doorknob Davey, Chaos, Sisters of Solicited..."

"There are so many of them!" Mikey moved along the trailer in awe, his mouth open. "They're mostly killers, with a few perverts and monsters thrown in for good measures, guys."

"This is too cool." Chunk rubbed his hands together. "Can we go back to the start and look at them all a—"

"Nobody fucking move!" A man pointing a revolver stepped from the shadows. "Or I'll turn you all into Swiss cheese."

Mouth couldn't help but laugh at that one. "Because it's full of ho—"

"Shut up, Mouth!" his friends shouted.

"Tie 'em up, boys!" Mama Fratelli stepped from behind the gang and threw a length of rope over their heads. It landed at Jake's feet where he now stood at his brother's side.

"What a sweet idea, Ma." Jake gathered the rope and pulled a section of it taut between his hands. "You're all ours now, children."

"*Argh*!" the group screamed collectively, backing up against a Perspex prison that held conjoined twins.

The Fratellis closed in on them: Jake with the rope, Ma with her cutlass and Francis with his revolver. They had awful, heinous grins plastered all over their disgusting faces.

The freaks were up against their windows, banging on them.

"Please!" Mikey begged. "It can't end like this…"

"Afraid it can, sonny," Ma countered, breaking the bad news.

"Gonna cut your fat fingers off, fatty," Francis threatened Chunk.

"Ugh, *no*!" The meaty lad shook his head and put his hands behind his back, his jowls wibble-wobbling.

"Cut this fuck's tongue out!" Jake grabbed Mouth by the chin and forced his gob open. "Let's see it, boy."

"Leave him alone!" Stef slapped at Jake's hands.

"Fuck off, cunt-bitch-twat sack of shit." Jake lashed out, catching the girl in the jaw with the back of his hand.

Stef's head slammed against the Perspex, her eyes rolled, and she collapsed to the floor like a sack of bricks. "*Ugh*!" Blood trickled out of her mouth and left nostril.

Chunk went for him but was shut down by a robust right hook from Francis.

"You ballbags are fucking *pathetic*. I can't believe it's taken us so long to catch up with you."

Ma Fratelli swooped in with her cutlass and removed Brand's head, which bounced along the floor until it hit a cell. The occupant slammed his arms against the solid window and growled. "Pipe the fuck down, pumpkin," she growled back, turning to face Raj, the mummy sun god. "You're not fooling me with those discoloured bandages!"

Raj hammered his fists against the see-through wall of his prison and let out an ear-bleeding roar.

The lights inside the trailer winked on and off a half-dozen times and then died completely, throwing the friends and Fratellis into total darkness. A back-up light kicked in, swamping them in an eerie, washed-out ice blue colour, which made them look dead and frozen.

The Fratellis were welded in place from fight.

"Ma," Francis squeaked. "What's going on?"

The generators grumbled to a spluttering death. Locks disengaged. The Perspex to the cells slid aside, releasing their captors.

Shadows crept along the walls.

"They're coming to get us!" Jake shrieked.

Francis fired his gun once, twice, three times: *bang, bang, bang*! Bullets pinged and whizzed. "*Die*!" he demanded, and then the mummy shoved him off-balance, giving the remaining gang members a chance to scatter. They made their way towards the exit, but became entangled in separate struggles with the freaks, killers and monsters.

"Come on, Francis, get up and moving. Follow me, Jake!" Ma Fratelli instructed, grabbing Jake by his vest and pulling him out of harm's way.

Francis, still on the floor, took aim with his revolver once again, putting a bullet through Raj's eye. An explosion of sand burst out of the sun god and did little to stop him—he kept coming. Francis screamed as he unloaded his gun into the monster. With each striking bullet, bursts of golden particles erupted from beneath the rotted bandages.

Before Francis could throw his pistol at the approaching threat, Raj stamped on his leg, crushing his calf and splintering bones, which ripped through his flesh.

"Ugh-*argh*!" he cried, his hands going to his hurt. Blood pumped out of him and his eyes rolled. "P-please..." He opened his mouth to speak again when a small, wooden hand entered him and latched onto his tongue.

"Mine now, fucker!" the doll, Harry, gleefully warbled, yanking the organ free. This prompted his keeper, Crystal, to step forward and stab Francis in his stomach repeatedly, until blood washed up her arms and face.

"*Francis*!" Ma Fratelli attacked with her cutlass, her sword slashing air. "I'll kill you all."

"Behind you!" Jake warned, feeling helpless with his rope. As he was about to step forward to help, a machete punched through his guts from behind. The mighty blade was ripped him his body, his guts splashing onto the floor, until it opened up his chest and more.

Blood trickled out of his mouth and dribbled down his chin, his fingers groping at the steel tip sticking out of his throat. "*Uch*..." Jake gargled, collapsing to his knees.

"Oops, sorry!" Simone chuckled, holding his toy clown. "Didn't see you there."

Jake continued to wheeze, and then fell forward, his face smashing against the floor.

"*Jakey*!" Ma wailed, slashing her sword as she walked backwards, keeping the threat at bay. "Back. *Back*!" She stabbed at the marauding horde of blood-crazed killers.

Raj stepped out of the pack, allowing her weapon to punch through his guts, where it lodged.

"Fuck—"

The mummy placed his hands on either side of her head and squeezed, cracking her skull like an egg. Her eyes popped out of their sockets on short jets of blood and pearly-white goo. Her body spasmed as he picked her up off the floor, allowing his freako friends to have at her with the weapons they possessed, shredding her flesh and body like cheap bedding.

When Raj was done, he threw the body aside.

Data, Mikey, Chunk, Andy, Stef and Mouth ran out of the House of Horrors screaming, their hands held high, and pushed by Sideshow Necrotic and Nightshade.

"They're free*eee*!" Chunk warned. "Run, for the love of mercy."

The crowd around them broke up with laughter, until the amassed berserkos gathered at the opening of the trailer. The imperial guards were hauled inside by unseen hands, and it wasn't long before blood poured down the ramp, mixing with the grass and hay.

"Oh. My. Fucking. God!" A woman dressed like Tank Girl pointed, and then slung her baseball bat over her shoulder in readiness to strike.

She was joined by a Hulk Hogan, Ultimate Warrior and the three Storms from *Big Trouble in Little China*.

"These fucks think they can mess with us and Chinatown? This is our turf," a wannabe Scarface declared. "Say hello to my little—*Ugh*!" A knife thundered into his chest, propelling him backwards.

The '80s geeks rushed towards the horrors, weapons and fists held high, and they met in the middle. Bone snapped. Blood squirted.

During the melee, Data, Chunk, Andy, Mouth and Stef were able to slip away, exiting the circus and running for home.

****

Mr Tickles poked his head from behind the House of Horrors and smiled. The carnage and violence erupting all around pleased him to no end, and there was still no sign of Hughes.

“Good. I need to get the bombs off the freaks,” he muttered, looking at the keys. “But how? They’re too wrapped up in killing.”

When he saw Raj standing on his own, watching the action unfold, he went to him and put the bunch of keys in his hand. “Set our friends free. If you don’t, Hughes will activate the bombs around their necks. Yours, too.”

Raj nodded.

"Necrotic, Nightshade—with me, now." Mr Tickles waved his Sideshows over, who were both involved in altercations with members of the crowd, but they came on his command. "I'd like to take as many horrors with me, but I can't. Shit. I guess they're on their own."

"What now, Master?" Nightshade asked.

"We get the fuck out of here. Make Chinatown a bad memory."

"Let's go, before we're made a part of this place's history," Sideshow Necrotic advised.

"Agreed. Follow me, ladies." Mr Tickles led the women towards the back of the circus—the bloodshed covering their movements—until they found his van. "Get in."

The clown got behind the wheel and wasted no time in starting the engine and pulling out. He ploughed through those who got in his way, but avoided his own.

"We'll never make it, guys," Sideshow Necrotic whined.

"Shut up, bitch." Mr Tickles put his foot down, powering the vehicle through the gates and into the streets of Chinatown, where an angry mob was gathering. "Shit."

"They're heading this way. They must have heard about what's happening back there," Sideshow Nightshade surmised.

Mr Tickles cut down a side street, leaving the roving pack behind him in a cloud of dust. "We'll get there." His van's lights illuminated the spot where the bridge out of Chinatown had been two nights ago. "What *the*?!" He jumped on the brakes, his vehicle screaming to a halt. "Motherfuckers have taken it—"

A roar from above stopped him, and a bright light descended on him. "Turn around and go back, or we will be forced to open fire!" came a voice over a megaphone.

Mr Tickles wound his window down, poked his head out, and looked up at the chopper hovering above. "We're with the circus!" he pleaded. "We need to get out."

"Go back—that's an order. Nobody leaves Chinatown once they've entered."

"We could swim?!" Sideshow Necrotic suggested.

As if on cue, boats appeared from nowhere, their spotlights and high-calibre machine guns trained on them.

"There's no escape," Mr Tickles declared, looking up and into his rear-view mirror. The enraged mob had almost caught up with them. "Fuck it." He put the van in gear, released the brake, and powered his way into the river below with a crash.

Slowly, the water around the van bubbled as it sank.

Nobody emerged from it...

The End

Lifeblood
By
Mark Fleming

Each flash preceded a monstrous rumble beyond the black clouds. McLean shivered, not at the rain soaking through every layer of his uniform, but that sporadic sound that made him think of a bombardment.

He watched Munro picking his way across grass stamped from green to brown by days of footfall. Puddles welled around hot dog and candy floss stalls normally thronged with customers. The relentless downpour had stripped the carnival of its brash allure, transforming the garish reds, oranges and purples painted on the ferris wheel, ghost train, waltzers and fortune teller booth to greys. Crows drifting like lost kites were the only signs of life. McLean shoved his hands deeper into his pockets in an attempt to counter their trembling.

Munro turned to his partner, the much younger constable grinning at McLean's laborious approach. "Jeez, Frank. I know you're coming up for retirement, but you look as if you should've jacked this in ten fucking year ago. Maybe you should've retired when you came out the navy. When was that? Just after Trafalgar?"

"Ha, fucking, ha. I'm just taking it easy walking through this swamp. Not wanting to end up flat on my back. Although I don't think I could possibly get any wetter." He took in their murky surroundings. "Where d'you think the staff hang out, then? This place looks like the fairground in a ghost town."

"There's a dose of caravans through that way." Munro's finger stabbed through the rain, shaped to imitate a gun. "Let's check them out."

Pools were coalescing into one ankle-deep pond. The pair swished through, cursing as filthy water crept into their boots. They arrived at a caravan where muted folk music sounded. McLean stepped up to the door, rapping on it with knuckles so numb only the insistent sound told him he'd made contact. The door squeaked open. A clown's face peered at them, its furtive disposition at odds with the lurid red smile.

"Mister Jaworski? Jan Jaworski?"

"Yes, yes. Afternoon, sirs. You got here quick." The clown poked his head outside, as if to make sure his visitors had remained unobserved.

McLean took the opportunity to glower around himself. If the guy was apprehensive for whatever reason, he needn't have bothered. Even the birds had vanished. The policeman felt as if they were the last people on Earth, never mind a carnival-site in Motherwell.

They stepped into a scene as shambolic as McLean's daughter's bedroom had been at the height of her rebellious teens. It appeared clean enough, although the newspapers stacked in a corner were so yellowed he anticipated headlines about the Moon landings. In another corner a clear plastic sack bulged with crushed beer cans.

"You are Jan Jaworski?" enquired Munro.

"I am. Sorry. As you can see, my humble abode needs a tidy. I just haven't had time, what with everything that's been happening around here."

Munro glanced at McLean, who shrugged. The older policeman fished out his notebook. "The clown make-up? You'll not have much of an audience today."

"Is true."

"Forecast says the rain is due to ease late afternoon," noted Munro. "You might get to put on your show later. There's a small big top at the centre of the carnival, isn't there? My laddies love watching clowns."

"Good one, Kevin. Small big top," McLean butted in. "Or is it a big small top?"

"Yes, yes. Clown show for little kids. The teenagers are just coming for the ghost train, the big wheel. The waltzers, the mirrors. Always chasing them for smoking among the mirrors. Or getting too frisky."

"So, Mister Jaworski. The call that came through was a bit… vague. Although the call-taker did mention you sounded… concerned?"

"*Concerned*? Oh, yes. That's a fucking understatement, sirs."

McLean appraised this man. Age-wise, it was impossible to hazard a guess through that caked-on warpaint. He checked the preliminary notes he'd jotted after their sergeant had briefed them. A message had come through that the carnival manager, Jaworski, wished to make a complaint against another member of the staff who was verbally and physically harassing him. McLean stared at the blank space on the crinkled pad he'd just retrieved from his uniform pocket. This guy looked as eccentric as the leering faces painted on the wooden horses on the carousel they passed earlier. Whether his statement would amount to a genuine grievance or an alcohol-fuelled rant remained to be seen.

Munro stood legs apart, the classic pose intended to let the interviewee know he was in no mood for bullshit. "Right, Mister Jaworski. Can we begin with the basics. Name?"

"Jan Jaworski. But you knew that. I already said."

"Just answer the questions, if you would, Mister Jaworski. We'll be finished here much quicker and you can get back to your... tidying. Date of birth?"

'June twelfth, nineteen fifty-nine."

Munro scribbled the details. "I take it your address is no-fixed-abode?"

"Yes. We travel around the country this time of year. So JJ's Carnival."

"And your capacity?"

"Me? I must admit, eleven, twelve cans each night."

"No. Not your *literal* capacity, sir. In what capacity does JJ's Carnival employ you?" McLean fought not to roll his eyes.

"I'm co-owner. With my partner, Jadwiga. Well, as of now, *ex*-partner."

McLean looked up from his own shorthand. "You've broken-up then, Jan? We *can* call you Jan?"

"Yes, yes. Is my name. We have big fight. Well. It's been long time coming."

"Why *are* you dressed as a clown, Jan? The fairground is deserted in this weather." asked McLean.

"I put on sometimes when I'm feeling the stress. I worry easily. Insecure."

"Why is that?" wondered Munro.

"Cause of Jadwiga. She's... she's been threatening me."

Munro and McLean exchanged looks. McLean squinted his eyes as he asked the next question." Jadwiga and yourself were in what sort of relationship?"

"Jadwiga and I have on-off relationship... for years. Since she joined carnival troop... ten, eleven years ago, and bought out my previous partner. She's also Polish. A fortune teller. Best in business."

"Her age?"

"That's hard to say. I think late seventies?"

"Wow," Munro blurted out. "Which would make you a bit of a toy boy?"

Jaworski's gaze slipped to his feet. Munro's attempt to inject flippancy seemed to have had the opposite effect, reducing him to shame. "I drink too much, I know this. Why else would anyone get stuck in relationship with a controlling... psychopath?"

The emotive word seemed to fill the caravan with malice. McLean followed up on it. "A psychopath?"

"Anytime I threaten to leave her, she threatens me with violence. She comes up to me, right to my face... I swear when she stares at you, right *into* you, she can reach into your soul. She can *hypnotize*. I've always thought that is how she sounds so convincing when she is reading her Tarot cards, her crystal ball. She tells her clients *anything* and they fucking believe. Boy, do they lap up. She's gone too far this time, though. We have huge fallout. Hence the make up, sirs. That's the real reason, actually. I'm so ashamed. She is, how you say, punching my lights out."

"Do you want to press charges, Jan?" asked Munro.

"Yes. And no. I should do right thing, I suppose. But I'm worried about how she would react. I mean. She once told me, in Volhynia, on Ukrainian border, during war, there was a Polish Home Army fighter who she fell in love with. This boy is breaking her heart. Into pieces. He fell for another girl in the village. Day of his marriage, Jadwiga got into his head. I mean, *right* inside. Fucking brainwash him. He threw himself into River Dniester."

At this revelation the policemen glanced at one another again, eyebrows raised. His stories were meandering along a fine line between a version of the truth and outright fantasy. McLean felt icy rain trickling down his neck. "During the *war*? Which war?"

"Against Ukrainian partisans. Against Nazi occupation."

"As in, seventy years ago? Jadwiga must surely be even older than she told you?"

"I believe probably is, officer. I believe she draws energy from the souls of her men. She's been doing this for decades. I've no idea how many young men she ruined back home. She told me she emigrates to Scotland after communists took over Poland after war. I move much later, in 1980s, as communists are leaving again. When she made her way up here and joined my carnival I only saw an attractive woman, with an uncanny ability, a *gift* for seeing into different dimensions. She was happy to live quietly among us. Then when we got into the financial problems, she bailed us out. She became joint owner. A business partner. Very passionate, too. Not just with me. With *all* the men in the troop. Some of the women, too. She was fucking insatiable. But she scared them all. I was only one who would stick with her. But if I didn't have this paint on my face you would see my bruises, black eyes. It started over nothing. We were drinking, here. I spilt her glass by accident. She raged."

"We'll need to ask you to come down to the station to make a formal statement about any alleged abuse," insisted Munro.

"Yes."

McLean gazed at the caravan window, seeing nothing beyond rivulets of rain slithering down its grimy pane. ”We’ll have to get Jadwiga’s side of the story. Where do we find her?”

”Caravan at end of this row. You won’t miss. It’s painted black. Like her soul, the witch.”

McLean winked at Munro, slipping his notebook inside his jacket. ”Right then, Jan. Don’t go anywhere, please. In case we have to go over anything else about this.”

”Where else am I going to go? The carnival’s over,” Jaworski replied mournfully.

”The Seekers,” murmured McLean. ”Love that song.” His remark was lost on his youthful colleague and the alcoholic clown.

The uniformed pair stepped outside, relieved to be departing the stench of stale beer and body odour. McLean scowled over his shoulder, and halted.

"What is it, Frank?"

"There's someone else in there with him, Kevin."

"What?" Munro stared at his partner.

"Someone else is in his caravan. I caught a glimpse of them, looking out at us, just for a second. It definitely wasn't a clown. Someone younger, without the fucking warpaint. Might even have been a female."

"You sure?" Munro peered back through the rain. "Little Mix could be in there, fucking starkers, and you wouldn't be able to see anything through these stair rods."

"Little who?" McLean looked at his partner, genuinely perplexed.

"Oh, nothing. We can go back and check once we've spoken to this *witch* of his."

"Well, Jaworski's making as much sense as the fucking Dead Sea scrolls would to you or me, Kevin. Polish Home Army? Exes throwing themselves into rivers? Until he gets wired into some make-up remover we've no way of gauging his claims of abuse, either. We'll see what this Jadwiga says."

They approached the caravan. As well as being daubed matte black, the exterior walls were festooned in stars, moons and demonic faces resembling gargoyles. Rain sluicing through their leering mouths created a disconcerting three-dimensional effect. This time Munro marched up to the front door. Before he knocked on it, a voice was heard from somewhere behind the caravan, although the relentlessly driving rain muted it.

Munro faced his partner. ”Did you hear that, Frank?”

”I may be facing retirement, but I’m not fucking deaf, Kevin.”

”Sounded like someone saying *help me*. I think.”

”Go check it out. There’s nothing else after this caravan, except the house of mirrors. What if I try getting some sense from the insatiable senile delinquent, then catch you up?”

McLean grinned, watching Munro pacing through the mud, then disappearing in the gloom. He thumped on the door. Expecting to be confronted by some ancient crone, fingers gnarled from decades of weaving elaborate tales while extorting money, he was taken aback to be greeted by a beautiful woman, surely no older than 40. Instantly, he doubted everything Jaworski had been garbling about.

"Police? Yes, I'm aware that spineless fool was making contact with you, spreading his nonsense." Her Slavic-accentuated words rolled from her throat like a purring cat. "Perhaps you come inside and hear truth?"

The contrast with the previous abode was like day and night. She beckoned McLean to a seat on a couch. The interior was homely, draped in tapestries, decorated with colourful plant pots. Scented candles flickered on the small table, casting a welcoming glow.

Her eyes shone like emeralds... comforting, enigmatic, alluring. He inhaled her intoxicating perfume. Being in such close proximity to this exotic beauty had a narcotic effect: the more he inhaled her scent and the more his eyes roved over her generous curves, the greater the feeling of a thousand butterfly wings brushing his guts. He imagined being strapped into a waltzer, the moment you felt it beginning to pick up speed.

Jadwiga's hair was black, with a wonderful blue sheen reminiscent of a raven's plumage. Gold necklaces were draped around her neck. His eyes were drawn to these adornments, following the plunging neckline of her unbuttoned purple blouse to the expansive cleavage where her large breasts trembled as she shifted her weight. As his eyesight grew accustomed to the sparse light he noticed piercings glinting around her ear, through her septum, pinning her dark lips as they smiled expansively.

"No doubt he told you we were lovers? In his mind. Yes. He gives his mind a treat."

McLean fumbled for his notebook, more to keep his attention diverted from her physicality. He'd never felt such a powerful sexual attraction. A divorcee of 17 years with grown-up kids, the last time he'd been so close to a voluptuous woman had been some time ago, during an Amsterdam stag weekend. He'd paid for the privilege. He watched her licking her full lips with her silver-studded tongue, toying with the hoops. The feeling of being deliberately, but wonderfully, anaesthetised increased.

Finally he shook his head and flipped the pages open, dismissing the scribbled summary of Jaworski's rambling interview. "Jadwiga, isn't it?"

"It is. And you?"

"McLean."

"Police Constable McLean, handsome and dashing officer of Her Majesty's Constabulary. I'd rather be less formal."

He sniggered. "Frank."

This boosted her enticing smile. "That's better. Frank. Now. How can I help you?"

Before continuing, he glanced beyond the lace curtains, searching for any sign of his partner.

"You look for your friend? Kevin? I saw him go round back. He is making his way to the special attraction here, no? Hall of mirrors. Did he hear something?"

"How d'you know his name?"

"I listen to you talking outside Jan's caravan. Is close. Even closer if you know shortcut through maze of caravans. Plus I have excellent senses for someone my age."

"*Your* age?"

"They say everything improves with age... intelligence, wine, sexual pleasures."

"I'm not following, Jadwiga." Although intrigued, he tried remaining focused on the formality of this interview. He shifted uncomfortably.

"I can prove the last two."

He felt the caravan lurching to one side and slapped his hands onto the table. "What was that? A mudslide?"

"Is nothing. Relax, Frank. Please. Close eyes a moment."

Again, he was conflicted between duty and her hypnotic allure. He debated whether to comply or refuse her request. Somehow it seemed so much easier to go along with her. When he opened them again, she'd placed her own palms over his hands. Although he hadn't felt any physical contact, there was a warm sensation inexplicably flowing from her fingertips, traveling along his limbs, then centering in his crotch. He was drawn to tattoos on the back of her hand, so livid their colours and shapes were almost shifting, like an animation. He shook his head.

"You will accept my hospitality, Frank?"

"Wh-what?" Looking deep into her eyes, he sensed a darker mood, far more dangerous than the beguiling tone she'd been adopting. But this anxiety vanished the moment her full lips drew back into a seductive smile. Now all her felt was an overwhelming desire to kiss her.

"Please. Take a drink. Krupknik. A delicious liqueur. Flavoured with honey and spices. I've heated for you."

Now he stared at the glass which had materialised on the table. Its quivering amber surface captured the candlelight, entrancing him. "I don't drink. Stopped a while ago. I had to." He licked his lips in spite of himself.

"Just a few sips then, Frank. It won't harm. Will help thaw out that frosty Scottish exterior, no? Krupnick is liquid gold. We used as antiseptic during war."

The next thing he was aware of, he was touching the glass to his lips. A rich aroma permeated his senses. Its taste was liquid summer: sunshine, golden meadows, humming bees, birdsong. The sensation of this sliding down his throat was exhilarating. Its warmth radiated throughout his body.

"My God!" he finally gasped. "That's the most beautiful thing I've ever tasted."

"I'll prove to you *second* most beautiful thing you've ever tasted."

"What do you mean?"

Her stare matched the intensity of the aftertaste. The need to press her with constant questions was dissolving like the tears appearing to course down the perspex pane behind her. Tracking one of these raindrops, he noticed statuettes, placed along the window sill, of tiny forest creatures: fairies, elves, fawns. The females were all topless and some of the figures were copulating with wild abandon.

"My figurines? These I sculpt myself, Frank. Those two... they could be you and I, no?"

He followed the direction of her pointing finger. The resemblance was uncanny. His notebook clattered to the floor. She moved closer, pressing her chest into his. Her eyes were boring into his. The background, muted as it was by candlelight, dissolved into shadows. McLean got the impression of being inexorably compelled inside a tunnel; but there was nothing sinister about this. Moments before, he had been chilled to the bone. Now a serene heat spread over him, bristling the hair beneath his cap, tingling his skin. It was like being overwhelmed by an incredible sense of calm, underpinned by desire. Perhaps her potent liqueur was the closest he'd ever get to experiencing a hit with Class As.

She was addressing him, soothingly, her words swirling inside his head. It became easier to simply nod in acquiescence rather than demand any explanation. Time had become unhinged, as if he'd blacked out without even realising it. He wasn't aware of her having altered her position, but the next moment she was indicating an object draped with a sheet of silk. It hadn't been there before. While murmuring in an unfamiliar tongue, she tugged the covering away, revealing a crystal ball. Although its surface was smooth as ice, the surrounding candle wicks were reflected in myriad points.

"Remove hat, Frank. Please. In Volhynia we say to guests, my home is your home, take from it whatever your heart desires."

His eyes were riveted to her reaching for his peaked cap, placing it next to her, then ruffling his wiry grey hair. "Such handsome man, Frank." Her other hand stroked his right thigh. "Please relax. I know so many people sceptical about the power of the globe. But I show you the truth. In this ball I can see all things, past, present, future. If you believe with all your heart."

"I *do* believe," he murmured, studying the object with awe, like some primitive presented with fire for the first time. This became the focus of his attention, so much so, he found his reasons for having arrived at this moment completely cryptic. Who was this captivating woman who oozed sensuality from every fibre of her being? Why was he even here? He was sure he had arrived with someone else, but that was another mystery. The more he tried to recall his companion's identity, the further the truth slithered from his grasp. Eventually he gave up trying. There was only this beguiling woman and her radiant sphere.

She waved long, slender, black-tipped fingers towards the ball and a picture formed at its core. Her other hand caressed the sodden fabric of his trousers until they were no longer wet, fingertips working between his legs, boosting his libido until his heart was drumming inside his rib-cage. When the shimmering colours coalesced, he was stunned to see an image of himself as a young man.

"*So* handsome... but you were very afraid, Frank, yes?'

McLean recognised the scene with a clarity that took his breath away. A horrendous explosion shuddered through the vessel. He joined the confused melee of panic-stricken men rushing along smoke-filled gangways. Alarmed, he wrenched his attention from the flashback. "I... I saw myself. I was on the Sheffield—the H.M.S. Sheffield. We were struck by an Argentine missile, an Exocet. We were the first ship sunk since World War Two. Twenty of my mates died. I... I joined the force after I was discharged from the navy."

"Just so. As soon as you walked in caravan, I knew. I knew you have cheated death once before. This gives you lust for life. Makes you *potent*."

"*Once* before?"

"What else you see?"

The vision altered again... revolving, drawing him in until he felt his entire body succumbing, spiralling into a vortex. He was sinking backwards into the deep, lustrous comfort of the cushions strewn over the coach. Moments later she was on top of him, grinding into his pelvic bone, grasping his hands, hauling his fingers towards her pendulous breasts. Again, time had distorted. He had no recollection of having taken off his clothes or watching her removing her own; yet they were voracious for each other's naked bodies. He grasped her nipples and relished the intricate tattoos emblazoned across her chest, shoulders and arms; vibrant floral patterns that were pulsating in time with her rhythmic thrusting. Seizing control, she writhed over him, rolling around in a rapturous wrestling match; forcing herself deeper onto him, her tongue coiling around his. He could only stare into her exquisite green eyes as her motion became ever more insistent, biting her lower lip, fixing him with an expression of craving so fierce it was almost hateful.

"You were lucky to survive, no? Fate was not yet ready for you. You wanted to *celebrate* life. Always. Living it to the full. Every day precious. What *ripeness* I feel in you, my lover… I want it all…"

It had been so long since he'd experienced intimacy, he felt the climax rushing towards him. His teeth clenched as he focused on the patterns splattering against the skylight, attempting to prolong the inevitable, until even this became futile. He groaned and jerked into her heaving thighs. As she rode his ejaculation, he stared into her intoxicating eyes.

"Yes, yes. Fill me with your life. I crave your life juices, your seed, your blood..."

Exhausted, McLean felt himself sinking into a delirious sleep. Some time later he came to with such a start his head slammed into the wall. He was alone in the caravan. Hastily, he dressed. What the fuck had just happened? Why had he *let* it happen? He was a police officer on duty, two months from his pension. Then he remembered his colleague. “Kevin,” he said aloud.

He stood up and was about to barge outside when the crystal bowl flickered. He stole a glance inside. There was Munro, pacing through a long, elaborate corridor, stalked by his own reflection. A shadowy figure joined him. McLean got the impression this second person meant his partner harm.

He rushed out of the caravan. The hall of mirrors was constructed on a long plinth raised from the field. McLean stooped inside. Instantly he was enveloped by a crazed world of false corridors and mirrored walls that continually led him into dead ends. Each abrupt halt left him confronting a purple-faced vision of himself.

"You're far too old for this fucking caper, McLean" he hissed to himself. Then there was a terrible wail. He started. "Kevin?" he cried out. "Where are you?"

Lurching to the end of an interminable wall of glass, he slammed into another mirror. When he opened his eyes, he saw his colleague standing stock still, facing away from him. Sighing with relief, he approached his partner. "Kevin, mate. I was starting to get worried."

His voice echoed, yet the other policeman remained rooted to the spot. McLean stepped up to him. Munro eventually turned about, the movement fatigued. The younger man gazed blankly at McLean.

"What's the matter, Kevin? Did you find anything? I thought this was going to be a routine call. I wasn't expecting anything to get out of control. Let's just head back to the station."

But Munro's image vanished as quickly as it had materialised.

"Help me." The plaintive cry sounded close by. He jerked his head around. His own despairing features confronted him. There was movement across a row of mirrors to his left. Two mysterious figures in chain mail, their tabards bearing a

ferocious double-headed eagle motif, marched into each other before disappearing. Footsteps sounded behind him. When he swivelled around, he glimpsed men in khaki tunics with white and red armbands, striding forward, then altering direction in a blink of an eye, their hollowed eyes catching his own before the ranks of identical soldiers were inexplicably replaced by Jaworski's heavily bruised face.

McLean shut his eyes to the hallucinations. The ground was spinning. Jadwiga had surely spiked his drink. When his eyes snapped open, the mirrors seemed to have tripled in number, stretching as far as he could see in every direction, each silver sheen intensifying. The harder he stared, the more people he could see making their way along the myriad corridors, their images appearing for fleeting seconds before altering into someone else.

Then Munro was facing him again. "Kevin! Thank fuck. We need to get the fuck out of here, buddy. I… I've been poisoned."

It was Kevin's eyes he noticed first, the irises suddenly altering from brown to green. Creases worked their way across his complexion, ageing him by decades. His frame was contracting into a much wirier physique. McLean thumbed at his eye sockets, convinced this was more than just the drugged liqueur: these mirrors were convex, distorting his perception. He reached out for Munro only to touch glass. McLean observed his friend's features transforming further until there was no sense of the policeman at all. His likeness had been replaced by a stooped, elderly woman.

There was something crumpled on the ground by her feet. McLean strained to see further inside this panel. A navy-uniformed figure was sprawled on the ground. Pulse quickening, he strained closer. Shock impaled him. *This* was Munro. McLean thrust a hand out to steady himself. Munro's throat had been torn out, as if by some ravenous animal, muscle and tissue ripped aside, blood spurting over his shirt, his lifeless eyes staring into the infinite reflections of his gory demise.

McLean drew his truncheon while the mysterious woman bowed to the butchered body. There came a disgusting sound of her satiating herself. When she raised her head again he saw Jadwiga's rejuvenated features, her lips bloodied.

"I need lifeblood. I feel *your* heart... driving your blood through you, *surging* with your spirit."

Every hair on his body prickled. His heart was thundering and with every beat she mutated into doppelgängers: a medieval lady, a musket-bearing guard, an adolescent in rags, the soldier with the armband, then Jaworski, returning to Jadwiga.

"Is why I lured fresh meat to my lair, to bait my latest trap. You now realise the true horror you have walked into?"

He stepped backwards, preparing to bolt. A mirror blocked his way. Feverishly he glared to the left and right, searching for an escape route. Her cruel face observed him mockingly from every angle. "There is no escape once I see you, I promise. I am ancient shapeshifter. I survive with the lifeblood— and seed— of mortals. You cheated death once before, which is why I crave your strong lifeblood."

McLean stared at her multiple likenesses as their jaws drew back to reveal vicious canine teeth, dark blood oozing from each tongue like tar. He snatched a breath and screamed in utter terror, shrieking like these were the horrific seconds after the missile attack. Surrounding him, myriad versions of himself mimicked this.

Careering backwards, his desperate eyes sought an exit. He stumbled blindly. Every so often he would flounder into another plate-glass mirror. His heart had transformed into a knot thumping agonisingly inside his ribs. He sunk to his knees, struggling to inhale. He'd evaded death by a few feet in 1982. Now it was all around. Whipping his head over his shoulder, he saw hundreds of demons gaining on him. He stared at himself. Grinding his jaws, he punched the mirror. The glass shards formed serrated teeth. He could feel her rancid breath on his shoulder, see her evil faces in the broken glass, so many it was impossible to tell which was real. He genuflected, the blood from his shattered knuckles spraying over his face, then launched himself forwards, the vicious blades severing his jugular vein an instant before she fell on her prey.

The End

House of Illusion
By
Andrew Lennon

Kevin paced back and forth across the laminated kitchen floor. His shoes clicked on the imitation wood with each step. Steve, Collette's father, gritted his teeth, trying to ignore the annoying pacing from his daughter's boyfriend. He pushed the volume button on the TV remote, increasing the sound in his attempt to ignore the impatient youth. It didn't work, he couldn't block this kid out.

"She'll be down in a sec," he said, trying to stop the pacing.

"Yeah, I know," Kevin said while biting on the corner of his thumbnail. "There's no rush."

"You okay, son?"

"I'm fine, just a little bit nervous, you know. It's our first real..." He blushed. "It's our first real date."

Steve was fully aware of this. At sixteen, Collette and Kevin had been friends for their entire lives. Kevin lived two doors down. Steve always had a feeling that something would happen between the two of them, was actually surprised that it had taken this long. Of course, Collette is his baby girl, but Kevin had always seemed like a good kid. If he could have handpicked a boyfriend for his daughter then he'd probably choose Kevin.

"Yeah, but you've been out together loads of times," Steve said trying to ease the boy's nerves. "This is no different really, is it?"

"It is different though." Kevin continued to pace. "I've thought about this for years. I just don't wanna mess it up."

"Don't worry. I don't think you could mess it up. Unless you hurt her, of course, then I'll have to hurt you." Steve glared at Kevin, then followed with a smile. He was just playing with him, he knew that he didn't need to threaten this kid.

"More like she'd hurt me," Kevin joked. "Have you seen her punch?"

“Yes.” Steve smiled. “I taught her. So, what have you got planned then?”

“Well there’s this travelling carnival in town, so I thought we could. . .” Kevin’s words were interrupted as Collette skipped down the stairs.

“Hey,” She said.

Her smile filled her face, flashing her perfect, white teeth. Kevin’s pacing stopped. He stared at her in awe. She wore tight jeans and a yellow vest top that hugged her perfect figure. Kevin had to stop himself from staring as he quickly became aware that both Collette and her father were watching him.

“You okay?” Collette asked.

“Yeah. You look amazing.” He almost went to her to give her a kiss, but he quickly decided against it. If the nerves hadn’t halted him already, the stare of Collette’s father would have.

“So, are you ready to go?” She took his hand.

“Yeah, let’s go. See ya later, Steve.” Kevin waved.

"See you two later. Be good!"

"Bye, Dad."

The two walked out into the sunshine. The house had felt relatively cool, but now, outside, the sun beamed down, smothering their bodies with warmth.

"It's a beautiful day isn't it?" Collette said.

"It really is, a perfect day for the carnival." Kevin grabbed her hand.

She smiled. "Yes, it is." Then she started running along the street, keeping hold of Kevin's hand and forcing him to run along with her.

This is what he loved about her, she was so different from all the other girls he knew. At sixteen, most girls were more concerned about how they looked, and they'd sit at home all day taking pictures of themselves to post on Instagram. They certainly wouldn't be caught dead running down the street. Collette wasn't like that. She was beautiful, and she must've known she was beautiful. It was common knowledge that she was the prettiest girl in school, but that didn't matter to her. She didn't cover herself in makeup. She didn't take non-stop selfies and search for online approval from people for filtered pictures uploaded night and day. She did use social media, but mainly to chat to friends and stuff like that. It hadn't consumed her as the vanity tool that had taken over so many kids today.

Kevin laughed and ran as fast as he could to keep up with her. He was by no means unfit, but it was still a struggle to keep pace with Collette. With her being practically perfect in every way, without the umbrella, she was also the school's athletics star. That was on top of being brilliantly intelligent, there wasn't much that she couldn't do, really. It still baffled Kevin that she even had the time of day for him. She could have anyone and do anything she wanted, but she chose him. Her childhood friend. Together they shared a bond stronger than anyone else they knew. Truth be told, they were so close growing up that they had been confused as brother and sister quite a few times, especially at school. There would no doubt be a few turned heads when they turn up after the summer holidays as boyfriend and girlfriend.

"Okay, okay, slow down," Kevin panted.

"You need to work on your fitness, buddy." Collette laughed.

"Hey, not everyone is a star athlete you know."

"Yeah, well you gotta keep up." She took both his hands in hers.

Kevin wanted to lean in for a kiss, the moment felt right, but he was also out of breath and didn't want to start coughing and spluttering in her mouth. With his stomach bubbling with nerves, he leaned forward and kissed her on the cheek. Collette smiled at him; her eyes smiled as well. They seemed to sparkle with the reflection of the sun.

"Come on, we're nearly there." She held his hand and they both walked slowly for the rest of the way. Kevin subtly took deep breaths when he could to catch his breath without letting Collette notice.

~

They turned the corner to the old school field where the carnival had set up. The field had been unused for a few years now. The old school building stood tall, watching over it. Its blackened face had been untouched since it went up in flames. Firemen worked hard to put the blaze out, but after the smouldering and smoking had stopped, the place was left untouched. It was on the far side of town and had been derelict for years before the fire. Since the new school building had been built closer to the town centre, there was no need for this old place anymore. Locals had hoped some developers would snatch the land up and build a retail park or something on there, but it never happened. No one was interested in this place. Police and fire marshals ruled that the fire was the result of vandals, but no one was ever caught. Thankfully no one was hurt either. After that, no one seemed to even think about the place, until now.

A large ferris wheel stood tall, its silhouette backing against the charred building. It gave for a rather haunting, but very effective visual. Kevin always thought that carnivals were a little bit creepy, and this image seemed to really show that.

“One sec, I gotta get a pic of this,” he said.

“Ugh, I thought we said no phones today,” Collette moaned.

“I’m not gonna be on my phone, honestly, I just want a pic of the wheel.”

“Okay, hurry up.” She walked ahead while he took his picture.

A couple of seconds later he’d caught up to Collette. He was expecting to walk under a huge sign or archway that said “Funland” or “World famous travelling carnival” or something like that, but they didn’t. They just walked onto the field and the carnival was set up. There was no entrance as such at all. Music filled the field. It was horrible 80’s disco music, or that’s what Kevin thought it was anyway. The sort of stuff that his parents listened to. He tried to ignore it, which was difficult due to the huge speakers that were placed around the field.

The first thing they came to was one of those hook-a-duck stalls. Kevin looked to Collette for a brief second before she dismissed him with a quick "no." He laughed and pretended he was joking, then took her hand again.

"So, what did you want to go on first?" he asked.

"How about the ferris wheel?" They looked up to the huge looming circle in the sky.

This filled Kevin with fear. He didn't mind roller coasters or any other rides, but he dreaded the thought of the ferris wheel. Just dangling there from so high and for so long. Other rides move fast and it's over before you know it, it's just a pure adrenaline rush. But the slow unsteadiness of the ferris wheel was torture, and those chair things rocked back and forth while up there. His stomach knotted. He really did not want to go on that thing, certainly not for the very first ride, but he couldn't start off the day by showing Collette that he was a wimp.

"Erm." He hesitated.

"Come on, look at that thing." Collette said. "It's huge."

"Yeah it is," Kevin muttered and frantically looked for an escape. "Hey, look at that place."

"What?"

"That over there." He pointed. "House of Illusion. Let's go and try that out."

The attraction looked like one of your typical fairground haunted houses. Its build was rectangular in shape, and it wasn't particularly tall. There was a single cart track which ran across the entrance with a skeleton stood at the doorway. The skeleton wore a purple wizard's robe and hat. The hat had gold, shining stars patterned on it. Running across the top of the build was a blue, sparkling sign. "House of Illusion".

The man who stood outside the building, who also wore a wizard's robe, suddenly turned his gaze to Kevin and Collette. It was as if he knew they were looking at his ride. He flashed them a smile and then gestured for them to come closer with his finger.

"Come and play in a land of confusion. You cannot escape the house of illusion," he bellowed.

Kevin and Collette looked at each other and laughed.

"Well that was a bit cheesy wasn't it?" Collette giggled.

"Yeah," Kevin replied. "But it might be fun. Come on, let's check it out."

The pair approached the ride. The man flashed them his smile again. He bowed and lifted his hat.

"Hello young sir and madam, and how are you on this beautiful day?" he asked in his deep voice.

“We’re good, thanks.” Kevin gave a narrow smile.

“Are you prepared to be astonished and amazed?” the man asked.

“Sure.” Kevin smiled again.

“And are you prepared to be shocked and confused?”

“Erm, okay.”

“Well take no more time, please enter, enter.” The man held out his palm.

Kevin saw the sign that said “ENTRY 5.00” he took a ten out of his wallet and placed it in the man’s hand.

“A grand gesture sir, but I do not wish for your money. I would like to take your hand so I can take you beyond. Beyond the realms of our reality, beyond comprehension, beyond...” He paused and looked around the area. “This place.”

"Okay." Collette smiled and took the man's hand. "He really gets into his role, doesn't he?" she whispered to Kevin.

"Remember, this is the land of illusion. What you see is not as it appears. Trust nothing." The man took Collette's hand and led her toward the cart. He helped her into the seat and she shimmied along. "Sir?" he gestured for Kevin to join her.

There was no bar in the cart, which didn't really surprise them. These rides always moved so slowly that there wasn't really any need for them. Plus, it looked so old that it had probably been around long before all the health and safety regulations from today's standards.

To add emphasis to the age of the cart, they quickly realised that there were no mechanics to move them along. The man walked behind the cart and placed his hands on the back. Slowly, he began to push.

"Time to enter a land of confusion. Good luck in surviving the house of illusion." The cart gradually picked up pace. He pushed them through a purple satin curtain. Then suddenly, they came to a complete stop. The pair sat in the darkness for a moment; nothing happened.

"Hey what's going on?" Kevin turned around, but the man was gone.

They could see the light from outside shining through the parting in the curtains. But the man was nowhere to be seen.

"This stupid thing's broken." Collette moaned. "I knew this would be rubbish. We should've gone on the wheel first like I said."

"Come on, we'll go and find out what's going on." Kevin climbed out of the cart and helped Collette out. The pair walked toward the strip of light in the curtain.

"Hello?" Kevin called. "Hey, your ride isn't working."

They opened the curtains and walked back to the entrance of the ride. Their jaws dropped as they looked around. The entrance to the ride was there, but no sign of the man. Or anyone else at all. Nowhere around the whole carnival. And the sky was black. They could see the glimmer of stars in the blanket of night.

"What the hell?" Collette said.

"What time is it?" Kevin asked.

"I don't know. We left my house at what? 10:00 a.m. We've only been out for half an hour. It can't be night-time."

"Maybe an eclipse or something?"

"You hear of any eclipse coming? It'd be big news wouldn't it? And where is everyone? This place was packed before."

"I don't know. Are we dreaming? Or drugged or something? Did that guy do something to us?"

"I don't know, Kevin. I don't like this. I'm scared." Collette began to cry.

Laughter came from behind the curtain. The pair jumped with fright; Collette screamed. Kevin grabbed her and pulled her behind him. For a brief moment he felt proud of himself for being so brave and protecting his girlfriend, a very brief moment. Now fear settled in and the laughter caused his knees to shake.

“Hello,” Collette called.

“Shhh.” Kevin turned to her. “What are you doing?”

“Well they may be able to help us.”

“Hmmm, yeah okay.” Kevin slowly approached the curtain, keeping his arm back in a gesture to tell Collette to stay there. Before he could reach the curtain, a face popped through the opening. It had bright blue hair that stood on end, dark red lips that were stretched from ear to ear, eyes so black that they just looked like holes in the middle of the face. The rest of the laughing clown hadn’t come through the curtain yet, it was still just a face.

“Hi, erm,” Kevin stuttered. “Could you help us please?”

The clown responded with laughter, a laugh that made Kevin’s bones rattle with fear. The laughter got louder and the clown’s mouth opened wider and wider. A moment later Kevin was able to see that the extremely elongated mouth hadn't been painted on, it was the clown's actual mouth. The bottom half of its face seemed to unhinge and the top half tilted back. The laughter grew louder and bellowed around the dark carnival. Suddenly the head snapped shut, and the clown walked through the curtain. It wore a green and blue all-in-one suit, the colours split down the middle. In its hand was a sledge hammer. A smile returned to the face, flashing razor-sharp teeth that glistened in the moonlight like some kind of metal. Kevin was frozen in fear, stuck to the spot. He tried to turn and run away, but his legs wouldn't work. It was like the ground had gotten hold of him and refused to let go.

A hand gripped his shoulder and pulled him backward. Almost falling over, he somehow managed to turn himself around where he saw Collette reached for his hand.

"Come on!" She screamed.

"Huh." Kevin, still in shock, turned to look behind him to the monstrous sight.

"Run." Collette grabbed his hand and began to sprint away from the clown. Kevin went with her, finally snapping back into himself.

"What the hell was that?" he panted.

"I don't know. Just keep running."

"Where are we going?"

"We're going to get out of here." Collette kept hold of Kevin's hand and ran towards the edge of the field. The darkness seemed to be lowering from the sky and started to swallow them like a blanket. They ran past the hook-a-duck stall. In this light it appeared to be a greyish blue colour, like it had aged and all the colour had run out of it. They continued their run until they hit a black wall. The impact knocked the wind out of the pair of them, and they fell to the ground.

"What in the hell?" Collette rose to her feet. She walked forward with her hand held out. The edge of the field was gone; the exit from the carnival was gone. All that remained was a huge wall of darkness. When she reached it, she pressed her hand against the blackness. It was smooth, like a mirror, but there was no glimmer, no pattern, nothing at all. Just black.

"Kevin, what the hell is going on?" she began to cry again.

"Collette!" Kevin called, the fear in his eyes causing Collette to turn around and see what he was looking at.

Above her, coming from the smooth, black abyss, hundreds of hands reached through the darkness. They were crawling along on their fingertips, slowly edging toward her.

"Collette, get your hand off there!"

She removed her hand from the smooth surface and stumbled backwards. As though they'd pushed an off switch, the hands slowly receded back into the darkness. The finger tips were last to be seen as they disappeared through the black hole, and then Kevin and Collette were left facing nothing again, a large, looming nothing that seemed to cover the whole carnival like a dome.

Behind them, they could hear that laughter approaching again, accompanied by the thud of oversized shoes. The pair turned around and saw the shadow of the clown approaching in the moonlight. They ran away from the black wall and towards the nearest structure they could see.

"Come on, in here." Kevin hurried.

Collette followed him into the house of mirrors. Kevin almost screamed when he ran through the door and came face to face with his reflection. He hadn't noticed the name of the attraction he'd run into and wasn't expecting mirrors at all. Collette ran into the back of him, forcing him to fall forward into the mirror. He smashed his nose against the surface and blood exploded all over his reflection. He wanted to cry out in pain but knew he couldn't because the clown with the sledgehammer would find them. He covered his nose with his hands, and the crimson liquid seeped through his fingers.

"We have to move." Collette grabbed his hand, ignoring the wet, sticky substance. "Come on."

They crept along, moving through the hallway of mirrors, focussed on nothing but moving forwards and trying to make as little sound as possible. Neither of them noticed the mirror images of themselves were not copying their movements. The images in the mirror stood side by side, their facial expressions blank, then slowly turned to follow the pair.

“Do you think he saw us come in?” Kevin whispered.

“I don’t know, but if he peeks, he’s gonna see the blood on that mirror. We may as well have drawn a sign on the door for him.”

“It’s not my fault, I...”

“I’m not saying it’s your fault.” Collette shut him up. “We don’t have time to bicker, we have to keep moving.”

They continued their slow crawl along the hallway, until they hit a wall. Collette stopped and stood face to face with the mirror.

“Ugh we must’ve missed a turn off somewhere.” She moaned.

Then something caught her eye. Face to face with her reflection, she saw it was not showing a face of concern or disappointment, as she felt. It wore a smile.

“Kevin.” She whispered.

Her reflection didn’t whisper with her. It held its sinister smile. As Kevin approached from behind, his reflection joined hers. It too was giving that terrifying grin. Suddenly, laughter filled the halls. A chorus of boys’ and girls’ laughter, it surrounded them, coming from every angle.

Kevin and Collette crouched to the floor and embraced each other in a hug of fear, surrounded by the reflections that looked down on them and laughed. The laughing mouths grew wider until the top half of the heads unhinged just as the clown’s had earlier. When they snapped back into place, the metallic teeth appeared.

“Run!” Kevin screamed.

The pair scurried back along the corridor. When Kevin placed his hand on one of the mirrors to keep his balance, another hand shot out of the glass wall and tried to grab him. He screamed again.

"Don't touch the mirrors. Keep your hands to yourself. Or just keep hold of mine."

Collette's hand found his, and she gripped it so tight that he could feel his knuckles grinding together. It didn't hurt, he was too scared to feel pain. He kept running around in circles and back and forth through the hall of mirrors. Eventually they saw a red curtain with the word EXIT above it.

The laughter was getting louder and rushing up behind them. Collette looked over her shoulder to see that she and Kevin were now chasing them. Those razor-like teeth shone bright as they got closer to them.

"Oh my God! They're out of the mirror!" She cried.

"What?" Kevin looked over his shoulder. The sight of his own face pursuing him filled him with dread.

They dived through the red curtain and landed on the damp grass outside. They both sat in terror, waiting for the moment that their doppelgangers would jump through that curtain and devour them with those terrifying teeth. But it didn't happen. Nothing came.

"I have no idea what's going on here, Kevin, but I really want to go home now."

"Me too. Did we get drugged or something? How can any of this be real?"

Their conversation was interrupted by a high-pitched laugh that came from behind them. They looked up to see the blue hair of the clown dangling over them. A laughing scream pierced their ears as the sledge hammer came slamming down. They rolled out of the way just in time.

"You're going to suffer multiple contusions and you can't escape the house of illusion." The clown giggled.

Kevin and Collette got to their feet and ran away from the menace once again.

"Don't run, join in, we'll have no exclusion. You're staying forever in the house of illusion." He shouted behind them, his sinister giggle still accompanying the words.

"There." Collette pointed. "The ferris wheel."

Kevin came to a halt. His fear came rushing back to him.

"What are you doing?" Collette screamed.

"I... I..." he stuttered. "I can't do it. I'm scared of them."

"More scared than you are of that?" Collette pointed to the quickly approaching clown.

Left with no choice, Kevin joined Collette and they ran to the ferris wheel. It was already moving, but very slowly. They climbed into one of the carriages as it passed by. Kevin almost stopped again, but the thought of that clown and its teeth forced him onto the ride. They both sat on the bench in the carriage and gave a deep sigh of relief.

The clown reached the ferris wheel and just stood, staring at them as they slowly began to rise into the air.

“Erm, Collette,” Kevin said.

“What?”

“What are we going to do when this thing goes back down?”

She hadn’t thought of that. In her head, they were going to climb onto the ferris wheel and they would stop when at the top. Quite what they would do from there hadn’t really entered her mind, she’d just wanted to put as much distance between them and the clown as possible.

“Oh, I, erm...” She couldn’t think of a response.

It didn’t matter anyway. As they neared the top of the cycle, the structure began to shake violently. When they looked down, they saw four clowns. All of them looked identical, the same blue hair, the same green and blue suit. They all had sledge hammers. In perfect time with one another, their hammers began to smash against the supporting beams of the attraction. The carriages began to sway from side to side.

From behind them, Kevin heard laughter. He turned around to see the doubles of him and Collette climbing from one carriage to another. They were getting closer to them. The hammering continued as well, all of the carriages swaying more and more from side to side. The doppelgangers didn't seem to be phased by it as they easily moved from one to the next.

The young couple held each other. Tears pooled in Kevin's eyes he embraced the love of his life, waiting for the moment that the carriage unhinged and they fell to their deaths.

"I love you, Collette. I'm so sorry I couldn't save you." Then he kissed her.

Their lips pressed together and their hold got tighter. They heard the snap. The carriage began to fall, neither of them opened their eyes, they didn't want to see it. They just held that kiss and waited for the end.

~

The cart rolled through the curtain. Sunlight shined on Kevin and Collette's faces. They opened their eyes and saw the wizard from the beginning of the ride.

"Did you kids have fun?" he asked.

The pair just stared at him in disbelief.

"Are you okay?" the man spoke again.

"Yeah, yeah, we're fine." Kevin climbed out of the cart and then helped Collette.

They walked away from the ride, staring up to the clear blue sky. The shine of the sun hurt their eyes, but it felt good. It was better than that darkness.

"That was the most trippy thing I've ever experienced." Kevin laughed. "How did they even do that? Virtual reality or something. It felt so real."

Collette didn't respond.

Kevin turned to her and grabbed her by the waist. He pulled her close and gave her a gentle kiss on the lips. Then he wrapped his arms around her and hugged her tight, so tight that he never wanted to let her go. She mumbled something into his shoulder.

"What did you say?" he asked and loosened the hug so she could speak properly.

"You got out of the ride but took the wrong one of the twosome. You cannot escape our house of illusion."

"What?" Kevin's heart raced.

Collette's laugh filled the carnival. The top half of her head unhinged and flashed sharp, metallic teeth. She lunged at Kevin.

His scream was stopped before it left his mouth.

The End

Sweetheart
By
Selene MacLeod

The Brunswick Hotel has stood at its current location since the 1920s; some jokers say the piano player has been there almost as long. In exchange for room and board plus tips, she plays three shows a day. Her barrelhouse piano playing is slowed by arthritis, and her voice--roughened by decades of whiskey and tobacco--cracks on the high notes. Sometimes she dreams about her twin, the other playing fast melodies in the upper register while she pounds out a boogie-woogie bass line, four feet tapping time better than a metronome.

"Come on, get happy," she sings to an indifferent after-work crowd. She plays whether anyone's listening or not. She plays all the old pop standards to the ghosts: "It Don't Mean A Thing (If It Ain't Got That Swing," "Happy Days Are Here Again". And the slower, sadder songs: "Smoke Gets in Your Eyes," "Let Me Call You Sweetheart."

That had been her twin's favourite.

* * *

Their birth mother screamed when she saw them, abandoned them at a hospital where the state took care of them until their adoptive parents swept in. Old vaudeville performers, Frank and Millie trained the twins to sing, play piano and trade quips. By the age of seven the girls, christened Lily and Rose, had joined Frank in his act.

Frank and Millie could have set them up in the freak show tent. Many of their friends made a comfortable living, enough to buy houses in Florida for the off-season and keep a nice trailer on the road. But Frank and Millie wanted their girls to be stars. They'd been a family show until 1936, when both parents died in a crash, leaving the girls on their own. At the height of the Depression, few circuses wanted to hire a couple of teenagers. Frank would be mortified to see the girls working in a fleabag.

"A nickel to see the show!" The barker's voice boomed in Rose's ears. She elbowed her twin. "Hurry up, Lily."

Lily was always behind on something, an unbuttoned blouse, an unhemmed skirt, stockings showing their seams.

"Shut up, Rose," Lily grouched. "The show won't start without us."

"I know, but I want to get a look at the people." She pulled Lily toward the rear of the barker's platform; Lily knew better than to dig in her heels.

They shared little that was vital, just a large section of the skin of their torso, parts of their stomach, and a few blood vessels. In 1920, though, separation had meant dangerous surgery beyond what modern medicine could safely provide. Both girls had two working arms, hands and legs, but Lily's left foot turned inward. The meaner roustabouts called her 'Clubby' and 'Hop-along'. Rose was forever pulling Lily, making her move faster. Rose wanted life to be an adventure.

She was always the first to try something new: a smoke, a drink, a kiss from a boy.

The girls found their pace and slithered sideways along the heavy curtain the roustabouts had set up the day before. When they reached the backstage area, Lily turned away so Rose could peek.

“Look at all of them out there,” Rose gushed. “And they're all waiting for us.”

“Uh huh.” Lily hated being on display like a zoo animal. Sometimes, the patrons threw rocks or food. Or worse. Little Timmy ("barely two feet tall") lost an eye and Gene the Lobster Boy was doing time for manslaughter, after a fight with a mark. Once, a drunken mark broke into their trailer after he'd been stiffed in the hoochie-coochie tent. Since then, the girls kept a butcher knife under the bed.

It was a living. Lily elbowed Rose when she heard the opening strains from the phonograph, a tootling bugle and swinging cymbal.

"Me And My Shadow," Lily sang, loud.

Rose turned her body toward the part in the curtains and sang the next line.

The girls continued their number. A practised march, one step back, mindful of Lily's foot. Turn, wave and wink at the audience. Big finish as the girls shouted the last line together.

"Say, Lily!" Rose said. "Who gave the Liberty Bell to Philadelphia?"

"I don't know, who?"

"Must have been a duck family."

"A duck family?"

"Didn't you say there was a quack in it?" Rose delivered the punch line, to laughs, applause, and groans from the audience. The sound effects man brought a duck call to his lips and made a farting squawk noise.

"Speaking of quacks," Lily said. "A duck goes into the doctor's office and says, doctor, can you fix this quack in my beak?"

"Quack in my beak?" Rose echoed. "You mean crack? How did the duck pay?"

"He put it on his bill!"

Someone in the audience whistled. Rose waved her hands in front of her face. "That was a stinker, Lily! PEEYUW!"

The silly jokes continued as the girls made their way to the twin pianos at the side of the stage and seated themselves on a custom-made bench.

With her left hand, Lily picked out a slow bass line. "Knock knock."

Rose waved at the audience with her free hand. With her right, she plunked out a counter-melody to Lily's bass line.

"Who's there?" Several people yelled.

"Banana!" Lily said, with a crash on the piano. Rose groaned.

The knock knock joke continued while the girls picked out a song.

"Orange you glad?" Lily sang.

"What? That you didn't say banana?" Rose replied. “I'm happy!” She sang the first line of “Get Happy,” to wild applause.

The girls sang and traded jokes for the rest of their performance, ending on a slow note with "Let Me Call You Sweetheart." They bowed. The crowd threw flowers, and the girls gathered them up before they ran off stage, blowing kisses at the audience. Rose swept an arm around Lily and kissed her on the cheek.

"What was that for?" Lily raised her shoulder, trying to wipe away Rose's lipstick.

"That was great!" Rose gushed.

One of the handsomer roustabouts, whom Lily had noticed around the mess tent, wandered backstage. He handed a flower to each of the girls. Lily blushed when he leaned in to kiss her cheek. Her gaze dropped and she wished she could hide her bad foot.

"Hey Joe, whaddaya know?" Rose smiled, reaching up to ruffle his hair.

"Wonderful, ladies. You were the cat's meow."

"Thanks. I didn't know you were watching."

"Just me and my shadow!" Joe teased with a wink. Rose pretended to hit him.

Lily noticed how Rose brushed her fingertips against Joe's arm. He tilted his head. Lily moved her torso around and brought her right hand up to block Rose and brush the hair from Joe's eyes. He shook his hair back and winked at Lily. She flushed, but forced herself to meet his gaze. A tingle warmed her from the top of her head right through her middle and her toes curled. She smiled at Joe.

"Listen, Joe," Rose started.

Lily interrupted her, pushing up her shoulder to block Rose as much as she could and bring herself into Joe's view. "Come with us to the matinee at the Odeon this weekend."

Joe looked down. "I'd love to, ladies, but I don't get my pay until next week."

"We'll pay," Rose offered. She shouldered Lily back. Lily pushed her again.

"That's right, chum, don't worry about a thing."

Joe beamed. "You're both angels." He kissed each girl on the cheek and jogged away.

"Whew!" Rose commented, fanning herself. "I'd love to cut a rug with him sometime."

"Wouldn't we both? But wouldn't that be weird?"

"Why? You act like he's never seen two beautiful girls before!" Rose laughed.

Lily pursed her lips.

"Why, I do declare," Rose said in a fake Southern accent. "You're sweet on him!"

Lily screwed her eyes shut, grinned and nodded. "I can't help it," she confessed, opening her eyes and batting her eyelashes. She held a hand to her forehead. "He sets me all a-flutter!"

"Crazy!" Rose exclaimed. Both girls burst out laughing.

* * *

It should never have worked, one boy dating two girls. But, on the day of their movie date, the girls spent hours getting ready, bumping elbows as each set her hair in pin curls. The girls had a custom- made vanity table, a gift for their sixteenth birthday. The bench matched so the girls could both look into the split mirror.

Lily watched as Rose applied eye makeup and lipstick.

“I'll never get the hang of this,” Lily complained.

Rose giggled. “It's not that hard. Be careful not to poke yourself in the eye.”

Rose was the beauty in the family. She had glossy black hair, a cute nose, full red lips and wide blue eyes, and she was always careful to pluck her eyebrows and curl her hair just so. When Lily looked in the mirror, she saw a distortion of Rose's features: the nose bumpier, the jaw more horsey, the lips not so full. Nor did she have Rose's confidence. Her name should be Violet—as in shrinking violet—instead of Lily.

She scowled and shook her head, undoing half the pin curls.

“What did you do that for?” Rose asked.

“I hate my hair,” Lily replied. *Along with everything else.*

“Your hair is gorgeous, kid,” Rose assured her. She handed Lily a hairbrush. “Maybe curls aren't what you're going for tonight.”

Lily took the brush and before long, her hair looked respectable, if not perfect. Digging in the drawer, she found a velvet ribbon and tied a neat bow on top of her head. She wrinkled her nose in the mirror, wishing she weren't so blah, then pinched her cheeks to give herself more colour.

“Wow, look at that,” Rose gushed, laying down her makeup brush and tossing her curls. “Have you ever seen two more gorgeous gals?” She bumped shoulders with Lily. Lily grinned back at their reflection—when Rose was happy, she made everyone happy.

At a knock at the door, and with a practised step—Rose in the lead—they stood up and moved toward the trailer's door. Lily reached forward and opened it, forcing Rose back to avoid being hit.

Joe stood in the doorway, the last of the day's sunlight caught in his hair, slicked down for the occasion. A grin lit up his handsome face as he greeted first Lily, then Rose.

“Hiya,” said Joe. “You look great.” He reached out with big, callused hands and grasped each of the girl's hands in turn.

Joe stepped back and stood to one side as the girls stepped out of the trailer. He shut the door behind them and gestured for them to go ahead, falling into step beside their crooked pace. Their shadows streamed out to one side as they walked across the midway, away from the staff quarters. Joe's shadow was all long limbs and fluid movements, while Lily noticed how awkward and crablike the girls' shadow looked. She hoped no one would stare.

On the hour's walk into town, Lily and Rose entertained Joe with stories about the carnies. Joe replied with a few of his own. He'd dropped out of school and gone to work, trying to help out his family. FDR's New Deal came along a little later, and they could eat until money ran out.

“A fellow in the neighbourhood taught me engines,” Joe explained, “so when I left home, I rode the rails, looking for work. Most places need a mechanic. So far Carl's been good to me. He can always use a man for odd jobs, putting up tents, mucking out cages.” Carl was the head roustabout. The only person he answered to was the owner.

Lily nodded her head, watching her shadow bob and trying not to look too idiotic.

“Look at me, doing all the talking,” Joe remarked. “How did you girls learn to play the piano like that? You sure are swell.”

Lily grinned. Rose answered, “Our parents taught us. I think we learned to sing and play before we learned to walk.”

A hot thread of embarrassment twisted in Lily's gut and she glanced sideways at Rose, reproachful. Rose didn't seem to notice. Because of Lily's clubfoot, they had taken longer than normal to learn how to walk. Lily was the better piano player, though, and Rose knew it.

“Do you keep in touch with your folks?” Joe asked.

“Um, they died. In a car accident last year,” Lily answered. She watched Joe's face fall.

“Oh, I'm so sorry. I didn't mean...” He was cute when he blushed. Lily felt her gut twist again, not in a shameful way.

“You couldn't know,” Rose said. “It's okay. Look around you. Death is part of life.”

Wind rustled through dead leaves on either side of the dirt path they followed into town. The grass was still green, but summer was over and soon it would all turn to brown and then grey. Even the air held an autumn chill. Lily rubbed her arms and felt goose pimples.

The trio made small talk until they arrived at the cinema, a small building in the middle of Main Street. They sidled up to the counter and requested three tickets. When they found the usher, Rose nodded and smiled at him.

Joe cleared his throat. “Hey, these seats seem to be all joined up. Won't that be a problem?”

Both girls laughed. Rose explained “We've been here before. It's okay, you'll see. We have to sit in the front.”

“Whatever works,” Joe said.

“Flip ya,” Lily said to Rose, digging in her purse for a penny. She placed it on her thumb. “Call it.”

Lily lost. She tried to look casual while Rose chatted to Joe. She was grateful when the usher returned with a folding chair and set it beside the row of seats.

“After you,” Rose said. Joe took the second seat from the aisle while Rose and Lily arranged themselves. Rose perched at the upholstered edge of the fold-down seat, her knees pointed inward, while Lily sat on the chair in the aisle, wishing she didn't stick out.

“Hey, that's a neat trick,” Joe said. “Are you comfortable, Lily?”

"I'll be all right once the lights go down," Lily replied. She turned her head to look at Joe and smiled. He smiled back, making Lily flush. She didn't think he caught her reaction.

Throughout the movie, Lily knew every movement Joe made. She tried to be interested in the film –*The Prince and the Pauper,* with the ever-handsome Errol Flynn—but she could feel the heat between Rose and their date. Whispers. Hot breath on Rose's neck. The sound of clothing rustling.

Shoved aside while Rose got the attention, again. Lily dabbed at her eyes and sniffed. What a fool she was. She sighed and turned her attention back to the film, trying to imagine a world where her twin was somewhere far away.

* * *

For several weeks, as Joe and Rose grew closer, Lily tried to be happy for them, but ached for Joe. The way he tilted his head when he talked to her, his scent of engine grease and tobacco, the way he moved his hands. These things delighted Lily and filled her with a sweet longing. She knew

Joe thought of her as a kid sister. He was always nice, doing things around the trailer—he fixed the short table leg, and popped the knob back onto the radio—but Lily wanted more. She wanted Joe to look at her the way he looked at Rose.

Date night again. The girls had the evening off, as they only played two shows on Sundays. Rose was chattering on about her decision to sleep with Joe. Lily looked at her hands on top of the vanity. Why bother even brushing her hair?

"You okay, kid?" Rose asked. She brushed face powder across her nose and cheeks to cover a pimple.

Lily shrugged. "I guess. I guess..." She and Rose had never had secrets.

"What's wrong?" Rose went back to fixing her makeup. "You'd better get ready. Joe will be here soon."

"That's what's wrong," Lily replied. "He's not interested in me."

Rose frowned, then smoothed her expression so as not to crack her makeup. “Joe likes you just fine,” she said.

“As a friend. As a kid.” Lily scowled at her face in the mirror. “He doesn't care what I look like.”

“Maybe not, but I do, and I say you'll feel better when you pull yourself together.” Rose smoothed down her dress and put the finishing touches on her hairdo.

Lily ran her brush through her hair but didn't bother to change her dress; she wasn't looking forward to the evening ahead. Long, painful hours of Rose and Joe looking into each other's eyes while Lily tried to make small talk and find a position that didn't hurt her back. And then the walk back to the trailer with Rose and Joe holding hands.

A knock at the trailer door. Rose perked up. Lily stayed seated.

“Come on, Lily,” Rose said. “I really like Joe. Why can't you support that?”

"It's just..." Lily felt like a heel, whining about her own life when Rose was so happy.

"When is it gonna be my turn?" Lily said.

"Oh, Lily." Rose settled back.

Another knock at the door. "Just a minute! We're not decent!" Rose called.

"What is going on?" Rose asked.

Lily looked at her sister in the mirror. Dear Rose, her other half. "Men never want me. They always want you."

Rose opened her rouged lips and closed them again. Her eyes met Lily's in the mirror and they passed a non-verbal communication. The corners of Lily's mouth quivered but her tears didn't fall. Rose's expression softened, and she took her sister's hand. She tilted her head toward the door and Lily nodded. With a deep breath, she resigned herself to the night ahead, shame and longing pressed down to a sour ball in her gut.

Rose opened the door wide enough to include Lily. Joe's grin widened at the sight of Rose. Without hesitating, Rose threw her arms around his neck and kissed him. Lily reddened and turned her face away.

The walk to town was excruciating. Lily's foot was bothering her, so she walked extra slow—or perhaps, she wanted to put off the inevitable invitation and seduction. Rose had had boys around before, but never “all the way”--none of them had wanted to do more with Lily watching. Still virgins at seventeen, the girls believed they might be old maids. They had talked of getting married, but it never seemed likely until Joe came along.

Throughout dinner, Joe and Rose tried to prod Lily to join their conversation—about movies and radio shows, about fairway gossip, about politics—but Lily was busy choking on her pride. She could hear Rose's foot, rustling under the table, and Joe's hand was often out of view.

Lily dropped her fork onto her plate with a clatter and pushed it away, stopping the dinner table chatter.

“Is everything all right, Lily?” Joe asked her.

Lily looked at Joe—at his laugh lines and the shock of hair that always fell over his eyes. "I'm uncomfortable about tonight," Lily tried to explain. It had sounded better in her head. Rose elbowed her hard in the ribs.

"No, Rose, we haven't talked about this and it's high time we did," Lily said. "I'm sure Joe's been with plenty of other girls but there's no point in pretending."

Joe looked at Rose with wide eyes. Rose finished chewing and wiped her mouth with her napkin. "Well, it was going to be a surprise," Rose said. She and Joe laughed, breaking the tension.

Lily slumped in her seat, feeling foolish. This hurt her back, so she straightened up.

"Lily, we can talk about this, but I don't think the dinner table is an appropriate time or place," Joe said. He reached around Rose and touched Lily on the shoulder.

"You're right, Lil, we haven't talked about this," Rose added. She finished her dinner and covered the plate with her napkin while Lily thought of a reply. They sat in silence.

"Lily, if it makes you feel any better..." Joe paused.

Lily swallowed around the lump in her throat.

Joe reached across the table and took her hand. "I really like your sister," he said. "And you mean the world to me. I would never do anything to make you uncomfortable, or put you out in any way. I'm trying to get a marriage license, even though they keep telling me no."

Lily stared at his hand holding hers, too ashamed to look at either of them. She was being childish.

"OK," she said. "I want you both to be happy, too." The words tasted bitter. In her rational mind, she knew they were true, but what about love is ever rational? She dabbed at her eyes with her napkin, then wiped her nose. Her hand in Joe's reminded her of a small animal, cowering.

"Why can't you have a marriage license?" Lily asked. Joe's hand withdrew and she followed its course across the table. Joe slumped back in his seat and sighed. "They told me it's an 'abomination,' a 'sin against God and nature', but I swear to you, I'm going to fight it!"

Rose patted Joe on the shoulder and smiled at him, her eyes bright in the lights. Lily felt the ball of shame in her gut turn to lead and she tasted her dinner at the back of her throat. Other diners stole glances and whispered. Fingers of disgust and hate twisted around her spine. She wiped her mouth and dropped her napkin over her plate.

"We should get out of here," she said. Both Joe and Rose agreed. They made a quick exit.

A cold wind blew; Joe took off his jacket and put it around Lily's shoulders. He slipped an arm around Rose's shoulders and they walked together like conjoined triplets. Lily felt even more freakish.

Lily's ears and the tips of her fingers were cold by the time they arrived at the trailer. She was reluctant to return Joe's jacket, which smelled like him.

"Come in for a drink," Rose said.

Lily looked at Joe's face and then dropped her gaze.

"Are you okay with that, Lily?" Joe asked.

Without looking up, Lily nodded. Joe opened the trailer door and stepped inside, holding it for the girls to enter. With a third person there, Lily felt how small the trailer was. The only place to sit was the bed. She and Rose arranged themselves while Joe moved to the kitchenette and found a bottle of scotch.

"I don't want any, thanks," Lily said as she watched him set two glasses on the counter and look in the cupboard for a third.

Joe nodded and brought the drinks over. He sat down beside Rose and the trio made small talk while Joe and Rose sipped their drinks.

* * *

The piano player finishes her set, has her drink and meal at the bar, makes her way upstairs to her tiny, over-stuffed room. Each time she climbs the narrow stairs feels longer, and the sounds of the living stretch away into silence.

She's accustomed to stillness, and the ability to sink into herself. A twinge in her chest—her angina has been acting up lately. She shuffles to the kitchenette, finds her pills and takes them with a glass of water, then takes her glass and pours a drink of clear brown whiskey. The bottom of her glass looks like pebbles; she drains half of it in one shot and takes the rest to an easy chair in the main room.

There's movement in the corners, the whispers of old friends coming to take her home. They're welcoming. Forgiving, not damning her for the things she's done.

* * *

Joe had hung a sheet above the custom-made bed; it offered an illusion of privacy, but there was no way to divide skin. Lily tried not to watch, to go "away" into herself, but she could feel. And hear. Each exquisite whisper, each breath on Rose's skin raised goosebumps. Each tear that slid down Lily's cheeks felt cold by the time it reached her jaw.

Rose cried out. Lily winced and drew her legs together. Her eyes fluttered as a deep tingle of warmth crept from her centre and radiated through her privates and lower belly. Her nipples stood up in hard bullets, pressed against the sides of the open robe she'd left half on and half off—she'd agreed to leave off her nightgown, for Rose. She heard Joe's breaths on the other side of the sheet, smelled his musk. And she couldn't help it. His hands on Rose's skin became phantom hands on her own breasts, her own thighs. She screwed her eyes shut tight and imagined Joe above her, smiling, his sweat... skin... scent, oh love...

The sensation turned to a cramp in Lily's belly, her vision darkening. She gasped, raised her right fist to her mouth and bit down. All the good sensation stopped; the sweetness turned to a fork of black lightning up her middle and a belt of steel across her lower back. She drew her knees together, trying not to squirm and let on that anything was wrong, rage and jealousy a bitter green-black monster biting at her.

"Death is part of life," Rose's voice whispered, her words so clear Lily thought she'd spoken them aloud. She clenched her teeth and a wire of pain dug its way through her jaws and into her skull. Shaking, she opened her eyes, her vision blurry, and looked toward the sheet. A yellow light shone beyond the sheet, throwing Joe and Rose's shadows wide above Lily, heads and limbs distorted into a menacing blob. Lily cringed, unable to move or scream for fear of interrupting them. Her heart in her mouth, Lily dropped a hand down the side of the bed, grasping.

She found the butcher knife's heavy wooden handle. Her fingers brushed the curves and she clutched it.
For she wanted to be loved. The only way was to be rid of Rose. With this certainty, her good left hand –*la sinistre, le gauche*-- curled around the knife and brought it up and across her chest. She threw all the force of seventeen years of bitterness at the two-headed monster that menaced her. Heart pounding, Lily tore down the sheet and with it, brought down the knife.

The first arc struck Joe in the smooth muscle of his neck, arched back as he made love to Rose. A fount of thick red blood burst from his carotid, spraying Lily and wetting her twin. Rose's eyes flew open. She brought her hands up for protection.

"Lily!" Rose screamed as the knife came down again. Her screams died down into liquid rasps around a mouthful of blood.

Lily felt every blow and screamed along.

When they found her, Lily was weeping and carving at the thick skin that connected her to Rose. The cut hurt too much and their skin was too leathery-tough. Saw and sing, resting every so often to cradle Rose's lifeless head against her.

"Let me call you sweetheart..."

* * *

The piano player hums the sad tune and rocks, her posture imitating the scene in her custom made bed, so many years before.

She told them she woke up with Joe on top of Rose and panicked, thought he was raping them, and her twin got in the way. No one suspected her unless you counted Carl, during his visit to her in the hospital. Surgery was a rousing success—much easier when you need not spare both the twins.

When Lily woke up, glassy from ether, Carl had been sitting at the edge of her hospital bed.

She smiled, bleary. “How long have you been there?”

Carl took off his battered hat and looked at the floor. “Not long. I wanted to apologize for Joe.”

Lily shook her head. “I don't know what you mean.”

“I'm awful sorry. If I'd known he was capable of hurting you or Rose like that, I'd have killed him myself.” His hands crushed his hat into a twist of brown felt. He swallowed and looked up from the floor.

“Hey, Lily,” Carl began.

“Rose.” She interrupted him, shaking her head. “I'm Rose.”

Carl's brow furrowed as he processed the name. He stared at the girl on the bed for a long time. She watched his expression change, from guilt and sorrow to confusion, to blank acceptance. Without another word, Carl stood up, turned his back and left the room, his broad shoulders shrunken in on themselves, leaving the surviving twin with the first of the ghosts to come.

* * *

It's been a long time since the piano player thought of Carl, though she thinks of her twin often, and of her first love, the handsome roustabout. She stands and straightens her aching back, and heads to the tiny kitchenette, dragging her clubfoot. Humming, she pours another drink to silence the voices and bits of music that flap around her like a swarm of late-summer bats. After a few more drinks she will sink into the welcoming dark.

"Let me call you sweetheart..."

The End

Vampiro
By
Kevin J. Kennedy

They call me Vampiro. It's not my real name, but you tend to find that real names don't matter much when you join a carnival. Not a lot of time and effort went into picking a name for me. I was stood in a grungy little caravan and when they asked what my skills were, I told them I was a vampire. The old carnival owner that hired me had asked what that entailed.

"Drinking blood," I told him.

"Drinking blood?" he asked, with a frown upon his wrinkly old face.

"Yes, drinking blood. I'm pretty strong, too, and I'm fast. But drinking blood is kind of my main thing."

There was a pause and I could tell he was mulling it over. Obviously trying to think of how that could be used in a show. At that point in time, every carnival had a freak show. Some were better than others, but the best ones pulled in the crowds. People have always had morbid fascinations and before the world became a more politically correct place to live in, no one was ashamed to tell their friends and neighbours about the oddities that they had witnessed. No one found anything wrong with it back in those days. I'm not saying that it was all good; it probably depended on the individual freak. Some had a better life after they joined the carnival and some had a worse life, but the same could be said for any of the human carnies, so it all seemed pretty fair.

"Vampiro! That's what we'll call you," came the outburst from the owner.

I knew at that very moment I hated the name. My real name is Eddie by the way. It used to be Edward, but I've been alive a long time and Eddie seems to fit in better with the modern day, when I'm not Vampiro that is. I sat with the owner for a while— who, I later found out, was called The Great Waldo. I didn't mind my name quite as much when I found that out and as I got to know the other carnies, I realised most of them had stupid names. It was all part of the act and looked good on fliers that were distributed to promote the carnival. The Malcasa Carnival that I had joined was pretty standard, but what made them stand out from the rest was their freak show. They hired the best and they made sure that each of the freaks had their own show. Some were only a few minutes long and others went on for a while and had several carnies involved. Some were actually quite intricate and while I'd love to tell you more about some of those shows, those are stories for another day.

I slid right into carnival life and I loved it. Before I was a carnie, and since I had become one of the undead, I had been living in the shadows, moving from one place to another before the body count got noticed, but in the carnival, though we constantly moved, I was always home. There were other outcasts like me, those who were different. Hell, we were all different. Even the supposedly normal carnies didn't fit into everyday life. The owner or the Ringmaster, The Great Waldo, as I came to know him, had decided that my act would be to terrify the crowd. He had put me through some tests to make sure I really did drink blood, all with animals rather than people. That's how the show started. He would have me come on and bite the head off of a chicken and drink its blood. The main problem was that people weren't that freaked out. There were geeks in other carnivals that did the same thing. People had seen it before.

My second act was to drink blood from someone before the entire crowd. Now this one had me excited. All the time I had spent sneaking around in the shadows, only to be afforded the opportunity to have my meal in front of a large crowd. It was a bit of a dream come true and I was old enough that I could drink from humans without draining them completely. The problem with that act was, no one in the crowd wanted to volunteer so I would have to get one of the carnies to come on stage and let me drink some of their blood. People then believed it was all faked because it wasn't an audience member so that act got canned pretty quickly, too. I can remember thinking at that point that I would probably never fit in anywhere. I had no memory of being turned into a vampire and had never met another of my kind, so I felt alone in the world. I had hoped that the carnies would become my family, but at that point I was concerned.

Act number three was a winner, though. I would prove I was a vampire by accomplishing feats that no human could. There were several ways of doing this, but the first one we tried that worked was to put me into a large chest with several poisonous snakes. The other carnies would then shake and kick the chest until the snakes went wild. When the lid was opened and I stood up they could see the snake bites all over my body. I could always hear the murmurs in the crowd.

"They aren't poisonous snakes."

He's already had the antidote before going in."

I bet he lies in a separate compartment from the snakes and those bite marks are fake."

I used to smile and watch their expressions change as the bite marks healed themselves in front of the crowd's eyes. Their murmurs would change to "oo's and a's." It was a talking point for the crowd when they left the carnival and it helped spread word about us. The Great Waldo knew we had to add more to the act to keep it fresh.

I had an act where I was submerged in a glass tank of water and left in there while other acts went on. I would stay in the tank for over an hour sometimes. The punters would watch the other acts but I could see their eyes coming back to me. I didn't have to breathe so I could have stayed in there as long as I wanted, but it was pretty boring. I'd eventually come out just after one of the other acts finished to massive applause. The applause did nothing for me personally,but it did give me the reassurance that I would be staying with the carnival.

People come and go at a carnival. Sometimes people join and will travel with the carnival for years and others join and leave within a few months. I can remember one particular carnie named Melissa, who joined not long after me. She was quickly renamed 'Cobra, the Serpent Girl'. I was taken by her beauty the first time I saw her. She looked like any normal woman, but like me, she had fangs, though she wasn't a vampire. Snakes seemed to listen to her and as soon as she was near them, a calm would come over them all instantly. They did anything she told them to do and the crowd loved it. She was far superior to any snake charmer that they had ever seen and she quickly became a favourite act of the punters. I was mesmerised by her. She seemed both innocent and deadly. There was a quietness about her however, wielding an army of snakes gave her a great deal of power in my eyes, not that she ever used it. It took me a while to pluck up the courage to approach her, but when I finally did, we hit it off. I didn't come onto her. We just became friends. Although we were treated well at the carnival and for all the differences we had among us, some of the other carnies were still scared of us both. We spent a lot of time walking between the tents and stalls just looking up at the night sky. She had a fascination with the gods and would spend hours telling me about various snake gods from different cultures. As time passed, I knew I was deeply in love with her, but the risk of pushing her away was too great so I never tried to make us anything more.

The acts Melissa and I performed did well for a while, and then the carnival started to struggle again. Carnivals tend to do that. Things are good for a while and then it tends to die off a bit. While both of our acts had been some of the most popular, as we continued to travel a similar route year after year, most people had seen them. Little did I know how much things were going to change and soon.

We had stopped at a few small towns and had pretty poor turnouts. Melissa and I were relaxing in my small caravan after a long walk when the Great Waldo appeared at my door. He let himself in as he always did though the caravan belonged to me. I bought it with my earnings, but I suppose Waldo believed he had a right to go wherever he wanted in his carnival.

"Vampiro," he said, then sighing before he carried on, as he always did when he had bad news. "Takings are down. Your act isn't pulling in as much money as it used to. I have a new idea and I want you to hear me out on it."

"Okay, let's hear it," I said, holding back my own sigh.

"We have this new guy, a clown. I haven't given him a name yet. The thing is, he seems a bit unhinged."

"What do you mean 'unhinged'? Aren't all clowns a bit crazy? Doesn't it come with the territory?" I asked.

"No, I mean yeah, but not like this guy. He's a monster. Looks like he has steroids with his cornflakes. Wears the regular clown makeup, but his costume's a little strange. Gives me the creeps, but we need new acts." The Great Waldo shivered as he finished speaking.

"What's all this got to do with me?"

"Well, I was thinking you could maybe fight him. I asked him what he does and he said whatever. Doesn't actually have an act. He's a big guy, though, and scary looking and you're super strong. I thought it would be a good crowd pleaser. Everyone loves a fight and a vampire going at it against a scary clown could be a winner."

"You want me to fight a fucking clown! Are you serious?"

"I'm telling you, it could be big. Think about it: Vampiro VS... uh... Koko... um, the Vampire Killing Clown! It will sell out."

"I think you have lost it, and I thought you hadn't named him yet?"

"Yeah, well. I've named him now. He's a clown... and a vampire killer. People love cheese. They will lap it right up."

"What if he gets hurt? You know how strong I am."

"Oh, don't worry about that. Judging by the look of him, he's the kind of guy who gets off on pain."

"Great, I can't wait!" I said sarcastically.

"I'll set it up. This will get us back on top." And with that he left. Not a thank you or anything.

It was a few weeks before it was all set up. The Great Waldo had to get fliers drawn up and printed and then distributed all over the next town we were traveling to, to build up some hype. He was right, though. People do love a fight and they love a bit of cheese as well. The fight sold out as soon as we opened up. The Great Waldo had kept Koko under wraps. As unbelievable as I found it, I hadn't managed to get a single look at this supposedly psychotic- looking clown yet.

We were the main show, starting at eleven in the evening. A standard boxing ring had been set up in one of the larger tents and seats had been placed all around it. Most of the other carnies were there. They were being used as extra security to stop those without tickets from trying to sneak in and to be available just in case things got rowdy outside of the ring. The carnival wasn't in the habit of running boxing matches and the Great Waldo didn't know what to expect, so he had made sure he had plenty of support that night in the hope that everything would run smoothly.

I was first into the ring. I had brought Cobra, but no one else. I didn't think there was much point. It was a show and that was all. My biggest worry was that I ended up accidentally hurting Koko. I'd have to pull my punches but still make it look good or everyone would demand their money back.

When Koko came out and I saw him for the first time, I was shocked. He was at least seven feet tall and he *did* look mental. His torso was covered in a typical red, yellow and blue clown suit but he had ripped the arms from it, possibly because his arms would have been too large to fit. He had muscles on his muscles. I had never seen anyone of such proportions. He had clown make up on his face, white with red, and black diamond eyes. His hair was the colour of fire and styled into thin spikes. I could see what Waldo had meant about him looking like the kind of guy who might enjoy pain. He was definitely the most psychotic-looking clown I had ever seen. He jumped into the ring and just started pacing back and forth on his side. He looked like he wanted to murder someone. Me, probably, but I was hoping he was just a great actor rather than taking this all too seriously.

The bell rang and he almost sprints across the ring at me. I put my guard up high and he smashes me in the ribs. Now, my organs are useless. I have no real need for them; they are just still there. The blood keeps me alive, but when that first punch landed, I felt like I was going to die, as if something inside was going to stop working. I knew right then that this was no human clown. He was something else. I pulled my guard lower as he threw body shots while I tried to recover. He then caught me with a right hook to the jaw that nearly took me off my feet. I started to move around the ring, keeping my distance, but he moved quickly for something so large. I'm not going to take you through the fight, blow by blow, but it went on pretty much like this throughout. He attacked and I was on the defensive... not how I had anticipated things would have gone. It was scheduled for fifteen rounds since that was standard for big fights back then. By the time we got to round ten I was on shaky legs. I had never experienced anything like this in all my time as a vampire, and I had never been put under such physical exertion or pain, either.

Round eleven started and I was wondering if I could do five more rounds. That was the round that Koko went absolutely berserk. He started grabbing me round the neck and throwing knees into my ribs. When the referee tried to intervene, Koko threw him from the ring into the crowd. Most of the crowd was on its feet. They had never seen a fight like this one. I threw a few elbows and one that caught the clown in the temple rocked him, giving me time to throw a series of body blows. It almost seemed like he was absorbing the pain. The last thing I remember is him grabbing me around the neck again and smashing his knee into my forehead—and it was lights out.

I came around about ten minutes later. The carnies were trying to clear the tent. There were screams and shouting. Cobra was kneeling over me smiling, but she had tears in her eyes. I later found out that when Koko had knocked me out, he had dropped on top of me and started raining blows down onto my face. Cobra had immediately leapt the ropes and fly- kicked him, her boot hitting him squarely in the chest. He had barely budged, as she tells it, but he did stop his assault on me to focus on her. She had tried to circle the ring, but he lunged at her and grabbed her by the throat. He lifted her off of the canvas, squeezing the life out of her with both hands... and then they were on him. Snakes. At first there were only a few, but they kept coming. The carnival had their own snakes, but they were coming from the surrounding fields, too. Koko had over one hundred snakes latched onto him in a matter of seconds, several different venoms pumping into him at the same time. Cobra was smiling down at him, even before his grip loosened. Seconds later he was lying dead on the floor with Corba standing over him. The snakes quickly departed. It didn't take me long to recover. I drank from a few different people and I was good as new. It made me wonder, though. I had considered myself immortal and it was almost all over, just like that. I tried to form a relationship with Cobra after that, something more than just a friendship, but she rejected my advances and eventually left the carnival. I wanted to go with her, but she had snuck away in the night. I think she loved me too, but for one reason or another, she had decided that it was best we parted ways. I'll never forget her and I will always be grateful for the day she saved my life.

Things were never the same after her departure and soon after, the Great Waldo died. He had kept us going for as long as he could, but the outside world had already put him under pressure to change the way the carnival was run. Once he had passed away the new owners swooped in and got rid of half of the old carnies and replaced them with people who had no idea how a carnival should be run, kids who were cheap to hire. I think the only reason they kept me was because I was still young and fit. It's true that vampires don't age.

The world changed, too. Carnivals can't have freak shows anymore. They would have protesters crawling all over them and it would be a PR nightmare. On top of that, technology had taken over kids lives and a trip to the carnival wasn't a big deal anymore. Young couples didn't go on dates to the carnival like they used to. I had ideas to revitalise the carnival, but the new owners didn't listen to me. It was a business for them, not a lifestyle like when the Great Waldo was in charge. I had been relegated to running one of the little amusement arcade tents. My acts were useless in the modern carnival. They barely had any shows anymore. The people that did come, came for the rides or to eat junk food and often just to wander around and barely spent a penny. There were still things we could have done to bring in more of a crowd, but what did I know? I was just an old act. For months I ran the amusement arcade wondering how I should approach the owners, how could I make them understand that the carnival could be grand once again, but in the end I knew it would never happen. I wasn't ready to let my dream go so easily. If the new owners didn't want to listen, they would need to go. I had thought about different ways of going about it, but each scenario resulted in my being found out and captured or killed. I took my time and I went about my day- to-day life as I pondered how I could bring real change...9 and then it struck me. I would create more of my kind and use the new vampires to replace everyone in the carnival. If we could take them all out in one evening and move on, leaving no one to talk of what happened, surely I couldn't be caught. I'd have enough people to run the carnival so I wouldn't need to bring in anyone new. It seemed foolproof. The main problem with it was that I didn't know how to make another vampire.

I decided the best way to work it out would be to start trying out methods I had seen in movies or read in books. I began working my way through them, but it took a while. I never wanted to kill more than one person per town and I'd often try and leave a few towns between kills. I can drink from people without killing them, so I only kill if I choose to, rather than out of necessity. The thirst lessens as each year passes. Since I didn't know what I was doing, I accidently killed quite a lot of people, but as I said, I had to spread it out, so it took me a few years to finally get it right. Once I had perfected the method, it was easy enough for me to start turning people, but I also couldn't just turn half a town, so I slowly began to collect my new family. One thing I hadn't planned for was how thirsty new vampires are. It was a nightmare keeping them fed without drawing any attention to myself. I kept them in my trailer at first. It was dark, for obvious reasons and there was space, but as my family grew, I had to start keeping them in the back of one of the empty trucks and I had to move them out before we moved town every time. It was a lot of work, but as each day passed, I felt happier and happier. I was going to take the carnie back to days gone by. The world never stops changing and moving. No matter how nostalgic everyone gets, we can never go back. It's a strange thing. Well… I'm going to set the clocks back. The new carnies will do things my way. We will have a freak show once again. When the entire carnival is run by vampires, no one will challenge us. No one will stand in our way. We will go from town to town and we will do things my way. My children will hunt and I will create more of my kind. Of course, it won't say any of that on the flier. Who would come? It will say something cheesy, like, 'Vampiro & the Carnival of Vampires.' The Great Waldo would have liked that.

The End

What a Price to Pay for a Fucking Teddy Bear

By

J. C. Michael

"It's not about the bloody bear."

"It isn't?"

"No, it's about the principle."

"The principle of what?"

"That they can't come over here and rip folks off, that's what."

"Why? It isn't like our own carnival gypos always played fair, so why should this lot?"

Both Carl and Ed stopped their bickering and turned to look at Wilf. It was the first sentence he'd spoken since they'd left Carl's house a good ten minutes ago, and clearly his mood hadn't improved during his spell of self-imposed silence.

"Who rattled your cage?" asked Carl. He had a face like thunder, a storm that had been brewing for the past hour after they'd left the fair.

“Yeah, who asked you?” added Ed.

“Fuck off, Ed.” Wilf would take the lip from Carl, they’d been friends since their respective fathers had parked their pushchairs beside each other outside the British Legion each and every Sunday dinnertime, but he was damned if he’d take it from the younger of the two Stephenson brothers.

“If you don’t want to come, piss off home.” It was an option Carl had frequently given Wilf over the years, and one he never took despite all the times circumstance came to prove that he should have.

“And leave you two clowns to get up to God knows what, yeah, that’d be a good idea.”

Carl smiled, his mood switching instantly as it so often did, “So long as we’re agreed this is a matter of principle, and not just about the sodding bear, then glad to have you aboard. Besides, wherever would I be without my conscience tagging along, eh?”

Wilf’s own conscience, the one pleading with him to go home, lock the door, and avoid whatever crap his best mate was bound to drag him into, was currently drowning in a sea of alcohol, its pleas going unheard. He grinned as he replied - “Prison, most likely.”

***

“So what do you and your friends make of all this kerfuffle?”

“What kerfuffle would that be, Reverend?” Wilf had no desire to engage the busy-body vicar in conversation, but it was hard to be rude to a man of the cloth. Reverend Whiting always attended assembly on a Friday afternoon and normally spent half an hour afterwards chatting to the young mothers, particularly the milfs, as Carl would put it. That said, whenever there was trouble afoot, he always sought out Wilf who normally stood alone as he waited for his son who would habitually be the last out, and even then only have half of what he should be bringing home with him at the first attempt.

“This carnival malarkey. I picked up a pamphlet earlier today,” he waved a gaudy coloured flyer under Wilf's nose as he spoke,

"Direct From Eastern Romania - the home of the traditional travelling carnival. It explains a few things, like Elsie Prattley panicking in the post office about Eastern European 'pickpockets and vagabonds' and Bob chiming in from behind the counter about how 'they' have a liking for young girls. It was all quite unsavoury."

Wilf shrugged. "You know Churchmoor; us locals aren't big on change."

"Well I do hope there won't be any problems caused for our new acquaintances," smiled the Vicar.

"You mean from Carl and Ed?" The comment was pointed but Wilf said it with a smile of his own. Both men knew that whenever there were 'problems' in town Carl and Ed were never far away, and where they were, Wilf would generally be pretty close too.

"Now come on Wilf," said Reverend Whiting leaning in close. There was an aroma about him that made Wilf think of communion wine, "You're the sensible one out of your particular trio, always far enough on the outside of things to avoid the more serious issues those two get involved in. I'm hoping you'll be the voice of reason if anything should develop over the weekend."

Wilf shook his head. "You never let up, do you? Anything goes wrong and Carl and Ed are prime suspects. You'd've had 'em blamed for those kids that went missing in Fryton if they hadn't been at that stag do in Blackpool. They aren't bad blokes, just a bit boisterous. We've all grown up y' know, we aren't kids n'more."

"All I'm saying is..."

"Well don't. Folk 'round here don't like change, we'd still be baiting badgers and hunting foxes if we could, but having a fair turn up in summer rather than that shitty one that comes at Christmas isn't the end of the world. And as far as Eastern Europeans go, a Pole fitted Carl's new bathroom last week, and Ed spent a very happy night with a Slovenian lass last time we were in Amsterdam, and she was just as good value for money as the plumber from what I can gather."

Reverend Whiting went red and turned on his heel. For his part, Wilf bit his bottom lip, as although he was in his mid-thirties, he still didn't want to have to deal with his mother if what he'd said got back to her. *Fuck it*, he thought, *can't unsay it now*.

***

When Wilf had told Carl and Ed about "his message from God" over their first pint that evening, the conversation had been laughed off. The brothers had no intention to cause any trouble. They never did. It's just a shame that trouble itself didn't have the same good intentions and tended to seek them out whether they went looking for it or not. Sometimes that trouble led to a black eye or two, for both them and others. Occasionally it was a little more serious and required a bit more sorting out than a knob of butter on some bumps and bruises. This time it was at a whole different level. Trouble had brought a friend of its own. Trouble came with death in tow.

***

On Friday night, the night Wilf told his friends about the Reverend's concerns, the three of them got no further than the pool room of the Awkward Turtle. They drank the usual amount, played their usual games of pool, and talked the usual nonsense of the kind that old friends develop over the years and can repeat over and over again without boredom setting in. It was only toward the end of the night that the fair was mentioned again.

"Young Wilf at his Mum's tomorrow night?"

Wilf took his shot, potting a red and lining up on another, before answering, "Yeah, back on Monday night so he can watch the match with me."

Ed chalked his cue, "Fancy a walk down to the fair then?"

Wilf looked up. It was no accident that Ed had raised the topic while Carl was taking a slash. If Wilf said no that'd be the end of it, if he said yes it'd be two on one and presented as a done deal when Carl returned. "Not really."

"Aw come on mate, what harm can it do?"

Wilf pondered the question as he lined up the shot. There were probably a hundred things that could go wrong, but if he said no, Ed would sulk all evening and likely or not take his aggravation out on some poor bugger who didn't deserve it and would end up staying at home for the next six months. If Ed was going to pick a fight with anyone, it was better to be somebody from out of town that'd be packing up and fucking off the next day. He took the shot, missed, and cursed. Carl was at the bar now, arguing with somebody about the price of takeaway pizza, of all things. Maybe a change of scenery wouldn't be too bad an idea. "No more than staying here, I guess. You can tell your brother though."

As far as planning went, that was all that was needed. They met again on Saturday night where Friday night had ended. They downed a couple of pints then bought bottles to take with them as they walked out of town to where the fair had set up along a wide stretch of grass along the roadside. The walk was pleasant – a blue sky with a few clouds drifting amiably across it as the sun sauntered to meet the horizon, and birds twittering in the hedgerows. The music from the fair got gradually louder as they approached. Old-fashioned music. Organ music rather than the dance and rap played at the usual fair and for once Wilf felt relaxed. Quite a few folk from town were heading the same way. Everyone seemed in good spirits, including Carl. It was never going to last.

It seemed most of the town was already there when they arrived, although that wasn't saying much when the word town was, in essence, an exaggeration for what was more a large village. A mix of kids, adults, and geriatrics, desperate not to miss out on what was going on, all appeared to be finding something of interest. Amongst the handful of rides, mainly roundabouts but also a waltzers, were the usual games and some open-sided trailers packed with arcade machines. It was the typical set up for a half decent travelling fair with only a smattering of more eclectic additions – a strongman billed as 'The Romanian Rambo' tearing up phone books and bending iron bars, a couple of female gymnasts-cum-contortionists, a knife-throwing act, and a fortune teller. The rides and machines were powered by a collection of generators, which hummed below the sound of the calliope music and added a faint diesel smell that lingered amongst the aromas of hotdogs with fried onions, burgers, and candy floss. Everything was of a scale that could be transported by a convoy of trucks and trailers with a day's set up and half day take down at each town the fair visited. It was more or less exactly what the three of them had expected.

"That clown flogging the balloons looks like fucking Pennywise," said Carl with a broad smile; the same Carl whose response to the previous evening's declaration that "we've decided to go to the fair tomorrow" was "for fuck's sake, what are we? Thir-fucking-teen?"

Both he and Ed actually seemed to be enjoying the carnival atmosphere. Even Carl's failure to hit the bell on the high-striker didn't soil his demeanour, he simply explained how "they stand on the air pipe so less gets through and make the men look weaker than the birds. It's all a bit of fun." It certainly wasn't what Wilf would normally have said was Carls idea of fun. Perhaps that's why he let his guard down.

Burgers and hot dogs bought to soak up the evening's lager, and more lager purchased to wash down the food, they sat and watched the evening unfold. Almost everyone there other than the stall holders was known to them. Things were calm. Things were relaxed. Things soon changed.

It started, as it so often did, with Ed saying something to his brother without considering if the topic was a wise one to raise; "Oi, Carl, isn't that Debbie Smith over there chatting to the shooting gallery bloke?"

"Can't be," said Carl, as if daring it to be the case.

"It is. How could you forget an arse like that? Maybe she's visiting her folks."

Wilf spotted the danger "Nah, can't be, she hasn't visited in years." It was too late.

"Fucking well is her," Carl growled, "smarmy bastard's taken a real shine to her too, ain't he." And that was that. The switch was flicked.

"They're just chatting," said Ed.

"What the fuck do you know?" snarled his brother, "Look at the cunt flirting with her. Who's he think he is?"

Wilf sighed inwardly. The problem wasn't the bloke innocently talking to the girl they'd all loved a little back in their teens. The problem was the sense of ownership Carl felt he had over her which harked back to school discos almost twenty years ago when she'd always agreed to a dance at the end of the night out of politeness more than anything else.

"Come on, let's go say hello," said Carl, his eyes fixed on the object of his teenage fantasies. He was halfway to her when two men walked over, the tallest and most handsome of which slipped his arm around Debbie's waist. Momentarily, his pace quickened, and then he stopped. Debbie's mother and father were joining them, laughing and joking. Alongside her father stood her Uncle, a silent partner in the building firm Carl worked for. "Fuck it," muttered Carl as the group walked away. "Fuck it."

His mood soured, Wilf and Ed expected Carl to tell them it was time to head back to the pub.

Instead, he drew himself up to his full 6'5", sniffed, spat on the ground, and began to head towards the stall once again. Ed shrugged. Wilf shook his head. They had no idea what Carl had in mind other than the fact it likely wouldn't end well.

***

"I'm telling you, I hit that fucking duck fair and fucking square."

"No, no," insisted the stallholder, a rat-like little man with a Hitler moustache and tatty tracksuit top over an out of date Barcelona shirt. "You hit nine out of the ten, you get small prize."

As Carl's face got redder, his knuckles, still clasped around the air-rifle, got whiter. Sweat ran down Wilf's back, *any minute now he's going to clock that twat around the back of the head with that gun and all hell'll break loose.*

"Are you fucking deaf? I heard it ping off the metal. It's fucking rigged, that's what it is." Carl leaned further forward as he spoke. A small crowd was gathering.

“I am hurt you would say such a thing. Truly hurt. The tent has a metal sheet at the back, to stop the bullets firing through and causing unwanted injury. Come, I show you.”

“I’ll fucking well show you in a minute. I hit the fucking duck, I want the fucking bear. The big one at the back.”

“You can have the small bear. It is good quality, see?”

“That twatting thing’ll give my niece nightmares. I want the good one. The big one.” Carl gave him a knowing smirk, “the one nobody’s supposed to win and that just hangs there to encourage people to try and then end up with one of the shitty ones worth less than what you charge per go.”

The crowd was building even more, the music seemed quieter, the smell of diesel stronger. Ed was scowling beside his brother, a rabid dog ready to lurch at a moment’s notice. Wilf felt the sickness he normally felt when it was about to kick off. He could look after himself, but his approach was more considered, with less bloodlust. “Carl, Ed.”

“What?”

“His mates?”

Carl spat as the crowd moved aside and half a dozen fair folk, including Rambo, approached.

“Oh right, I see, here comes the fucking cavalry. Rushing to rat-boys rescue.”

Rambo stepped ahead of the rest of the group and looked directly into Carl’s eyes, “My friend, surely we can resolve this peaceably, eh?”

Wilf quickly took in the scene. A couple of blokes in overalls were stood off to one side, guys who surely knew how to use the spanner and crowbar they carried as tools to break heads as well as fix machines. The others stood behind Rambo looked rough and ready, nothing that couldn’t be handled one on one, and Carl could probably hold his own against three or four, but the odds weren’t in their favour and still more stall operators were approaching, including the high striker operator with his heavy mallet and the knife thrower twirling one of his blades across his fingers.

“Come on Carl, let it be,” said Wilf.

“Why the fuck...” said Ed before Carl hit him on the shoulder as if he had to hit someone to ease the tension.

Rambo continued to stare. He matched Carl in height and was better built. Wilf knew Carl wouldn’t be afraid, he’d taken on bigger men, sometimes successfully, sometimes not, but with the back-up Rambo had, and a crowd of witnesses, it wasn’t a fight they could win.

“Yeah well, don’t think we don’t have mates too,” growled Carl, “probably for the best you’ll be gone tomorrow and maybe think twice before coming back, yeah?”

“There’s no need for threats,” said Rambo with a smile that was begging to be wiped off his face.

Wilf started to back away, as did Carl, saying nothing.

"Don't turn your back's on 'em lads, filthy bastards'll fleg on y' soon as it's turned,"

Carl punched his brother's shoulder for a second time "Shut up Ed, let's drop it."

***

As they walked back to town, Wilf knew damn well there was next to no chance that'd be the end of it. It wasn't in Carl's nature to back down. The only thing that could cause Carl to drop it was if he drank enough to fall asleep and couldn't face daylight before the fair had packed up and gone, the irony being that drinking more would make matters worse before there was a chance of him passing out.

"Fucking snide cunts," Carl mumbled through a mouthful of pizza.

"Not worth the hassle, mate," said Wilf, but it was an empty gesture, he was well aware where this was heading.

Carl had complained about his "overpriced takeaway pizza when you can get them for a quid at the freezer shop" from the first bite. He'd railed at the Middlesbrough defence as he watched them get stuffed by Man City on Match of the Day, and he'd looked ready to kill Ed when he'd spilt tomato sauce on the carpet.

"Come on lads, time we paid them arseholes a visit."

Ed readily agreed, it would distract his brother from the mess he'd just made worse by rubbing at the sauce with some kitchen roll. Wilf said nothing, he was knackered and could do without the aggravation, but he hadn't let his friend down in the past and wouldn't now. Besides, Carl had clearly hit the damn duck so his irritation was justified, and that's all it needed to be.

***

When they'd left Carl's flat, the stated aim was to find, and liberate, the bear. Then, somewhere down Westfield's Lane, things changed. Carl and Ed had started bickering -it wasn't about the bear now, it was a matter of principle. Carl had always been like this, always convinced himself that he was the oppressed and was standing up for what was right and proper. On this occasion, he had a point, but it didn't change the fact that he was a thug with an overwhelming capacity for self-righteous justification and propensity for violence. Wilf had kept his own counsel, well aware that a bully with principles is a dangerous thing: a creature inclined to find problems and see only a single solution - that somebody would have to pay the penalty. Eventually, he spoke up, not that it changed anything. Despite his reservations, he still didn't go home when Carl suggested it. If he'd walked away then it would've been the end of their friendship. Carl was like that.

"So long as we're agreed this is a matter of principle, and not just about the sodding bear, then glad to have you aboard. Besides, wherever would I be without my conscience tagging along eh?"

"Prison, most likely."

Carl rested a hand on Wilf's shoulder. "They'd never take me alive. Now come on and keep quiet. We'll go in through that gate hole and work down the inside of the hedge so we can recce things from cover."

With that he was away down the path in a half crouch, beckoning Ed and Wilf to follow with two raised fingers. Ed shrugged and Wilf gave him a knowing look in return. Carl had loved to act like he was in the army since he'd been a little kid obsessed with the Falklands and then the Gulf. He'd even set his watch to Iraq time while at school to keep track of when the bombing raids would take place and asked Miss. Ellis in R.E why "we don't just march in and shoot them all while they're doing that praying thing". He'd tried to join the Army at 16 but left after a few months - Carl Stephenson and discipline were barely passing acquaintances.

The hedgerow led them along the back of the fair, the soft putt-putt of the few generators that were still running helping to mask their less than silent approach. As luck would have it, the shooting gallery backed onto the field they were in and, producing a wicked looking combat knife from his jacket inside pocket, Ed began to slash at the fabric.

“That ticks criminal damage off the nights to do list,” said Wilf

“I’ll tick off fucking GBH if you don’t shut up,” said Ed as he stuck his head into the tent and began to crawl in.

“Give over you two,” whispered Carl, “Ed, get the bear.”

Ed’s head popped back out of the tent, “It’s dark in there, besides, I thought it wasn’t about the bear?”

Carl scowled. “It isn’t, but ‘avin away with it teaches ‘em a lesson don’t it? Use your lighter.”

Ed smirked, “You want me to torch it?”

“Don’t be daft,” said Carl before Wilf could protest. “You know what Uncle Tom said about arson.”

Ed looked disappointed, “I know, ‘arsonists are arseholes’. Only bothers him cause of the fire at that fucking club. Wasn’t bothered before.”

It was a damning statement for a local copper, but Wilf knew Tom was as corrupt as a politician. The three of them would've had a free holiday in the big house by now if he hadn't been.

"Maybe a bit of target practice though. Are the guns in there?"

Ed vanished back into the tent, "Yeah, but chained to the counter."

"How's the chain fixed?"

"Screwed in."

"Take the screw out then."

As the brothers spoke Wilf acted as lookout, falling into his familiar role as Ed and Carl took the lead in making mischief.

"Here," one of the guns pocked out of the back of the tent. Carl passed it to Wilf. Another followed, and then Ed carrying a third.

Wilf looked at Ed, then Carl, then Ed again, "Pellets?"

***

Wilf had been landed with the task of writing some risk assessments at work, and if he'd been asked to write one for a shooting gallery where guns, even simple .22 air rifles like these were left lying around, he'd have noted that the pellets shouldn't be kept with them. Clearly, the fair's Health and Safety Manager didn't think it was a precaution that needed to be taken, or, more likely, he didn't exist at all. Ed found the pellets in a box under the counter, and they grabbed a handful apiece before hunkering back down behind the hedge.

"So what's the plan?" said Wilf, his heart pounding in his ears at the feel of the weapon in his hands.

"Take a few pot shots, take out a window or two, and then leg it. Keep hold of the guns and club any fucker who catches up with us."

"Right. Spread out or stick together?"

"Stick together. Ed, you ready?"

Ed nodded and Wilf could see the sweat gleaming on his brow and a focused look in his eyes that was only ever seen when something like this was about to go down.

Carl moved around the back of them, gently tapping each of them on the back. "You ready? Aim for the caravans over to the left."

Neither man answered, their silence giving their de facto leader his answer.

"Ready. Aim. Fire."

Three shots rang out at once followed swiftly by the sound of broken glass and two pings from hit metal. They reloaded quickly, all of them quite comfortable using the rifles after hours spent lamping and poaching in the woods around town. By the time the next volley was fired, the lights were on in two of the caravans and another window smashed as one of the doors flung open.

"That's him, greasy twat," shouted Carl as he stood and shot. The shooting gallery operator yelped and put his hand to his face, jumping back inside. Their shots were more spread out now, pellets pinging and ricocheting off the nearest caravan while lights came on and doors opened amongst shouts and what could be assumed to be curses in a mixture of Romanian and English.

"Where are you?" bellowed a loud voice, and there, stood in one of the caravan doorways, was Rambo, naked but for a pair of black boxer shorts. "Come on. I fight you."

A shot rang out and his shoulder flinched back, but rather than duck back, he stepped forward. "What are you, chicken? Cluck cluck fucker. Come face me." Another shot. Another hit. He didn't break stride.

Wilf pulled on Carl's sleeve, "Carl, let's go, there's too many of 'em coming out now."

And then another shot rang out, but not from one of the three air rifles. This was a boom, not a crack. The sound of something far bigger. The sound of something big enough to take Carls head off.

***

Blackness.

A ringing in his ears as blurry eyes tried to open.

The back of his head hurt.

He could hear crying.

Bright lights shone in his face causing him to squint in order to see.

The crying was coming from a body curled up in the corner of a rough square made of caravans. Wilf recognised the figure as Ed and moved towards his friend. Something hit him in the ribs, causing him to go down, and a pair of scuffed up steel toe capped boots stepped in front of him.

"Let me tell you a story," said Rambo as he hunkered down. Behind him stood rat-man, a handgun in his hand that looked straight out of a Clint Eastwood movie. Wilf noticed two things about his face – the welt on his temple where the pellet had hit him and a sadistic smile.

"Your friend. He decided to run away with the carnival. He ran away with a very pretty girl called Magda. That is what we will tell the police. We will tell them how Magda wished to return to Romania to visit her sick mother and how your friend went with her."

"Nobody's going to believe that," said Wilf. Ed had stopped crying but wasn't moving. There was blood on his clothes. “You think people will believe he went without packing? Without his passport?”

“Passport, no matter, we don’t enter your country legally, and we don’t leave it that way. Clothes, they buy on the way. We gave them money for their adventure. It’s bullshit, but it doesn’t matter. That will be the story and that will be what we say.”

“And what about us? We all going to run away to Romania?”

“No, that would be implausible.”

At that, Rambo turned and began walking towards Ed. Rough hands grabbed Wilf from behind and pulled him to the edge of the caravan square, and he began to take in more of what was around him. Faces peered out of windows and doors. The putt-putt-putt of generators chuntered away in the background. Rambo stopped and nodded his head towards one of the caravan windows, the gesture repaid with a knife thrown out and into the dirt in front of him.

"You have a knife of your own little man?" He was taunting Ed.

Wilf tensed. Ed was ignorant and stupid. He would be distraught at the loss of his brother. But he was also dangerous, a cornered animal out for revenge. His friend got to his feet. His face was dirty but for the clear tracks of his tears, and one of his ears was caked in blood.

"Seem to have misplaced it. You got a spare?"

Rambo looked at the knife in his hand and then threw it at Ed, catching him in his shoulder. Ed went down but grabbed at the knife, pulling it free as he leapt to his feet, and charged. Rambo sidestepped and tripped the smaller man sending him sprawling in the dirt. He laughed, and realised he'd underestimated his opponent when Ed span and threw the knife himself. It struck Rambo in the gut and stuck there hilt deep. Blood began to run from the wound and collect around the band of his shorts. And then he started to laugh. They all started to laugh. Cackling and shouting, yelling and cheering, hollering and howling. Howls that changed from those of men to sounds more animalistic in nature. As the gathering howled, Rambo bent over, and Wilf expected him to topple face first in the dirt like a felled tree, at which point he expected everyone to attack at once and tear him and Ed to pieces. Neither thing happened. Instead, all that Wilf thought he knew about the world shattered.

Pulling the knife from his stomach and causing blood to pour onto the floor, Rambo lifted his head and howled, and as he did, he began to change. His face began to jut forwards, stretching out from his nose, which seemed to shift and twist into something that bore more resemblance to a snout. The muscles on his shoulders rippled and expanded from already significant proportions to something all the more unnatural as he moved to kneel on the floor and place his palms on the ground, where his fingers grew and claws erupted from their tips. Black hair sprouted from his body and those gathered around him howled at the sky with an ever increasing intensity and volume, as if summoning the wolf he was becoming. Ed was frozen in place while the creature morphed from man to beast and then it too began to howl, its jaws wide and full of dagger-like teeth dribbling strands of saliva.

Then, slowly and deliberately, the monster advanced. Only now did Ed begin to scuttle backwards before stopping and making the sign of a cross with his fingers, fingers that were then bitten clean off as the huge black wolf lunged forward and snapped its jaws.

It was now Ed's turn to howl, but it was a howl of pain that was given chance to pierce the night before a chorus of other howls drowned it out. Then, as Wilf could only watch in disbelief, the Rambo wolf began to walk slowly around Ed, who was holding the bleeding stumps of his fingers to his chest. And then Ed began to convulse. Wilf moved toward him but was hauled back as his friend writhed on the floor. Ed was foaming at the mouth and then he too began to change, the bite transferring the ability to transform and twisting his body into shapes it had never been designed to construct. Wilf could hear Ed's bones snapping as they moved, his friend screaming through a deformed face that soon became incapable of making such human sounds.

The screams had now become howls that were far more in keeping with the form Ed's body had rebuilt itself into. And then the transformation stopped. The black wolf continued to pace, its yellow eyes staring at its newly created kin. Ed, or what had once been Ed, for Wilf had no idea what remained of his friend inside his new form, began to rise. As they had been as men, the black wolf dwarfed the smaller creature Ed had become. The moonlight reflected from the brown fur that now covered Ed's still partially clothed body. The smaller wolf shook itself and stepped out of what had been Ed's jeans before grabbing what had been his shirt in its teeth and pulling it away. It bared its teeth and growled, its intentions clear, and then the two wolves attacked.

Wilf had once accompanied Carl and Ed to a dogfight, and this wasn't too different. The wolves turned and twisted, snapping their jaws and flailing their clawed paws at one another. Yelps and howls split the night air, and jeers and shouts came from the caravans surrounding what was now nothing more than an arena. The Ed wolf was fighting valiantly, but it was clear that the bigger animal held all the advantages of size and experience. Blood streaked from both, but the wounds on Ed were deeper, the loss of blood slowing him until eventually, he was down and out, his long tongue lolling from his bloodied jaws as he panted for breath. The black wolf, the alpha, circled him once, then twice, and then tore out his opponent's throat in a fountain of blood.

***

They must have hit him again. His head pounded. It was still dark, but the vans had been moved. Shadowy figures moved around in his blurred vision. There were bangs and clangs, clattering noises and shouting. The fair was getting dismantled, the vans loaded.

"We will be gone by daylight." Rambo stood in front of him in his human guise and Wilf shrank back as he tried to piece together memories of blood and beasts, of what could, and what couldn't, have happened to his friends.

"Where's Carl? Where's Ed?"

"There is no need to ask. You know the answer. You can try and convince yourself it was a nightmare. It was not."

Wilf's mouth felt dry. His head hurt. "So what about me? Is it my turn now?"

Rambo smirked, "No. You will not run away with a young girl. Nor will drunkenly stumble into the road where a speeding lorry will crush your body and wild animals will feast on your carcass before it is found dead in a ditch."

"That'll be your story?"

"Yes. We have told many tales, and will tell many more," Rambo paused as if in contemplation and then glared at Wilf. His eyes flashed yellow and his teeth extended, he pointed with a finger, the nail of which became a black claw. "You my friend, you get to go home. You get to sleep in your bed knowing what happened to your friends. To lay awake knowing that nobody would believe you if you told them the truth and nobody will believe the lies you tell to hide it. Your community may even blame you for what has happened, make you an outcast, or perhaps they will be glad to be rid of your brutish companions." The man's features settled, the direct opposite of Wilfs nerves which were by now shredded. Bed sounded good. To wake up from this nightmare would be even better. Rambo began to walk away from him. Truck engines were firing up. Vehicles were leaving the rubbish strewn site. "The world of your tomorrow will not be the same as that of your yesterday," shouted Rambo as he strode away and began to climb into a lorry laden with the waltzers. "You know what we are. Send your police, and we will send our brothers. You have family? The big bad wolves will descend on you, take your babes from their cribs, rip the throats of your parents and grandparents, and your women, we will fuck them in both our forms and leave them to tell you which was better, beast or man. We'll make sure it looks like your friend had an accident, we know how to cover our tracks. Our kind has been hunted for centuries, we've learnt how to live with that." The can door of the lorry shut behind him with a solid thud and the engine roared. The sun was rising as the convoy left the field, the waltzers in the rear. Wilf curled up and wished he was dead.

***

Every few years the fair comes again. There's never any trouble. It isn't new anymore. Wilf always stays away. Newer friends tell him to let the past go. They tell him there's nothing to be afraid of. He knows that there is. When those same friends next see him, they tell him that the fair folk ask after him. That they tell them to pass on that Carl is doing well. That he and Magda have a child. That they called the child Ed. And every time the fair comes all he can do is wait for them to leave, and when they do they always drive past his house, and as he lies awake, he hears them howl.

The End

The Voodoo Man
By
Steven Stacy

Elvira laid the tarot cards out in front of the dumpy middle-aged woman in front of her. Elvira could see that her own hands were shaking, and she wondered if the paying rube would wonder if she were a fraud too. She closed her eyes and tried to concentrate, *had she lost the gift?* She tried to focus on the woman and what the cards were telling her, but her mind was fraught with worry. Her father would find out if she had lost the gift, like her mother before her and her disowned older sister, Elena. When they found out Elena had lost the gift, her parents had packed her things and dropped her with no money at the nearest bus station; although Elvira and her other sister Serena had given Elena every penny they owned, not to mention their jewellery to sell.

"Can you see anything?" the woman in front of her asked.

It was the Carnival's last day in New Orleans. The people here loved the psychics. They were always the main draw and they always made good money.

"If you could concentrate on the question you want answered," Elvira said through gritted teeth.

"I haven't got all day, sweetie!" The woman said abruptly, standing and pushing her chair back with a squeak. She placed her hand out with an exasperated sigh, and Elvira returned the twenty-five dollars she had given her for the reading.

After the woman left, Elvira closed the voile and changed the sign to busy before bursting into racking sobs. "I want to die!" she cried, and a shudder went through her. *What was she to do?*

Later that night, Elvira lay on the small sofa in her family's large Romany caravan, alone. The entire sideshow was on the move, everything fixed to the railway carriages. On to the next town. She could hear the rumble of the tracks underneath them. Her father was in the front carriage playing cards with the boys. She was in their Romany caravan which was tied down with wire cables to keep it in place, attached to the train. Her sister, Serena, was in one of the carriages, no doubt, with her acrobat boyfriend, Jamie. Elvira was alone though, and although she put on a brave face for the punters and her family, she felt completely alone in the world. Her hands lay under her head in a prayer as she quietly wept, fraught with worry. She had been brought up in the Carnival with freaks; Charlie the dwarf, Two-Face, the Siamese twins, Croc – the human crocodile, and others. Her mother was also a psychic, although all the family used this term loosely, because her father had accused her mother of being a fraud in more than one argument. She and her sister danced and did gymnastics together, which was a favourite with the men; as they balanced on top of one another, flipped, and danced to old Romany music. Her father played it brilliantly on the violin. And, of course, Elvira read the Tarot cards. Or, had been able to until Dimitri had taken her virginity.

Her father and Uncle Benny (who juggled with one arm) were the owners, and the entire troupe travelled together. There were many more Carnival performers; it had grown over the years, becoming more and more successful. All the vehicles were loaded onto the train and some chose to drive together, trailing behind one another or towing materials (such as small rides) and animals. The carriages near the back of the train transported the animals; the two headed sheep – Fluff, and a beautiful horse named Uni who had a strange growth on its head, which, when painted with gold paint, looked like a unicorn. There were more, but these were her favourites. Sometimes, when she could, she would brush Uni's mane and whisper secrets to him, though she hadn't dared whisper to even Uni that she had given up her gift for love. The irony was, she should've seen it coming.

Her depression had risen up like a monster after Dimitri had finished with her in a furious argument she had lost quite superbly. His cruelty and coldness to her was shocking compared to the loving words and caresses he used to get her into bed. He had been her first love, a childhood crush which had developed into a mutual lust. Her with her undeniable beauty and him with his elemental sexuality. She had tried to resist the temptation of having sex with him, but she had given into her body one night when they had been camping on the beach. He had snuck into her tent and seduced her.

If her father found out he would disown her, because along with losing her virginity, she would have lost the gift of the second sight. The way things were going, they were sure to find out soon; customers were complaining, and her sister had already found her sobbing more than once. Though she trusted Serena completely, she didn't trust Serena's boyfriend Jamie; the brother and fellow acrobat of Dimitri.

Her chestnut hair was tied back in a black ribbon, and she lay in ripped jeans and a white silk shirt in front of the TV as she fidgeted anxiously. She stared up at the skylight, watching the moon as the caravan gently rocked back and forth. A shadow blocked out the moon suddenly, and Elvira sat up with a start. It sounded as if there were an animal on top of the van. She wiped her eyes, wondering if she'd imagined it, or if her tears had blurred the light for a moment. She stared with her cobalt-blue eyes at the window in the ceiling, defiantly daring something to happen. She got up and looked outside. Past her own reflection, she could see only dense forest moving along in dark shapes. All at once, she felt quite fearful and even more alone. Of course, she could travel through the connecting vestibule cars and get some company, but she was afraid her shame was visible to everyone. She was certain her sorrow would be.

Her phone vibrated abruptly, giving her a jolt, then started singing 'lollipop, lollipop' on the table beside her. She moved to answer it. Number withheld. "Hello?" she answered; a traveller's accent in her curious voice.

"Hello, may I speak to Elvira?" A male voice asked.

"Yes, this is she."

"This is the suicide helpline calling Elvira back?" The man said gently. Elvira's mind raced. *Who had given her name to this organisation? Was it a trick, or was someone genuinely worried about her?*

"Can you tell me who gave you my name? Because it wasn't me."

"I'm sorry, due to the data protection act and obviously the sensitive nature of the call, I'm unable to do so. Do you need to speak to someone about harming yourself or suicidal thoughts?" The man asked, as if speaking to a child or an elderly person who wouldn't quite understand the question.

"I, uh..." Elvira couldn't help it, she burst into tears. "...Suicidal," she exhaled.

"It's okay child, whatever is worrying you we can help take all those worries away."

"That's very kind of you, but I'd rather not discuss it..."

"We run a unique program for certain. . . *important* clientele, and luckily for you, someone has paid your bill and settled the *'Departure from this World'* program for you," the stranger said, still as chirpily as he'd been since he'd started.

Elvira stopped crying, aware that something very strange was going on. She placed a hand on her hip and straightened her back.

"I'm sorry what program?"

"The Departure from this World."

"And what exactly is the 'Departure from this World' program?"

"Well, that's the fantastic part! It can be anything the client asks for. The client paying for your case mentioned your enjoyment of horror, and naturally picked the *Slasher Death* package for you. But it can be literally anything! We could arrange someone to strangle you, stab you, slash your throat, throw you from the train etc. etc."

Elvira gasped, her hand naturally going to her throat protectively. They knew she was travelling by train! Her mind whirled, she felt dizzy and sick. She sat back down. "Is this some kind of sick joke?"

"Oh no Miss, I can assure you this is completely real. We run a very private clientele. Very private you understand?"

"But I don't want to die!" Elvira blurted out, sounding more sixteen than nineteen.

"Well then, you shouldn't have asked for it."

"I didn't!" she protested.

"Please hold..." There was a beep and then music started, Elvira found herself listening to The Smiths singing 'Asleep.' She sighed and raked a hand through her hair. Suddenly, there was a loud crackle and Elvira could hear the fuzzy recording of a party. She immediately went back to the night at hand in her mind.

Elvira had just got off the stage from doing her solo number, a gymnastic, sexy piece to haunting violin music played by her father. She'd made a lot of money that night, and as she was walking off the stage, a young lad slapped her ass. "I'd fuck you good and proper!" he yelled to the delight of his friends, who had started a campfire on the beach nearby. She moved to slap his face, but Tri-clops was faster. He was named Tri-clops because of his third, pale blue eye, which sat just under his left. He punched the boy, sending him falling backwards into a group of his friends, some of whom laughed in uproars.

"Don't touch the ladies!" Tri-Clops yelled, his voice loud and angry.

"Fuck off, three eyes!" one of them shouted.

Then, the one with the bloodied nose threw his beer can at Elvira.

"Whore!" He screamed as the can span through the air, beer slushing out. The can had hit her head, cutting her just below her hairline, and a tiny trickle of blood crept down her face. Elvira listened to the tape transfixed. *Who had recorded it?*

Then Jamie and the acrobat family got into the fight with the boys as Elvira's sister led her away. "Why are people such bastards?" Serena asked. She had Snippy the albino snake around her shoulder as she led Elvira away by the hand.

"I have no idea, but I'm sick and tired of the whole thing!" Elvira whined.

They got to the caravan and climbed inside. Serena started making tea for them both. *No one could have recorded this unless they'd planted bugs all over, and that was an impossibility.* "Elvira, I know you and Dimitri have something going on, and I know it's not really any of my business, but I am your sister and I've never seen you so depressed." Serena poured the hot water into the cups as her snake writhed through her long dark hair and over her shoulders.

"I've never felt so depressed, sometimes I wish I was strong enough to end it all..." Elvira said, palms in her face, knees up on the couch. The moonlight picked up the highlights in her hair.

"You don't mean that. You're not at the 'Thirteen reasons why' stage yet, are you? Because I'm asking you and I love you and I want to help. I can't lose two sisters."

"It'd certainly be a lot easier, just close my eyes and let the problems fade away. I can't stand much more." Elvira sighed deeply as Serena brought the cups over to the table.

"I'm not being funny, but I hate it when people threaten suicide - "

"It'd be too late if I was gone, then you'd all feel guilty!" Elvira shot back.

"Is this about Dimitri, is he pressuring you into having sex? Because he knows you'll lose your second sight, just like our mother... and our sister," Serena added in a whisper.

“Perhaps I’m telling the truth Serena! Perhaps I’ve had enough of this world. It’s exhausting, it’s depressing. It’s a constant uphill battle for some people, and I’m including myself!”

The tape recording came to a loud cracking stop, which caused Elvira to hold her mobile away from her ear. The stranger’s voice came back on the line. “You see Miss Elvira Loveridge, you asked for this. Plus, you asked for it only earlier this day.” Panic seized through her – these people were for real, at least this guy was.

“Well, I’ve changed my mind – I don’t want to die, I said that when I was upset! If you just tell me who your client is I can explain it to him.”

“I’m afraid that’s not how we work Miss Loveridge, but I will give you a heads up. I’d start running if I were you – you have about five minutes. Our dispatcher is usually very quick.” Abruptly, the line went dead.

“Hello? . . . Hello?” Elvira called angrily, but the stranger was gone. She looked up her call log, but the number was withheld. “Bastard,” she whispered. Then she looked at the three entrances to the caravan. There was the front door, the back door, which led all the way to the stables, and finally, the skylight. She hurried over to the front door and locked it, then peeked outside through the peephole and could see nothing but darkness. The sound of the railway track was louder than ever. She hurried to the galley kitchen and grabbed a kitchen knife from the block then used her free hand to dial the police. The number went dead immediately. "What the. . .?" She raced over to the window, opened it, and leaned outside. "Daddy!" Her hair whipped around her face, the air was freezing. "Daddy!" she screamed again, but her voice just came back at her. All she could see was the edge of the carriage ahead. She pulled the window closed and locked it.

This must be a sick joke, just the kind of thing a multitude of staff from the freak-show would pull on her to try and cheer her up. That was when she heard the tapping sound start up. She looked to her left and walked slowly over to the right. The sound grew louder as anxiety climbed up her spine like a little spider. "Hello?" she whispered. She walked slowly over to the door which led to the stables. There was a small walk, which was dangerous, but then you were in the next carriage. She pulled open the door with trepidation, and was met with a gust of wind. Someone had opened one of the windows in the cart next door and Elvira could hear the lambs screaming. Lightning lit up the sky, bluish-white, and Elvira jumped back inside, slamming the door. A few moments later thunder rumbled, causing her to jump. She held the knife up to her chest, her eyes searching the caravan.

A 'rat a-tat-tat' above her, on glass, made her body fill with fear. Elvira looked up slowly to see a black man wearing white voodoo paint over his face, painted like a skeleton. He smiled down at her, a cowl surrounding his face like death. His wide grin was filled with teeth and pink gums. Elvira gasped with shock and screamed. She backed away towards the back of the caravan as the voodoo figure disappeared into the darkness. There was a beat and then a scythe smashed through the glass, shattering the skylight completely. Elvira covered her face as glass and rain showered inside her home. The scythe came down again making more glass fall like rain on the hardwood flooring. She turned around and opened the door towards the cattle van. Using the vestibule between the carriages, she walked outside, the steel frame felt unsteady under her feet and the hand rails were wet and rusty. The smell of forestry smelt ironically pretty. The figure dropped down into the caravan with a thud as she pulled the door tight behind her with a slam. She locked it from the outside as the figure, now visibly dressed in a death shroud, tapped the window with the edge of the blade and smiled. He was wearing a necklace of feathers and beads, and a large white wooden cross like a Loa Haitian God dressed as Death. Even his muscular chest had white body paint marked like a skeleton on his dark skin. He pressed his face against the small round window, stretching his large lips and licking the glass with his pink tongue, then rapidly he dropped out of view.

Elvira turned quickly and walked across the metal beams toward the cart with the animals in it. She raced inside and slammed the door as the rain started lashing down heavier outside. "Please God, I never meant it. I want to live. I want to live," she prayed, thinking of all the times she wished to not wake up or heard other people make similar wishes, and feeling guilty. She raced through the stables and ran to her horse, Uni. Uni whinnied when he saw Elvira, and as she stroked his hair, he gently sighed. "I love you baby boy," she whispered to him. Then, she moved into the darkness to see if the voodoo man had followed. She peered over Uni at the still closed door. Dramatically, it burst open, letting in the wind and rain. The door banged back and forth, but there was no sign of the Voodoo man. Lightning illuminated the stables, and then she heard scuttling on the roof. He was above her, on top of the carriage.

Elvira tried her phone and saw that every call she tried to make was blocked, *either the train was out of signal or Voodoo was using a scrambler to stop her calling for help. Or it's really magic*. No, she couldn't allow herself to think that. She'd seen enough sideshow pranks, enough carnival tricks to know there was always some way to make someone think what you wanted them to think. And this guy wanted her terrified. She stuffed her phone in her pocket and looked up. The scrambling noise on top of the carriage was going towards the next carriage, so she slowly moved backwards, the way she'd come. Then, her mobile phone burst into action, vibrating in her pocket and singing 'Lollipop, lollipop' – he had her number. She threw her phone and it skidded across the dusty floor, back towards the way she came. She heard movement on the ceiling towards the phone as she ran the other way, towards the next carriage. She unbolted the door, ran across the gangway connection, and burst into the next carriage, where a surprised Serena, Jamie, Croc, and Tri-Clops were playing cards at a round table. They looked up at her, shocked. The cards blew off the table in a gust from the wind and scattered around her feet. All except one, which landed on her chest. She grabbed at it. There was an image of a skeleton in a hooded shroud with a long scythe hovering over a young woman. She dropped it like a hot brick. *Coincidence*, she told herself. *Mere coincidence*.

Elvira took a deep breath, determined not to sound hysterical. She kept her voice level as she spoke to them. "Someone's trying to kill me," she announced as calmly as possible with her shaking voice. She braced herself for what would come next.

Serena got up, shocked by her sister's appearance. Jamie's liquid brown eyes wouldn't quite meet hers, and she knew in that instance that he knew what she and Dimitri had got up to; which probably meant her sister also knew.

Serena ran to her sister, wide-eyed and speaking at a rate of knots. Serena slammed the door.

"Who? Who is trying to kill you? Are you okay? They haven't hurt you, have they?"

"I'm fine, honestly," Elvira lied, as her sister guided her to the table. Tri-clops, dressed in a shapeless black suit, stood up, towering over the two petite girls. He punched a fist into the palm of his hand.

"Come on, Croc. I'll kill whatever bastard tries to hurt my little dancing El," he roared in his deep voice. "Where is the fucker?" Tri-clops had spent his life in the carnivals, sideshows, and freak-shows and he was one tough bastard

"Where is he, darling?" Croc asked.

“I don’t know where he is. He broke through my skylight dressed like death with a shroud and a scythe. I barely got here alive,” Elvira explained. Jamie turned his eyes on her, disbelieving.

“Do you know why he would want to kill you?” Jamie asked. They all looked at her.

“Of course not!” she shouted a bit too loudly and defensively. “He must be a lunatic who likes to taunt his victims.” The light in the caravan was dim, but she could see that Jamie didn’t believe her. Serena found a brush and began brushing Elvira’s hair.

“I’m gonna go look!” Tri-clops announced, much to both girls’ distress.

“No, don’t!” Both girls shouted in unison. He ignored them and walked outside into the dark and rain.

“I’ll stay with them,” Croc called after him, beginning to pace the floor. Croc, who could put on quite a show wrestling alligators, was actually a very gentle soul, and Elvira could tell he was scared. A silence descended on the group. No one looked at each other. They busied themselves;

Jamie with his cards and Serena brushing her sister's hair. Elvira took a deep breath and the smell of Diesel petrol and cleaning products filled her nostrils.

"Where is he?" Elvira demanded, looking towards the heavy door swaying in the wind. Something huge and dark suddenly crashed through the window. Glass flew everywhere, sending everyone diving to the floor. Tri-clops dangled from a noose around his neck, his long legs reaching for the glass-covered floor. His hands scraped at his neck and the rope around it as he desperately tried to breathe. Elvira saw his third eye had been gouged out and he had a dark red slash across his face and chest. "Someone get something to cut him down!" Elvira ordered as she ran to him and used her knife to try and cut through the rope. As she sawed back and forth she could see something like a torch moving along the top of the caravan, from the outside. Tri-clops was now gasping horrifically for breath. Her mind went into overdrive as it came to a terrible conclusion. It wasn't a torch, it was flames, and that smell of petrol had not only been leaking into the caravan, it was all over Tri-clops writhing body. “Run! He’s going to set the carriage on fire!” she screamed. She saw the flame spread like a boy-racer going down-hill, it consumed Tri-clops, forcing her away from his body. Croc picked her up and as the trailer went up in flames, Elvira felt cold air hit her face. Serena and Jamie were with them, talking to her, as they moved along to the next trailer on the train.

This car, lit in luminescent green, was where the sideshow kept all of their freak-show exhibits. Baby hammer-head sharks which looked like ‘Aliens’ in huge test tubes. A double headed cat. A puppy with five legs. They all glowed from their Formaldehyde liquid tubes. Jamie helped set Elvira on a dusty sofa and Serena sat next to her trying to get her to come around fully. Elvira felt sick. Tri-Clops’s death was on her. The entire side of her face and arm felt alive and sore from the heat of the flames that had engulfed him.

Jamie was bolting the door they’d just entered through, which Elvira didn’t think was a great idea, seeing as the killer following them had just used fire, but she was too deep in shock to say anything. “We need to keep moving,” Jamie said, panting for breath. Then he turned his face to Elvira, "Who would want to do this to you?" Elvira turned to him from the dusty sofa he'd lain her on.

"I have no fucking idea!" Elvira yelled, not liking the tone of his accusation.

"Give me a break! Someone just set one of our family on fire and you said you'd had a death threat!" he countered.

"The only person I can think of who would want me dead is your sexist pig of a brother!" she shouted. Jamie raised his hand to slap her, and Croc stepped in and grabbed it, holding on to him as he swung him around. Serena jumped up also, leaving Elvira alone.

"Don't you dare touch her!" Croc screamed at him. "You hit a lady, I hit you."

"What the fuck are you playing at, Jamie!" Serena asked. "We need to stick together!"

Then, as if he'd seen a ghost, Jamie stopped fighting and pointed behind the three of them, toward the other end of the trailer, where the door swung open silently. In the doorway, the Voodoo man stood with something like a flute to his lips. There was a whistling sound and Jamie's hand flew to his neck as Serena screamed, then Jamie's eyes rolled backwards, up into his head, and he fell to the floorboards; dust flying up around his body. He pulled Serena down with him, just as a dart flew past her head and landed in the door. "Get down!" Serena screamed, as she pushed Jamie off her legs. Croc charged at the creepy man in the doorway, but he was too slow. A dart hit him in the neck and he landed heavily at the Voodoo man's bare feet.

Elvira pushed the sofa backwards and landed with a thud on her side, as two darts embedded themselves in the fabric of the sofa, causing dust to fly outward right beside her face. Poison darts, she deciphered, or at least something to knock someone out. Serena hid behind the tanks, pushing herself flat against the wall, as the Voodoo man advanced slowly towards the sisters. He walked right over Croc's body, his bare feet positioned perfectly as he crept along, back bent enough so it looked like only a skull and white eyes were looking out from underneath his dripping wet hood.

Serena started talking to her sister in Romani, praying the advancing Voodoo man couldn't understand her. "Elvira, I'm going to distract him – when I do - run!"

"No, I won't. I'm not leaving you!"

"There's no time to argue, he's after you! Just do as I say. . . God damn it Elvira, for once in your life, listen to me!" Serena insisted.

"Okay... I love you!" Elvira called, tears creeping down her dusty face, as she crawled behind the overturned sofa.

"I love you too!" Serena called tenderly, as she watched the distorted figure of death enlarging and shrinking in the reflection of the tanks. She brought both her hands back, readying herself. Elvira prepared herself, crouching on bent knees as she saw the man approaching, his wide eyes searching for her through the many deformed bodies floating in tanks. The trains whistle sounded out like a forlorn, unheard call in the night. Serena waited until he was practically on her and pushed one of the tanks holding the baby Hammerhead sharks. It only tittered at first and she doubted she would have enough strength, but then she saw the Voodoo man's eyes open with glee as he spotted Elvira and she pushed with all her strength. "Now!" she screamed, as the tank smashed over onto the Voodoo man and exploded in a mess of glass and liquid. Though he never made a sound, he went down under its weight. Elvira ran for the door, working her way through the maze of floating freaks. She hesitated for a moment to look guiltily at Croc, noticed he was still breathing, and ran outside into the cold night air, lashing rain, and terrifying thunder.

Serena moved around to see what damage she'd done to the intruder and bent down to see with horror that he wasn't there. Shivers tap-danced along her spine. She'd never seen a magician that good. She lifted his empty shroud, and he appeared inside it again, the garment taking form. "Like tricks?" he mocked, looking up at her. Holding his palm out as if to blow a kiss, he blew green dust into her face and cackled with laughter. Serena's hands went up too late, and she felt dizziness overcome her, a sinking feeling dragging her into unconsciousness. Serena realised this was no ordinary person who had come for her sister. She tried to scream "Run", but her word melted into a coherent mess. She fell to the floor with her friends, her dark hair fanning out.

Elvira heard Serena scream and then felt something like a bee sting in her lower back. Her hand went to it instinctively, as she felt a rush of fresh air hit her face. She pulled it out and looked at a distorted, primal looking dart with feathers of black and white. A beautiful wave of sleepy relaxation swept through her body and the world went dark. The Voodoo man grabbed her before she fell from the train.

The first thing Elvira felt was a dull ache in her armpits and thighs. The pain spread up to her wrists and down to her ankles. The rain lavished drops down onto her, soaking her shirt and jeans until they stuck to her flesh. She was scared to open her eyes, for she could hear the roar of the train and every now and then her body would move with its motion as it chugged along. She could also smell the pines from the forest, and if the rain hadn't given it away, their scent on the cold air would've told her she was outside. Elvira slowly opened her eyes to see the predicament she was in, her hands tied to one carriage, her feet to another (the only thing holding the carriages together were the four emergency pegs.) She also saw the Voodoo man stood at her feet, his eyes wide in her blurred vision. She screamed, as loud and as long as possible, but the howling wind seemed to grab her scream and carry it away.

"I didn't mean it, I didn't mean it, I swear, I swear. . ." She sobbed. The Voodoo man threw back his head and laughed, a mocking, cackling laugh.

"You wished for death, well here I am!" he announced proudly, speaking in an accent Elvira didn't recognise. Then he bent down and pulled one of the pegs out from the train.

"Please don't!" Elvira begged. "I'm pregnant!" Elvira confessed, playing her last card.

The Voodoo man first, slowly turned his head to the left, and then repeated the gesture to his right. "And pray tell, why should I care if I take two lives? Death has no feelings of remorse or pity. Death delights in his job."

Elvira looked at him with shocked eyes.

"A baby, you evil bastard!"

"Don't millions of children die every day? When wishing for your own death, you cared nothing for your baby's life then, did you? Death takes the young and innocent just as much as he takes the old and corrupt. Won't your youthful skin soon begin to wrinkle and decay? You are no different from millions in this world, you just think you are."

"The only blessing you will have tonight is that when these pegs are all free, I don't think that rope will hold long. Then you will be ripped apart, and your baby will splatter on the railroad tracks. Think, what a blessing that will be to you, you have wished for me so many, *many* times, and tonight I have finally come. Many people with disease and pain still pray that I never darken their door, but you, a healthy young girl with pathetic troubles call for me?" Elvira threw her head back, her rain-soaked hair heavy on her neck, and she screamed. She wailed for her life and that of her unborn child. The Voodoo man, or death himself, as he was now thought as by her terrified mind, pulled another peg out, all the while laughing hysterically. Her body became taught and she could feel the immense pressure around her ankles and wrists. She didn't think he would need to pull the other pegs out, she was sure to be ripped in half – no rope was strong enough to hold two train carriages together. Of course, she *was* now the rope. She looked at her feet which were turning inflamed and red. She tried desperately to wriggle them free for the pressure was too much. Death leapt over her body, a black shape in the dark, and crouched down. He pulled another peg out and she howled in pain as it swept through her.

"You should delight in this pain, my girl. So many never get to experience it."

"Who hired you? I beg you, tell me," Elvira screamed at him. He bent his head towards hers and placed his lips next to her ear. His hand rested on the final peg.

"You did!" he announced, before pulling the final peg free and flying up into the air cackling that malevolent laugh of his.

Tears streamed down her face as the rope creaked and her body tried to hold the carriages together. She let out a low, guttural howl, before her body ripped, tearing her arms from their sockets. Her head hit the tracks in a blast of blood and she and her child died, almost instantaneously.

The next morning, as Serena was being placed in the back of an ambulance, she realised there had been one final carriage in the crash the night before. "Who was in the final carriage Daddy?" she asked as she wept silently. Her father climbed in and sat beside her.

"We won't talk about that now honey. Try and get some rest," he placed a cool hand on her wrist, avoiding the drip. She knew her sister was dead, but there had been another casualty. Serena had heard the police tell him but had missed the name.

"Tell me," she pleaded. When he shook his head, she sat up and demanded he tell her. "Who was in the final carriage?"

"Dimitri," he said slowly and sadly, but his daughter looked at him and burst into laughter tinged with hysteria.

"Good. At least that bastard had a sense of humour. Good," she smiled, laying back down. The ambulance turned on the siren and drove away as morning slowly lit up the sky and Serena prayed for life. A long and healthy life.

The End

Frimby's Big Day
By
John Dover

Brother Tom looked upon his congregation of clean-shaven scalps, feminine faces stretched tight by meticulously-spun hair buns, and freshly pressed overalls; he was proud of his flock. They took in the word. They were stalwart in their faith. They were strong and unquestioning. Soon, they would descend on the masses, eager to take up the call of the Cleansing. The large barn resonated with the warm hum of their meditation. He reveled in their devotion.

"It is time to go forth. Today will inspire the un-woken to rise and take up the call. Your sacrament will be blessed, and your sacrifice will be pure."

A unison of "Amen" shook the walls as the Overalls recited their thanks to Brother Tom for his guidance.

Brother Tom beamed as the mass of blind faith filed out to join the rest of the county at the merriment being erected down the road.

*****

"I hate these Podunk towns. I work twice as hard for half the cash," Frimby said, curled over the steering wheel of his vintage, rust-worn RV.

"Stop bitchin'. It doesn't suit you," Tara hollered from the kitchen table where she waged an epic tournament of cribbage with Ed, the Tilt-O-Whirl operator.

"Whatever, Tara. What do you know, anyway? Have you ever tried to warm up a five-person crowd with a collective IQ of sixty-two?" The RV lurched as Frimby bounced over an unlucky groundhog haplessly making its way across the pock-marked gravel road.

"What, you don't like playing to a crowd of intellectual superiors?" Ed chimed in.

Ed and Tara scrambled to rescue their game from the violent jostling and gathered up their cards to reset for the next hand.

“You wanna switch, smart-ass?”

They continued their banter, Ed and Tara ganging up on the disgruntled clown. They had been needling him for most of the drive since he had opted to get himself costumed up before they left on their six-hour haul. He figured they would be pushing their timeline with such a late start.

Tara shuffled and dealt. “You’re always an unruly cuss when you gear up early. You don’t have to take it out on us, ya know.” She grinned at the points fanned out in her hand, her victory a forgone conclusion.

“Don’t you dare talk bad about my prof-ess-ssion-nalism,” a grouping of erratically-sized potholes dribbled Frimby’s vocal chords.

“Jesus, would you watch where you’re going?” Ed shouted, feeling sore — he was about to be skunked by Tara and her run of high hands.

"I *am* watching where I'm going. This road is ridiculous."

The RV took flight, launched by a horse-sized crater that stretched across the road. The galley exploded in a hail of breakfast cereal, macaroni and cheese boxes, and instant coffee. The shower of off-brand groceries washed across the table and the cribbage board was sent hurtling, nearly clocking Tara in the forehead and scattering the game pieces out of sight.

Frimby wrestled his bulbous-toed clown shoe onto the brake pedal, skidding the clumsy vehicle to a halt. The rattle of gravel and dirt belching up from the wheels echoed across the sea of winter wheat and alfalfa that that stretched out and away from the road. A murder of crows, startled by the ruckus, fired up into the sky, flying off to find a more peaceful resting place.

The battered engine coughed and sputtered as the dust from the road blew away from the hot tires. Frimby stood on the brake pedal, holding his full weight down to the floor. He breathed hard, gripping the wheel in his multi-colored, gloved hands.

"What the hell, man?" Ed brushed away the edible shrapnel from the cabinets' eruption. His feigned anger almost hid his pleasure at the forfeited game he had been about to lose.

Frimby pried his hands from the worn vinyl steering wheel, grabbed the gear shift and clicked it up to 'Park'. His legs shook as he released the brake. He turned to face his friends. "You think you can do better?"

"Settle down, Frim," Tara said, casting away the crumpled cards she had mashed in her death grip.

Ed watched the cards drop. He grinned and said, "So you forfeit then?"

Tara shot him a scowl to advise him that he best not push his luck.

Frimby looked out the windshield, breathed out a sigh to release the last of his adrenaline-laced frustration. "Never mind. We're here."

He shoved the RV back into gear and cautiously edged forward. He took the next side road, aiming the snub-nosed vehicle towards the waving flags and the faded, red-and-white tents that marked where the carnival had landed.

*****

Twisty's World of Wonder traveled the country chasing the seasons, North to South, East to West. Their route was cultivated to keep the carnival working through most of the year, with the exception of December and January. The other months they stayed busy enough to keep boozed, fed, and gassed up.

The band of merry carneys had been on the road for six straight weeks without a break, and Frimby was ready to snap. He couldn't wait to be done with this last town on the circuit. It had been a hard season for him, marked with strained muscles, unshakeable colds, and the arrival last week of the divorce papers from his disgruntled ex. It was a banner year, and he looked forward to this being the last weekend he would don his clown regalia for a while.

The RV pulled into the long grass of the field adjacent to the carnival grounds, where the staff vehicles were stowed. Frimby ignored the hissing steam and screeching belts as the disgruntled engine shuddered to its spot. There was nothing he could do about the decrepit vehicle now. The battered chariot shuddered to a stop and the engine rattled to sleep, wheezing goodnight to its shaken passengers.

"Everybody out!" Frimby called over his shoulder. He stashed his keys above the visor of the driver's seat and was off.

"Thank God!" Tara kicked out of her seat and crunched through the coating of Yummy-O's and coffee grounds that colored the floor. She swung the rickety side door open and the cabin was filled with the smells of fresh-cut hay and grease drifting from the food stands.

The trio surveyed the neat rows of canvas tents and booths assembled in their usual order.

Rigged games and novelty attractions were already humming with an early evening crowd ready to partake in the carnival's offerings.

"So, what are your assignments tonight?" Frimby asked as they moved towards the maze of tents.

"I'm at the Tilt-O-Whirl, as usual," Ed said.

"I'm filling in for Madame Mist in the fortune telling tent," Tara bugged her eyes out, dropped her voice to a husky rasp and gave a flowing gesture, evoking the mystic charm of Madame Mist.

"She out sick again?" Frimby asked.

"Yeah. She told Twisty he could take a flying leap."

"Shit. Did he hit on her again last night?"

"Worse. She said yes."

The three gave a collective wince at the thought of seeking pleasure in the arms of the three-hundred-pound chain smoker they all referred to as Twisty. He had taken up the carnival and the name when his uncle had gotten killed by a jealous lover on the road a few years back. Since then, the semi-lucrative operation had been following a downward trajectory, barely keeping afloat, each season promising to be the last. He seemed to pull it out of the fire each year, but no one was convinced that his health could withstand too many more disappointing seasons.

"So, you get the 'look into my crystal ball' schtick this weekend. There are worse jobs, I guess," Frimby gestured to his clown getup.

"I guess, I always feel like such a fraud."

"That's because you are," Ed chuckled and braced for Tara's retort. He was rewarded with a pointed punch followed up with a hard kick to the ass. "Hey!" he yelled and scurried off, evading a follow-up shot and giving a quick flip of the bird as he jogged off to start his shift.

"Don't listen to him, Tara. You know your stuff. Just don't push too hard and stick to the script," Frimby gave Tara a gentle squeeze on the shoulder as he wrapped his arm around her to both reassure her and keep her from giving chase to Ed.

“I know. I bet you’re ready to be done, huh?”

“I am. I just want to disappear down the road and spend the next couple months stoned and drunk, watching sun set on the coast of Galveston.”

“That sounds nice,” Tara leaned in to Frimby’s comforting half-hug as they neared her fortune telling tent. “You don’t want some company in your down time, do ya?”

“I thought you hated the idea of wasting away during the dead months?” Cautious optimism colored his question. Their dalliances were part of the reason his marriage fell apart. But the thought of Tara as a traveling companion was a welcome addition to his plan.

“Well, I don’t know if I can be wholly unproductive for two months straight, but I don’t see anything wrong with a nice coastal detour with you to unplug and maybe see what’s next for us while we’re at it.”

They stopped at the rear entrance of her tent. A small line had formed at the front and she still needed to get suited up in her gypsy getup.

"That sounds pretty good. Why don't we sit down after the show tonight and talk about it? See if you really want to be the road companion of a clown or not."

"Oh, I'll only do it if you keep the costume on full time. Never noticed what a turn on this thing is," Tara gave an aggressive squeeze to his buttocks and chomped at the empty air between them.

They laughed at the morbidly humorous imagery of playing slap and tickle with Frimby in his full clown regalia.

"You're quite wrong. You know that, don't you?" Frimby said, cupping her mischievously grinning face in his felt-laden hands.

"Wouldn't *you* like to find out," Tara winked and gave him a playful smack to the ass before disappearing through the tent flap.

Frimby spun and got into character as he traversed through the growing crowd of overall-clad pedestrians that churned through the manufactured passageways of the carnival's footprint. He noticed the Overalls, but figured it was the adopted uniform of the local farmers, or perhaps it was something else. He was too wrapped up in the limb-tangled visions that Tara had sparked in his imagination to truly notice the monochromatic nature of the people who were gathering in the nooks and crannies of the fairgrounds.

Throughout the grounds, similarly dressed farmers were popping up. They materialized in groups of three: two men and one woman. The men were decked out in pristine, pressed, pale blue overalls, rolled up a bit too high, just above the work boot, a porcelain white t-shirt, bald heads with shaved eyebrows and meticulously manicured beards outlining their jaws.

The women were in similar overall getups, but their hair was pulled back in tight buns without a single hair out of line. The trios walked through the rows of tents, taking in the carnival's looks and smells, circling, and rarely stopping to partake in the activities being offered.

Frimby wove through the crowd and arrived at the back entrance to the main tent. The live show involved a series of acts: ground-based acrobatics, comedians, jugglers, and Frimby breaking up the time between each with his pantomimed hijinks.

"Where have you been!" Twisty growled at Frimby.

"Had some trouble finding this place, boss."

"Then you should have come with us last night!"

"I told you — I had a gig yesterday half a state away."

"You taking gigs on my dime?"

"It's not your dime when it is my time."

Twisty chomped on the mangled log of a cigar that dangled from his lips. "You give me lip and I'll find someone else to take your spot next season."

"Promise?" Frimby rounded on the rotund owner. Frimby was a good six inches taller, but Twisty was not one to back down when stood up to by one of his employees.

"Screw this! You're out!" He spun away from Frimby but was stopped by Cameron, the show's emcee.

"It's the last weekend before break. Can we have one show where you two drama queens don't go after each other?"

"Who you calling a queen?" Twisty smirked.

"Seriously?" Cameron said, his fists balled on his hips in flamboyant defiance.

"It's fine, Cam," Frimby ignored Twisty's tantrum and moved past his boss to confer with Cameron. "What's the crowd like tonight anyway?"

"Hey, we're not done!" Twisty attempted to assert his control again.

"Then take it up with me after the show or you'll lose more money than just what you'll owe me for breach of contract, big guy."

Twisty gnashed on his cigar, a trail of brown spittle edging past the corner of his mouth toward his chins. But the contract comment shut him up. He stormed out of the tent, his howl of aggravation chasing him out and down the alleyway to his trailer.

Cameron and Frimby relaxed and fell into sync as they discussed the evening's show.

"We'll stick to the usual lineup. Everyone is here, so we don't have any holes to fill. There's just one thing,"

Frimby looked at Cameron quizzically. "What's that?"

"Have you taken a look at the crowd yet?"

The concern in Cameron's voice prompted Frimby to go towards the entrance to the inner tent and take a peek. "What about it?" He pulled the flap back a hair to get a look, and then his question came back at him with an answer before Cameron had a chance. "What the hell?"

The stands were full, which was a welcome addition to his shitty afternoon, but it was the characters who filled those seats that made him take notice. While he hadn't paid attention to the obscure townsfolk on his way into the tent, now he was smacked in the face with a full audience of almost nothing but the cast from *Amish Gone Wrong*.

"Is there some sort of dress code I wasn't told about?" Frimby asked as he turned back to Cameron, a perplexed look that not even his thick layer of makeup could hide.

"No clue, my friend. But this whole place is teeming with those folks. It's like someone dropped a Quaker community into the script of *The Hills Have Eyes*, but with a better dental plan."

"Weird," Frimby said, letting the flap fall flat as he turned back to his friend. "Well. The show must go on, I guess. I hope they at least know how to laugh." Frimby squeezed his nose and a gurgling fart sound expelled instead of the usual honk.

Cameron gave a smirk and clapped Frimby on the back. “Indeed, my friend.”

They chuckled together and conferred with the other entertainers, passing around a jug of moonshine for courage as showtime approached.

*****

A chill breeze nipped at the heels of the autumn sun as dusk settled over the plains. The transient lights of the carnival popped on, illuminating the grounds with a soft glow. The grounds percolated with bodies. Ride operators, vendors, and game runners alike should have been ecstatic; this many people generally signaled a banner night. But not everyone was buying what they had to sell. Very few game buzzers or bells clanged from winners and losers. The majority of the sound came from the carneys’ own demonstrations. The crowd buzzed, the carneys barked, and few took notice of the tall man at the entrance.

*****

After a couple of shots of cheap booze, Twisty was ready to mingle and check in with his operators to see how the night was going. It should have been pretty good, based on the rubes he counted moving through his streets. His cheer was stoked as he threw down a third shot and then smoothed himself out to go make the rounds. He figured a preliminary tally of ticket sales would help to quell the remainder of his anger at Frimby.

He opened his door from his trailer and headed out to get the scoop, a fresh cigar mashed between his crooked teeth.

*****

"Step right up and win a prize!" barked Joe, who ran the shooting gallery.

He looked bigger than he was, due to the bulky, weathered flannel shirt that was draped over his skeletal frame. His nimble fingers juggled and spun an air rifle. Even with his sparse musculature, he could whirl the weapon with the ease of a baton twirler leading the marching band onto the field at halftime. Passersby could not help but be mesmerized by his hypnotic routine.

A trio of Overalls approached. Blank faces stared him down, which he mistook for the typical trance he was known to put visitors in with the fluidity of his weapon-based acrobatics. He grinned a scant-toothed smile that stretched his tanned and bristled face.

"Well hi there, strangers. Are you interested in giving a go at my little game?"

The quiet trio moved their stare from his hypnotic twirling to his beaming eyes.

Joe hesitated at their silence and spun his gun to a halt, presenting it to the them in a gesture of welcome. They stood looking at him for a long second, the bustle of the crowd rolling on behind them.

"Are you up to test your aim, gents?" Joe prodded for a response. His rehearsed smile burned with the effort of holding it too long. He bobbed the rifle, luring the rubes to take up the challenge.

The man in the middle brought his hands up under the stock of the gun testing its weight and a relieved Joe let the slight heft of it drop into the muscled grip of the bald man. The man cradled the toy in his thick paw.

"Why don't you take a shot for free to get the feel of it?"

The man lifted his eyes away from the gun to meet Joe's gaze, his dilated pupils devouring whatever color tinted his irises. Joe blinked rapidly and gulped back his discomfort at the awkward stare. Shivers ran up Joe's spine, raising the hairs on the back of his neck. His smile twitched as he futilely worked to disguise the entrapped discomfort he felt from the man's eyes.

He squirmed backwards, out of the line of fire. "Just aim for the red target on the bad guy as he moves past the window," Joe motioned to the rendering of an early century building with the word BANK emblazoned across the top just as a group of cardboard rogues in black-and-white-striped shirts and bandit masks slid past on their motorized track.

*****

The warm weather took a turn. A cold wind blew in, shaking the canvas walls of the carnival. Dust gusted through the corridors, biting at any bare skin that it blew past. The few visitors that were not in overalls yelped at the stinging wind as it gnawed at the exposed flesh from their skirts and tank tops. Dime-store trinkets and down-market stuffed animals blustered on the shaking walls of the game dens. Glass milk bottles rattled as the wind whistled across their tops. Balloons popped, and children cried.

The man at the gate smiled, the glint of his misshapen teeth winking at the discomfort of the lambs that hustled to find shelter. He could not have planned for the timing of the weather, but he was not one to question when the Fates were with him. The shift in the day would add chaos to his plan and energize his followers. His stomach rumbled with the anticipation of the coming sacrament. He licked his lips and moved forward into the fray of what was brewing.

*****

The lights in the big tent rippled with the movement of the walls. The few attendees that were not Overalls looked concerned and clung to each other as the winds outside rapped on the walls to come in.

“We should shut this down and tell everyone to go home if the weather is gonna be like this,” Frimby said to Cameron.

“Are you crazy? I don’t want to tell Twisty that we turned away a full house. He’ll lose his shit over refunding that many tickets.”

“Better his shit than they get spooked and make a run for it and trample someone.”

The howling wind tore at the rippling canvas. The rhythmic rumbling overtook their conversation and Cameron conceded the win to Frimby’s common sense.

Then, the crowd rose. But not the whole crowd — just the Overalls.

A light popped and rained down a dramatic shower of sparks, enhanced by the high shrieks of a couple of skittish attendees. Frimby and Cameron stood in shock, unable to move as the room appeared to move in slow motion.

*****

Joe grew frustrated at the creepy man in the overalls, as he had plugged away at the shuddering targets — without paying — for the past ten minutes. Even as the wind escalated, and people ran for their cars, the man continued to gun down the paper bandits.

"Ok. *Nice* grouping buddy," he pandered to the Overall, "but you either have to pay up or move along. I'm not wasting anymore ammo on you."

The man ignored him and scooped up another cartridge, dropping his empty one on the ground with a metallic thud. He slapped the fully loaded cartridge into the chamber and primed the gun to fire.

Joe's creep-o-meter was on overload and his anger turned his face beet red. He moved over next to the bent-over interloper.

"That's enough. It's time to go," Joe set his hand on the barrel of the BB gun, forcing the man to miss.

The bald man looked up. Joe could swear that the black pools of the mans pupils had grown, swallowing most of the white as well.

The Overall let loose of the gun with his left hand and whipped it around the back of Joe's head, knocking Joe's sun-bleached trucker hat to the ground to join the empty clip. The man's face remained blank as he shoved the small barrel of the rifle into Joe's nasal cavity. Joe looked into the dark eyes, pain ripping through his skull and fear holding his voice captive as the man pulled the trigger, again and again.

The copper projectiles hammered away at the soft tissue behind Joe's eyes. Tears streamed down his face, BB's lodged in his olfactory bulb and ricocheted out through his other nostril. His screams finally came as he fought to free himself from the assault. The monster pushed the gun further into Joe's head until it caught, and he lifted Joe's flailing body from the ground. The click and pop of the air-powered gun echoed through the booth as its payload was emptied into Joe's head.

The man flung Joe up and over the barrier that had separated them, slamming him to the ground. Joe's final painful glimpse of the swirling world around him was of the three heads, two bald and one bun-stretched face, standing over him, brow-less eyes accentuating their flat expressions. Joe's world went dark with a sharp 'pop' as the Overall rammed the gun's barrel through his head, pinning him to the earth in a twitching frenzy. The dry grass beneath him was colored with shining copper BB's rolling out his ear, drowning in a pool of blood and brain.

*****

Twisty's World of Wonder erupted in coordinated carnage, the Overalls turning the family fun zone into a technicolor nightmare of viscera, bone, and immolation. Phillis, who ran the balloon popping tent, had her eyes gouged out with her own darts and was left pinned to the dart board, bleeding on her array of foreign-made prizes. Tim, who manned the funnel cake stand, was dipped headfirst into the deep fryer and held there until he stopped wriggling. Ed was fed to the spinning gears of the Tilt-O-Whirl, his cartilage and tendons torn away from his joints as his limbs were pulled apart, cheered on by his own screams as he watched his body being fed to the powerful machinery that spun the ride. The Tilt-O-Whirl shuddered to a halt when the gears got hung up on his sternum and the passengers were thrown from their cages. A freckle-kissed female Overall took over the controls of the Ferris wheel while her two bald counterparts stood on either side of the ride with machetes. They swung at the passengers as their cars rolled past them, coating the steel carriages in blood and littering the ground with fingers, arms and heads.

Not even Twisty was immune to the Overalls havoc. After arguing about the lack of ticket sales with Alice, the bookkeeper, he wove his way through the booths confirming the disappointing numbers. The violence broke out as he rounded the corner to the Strong Man game, distractedly grumbling at the pages of his log book. The oversized hammer of the bell-ringing attraction crushed Frankie's skull, shocking Twisty into attention as the bell rung 'winner'. Brain matter and bloody bone shards coated his log book and dripped down his face and shirt. He dropped the Frankie-colored booklet and was off in a labored run, the momentum of his heft carrying him towards the park's entrance. A trio of Overalls caught up to him as he reached the *Twisty's World of Wonder* arches and secured him to the flag pole that welcomed guests to his playground. Instead of raising the flag, they raised Twisty high above the tops of the tents, kicking and gurgling as he wheezed his last breath out of his stretched neck. His cigar dropped to the ground as his rotund body swung in the wind, his heels chiming 'goodbye' against the metal post.

Terror ran rampant as the Overalls took control of the carnival. Brother Tom strolled through the mayhem, his arms outstretched as he soaked in the shrieks and cries that fell on his ears like a hymn of praise. The wind blew at his back and carried the macabre lyrics across the waving fields beyond the carnival structures, dissipating into the open terrain with nothing but the birds to call back to the howls of anguish and pain.

*****

Frimby watched as the glimmer of long blades reflected from the hands of the Overalls. The polished glint of steel was transformed into a crimson glisten as the blades were coated in the blood of the innocent that stood among the Overalls in the stands.

"What the fuck is going on?" Cameron asked, fighting back the instinct to vomit as his mind was flooded with the horrific imagery of arterial spray coating the walls of the tent.

"I don't know, but we need to get the hell out of here," Frimby said, pulling his friend back from the small canvas flap. The two turned to face the small crowd of performers. Their looks of confusion and concern prodded Frimby and Cameron for answers.

"Something very bad is happening," Frimby said. "We need to get out of here and find someplace safe to hide or get to our cars if possible."

"What is it?" the pixie-esque contortionist asked, her lower lip quivering and her glitter-highlighted eyes damp with the anticipation of tears.

"I don't know, but I don't feel like sticking around to play twenty questions with these psychos either. Does anyone have any weapons handy?"

A grumble scoffed through the small group. "Does it look like I can hide a saber in this outfit?" Pixie motioned up and down across her skintight, iridescent unitard.

"I've seen your act. Who knows what you can hide in there," Frimby couldn't help himself with the inappropriate joke.

"This is not the time for that crap, man," Cameron said. "Frimby is right, though. Who has anything to swing?"

The juggling team of twin brothers stepped forward. "We have these," they said in unison, presenting their bowling-pin-shaped implements. "They aren't much, but they're something."

Frimby took one and tested the pin's weight. "That'll have to do."

The canvas wall behind them shook. The group turned as a blood-stained chef's knife sliced a fresh portal from the other side. A six-foot-tall Overall stood panting and splattered in blood, looking through the small crowd for his next target. No emotion at all tinged his face — just intent. He homed in on Frimby, the most distinct target, and he moved forward. Frimby hauled back with the juggling implement and swung through, first knocking the sharp blade from the man's hand, then spinning around on his follow through, cracking the pin in half across the man's brow. One blow and the giant slumped to the ground.

Frimby stood over the motionless body.

Cameron and the other performers stood back, mouths agape. "Well, ok then."

"No time to clap me on the back. We need to get moving!" Frimby snapped at them. "Grab up whatever you can to fight with."

Frimby reached down and procured the long blade, slipping it into one of his oversized pockets for safekeeping. He gave a kick to the downed Goliath's head for good measure, picked up two more juggling pins, then followed his friends out to the main tent's stage. They were welcomed to the show by the final screams of the last non-overall-clad attendees as they pleaded with their tormentors until silenced by the quick stroke of a blade severing their vocal chords.

*****

Tara listened to the madness outside the canvas walls of the *Madame Mist: Futures Unveiled* tent. As things escalated outside, she had gone unscathed—so far. She crouched against the wall of her tent, hiding behind the changing screen. The thumps and bumps grazing the canvas walls rattled her nerves and she fought back the yelps and tears that begged to escape her. She clutched at her clothes and winced at the sound of the outer flap drawing open and the muted footsteps of the suit-clad man entering her domain.

“You don’t need to hide, prophet,” Brother Tom’s raspy drawl scratched at the air around her and she held her breath. He smoothed back his waxy salt-and-pepper hair. “I’m just here for a simple reading from a fellow seer.”

He looked around at the campy mystique of Madame Mist’s domain. The room was draped with silk scarves, painted with symbols, and illuminated by a dim lamp and the glowing orb of a crystal ball sitting in the center of the table as it awaited its next telling.

Tara gathered her strength and stood, containing the wobble in her voice that threatened to give away her fear. “What do you want here?” she said as she came out of the protection of the changing screen.

Brother Tom's yellowed teeth gleamed past his slapped-on grin. "I told you. I am here for a reading." He pulled out his chair at the table with the glowing orb. He settled into a relaxed slouch to show he was no threat.

"I didn't mean what you wanted in here. I mean, what is going on out there?" She held her ground, well out of reach of his long arms.

"This?" He gestured his arms around, recognizing the screams, thumps, squishy slashes and gurgling cries of the dying. "Why, this is nothing more than a gentle cleansing of the world." His syrupy drawl oozed past her ears, giving her a chill with each syllable.

Their silence was broken by the tortured screams of the passengers on the Octopus being flung through the air one by one as it whirled out of control.

"A cleansing?" Tara motioned around at the unseen chaos, her fear speckled with anger at the arrogant man who sat in front of her. "A cleansing of what?"

disembowelment of each of his followers upon the promise of reward in the next life. He was proud of this flock in particular. They were the most efficient and the least questioning so far. He beamed at his creation as he wandered the canvas alleyways, the innocents crying for mercy before silenced by the merciless response of their tormentors.

Once in a while he would stop to give his blessing to the final moments of one of the Overalls' victims. They would look to him for approval. He would nod his benevolent appreciation for the work they were carrying out. Then, they would commence with the gruesome act. They would pluck out someone's eyeballs and feed them back to them in a suffocating feast. They utilized the spinning wheels and gears on the carnival rides to flay victims. His pride in their ingenuity and improvisation beamed forth and the Overalls soaked in his paternal adoration of their acts.

This was his *pièce de résistance*, and he almost regretted the inevitable conclusion to his work. Almost.

*****

Inside the main tent, Frimby watched as his friends fight for their freedom from the hellish onslaught of the Overalls. He said silent goodbyes to them as they fell under the strength of the cult's numbers. But, he had said goodbye before. He knew the price of war and was not going to lose this one. He would pay the utmost respect to his fallen comrades by honoring them with the death of one bald-headed psycho after another.

His clown costume drifted from the vibrant rainbow of shining satin with which he had entered the day to a damp, crimson-speckled karate-gi that clung to him in its bloody wetness. He wielded the juggling pins in a spinning spectacle of skilled, death-dealing execution. Cheekbones crunched, skulls split, and knees buckled under his blows. He led his friends through the fray, doling out revenge for the fallen that he could not protect during the siege in the tent. Mourning would be reserved for the victorious and a bottle of single malt, but until then, Frimby continued to mow through the relentless Overalls, until there was just one left. The injured woman knelt before Frimby and Cameron, the only two performers to survive the brawl.

Frimby and Cameron, drenched in their conquests, approached the woman. She knelt, unable to stand, but held out a long, curved blade. It glistened with the blood of her last victim, a Bermuda-short-and-trucker-hat-wearing farmhand who was trying to make time with his girl on his day off. Her defiance and pride in her actions enveloped her in a murderous aura.

"It's over, lady." Frimby said to her.

Her black, dilated eyes stared, unblinking at him. "For you, yes. For me, the pilgrimage is just beginning."

Frimby stepped forward to stop her, but she plunged the blade into her gut, letting loose her insides, splashing the ground in a gooey mess as she spilled out in front of the two men. She slumped over dead.

"Holy hell, man!" Cameron uttered, fighting to hold back the flood of bile, so he would not vomit. "What is going on?"

"I have no idea, but I think we need to see if there is any more we can do outside. I don't think these were the only ones."

Frimby dropped the pins and took up two machetes as they moved towards the tent's entrance.

*****

Tara did not waste any time. She took her chance with the darkness in the room to slip under the nearest wall. She stood just as a trio passed and turned the corner away from her. She dusted herself off and scanned the alleyway for any type of weapon. She was not a trained soldier by any means, but anything was better than nothing, and she was not going to go without a fight. Her gaze landed on a tent spike that had pulled loose when some poor sap had tripped over it. She pulled the eighteen-inch steel spike from the ground and unknotted the securing tether. It was heavy, long, and sharp. That would work.

She looked for the best path back to the RV. That's where she wanted to make her stand. She hoped Frimby would have made it there by now, so they could get the hell out of there. She had to take that chance, if for no other reason than she knew he left it unlocked and the keys stashed in the driver's visor.

On the other side of the tent, she noticed the sound of Brother Tom addressing his followers. "Yes, Brothers and Sisters! Drink of your sacraments and reap the Cleansing!" His gravelly voice boomed as if he was next to her.

She took a beat and scooped up the folds of her peasant skirt, securing the cotton fabric into her waistband forming a loose-fitting pair of culottes. She shook off the chill his voice had sparked, and she bolted in the opposite direction of his hair-raising voice.

Across the park, Frimby and Cameron stopped in their tracks as Brother Tom's words shook their eardrums.

"We gotta see if anyone else made it," Frimby said to Cameron.

"You sure? We could just make a run for the parking lot and go for help."

"Help? Out here? There ain't a town for at least thirty miles! That's almost an hour to get help out here."

Cameron looked disappointed. "I know. Thought I would try. Let's go."

The two headed to the center of the carnival, where the sounds of the Cleansing were less frequent. However, Frimby wanted to make sure there weren't any survivors tucked away in the recesses of the game tents.

As they stalked forward, the scene that unfolded turned their stomachs and heightened their caution. Bodies and blood colored their path: mothers killed protecting their children; young lovers struck down in mid-stride, the life sliced from them in an instant; farmhands and their bosses off for the evening, dispatched with all prejudice. Looks of terror, surprise, and pain mixed with tears and blood splashed across their faces.

“These sick bastards.” Frimby said, shaking his head at the carnage.

“Who would do this?”

“I have no idea, but I plan on taking as many of them down as I can.” Frimby’s grip tightened on the machetes in his hands.

*****

Tara ducked, crouched, and wove through the quieting rows of canvas, making her way to the high grass of the parking lot. Staying low, she arrived at the side door of the caravan. The wind played with her eyes and ears in the grass, teasing her paranoia-stricken psyche. Cautiously, she raised her hand above the line of the grass to test the latch on the door. She did not recall them locking it when they left, but when she jiggled the rickety handle it did not give.

She tried again, but with less subtlety this time. Then she raised up straight to test the door with her full weight. It did not give. Then it shot outward. Tara was blown backward, landing hard on her back, the wind rushing from her lungs. The spike sprung from her grip and rolled a couple feet to the left, just out of her reach.

"Where'd you think you're going, little lamb?" A thick voice rumbled from two hundred and fifty pounds of farm-made muscle wrapped in crisp overalls. His bald scalp and face was speckled in the brown red of drying blood.

Tara coughed, struggling for air to make its way back into her lungs. She looked right and left, searching for her lost weapon.

The giant stepped down, rocking the aged shocks to their limit under his grain-fed girth. The dust on the ground rose with a poof as he dropped from the step, the struts sighing in relief as they rocked themselves free of his heft.

Tara's eyes locked onto her spike. She measured the time it would take to retrieve it compared to when the Overall would be able to reach her. She looked back to him and he stopped. A second bald man rounded the front corner of the RV and a woman, her facial features pulled taught by hair bun, rounded the other side.

"Fuck this!" Tara said. She dove for the spike, swiping it up as she rolled off to the side and bolted back towards the carnival. The three Overalls marched in unison after her. They were in no hurry — she was aimed back toward the park and there were plenty more of them there. Then, she stopped. She spun to face them, braced herself, and wound up with the spike, primed for a throw. She hurled forward and flung the spike in a spinning arc towards the trio. The giant reached out to retrieve the spike, but he was too slow. The spike drove itself through his hand and into the forehead of the bun-head. The giant stood holding her dead weight up, shackled to her corpse by Tara's lucky throw. He shook to loosen the spike's hold. The woman's limbs flitted about like a grotesque marionette. While the giant struggled, the third Overall broke into a run, in pursuit of Tara.

Tara was almost back to the carnival grounds. There was no way she was going to go back to the RV until she knew it was safe. Instead, she figured she would play hide and seek with the Overalls and hope she found other survivors in the process. That was, if she could shake the speed demon that was closing her lead.

*****

"Did you hear that?" Frimby hissed to Cameron.

"I heard something. Where did it come from?"

"I think it came from the direction of the parking lot. Sounded a bit like Tara." Frimby stopped. He turned in the direction of the yelp, the hope of Tara's survival drove him towards the parking lot.

"Hey, what about the others?" Cameron said.

Frimby did not answer. He was hauling his Saturday-morning-cartoon clown getup halfway to the parking lot already, Cameron hot on his heels. They caught their first glimpse of her about ten yards before she hit the camp again.

"This way, Cam. I think we can help her out."

*****

Tara's lungs burned from the sprint. She knew she could not go much longer, but she was not going to make it easy for these assholes. She crossed back into the carnival grounds, and wove in and out of the tents, trying to gain space between her and her pursuer so she could hide and wait him out.

Frimby appeared in front of her, "Duck!" he shouted.

She wanted to tackle him, but she did as he said. She flung herself at the ground just as he swung for home with his machetes.

She hit the ground and a second later was face to face with the bodiless head of the bald man who had given her chase. She scrambled backwards to escape the squish of blood that leaked out from under his chin as his dilated eyes shuttered with rabid intensity.

"Tara, you okay?" Frimby asked.

"No, I'm not okay!" She got herself up and shook off the adrenaline and dust. "What the hell is going on?"

"We were hoping you might know. We were about to start our show when all these wackos stood up and started killing the rest of the audience," Cameron said.

"Jesus. I was getting dressed to do readings and the shit hit the fan. Then there was this crazy guy in a suit that busted in asking for me to prophesize for him."

"Wait, not one of the bald freaks in overalls?" Frimby asked.

"No. He had this slicked back grey hair and smelled like my creepy uncle Rick."

The three exchanged confused looks.

"We need to get out of here." Cameron said.

"I tried. I went out to get the RV but was greeted by this guy and two others. I took one out but there is another giant out there somewhere."

"Good work then." Frimby said. The two men nodded their appreciation.

Their debate concealed the heavy footsteps of the bleeding giant making his way towards his quarry. His lower lip protruded as he pouted the loss of his female counterpart. He hoped his other friend had caught up to the mean lady so they could make her pay for her rash actions.

He clomped through the paths and wove around to find Tara with two other heathens, discussing what they should do next as they stood over the desecrated body of his bald brother.

"Noooo!"

The three turned as the giant rushed at them, one bloody hand wielding Tara's spike.

The Overall reached Cameron first. He batted him away, sending him sprawling. Frimby pulled Tara out of the path of the giant and spun, swinging one of his blades into the back of the man's thigh. The Overall stumbled forward, cushioned by the body of his beheaded friend. Before he could get back up, Frimby drove a machete down and through his thigh, pinning the screaming man face down in the dirt, the handle of the blade just out of his reach.

"Arrgghh! Let me go, heathen pig!" the Overall shouted, pounding the ground in protest.

"Shut up," Frimby said and he moved over to Cameron to check out the damage. "Cam, you still with us buddy?" He sat him up and gave a couple of light slaps to his cheeks. Then, he cracked a sharp slap on him and Cameron's eyes fluttered open.

"What? Ow, knock it off, you dick!" He grabbed at the cut the Overall had opened on his brow with the hit.

"Yep, he's still with us." Tara said with a gentle chuckle.

Frimby threw Cameron's arm over his shoulder and helped him up to his feet.

"Cam, can you make it to Twisty's trailer?" Frimby asked, steadying his woozy friend.

"Yeah, I think so, but why not make a run for the RV?"

"I doubt they're the only ones keeping a watch on the parking lot. Plus, I'm not confident that pile of shit would make it to help."

"Why are we heading to Twisty's?" Tara asked.

Frimby turned to her, a wicked grin playing across his blood-stained face. "For supplies."

*****

"My children gather 'round." Brother Tom hailed his followers. The carnage left behind by Frimby and his friends in the main tent had him concerned. He had not anticipated such resistance. There never had been before. He needed to assess the damage and regroup his followers to make sure there were no strays that could cause future trouble for him. He was nervous. But he could not let the actions of a couple of stragglers ruin the day. "Come, come, my children. Time to gather and praise the ascension of your fallen brothers and sisters."

They filed in after him to the main tent and held back their shouts and screams. How could their brethren have fallen to the sheep? The sheep were being saved by them. Why would they stand up to their enlightened fate? How could a sheep cause this much damage?

"Don't fret your fallen brothers and sisters." He motioned to the bloodied Overalls that littered the floor. "They have ascended to their next stage, as you all will get to do soon." His tone lifted as momentum built in his speech pattern and he found his evangelical groove.

"There are still those amongst us that are working against our efforts to help them be cleansed." The room came alive with the energy of the remaining Overalls. The remaining followers stood tall in a circle around their leader and let him feed off their energy. "It does not matter why they would resist. It does not matter that they have aided your brethren's ascent. It only matters that this world's surface is bleached of their rotten souls, that Hell's flames be quenched with their blood and their cries of pain carry your souls to the next plane."

The Overalls beat their chests in a steady rhythm, ringing through the dead stink of the tent. Their eyes were wide with the need to extinguish the sheep's lives that knew no better than to strike back at their liberators. A guttural hum thumped with their heavy pounding, offset by the crescendo of Brother Tom's call to action.

"We will go forth, my children. We will go forth with the sanctity of grace and we will bathe in the blood of the lambs and cleanse our world of the whores and the thieves that have tainted our lands."

WHABOOM!!!!!

A bald head vaporized in an instant, raining a light pink haze on the ground. All attention turned to Frimby and his pump action, sawed-off shot gun procured from Twisty's trailer.

"Who you callin' a whore?" Frimby growled at the crooked preacher as he cocked another round of heavy gauge buckshot into the chamber, preparing for the retaliation for his insolence.

"Time to earn your place in the realm of peace my brothers and sisters," Brother Tom sneered at Frimby. "Rip his head off."

*****

Eugene Beauregard Clemons, A.K.A, Twisty, was wanted in fifteen of the continental United

States for multiple counts of drunk and disorderly, shoplifting, driving while under the influence, racketeering, public urination, indecent exposure, and — last but not least — the purchase of illegal firearms with the intent to sell. His uncle's death was untimely for his uncle, but more than timely for Eugene.

Eugene saw his inheritance of the aged carnival as an opportunity to wipe his slate clean and get off the radar of the local and federal law enforcement that was ready to close their noose around him once and for all and send him up the river for what probably would have been life, what with the state he kept his health in.

The carnival was Eugene's way of continuing to build his network of buyers and sellers and move his merchandise across state lines under the nose of the authorities. The rumors of the carnival being on shaky financial ground were well warranted, but Twisty subsidized the failing business with the profits from his side business in order to keep his money clean and to keep up the front he needed to continue his nefarious dealings as he traversed the great American countryside providing family-friendly entertainment and a wide assortment of questionable weaponry to those who wanted to exercise their second amendment rights.

Frimby had stumbled upon Twisty's dealings one night outside of Circle, Montana. In exchange for a bump in pay, he promised to keep his trap shut about the guns as long as Twisty kept him on the payroll. He knew Twisty's trailer would have the supplies the three of them would need to throw a wrench in Brother Tom's Cleansing, so to Twisty's they went.

While raiding Twisty's trailer, Frimby, Tara, and Cameron helped themselves to assorted, illegally procured, recreational toys. Frimby was smitten with a sawed-off shotgun with a walnut stock and a box of heavy-gauge buckshot. He duct-taped a long chef's knife to the short muzzle as a makeshift bayonet. Tara outfitted herself with a matched pair of vintage Colt .45's with alabaster grips. In her gypsy garb, she was the picture of an 1800's-era prairie woman on a rampage. She had also sheathed a machete that was strapped to her back in case she ran out of ammunition before the party was over. Cameron had raided the first aid kit and donned a headband of thick bandages making him look like an extra from the crowd scene from *Les Misérables*. To accompany his off-Broadway look, he had strapped on a bandolier belt slung across his chest, loaded with cartridges for his *Dirty Harry*-style Magnum .45 that looked comically big in his small, wiry hands. Frimby could not help but rib him for his choice of a bullwhip that was on Twisty's wall. Neither Frimby nor Tara believed the whip was meant to be used for anything besides a bedroom prop, but Cameron was convinced that it made him look like Indiana Jones.

*****

Brother Tom stood his ground. His followers burst forth with roars and the glint of steel blades swishing back and forth as they drove towards the heavily-armed trio.

Tara was calculated and breathed through every trigger pull. She was focused on shots that would take the threat out, whether fatal or not. Most fell to a well-placed chest shot, but those that got too close were ventilated with a well-placed head shot.

Cameron flung his whip in a wide circle to keep his targets from getting too close. He brought it down and followed the disorienting crack with a thunderous boom from the Magnum. The over-powered hand cannon stripped limbs from bodies with its hollow-point ammunition.

Frimby had one goal, and he would to chew through a wall of Overalls for fruition. Tara gave a nervous directional nod towards the twisted man in the center of the Overalls' circle, marking Brother Tom as Frimby's target. Marching orders silently bestowed, Frimby drove forward. A female Overall lunged for him. Frimby ran the tight-bunned Overall through, her pained cries were silenced as he offloaded her head with the pull of his trigger. Her headless body flew backwards. Frimby locked his aim, center-mass, on another bald man and reloaded in time to spray the ground with the inside of the Overalls' chest.

Overalls fell, one after another. The scent of burned flesh and sulfur coated the air around them. Frimby and his friends stood over the vanquished followers.

Brother Tom stood tall and defiant in the center of the room. He looked upon Frimby and his friends. "Brothers and Sister," his smooth drawl concealed a slight tremble in his voice.

Frimby pulled the pump stock to reload and clicked in an empty chamber. He did it again and he growled in frustration at not being able to silence the slicked-back man.

Tara primed her six shooters but clicked on empty chambers.

Cameron took the cue that it was his turn, he pulled back the thundering behemoth's hammer and was rewarded with an unsatisfying clack.

Frimby stood there, the sawed-off shotgun clicking empty in his hands, panting from his rush of adrenaline, sweat, and pancake makeup stinging his eyes.

"You're empty," Brother Tom snarled, his tailored suit rumpled from the wind and the evening's chaos, his salt-and-pepper hair glistening from the healthy ladling of hair product, held in place except for one rebellious lock that dangled between his eyes. His muscles tingled with anticipation.

"Looks like it," Frimby said. "So now what, preacher?" He dropped the weapon with a heavy thump.

The two men stood panting and sizing up their odds.

"I won't let you out of here!" Frimby declared, droplets of blood tracing pink trails through his makeup.

"You don't have a choice, my son. Fate is my king," Brother Tom proclaimed. "'Tis the hand of God that shields me from the wrath of the unworthy," he continued, his arms out and his face raised to the skies. He brought his dark gaze to lock with Frimby's.

"I'm not your son." Frimby balled his empty fists, defiant and unwilling to submit. "Fuck Fate." Frimby raced forward, splashing the damp ground where stood the preacher. He punched down into the man's face, loosening the last healthy teeth in his head. He stood atop the sputtering man who reached up to shield himself from the assault. Frimby grabbed the man's wispy arm tightly. "And it's not the hand of God that will strike you down, you blasphemous son-of-a-bitch!" Frimby looked down into Brother Tom's terrified eyes. Frimby held the man in place with his oversized clown shoes and yanked up hard. The man screamed as the shoulder popped out of its socket and then, with a sickening tear, was liberated from his body. Frimby hobbled backward with the preacher's flopping arm swinging free in his grip. Brother Tom grasped at the moist, empty socket and screamed. Frimby stood above him, the mocking farts honking from his clown nose and waving goodbye with the disembodied arm.

Frimby wielded the arm like a bat, and swung it across the man's jaw, dislodging his loosened teeth and breaking his jaw. The man couldn't utter the profanities he was thinking. Blood and teeth dribbled from his broken maw. He knelt in the center of the tent, one arm outstretched, the other's socket spraying away the last of his life. His immobile jaw worked to croon a final prayer to whatever God he thought he worshipped. As Frimby stood behind the morbid man, he extended the middle finger of the limp arm then hammered the lifeless limb up, tearing through the seat of Brother Tom's disheveled suit pants, and lodging it in the man's anus. "Turn the other cheek now, asshole!"

Brother Tom gurgled a grunt of horror, disgust, and anguish, sodomized by his own arm.

Frimby stood and walked around to face the fallen monster. Tara came up next to Frimby and placed her soft hand on his shoulder. "He's had enough."

Brother Tom shook with an inaudible laugh, tears streaming down his cheeks. Frimby reached over Tara's head and unsheathed her machete.

"Go in peace, you son of a bitch!"

Frimby stabbed the machete down through Brother Tom's mouth, pinning his body in a knelt position, looking up to the heavens, the handle protruding from his mouth.

*****

Frimby, Tara, and Cameron left their dead friends, the Overalls, and the refuse of Brother Tom where they had fallen and made their way to the nearest town. It was all the local sheriff could do to not lock up the blood-soaked clown when he walked in the door. It took three hours of interrogation for them to send out a patrolman to survey the damage and another couple of days in lockup before they believed Frimby's story and let him out.

It took three days and countless ambulances to cart away the carnage from Brother Tom and his followers' Cleansing. When the police arrived, the air stunk of vomit for hours. They couldn't contain their own lunches at the site of their county's farmers and families torn limb from limb at the hand of the Overalls. They were also astounded by the carnage that a clown, a sham fortune teller, and a comedian could rain down when provoked.

"You're free to go, but we'd like you to stay in the area for a while," Sheriff Francis told Frimby as he signed him out of lockup.

"No problem. I'm on vacation anyway." He signed for his personal items. "So, who was that whackadoo anyway, and how did he not hit your radar before this?"

"Not sure what you're talking about." The sheriff said, a puzzled look on his face as he handed the clean-faced Frimby a paper envelope with his items. "All we saw out there were a shit ton of weirdos in overalls and the local townsfolk and farmers that they killed, like you said we would find."

Frimby went pale. "What about the man in the suit with one arm in the middle of the main tent?"

"No man like that there. You sure you got your story straight?"

Frimby grabbed up his stuff and rushed out to rejoin his friends, his face still pale, as if he had donned his clownish armor again, but instead, washed out from the news of the missing cultist.

The End

The Pinch
By
Ike Hamill

Connor had one foot on a pedal and the other on the ground. His bike was too short for him to rest comfortably in that position, but he shifted his weight again, trying to look as casual as the rest of his friends. The excavator was digging a hole right where the pitcher's mound had been. The dump truck was positioned at short stop, like it was ready pick up anything that tried to bounce through the gap.

"I gotta roll," Michael said.

"I'll go with," Devin said.

The two of them picked up their front tires and spun their bikes around. With a bunny hop off the curb, they were gone.

Connor was left there with Tyler.

He settled on an excuse.

"I better get going, I guess," Connor said. "Mom wants us to go to a thing tonight so my Dad will make me do chores before, you know?"

Tyler never had anywhere to be. He was always hunting for a co-conspirator.

"You don't want to see where that culvert is going to go?"

"Nah. It's depressing. I got my first home run on this field. It sucks that it's going to be another set of stupid townhouses."

"Baseball is boring," Tyler said.

Connor was beginning to notice a trend. Anything that Tyler was terrible at was deemed boring.

"I'll catch you tomorrow," Connor said. He started to turn his bike around.

"You know what this means, right?"

Connor paused.

"Think about it. Where are they going to set up the carnival now that this lot is under construction?"

Connor shrugged. He hadn't thought about it at all. The carnival was a fun diversion back when he was in grade school, but it was only in town for a few days. It didn't matter nearly as much as losing their best baseball field. Connor only had one summer left before high school. He had to improve his fielding quite a bit if he wanted to make the JV team.

"You of all people," Tyler said. "It's going to be right behind your house, idiot."

"Okay," Connor said. "Whatever."

#

It took him forever to pedal home on the old BMX bike. It just wasn't meant for any kind of distance riding and it was way too small for him. Now that the good baseball field was being torn apart by excavators, he would have to pedal all the way over to the rec center to practice with his friends. That would require a better bike. A better bike would require more money.

The logic of his request was completely solid by the time he rolled down his driveway and jogged up the back steps.

He paused on the back porch, looking over the fence. The fields there were private. They didn't even let kids take shortcuts across that field. The last time Connor had tried, they had chased him all the way to Miller Street.

It would be weird to have a carnival there. Tyler couldn't be right about that.

Inside, his Dad was busy at the stove.

"Hey, Dad?"

"Run upstairs and shower before dinner. You smell like a locker room."

"Okay. But, Dad? Do you think you could loan me twenty-five dollars?"

"Shower."

"You told me I had to pay for it myself, but if you loan me the last twenty-five dollars I'll have enough to buy Sully's old bike now, and then I can bike over to baseball practice this summer so I can make the team and..."

His father raised a wooden spoon, cutting him off.

"Remember--all prices are a negotiation. We have bigger fish to fry right now. Shower. Dinner. Discussion. In that order."

Connor turned and headed for the stairs. He actually felt pretty good about the interaction. He had gotten out the major points of his argument and he could let them simmer with his father until after dinner. The hard work was done. His father usually responded to logic eventually. It just took some time to simmer.

#

He ate fast, keeping his eyes on his parents while he ate to gauge their mood. What he saw wasn't good. His mother had come in just as the plates were being set and she had sighed when his father asked how it was going. Her eyes kept landing on the empty seat across from her. It was Helen's chair.

The last time he had seen his sister had been three days before. His parents wanted to make sure that his sniffles were only allergies and not some kind of virus. They couldn't risk infecting Helen when her immune system was so depleted.

Connor's thoughts wandered. All prices are negotiations--that's what his father liked to say. It drove his mother crazy. They would be over at the hardware store, trying to rent the rug cleaner for a day, and his father would attempt to haggle with the clerk. If the cleaner could be rented for a full day or half day, why not for just two hours? What would be the price for ninety minutes? His mother would always make the point that this big, nationwide store set their prices in some faraway headquarters. A local clerk didn't have discretion to set their own pricing.

The worst part was how often his father managed to secure a discount.

Connor was much more like his mother. He would rather pay the regular price than suffer the shame of trying to haggle. When his father had asked about the price of the bicycle, Connor had made up a higher price and then bragged that he had negotiated down to the real price.

Pressing a napkin to his lips, his father finished his dinner and pushed back slightly from the table. Connor had been done for several minutes, but he had been sitting quietly, waiting for the right moment to bring up the loan again.

"We want to talk to you about the next few weeks, Connor," his father said.

His mother's eyes went down to her plate. This was a bad sign. When bad news came, she always lost her voice.

"It's good news," his father said. "Your sister is going to be able to participate in the new protocol."

Connor blinked. He wanted to believe his father that this was good news, but his mother's demeanor was much more persuasive. A memory flashed through him--they were sitting around Helen's room when the oncologist had talked about the new protocol. Helen would be eligible if her condition took a turn. So it was both good news and bad. The good part was that the new protocol had an excellent success rate for the patients they accepted. The bad part was that when they said, "took a turn," they always meant a turn for the worse.

His father was choosing to look at the bright side. His mother was focusing on the dark.

For Connor, the worst part about seeing his sister getting so sick was watching the way she changed. She used to be so playful and innocent. Now, she was sarcastic and weary. The cancer had eroded her childhood, leaving her like a cynical adult trapped in a kid's dying body.

"That means that we all have to go to Turner General for three weeks so they can get her started."

Connor didn't mean to drop his water glass. The sides were slippery from condensation and his grip must have faltered. The glass slammed back down to the table, only spilling a little. His mother was so startled that she looked at him with wide, frightened eyes. A moment later, her concentration was back on her plate.

"We've talked about it, and you don't have to go. We know you're looking forward to baseball practice this summer and we want to support you in that."

When he started breathing again, his heartbeat thudded in his ears.

"We'll make some calls and see if you can stay with one of your friends for a few weeks while we're gone. Worst case scenario, your aunt will come stay with you here."

His mother stopped chewing as she shot his father a look. She didn't like it when he referred to her sister as the "worst case scenario." Connor was inclined to agree with his father. His aunt was absolutely the worst. Then again, she was likely to be the only scenario. His friend Michale was out. Michael's father was currently feuding with every other parent. Connor's mother considered Devin to be a bad influence. Tyler's mother didn't even let anyone spend the night at their house.

Connor struggled to think of who his parents would even call. He was so preoccupied that he forgot to bring up the loan at all.

#

From his bedroom window, Connor could see over the fence and across the field to where the workers assembled the ferris wheel. They pulled two trailers side by side and took forever placing and leveling them before they raised the arms that held the center axle. When the trusses were tilted into place, they unfolded like a giant fan. Connor spotted some kids at the edge of the field.

He tried to sneak outside, but his aunt caught him.

"Where are you going?"

"Nowhere. Just the back yard for a minute."

She was like a warden. He couldn't even turn on the TV without her checking to see what he was watching. The last time he had stayed with his aunt, he had been eight or nine. It seemed like she still thought he was the same age.

Connor crossed his back yard while the workers were hanging the first basket on the ferris wheel. They rotated the wheel all the way around to attach the next one on the opposite side.

"Hey," he said, over the fence.

Only Tyler turned around.

"Where have you been?"

"Prison. My aunt won't let me go out on my own," Connor said, hooking a thumb over his shoulder.

"How long are your parents at the hospital?"

"A few more weeks."

"You better find a way to catch up with Sully," Tyler said. "He said he's going to sell his bike to that kid on Wakefield Street."

"I don't have the money. My Dad said he would loan it to me, but then he forgot. My aunt was supposed to give it to me, but now she says that it seems irresponsible or something. I think that she doesn't have it."

"Just make her give it to you."

"How?"

"I don't know. Just take it. When my parents go away, I stay on my own. We're practically men, for Christ's sake. In some parts of the world, we would be married and having kids by now."

"They have bikes and baseball in that part of the world?"

"Bikes, yes. Baseball, probably not. You'll have to take up soccer or that game where they roll around a goat's head," Tyler said.

Connor rolled his eyes. "I'll stay here then. I'm not ready to have a family of my own."

Tyler nodded.

"You're coming to the fair tonight, right?"

"Can't. Irresponsible, according to my aunt."

Tyler shook his head. "You don't have to put up with this, you know?"

It was a tantalizing idea. Connor thought about what that might mean. He could defy his aunt to her face. That would make her panic and call his parents, who would probably support him. He had proved himself to be responsible, so they were pretty good about letting him do what he wanted to. Then again, the last thing they needed was extra stress and worry about drama at home. They had their hands full with Helen, and his sister needed all the help that she could get.

Tyler voiced a new idea just as it was germinating in Connor's head.

"Didn't you say your aunt goes to bed ridiculously early? The fair is open late. Why don't you sneak out and meet us?"

As he said no, he was already picturing it. She was on the opposite side of the house, and he could easily slip through his window, cross to the garage roof, and then climb down where the stockade fence met the back of the garage. His aunt would never know, so nobody would be stressed out.

Even if his parents eventually found out, they probably wouldn't care. They were always encouraging Connor to make responsible decisions and take care of himself. In the current situation, the best approach was to leave his aunt out of the process because she would worry too much about him.

The other kids that stood beyond Tyler were beginning to move across the field.

"I gotta go," Tyler said. "I'll be out here tonight if you get sprung from jail."

Connor nodded. "Hey--tell Sully I'll get him the money, would you?"

Tyler raised a hand in answer as he walked away.

#

It all went exactly the way he had pictured it. The hardest part was manipulating the screen so he could pull it back through the open window without dropping it. Once that was done, Connor shuffled easily across the roof on his butt, transferred to the garage roof and then found the top rail of the fence with his foot without even looking. Dropping to the ground, he figured that things were going so smoothly because he was doing the right thing. He was taking care of himself and not causing anyone else stress in the process.

The excitement that built up inside him as he crossed the field was a buzzing current of energy. This was his carnival. For the first time, it was practically in his back yard and he was on his own. Everything was falling into place.

Over at the ferris wheel, in the snaking line, he saw Devin and Andrew. Connor picked up his pace when he saw Michael and Tyler walking up to the guys with snow cones in their hands. All his best friends were there. They waved Connor to their place in the line when they spotted him.

"Hey."

"You made it," Tyler said.

"You weren't at baseball today," Michael said.

"My aunt wouldn't drive me," Connor said. "She had a migraine."

"My dad gets those," Andrew said. He was trying to negotiate a bite of Tyler's snow cone, but Tyler kept turning his shoulder on him.

"We have to break into two groups," Devin said. "Only four can go in a car on the ferris wheel."

The couple behind them in line were shooting them dirty looks. The line was long, and they had just been bumped back a place by all the new kids who had cut in with their friends.

Connor spoke quickly to mollify them. "It's okay, I'm not riding. I don't have a ticket."

"I'll spot you one until you get some," Tyler said.

"That's okay," Connor said. He was still saving every penny, hoping that Sully would keep his promise and sell him the bike. If that was going to happen, Connor would need every bit of his savings.

"I heard you can see all the way to the river from the top of the ferris wheel," Michael said.

The wheel stopped and the line moved forward as one of the baskets was emptied and refilled.

"I gotta see that," Andrew said. "Come on, Connor. Borrow a ticket and you and me will go up in the second car. When we get to the top, we can see who can spit the farthest."

Connor rolled his eyes. "Don't you remember what happened when you wanted to see who could spit the farthest off the back of the bleachers? Some of it got on that guy and he chased us for three blocks. You ran so hard that you puked. And, Michael, you live, like, a block from the river. You see it every day, as close as you want. Why do you want to see it from way up in the air when it's dark out?"

Michael shrugged.

The line moved forward again.

The other boys stepped up on the metal ramp. Connor held his ground on the grass.

"Come on," Tyler said, waving one last time.

"Forget him," Michael said.

The boys advanced in line. Connor almost reconsidered and then remembered the bike. He shoved his hands deep in his pockets and felt the money. He had brought it along in case he saw Sully. A downpayment might keep Sully from selling the bike out from underneath him. It was a risky thing to do--the money seemed to want him to get on the ferris wheel with his friends.

Connor turned before he could change his mind.

The other boys had already forgotten him. They were laughing about something and making guesses at which basket they were going to get to sit in, hoping it wouldn't be the dirty yellow one.

#

It was difficult to make his way down the crowded lane between the rides. With a group, people would split around them and they could join the flow of traffic. Alone, everyone expected Connor to get out of their way. He was constantly dodging left and right. Couples holding hands were the worst. They made a blockade that forced Connor to reverse direction to get around.

Everything cost money.

The food, the games, and the rides were all useless to Connor. He spent a few minutes walking through the petting zoo, but even the animals turned a cold shoulder. They nosed up to the kids who had handfuls of feed that they purchased from the dispenser. Connor was left petting a lazy calf who was stretched out on the straw, taking a nap.

Even though he couldn't play the games, the callers drew him out to the midway. He watched a young man desperately trying to knock over a stack of wooden blocks with a baseball. No matter how hard he hit the stack, he couldn't drop more than one or two blocks with each ball. It wasn't like bowling, where a person could hit the lead pin and watch the rest cascade. These blocks seemed oblivious to the ball, spinning and teetering, but never falling.

Connor watched as the young man failed. A group of spectators were taunted by the caller.

"Who's next? Who's next? The young lady in the back? You look like you have a sturdy arm. Don't let the young man's failure put you off. He had clearly never thrown a ball in his life."

The young man shot a dirty look over his shoulder and then moved away fast before he could be taunted again. A group of girls were trying to push money into a mother's hand. Connor recognized her. She coached the softball team and could strike out even the boys varsity baseball team. She pitched underhand with a windup, which the baseball players claimed was unfair.

"Come on, mom!" one girl said. She was a couple of grades younger than Connor. He hadn't realized that the coach was her mom.

"No. I told you, it's not about speed. Those blocks don't care how hard you throw. It's just luck, or it's rigged."

"You can do it."

Connor wanted to see her try.

"Why don't one of you try?" the coach asked.

The girls were still trying to egg her on.

"Maybe it's the angle," Connor said. "Or the spin."

The woman actually heard him. She glanced at Connor and he saw her thinking about what he had said.

She pointed at him. "You play ball, right? Do you pitch? Why don't you try?"

Connor shook his head. He had tried pitching, but he was terrible at it. His arm gave out fast and he had no control whatsoever. When he played outfield, he was lucky to get the ball anywhere near the cutoff guy.

"I don't have any money," Connor said, instead of explaining his shortcomings.

"You try, mom," the girl begged again. She was holding out her own money to her mom.

Connor nodded at the coach.

She finally accepted the dollar and advanced.

It was over fast. The coach had been right. It didn't matter that she put the ball exactly where she wanted, or hit the blocks with amazing speed. Only a couple of blocks fell, while the rest wobbled, spun, and stayed upright. After the third throw, the coach had to settle for a small rubber bracelet. The woman seemed disappointed. The group of girls were already onto the next distraction.

Connor leaned against the side of the stall, hoping that someone else would try. There was something funny about the way one of the blocks had nearly toppled and then stayed standing. It didn't have a string or pin holding it up. The caller working the booth had swept down all the blocks with his arm before setting them back up. There had to be some kind of trick though.

"You're not playing?" someone asked him.

He turned and saw a kid about his own age.

"No. Go ahead."

"Why don't you try? That lady said you play baseball, right?"

Connor paused. He hadn't realized that his conversation with the coach had been overheard, and he didn't recognize this kid. He had the sense that he shouldn't answer, like it was a trick somehow. But it seemed impolite when the kid was standing there, waiting for him to say something.

"Yeah, but I'm better at batting than throwing."

The kid nodded.

"Still, you could try."

"No money."

"It's only, what, a buck?"

At the conversation about money, Connor's hand itched to be back in his pocket, making sure that his wad was safe. That was a stupid impulse, and he knew it. If this kid wanted to steal his money, the worst thing Connor could do would be to reveal where he kept it.

"I don't even have a buck," Connor said. "Completely broke. That's why my friends are up in the ferris wheel and I'm down here."

"Good," the kid said. He glanced around and then leaned in. "You want to make some money?"

#

He knew it was a mistake even as the word crossed his lips.

"Yeah."

The kid smiled.

He spun around and stood next to Connor. Leaning back against the wall, side by side, they were just two friends, having a conversation.

Connor realized that he was taller than the kid. He was bigger, too. If it came to a fight, he could hold his own. For the moment, he decided to hear what the kid wanted to say.

"My dad runs one of the other booths. On a good night, he makes plenty of money. On a bad night, nobody will give him a dime. It's all about the crowd."

"Yeah?" Connor asked. He wondered what kind of scheme was coming his way.

"It's all about getting one or two key people to play. Once the dam breaks, a constant stream of people will want to try. Like you just did with that lady, you know?"

Connor shook his head. A young woman, maybe just out of high school, was talking to the caller and handed over her money to give the game a shot. She was the first one to play since the coach had failed.

The kid leaned closer so only Connor would hear.

"If you hadn't gotten that other lady to play, this girl here wouldn't be playing. Once she goes, one of her friends is going to go. In twenty minutes, you watch--there is going to be a line of girls wanting to play because the softball lady played. These other girls look up to her. These games are contagious."

Connor shrugged. He had no reason to believe or doubt what the kid was saying. He had forgotten the reason that he was even listening to the kid in the first place.

"That's what we need you for. You, or someone else who wants to earn some money. We travel around and people don't trust us. These games are fair, but people want to believe that we're all crooked and out to steal their money."

"Okay?" Connor said. He guessed what was coming next. This kid wanted someone to vouch for the games or something.

"So my dad needs someone to prove that the games are crooked."

"Huh?" Connor asked.

"Come on. I'll explain."

Connor stayed put as the kid started to walk away. The kid stopped and waved to him, coaxing him along. Connor frowned. His fingers were itching again. He stuffed his hands into his back pockets as he pushed away from the wall and reluctantly followed the kid. The kid might be small, but he was surprising. Connor reminded himself to stay on high alert for any trickery as he followed the kid into the stream of foot traffic.

Everyone else seemed to have the same immediate sense of the kid that Connor had. He wasn't from around here. Traffic parted around the kid like he was the school pariah and might have cooties. Connor was swept into the slipstream. The kid talked over his shoulder and gestured with his hands as they walked.

"If everyone believes that the games are winnable, then they also believe that the prizes aren't worth anything. We want them to know that the games are rigged but there's chance to get something valuable if they could beat the system."

"Okay?"

"Like those blocks. There are magnets in them. That's why it's hard to knock them down. But it's not impossible. You just have to finesse them and they will fall."

Connor looked back at the receding booth. It made sense. Still, he wondered how one might finesse magnetized blocks. Maybe he had been right about putting a spin on the ball.

The kid seemed to read his mind.

"You were right--it's all about the angle and spin. It's the same thing with the ring toss. That's the booth that my dad works."

The kid pointed at the stall on the end. It was easy to believe that the man calling and gesturing was the kid's father. They shared the same eyes and black hair. He also gave his son a tiny nod as Connor and the kid approached.

Nobody was playing the game, despite the kid's dad calling out to everyone who passed by.

"The rings are super bouncy and they just barely fit over the tops of the bottles. Watch when my dad slips them over to demonstrate. You see the way he holds the ring perfectly flat? That's because if the ring is tilted at all, it doesn't go. The way people throw, they always tilt them back a little. It's hard to get them on. If you show people that it can be done, they will play. Every five people who play, dad will give you a cut."

"I can't."

"What do you mean? You have something better to do?"

Connor shrugged. "No, I mean I'm not going to be able to throw the ring flat either."

"That's not what I mean by showing them. You just have to show them that you figured it out. You don't have to do it."

"I don't understand," Connor said.

"Keep walking. We don't want too many people to see us talking together, okay? Then you'll get the stink too. My name is Shawn, by the way. Let me tell you exactly what to do."

#

Connor wandered back towards the booth just as a pack of older kids was walking past. He wanted to call out to them, but that's precisely what Shawn had told him not to do. The booth already had a caller, and it was Shawn's father. Connor's role was to only engage with people once they were already halfway ready to play.

He positioned himself to the side, so he could get a good look at the way that Shawn's father demonstrated the rings.

It was a tight fit. In fact, it seemed like maybe only the bottles in the back row had necks small enough for the ring. Shawn's dad never leaned far enough forward to demonstrate the ring on one of the closer bottles. It seemed like there were multiple tricks at play.

"Sir! Sir! Wouldn't like like to win this giant panda for your lovely daughter?"

"Son," the big guy looking at the booth said.

The caller shielded his eyes against the light and blinked. "My apologies. So sorry. Still, it looks like your boy has his eye on one of these stuffed animals. I'm not going to lie--they're hard to win, but worth the effort."

Connor pushed away from his spot, where he had been eyeing the bottles. He set a path that took him close to the family. The kid was several years younger, but Connor caught his eye as he passed and said, "It's a trick."

"Huh?" the kid asked.

Connor kept his voice low. "The rings only fit on the bottles in the back, and only if they're perfectly flat." He demonstrated with his hand.

The father looked down, having overheard. Connor gave him a nod. With that, Connor left the family. None of it made sense. He had followed Shawn's instructions, but he had clearly just talked them out of trying. Nobody would be stupid enough to spend money on the game once they knew how it was rigged.

He was supposed to keep walking, but he couldn't help himself. Stopping in front of the balloon-popping booth, Connor knelt to tie a shoe that was already perfectly tied.

Back at the ring toss, the father leaned down, had a brief exchange with his son, and then approached the booth with money in his hand.

It didn't make sense, but it was happening. Connor stood up and watched with a blank expression as the man paid, tried, and failed miserably. He hadn't even gotten one of the rings to stay in the bottle crate, which would have won a plastic dinosaur for his son. The father and son walked away. When they passed by Connor, the father said, "You were right."

Connor was mystified. He wanted to try it again.

#

Connor hung out near the booths all night. Even when his friends found him and tried to talk him into going on other rides, Connor stayed put. He worked for the woman who ran the stall where people tried to pop balloons with darts. Then, seeing his ability to sway customers, the guy at the sharpshooter stall called him over. Before long, Connor had a circuit going. He wandered between a series of stalls, gentle swaying people who were on the fence.

These people considered themselves too smart to be manipulated by the operators who called their patter out to the passing crowd. But with a few words from a kid, some of them could be swayed. The idea was fascinating to Connor. He had never thought of himself as persuasive, but maybe he had been approaching the process all wrong.

Connor was lost in thought when Shawn found him again. Truth be told, he had forgotten all about the money promised him. The work itself had drawn him in.

"Come over to the fire circle and my dad will give you a cut," Shawn said.

Connor glanced around. The carnival had thinned out substantially. His friends had gone home. The families dragging around sticky toddlers had left long ago. The only people left were lovestruck couples, holding hands and strolling, oblivious to the world around them.

"I better get home," Connor said.

"You're kidding, right? Come get paid. You were hustling all night," Shawn said.

"Where is it?"

"See that little campfire, behind the Pharaoh's Chariot?"

Connor nodded. "I'll be there in a second."

Before Shawn could try to persuade him, Connor dashed off. He ran down the line of stalls, back towards the ferris wheel and then continued into the dark field before he took a sharp left and headed back towards his house. He didn't want any of the carnival people, especially Shawn, to know where he lived. Crouching behind a bush, he took out the money buried deep in his pocket and secured it under a flat rock next to the stockade fence.

To see the window of the guest room where his aunt was staying, he had to climb halfway up the fence and peek over. Her light was out. Except for the blue glow of his own window, the whole house was dark. She hadn't woken up, discovered him gone, and searched the house. There were no police cars parked in the driveway. For the moment, he was safe.

Walking across the field, back towards the ferris wheel, he watched them turn off the lights of the rides, one by one. The giant wheel of lights was the last to go out.

Connor remembered something his father had said to him--"Don't ever be embarrassed to admit that you're afraid. It could save your life."

The advice was referring to a very specific event. When Connor was a little kid, his father had taken a nap and woken up unable to pull in a deep breath. Sitting there sweating, between dry heaves, he had grown pale and then a disturbing shade of gray. Connor's mother wanted to call the ambulance, but his father kept saying no. Eventually, she called without his permission. The nausea and shortness of breath were from a heart attack and the call saved his life.

His father hadn't wanted the call because he had been embarrassed to admit that he was afraid.

The advice had a second line that was tacked on maybe the third or fourth time his father had conveyed it.

"And, once you admit it, don't ever be afraid to stand up to what scared you."

Connor was afraid of going to the fire and he was embarrassed to admit that to himself. Now that he had, his next job was to stand up to what scared him.

A dark shape stepped out from behind the popcorn stand and Connor sucked in a startled breath.

It was only Shawn.

"Hey! You came back. I didn't think you would."

They circled the Pharaoh's Chariot and Connor saw a bunch of people sitting on stumps and rocks around the campfire. People were laughing. A woman passed a big bottle to the man sitting next to her. An gray haired man in overalls stepped up to the fire, crumpled something, and tossed it in.

"Of course I came back. I have to collect my pay, right?"

"Yeah," Shawn said, he tugged on Connor's arm and pointed him towards where his father was sitting. Shawn's father pointed and smiled when he saw Connor approaching.

"The boy!" the man said, pointing. "He's the reddest shillaber we've ever stumbled on. You want to hit the road with us, boy?"

Connor felt heat rush up to his face. It wasn't from the fire.

The man next to Shawn's father was shaking his head. "Wouldn't work. Two days of road grime and the buzzards would smell him."

Shawn leaned closer Connor and whispered to him. "You have to mention that a worker should be paid."

"I have to ask for my money?" Connor whispered back.

"No. You don't ask for it. Just say that a worker should be paid."

Connor cleared his throat and waited for the men to stop laughing.

"Excuse me," he said. Connor stood up straight and made himself continue. "A worker should be paid."

After a tiny pause, everyone surrounding the fire burst out laughing. Connor felt another wave of hot embarrassment rush through him. The only thing that kept him in his spot was Shawn's hand slapping him on the back.

"You're a gem, kid," Shawn's father said with a cough. "And, for a great night's work, I'm going to give you your cut with an extra five."

The man counted out three fives and a stack of ones that brought the total on the rock in front of him to twenty-five dollars. Shawn's father collect the stack, rolled it so that the fives were on the outside, and then held out the roll for Connor. Shawn elbowed him and Connor took his pay.

He realized that he had precisely enough money. All he had to do was find a way to get it to Sully and he would have his bike. With that hurdle cleared, he was sure that his aunt would let him go to practice on his own. Maybe his parents would have to order her to let him ride alone, but that would be the easy part once he had his own transportation.

With the money in hand, Connor slipped backwards, away from the laughing men, and felt almost like his feet were floating over the ground. He never could have predicted any of the events of the night. It felt like he had stepped into a movie. Things like this didn't happen to kids that he knew.

"Hey," Shawn said.

He caught Connor's elbow just before he slipped out of the circle of light from the fire.

"Thanks again," Connor said. "This was fun." He stuffed his new roll of bills into his pocket.

"Just one more thing though," Shawn said. "You have to give a pinch."

"What?"

Connor was ready to run. It had been fun, but there's was always one more thing with Shawn. It was time to end the night while he was on top.

"This is important," Shawn said. In the flickering firelight, the smile was gone from the kid's face. For the first time, Connor thought that Shawn was being completely sincere. The idea frightened him a little.

"We all give a pinch of any money we earn to the Deuce, you know? You have to bribe the Deuce to stay safe. Some people say that you also have to thank him for your good luck. I never bother with that, but if you don't give the Deuce his pinch, he tracks you down in the night. Bad things happen if you don't pitch in four cents."

"I don't have any change," Connor said, still not understanding what Shawn was talking about.

"No, not change. You got twenty-five, right? Four cents of twenty-five is a buck. You have to pitch in a buck."

Connor thought for a second and realized that Shawn didn't mean four cents, he meant four percent. He was supposed to give four percent to someone.

"Wait. To who?"

"Not to anyone. Just to the fire. You give a buck to the fire for the Deuce. It's a tradition and it's really important. If people don't give a pinch, bad things happen to the rigs, you know? Whole wagons have gone down because someone shorted the Deuce. He always finds a way to get his pinch."

Connor shook his head. He couldn't make sense of any of it. There was too much lingo in the kid's sincere speech.

Shawn took a breath and started over. "Listen, you see what Miss Nan is doing?"

He pointed at a woman who was holding back her skirt and long sleeves so she could lean towards the flames. When her hand was over the fire, she dropped something in.

"Everyone gives a pinch. Your pinch is just a dollar. Do it. Trust me."

"Throw a dollar in the fire?"

Shawn nodded.

Connor had no basis on which to argue. It didn't seem like Shawn was trying to trick him. It was all found money. Giving back a dollar of money that he hadn't been expecting to earn wasn't the biggest hardship.

Connor shrugged and walked over to the fire. Deep in his pocket, his fingers found the roll of cash and kept going. There was something else down there--some forgotten scrap. He pulled the paper from his pocket, crumpled it, reached out, and dropped it in. Someone laughed and Connor shot a look. The man didn't seem to be laughing at him. As far as he knew, it hadn't been a joke.

"Cool," Shawn said. Connor walked right by him. Once he was in the dark field, Connor sprinted back to his house. He climbed the fence, crept across the garage roof, and slipped back into his bedroom.

For several minutes, he laid on top of the covers, convinced that he would never fall asleep.

#

When Connor woke up, the clock told him that it was several minutes past two. The moon had nearly set and the shadows from his window were long. He had the terrible feeling that he had forgotten to do something.

He had dreamt of the Deuce. Shawn hadn't described the man, but he had a very clear form in Connor's dream. The Deuce was tall and wide, with a stubbly face and a deep brow. His eyes were hidden in the shadows under that brow. There was a man like that who worked at the grocery store, collecting carts. Connor's mother always said that the cart man was really nice for a man with no neck.

Connor realized that he was still wearing his pants. He put his hand deep in his pocket, found the roll of cash, and remembered the fire. He had tricked all the carnival people, sitting around the fire. Instead of throwing in a dollar, he had pulled a scrap of paper from his pocket and crumpled that up before throwing it in.

He needed every dollar. With the twenty-five from the carnival, he had exactly enough to...

"My money!" he whispered, sitting up straight.

The bulk of his cash was still hidden under a rock, next to the fence. Would it be okay until morning? He didn't want to risk it. Besides, it was probably easier to sneak out at night when his aunt was asleep. Once she was awake, she watched him every second.

Connor slipped through his window for the second time.

In the distance, the ferris wheel was a black outline against the shape of the moon. Connor turned his back on the carnival in order to reach his foot down to find the top rail of the fence. He froze when a light came on in his aunt's room.

Connor held his breath until it felt like the air would burst from his chest. He finally let it out when he saw the bathroom light come on. After a minute, his muscles vibrating as he held himself perfectly still, he watched the lights go off again. Connor waited another minute, to be sure that she was back in bed. He lowered himself down.

Behind the bush, panic flooded through him when he didn't see the rock. He had to reach down and feel around to find it. Connor had forgotten that he had strewn some leaves overtop the rock to further disguise his hiding place.

Connor flipped the rock. His money was safe. He gripped it in both hands and whispered, "Yes!"

Standing up, he clutched his money to his chest.

Connor blinked at the darkness. Instead of seeing the ferris wheel framed against the moon, he saw nothing but black. Stumbling backwards, Connor stopped when his shoulders hit the stockade fence. The halo of moonlight surrounded the head and shoulders of someone big.

It took him a moment, but he finally thought he figured out who it must be.

"Are you..." he stammered, "Shawn's dad?"

As the shape stepped forward, Connor realized that it wasn't.

"No."

The voice was so deep that it felt like it vibrated Connor's whole body.

No--of course it wasn't Shawn's dad. Connor knew who it was. He just didn't want to admit it to himself.

This was the man he had dreamed about.

It was the man that Shawn had warned him of.

This was the Deuce, and Connor had failed to bribe him by pitching money into the fire. He shivered even though the night was warm. His blood had gone cold. Before he could say the name, the voice rumbled again.

"You owed me a pinch."

"Yuh-yes," he said, barely getting the word out between chattering teeth. "Suh-sorry. I forgot, I guess."

He hadn't forgotten--he had kept the bribe intentionally. Now, he held out all his money with both hands, not stopping to wonder if the man could even see it in the dark.

"You can take whatever you want," Connor said.

"It's too late for money," the voice said.

Connor couldn't see him clearly, but he pictured the face from his nightmare. The jaw was wide, stubbly, and square. The brow extended so far that it shadowed the man's eyes. His neck was so thick that his head formed a triangle on top of his shoulders.

"Please," Connor said, holding out all his money. "Please."

The man only laughed.

#

His hands were trembling around his wad of cash. Goosebumps sprang out on his arms. Connor struggled to remember the conversation with Shawn. Had the kid told him what would happen if he didn't pitch money into the fire? Something bad would happen to the carnival? Was that it?

"What do you want?" Connor managed to ask.

"More," the man said.

"More than what?" Connor asked. Before the man could answer, Connor guessed. "Five percent? Six?"

"No," the man said. Slowly, the man explained, "Four percent, but something more valuable than money."

Connor saw the silhouette shift and then heard the hand stroke the stubble on the chin. The sound was a raspy whisper, almost more terrible than the low voice when it spoke again.

"Flesh is worth more. A hand would be about four percent. Maybe a foot."

"No," Connor whispered, shaking his head. "No."

He spun and jumped for the top rail of the fence. If he could grab that wood, he could kick the man's hands away and get up on the roof of the garage. His money fluttered away, forgotten in panic.

Connor got his hands on the wood. He scrambled upwards, and when he felt the hand on his foot he kicked up and back, delivering a solid blow to the man's face. His other foot caught the middle rail and he flew upwards. For a fraction of a second, Connor's heart soared, knowing that he was almost free.

A hand closed around his other ankle. Connor was jerked back down so savagely that a chunk of wood came free from the fence, still clutched in his fist. He crashed through the bush and landed in a heap on the ground. His ankle was still in the steel grip of the man's thick fingers. The stars were blocked out as the giant man leaned over him.

The End

The Scare Machine
By
Megan Franzen

The heat of that September day was unusual, creating the disorienting illusion that Pierz, Minnesota might never again experience the horror of winter. They all seemed to be like that in the year of 2012, though. August may have been over, but it hung on with all of its might, and the only thing that was able to bring the people out of their air-conditioned houses was the carnival.

That carnival brought life to that wretchedly small town, and the population of 200 seemed to quadruple over the weekend, with people flooding in from the entire Central Lakes Area. Though this was an important event for the entire surrounding community, it held a special place in the heart of four teenage boys in particular.

Willy, Casey, Joe and Bobby weren't even old enough to drive yet, but they were old enough to feel like they ruled the world. Having attended that very carnival every year since they were three, the four friends felt as though they ran the place, joining in the good, old-fashioned fun every day from open to close as their parents and school permitted. They ran through all of the tents at least five times before the carnival left town, and they came home with enough candy and prizes to rival Halloween.

The Pierz Carnival of 2012 fit right along with this custom. The moment school let out that Friday, the four of them ran to the carnival, jumping on as many rides as they could before stopping at one of the stands for a foot-long corndog and a 24 oz Coca Cola. (They figured this out after the carnival of 2009. After two gyros and three rides of the Ferris wheel, Joe walked away looking as green as a frog, and Willy walked away covered in the byproduct.)

Their plans for staying out until curfew, however, had been foiled. As the final rays of the sunset started sifting through the surrounding haze of smoke, Casey let out a sigh and stopped his group in the middle of the crowd.

"I've gotta go home soon, guys," he murmured, looking at his watch.

"Why?" asked Joe.

“It’s almost 5,” Casey replied. “I have to be home by 5:30; you guys know that.”

“Even when the carnival is in town?” Willy whined, reaching a hand to his face to wipe his sweaty, red hair out of his eyes. “Your ma can’t be soft on you for just one weekend?”

“Especially not during the carnival.” Casey remembered the look on his mother’s face exactly a year prior when he came stumbling home with blood stains from his nose on down his shirt. Her eyes were filled with such a gleam of terror that he was surprised she ever let him leave the house at all. He was an only child, after all, and the only child that his parents were ever going to have. It broke his mother’s heart every time she found out he had a paper cut; a fight was a horror all its own. “I think it’s going to take her a lot longer than a year to forget about that fight.”

“That fight between you and Aiden? Oh, that one wasn’t even a big deal,” Bobby groaned. “The fight I got in with Jesse six months ago was ten times as bad as that one, and my parents punished me with a bowl of ice cream and a high five. What were you two even fighting over anyway?"

"He was messing with Joe," Casey murmured, shooting a sympathetic glance at his best friend who walked with his eyes glued to his shoes. "What did you and Jesse fight over?" he asked, turning back to Bobby. "Wasn't it over who got the last piece of pizza in the lunch line?"

Bobby scoffed and glared at Casey. "It was a battle over ego," he growled. "That asshole needed to be knocked down a notch."

Casey rolled his eyes. The fight between Bobby and Jesse was barely more than a slapping contest, but he brought it up with every opportunity provided to him. The fight between he and Aiden, however, had ended with two broken noses and a fractured wrist. Casey hadn't shown up to school for three days after that fight, and Aiden for six.

"Yeah, well, my mom seems to think that it *was* a big deal," Casey growled back.

Willy stopped the group, pushed up his thick-rimmed glasses, and looked at each of his friends.

"Okay, boys, enough about fights. Casey has to leave within 15 minutes, and that means that we have enough time for one more thing. What do you want to do? Another round on the Ferris wheel? Do you want to go see the hairiest woman in the world again?"

"*Nobody* wants to see the hairiest woman in the world again," stated Bobby.

"Okay, smart guy; what do you want to do, then?" Willy retorted.

Bobby looked around the bustling crowd, and his eyes rested upon a small tent sitting complacently behind the ring-toss stand. They were unable to see what was inside from where they sat, but Bobby seemed intrigued.

"That one," he stated as he gestured in front of him. "Let's go check it out."

Casey, Joe and Willy shared a look as Bobby pushed ahead of them and started towards the tent.

"Our fearless leader, ladies and gentlemen," Willy whispered sarcastically.

Bobby strode ahead of them, gaining distance quickly with his long legs. At only 14-years-old, he was already pushing six feet tall, and his head of short, brown hair bobbed above the crowd like a buoy.

Fearless leader, all right, Casey thought with a sneer. The only reason Bobby was even allowed to hang out with the three of them was because he was Casey's cousin. Casey's mother was adamant that he could never be mean to family, so he was forced to be nice to the boy who was convinced that he was on the same level playing field as Genghis Kahn himself. Willy and Joe hated him as much as Casey did, but they were fond of Casey enough to deal with it.

Bobby disappeared into the tent, and the three others were following closely behind. It didn't have any sign as to what it was, nor did it look like it had been trafficked at all. There was a cloth barrier between them and the inside, and when they swept it away to enter, they were hit with a wave of cold air as their eyes adjusted to the darkness.

When they were finally able to see, Casey noticed that there were only two things within that tent other than he and his friends. A relatively small game machine with a glowing sign that read “Your Biggest Fears Come to Life!” sat in the corner, and an old man stood solemnly next to it.

He didn’t know why his body was overcome by one, painful shiver, but as Casey stood in that tent surrounded by silence and an air of mystery, he suddenly felt terrified.

“I don’t know, guys,” he whispered to his friends. “I don’t know if I have time for something like this. Maybe we should be going.”

“Oh, don’t be such a baby,” snapped Bobby. He turned to the old man and motioned towards the machine. “So, what’s this?”

The old man cleared his throat and took a small step towards them and out of the shadows. It was apparent that he was frail and weak, moving with a measured slowness that conveyed an aged apprehension. His thin, white hair fell over his face like a mop, and as he used a withered hand to brush it away, he revealed to them a wrinkled face that had been contorted by time. He showed no level of emotion as he looked them over, and when he finally spoke, his voice came out low and gruff.

"This here, boys, is the most spectacular machine in the whole carnival."

His words made Casey uneasy. There was something false about them – something forced.

"What does it do?" urged Bobby.

"Exactly what it looks like it does," the old man continued. "It brings your biggest fears to life. Now, isn't that something?"

Casey looked at the machine more closely. It was built like a slot machine at a casino; it had a large lever on one side, and four levels to pull it down to. The closest one to the top of the machine were the words "Slightly Scary," and the next in line were the words "Very Scary." Following that was "Extremely Scary," and nearing the bottom of the machine-the farthest point where the lever would pull down to-was "The Biggest." Taped over this last option, however, was a piece of paper that had "OUT OF ORDER" written in big, bold letters.

As he looked it over again and again, Casey realized that printed in small, red letters in the top right corner of the machine was the word "Deimos." He recognized that name from somewhere, but he couldn't exactly recall where.

The shiver overcame him again, and he turned questioningly back to the old man.

"How does it work?" he asked.

The old man turned to him, and his deep, blue eyes brought that painful terror right back. "You see that lever there? You pull it down to whatever level of fear you want to experience; we have slightly scary, very scary, and extremely scary. Every option is unique to your very own fears. We used to have the option for you to experience your biggest fear, but that has been out of order for years." There was a slight pause as the man's eyes glistened over and he zoned out. The pause was short, and Casey didn't know if any of his friends had even noticed it, but it made that machine before him an even stronger enigma. "You pay for however many minutes you want to the experience to last for," the man continued, his eyes refocusing, "and it's as simple as that. Once you pull down the lever, the illusion commences, and it doesn't end until the time is up."

There was a moment of hesitation as the four teenage boys mulled it over.

"That doesn't make any sense," Willy finally stated. "How do these apparitions come? You're making it sound like it's magic or something. And how do you control how long they last for? What are they really? Some circus freaks that come parading through here wearing masks and Halloween costumes?"

A flicker of anger raced across the old man's gaze, and Casey noticed Willy shrink back slightly. His smart mouth was always getting him into trouble, but Casey didn't think that *this* was the kind of trouble that Willy would mess with for long.

"If you don't believe that it will work, boy, you don't have to be in here," the man snarled, his voice taking on a sinister octave. "I'm not here so that teenagers can tromp on in and question what I do for a living."

Normally Willy would have retorted with another smartass comment, pushed his glasses up, and trotted out of that tent with a victorious smirk. This time, though, all he did was nod his head and look at the ground. Casey had never seen his friend like that before; he didn't like it.

"Why is the biggest fear option out of order?" Bobby asked, seemingly unaffected by the atmosphere encompassing him.

The old man sighed and rolled his eyes. "Boys, I don't have any time to waste on needless questions. It's a dollar per minute if you want to try it out, otherwise you all can go to another tent if you'd like."

Willy, Casey, and Joe all exchanged looks, partaking in a mental conversation that Bobby would never understand. Casey could see a curious eagerness in Willy's eyes, and with his raised eyebrows, Willy was asking the two of them if they would try it too. When Casey looked at Joe, though, he saw a nervous fear. Joe was always the quiet one of the group, and he would go wherever his two best friends took him, but even now he looked as though he were ready to fight it.

“Joe...” Casey started in a hushed whisper.

In just that word Joe knew what his friend was asking, and he began to shake his head. “It’s alright, Case,” he murmured. “If you guys want to do it, I’ll do it. I’m not some pussy or something.”

Casey studied his friend, and with his eyes glued to the floor and his feet twitching back and forth, Joe had never looked so terrified.

“I don’t know, guys,” Casey stated for the group. “I don’t know if I like the sound of this.”

“Aw, come on, cuz,” Bobby groaned. “Don’t be a pansy-ass right now. Let’s just check it out, huh? What’s the worst that can happen?”

“He may be dumb, but he’s got a point,” Willy grumbled. “I want to try it just to see how the hell it works, you know? You don’t have to try it if you don’t wanna, but for a dollar...” he shrugged, “I don’t know – it sounds interesting.”

Casey looked at Joe one last time, and Joe looked back at him with a submissive shrug. He knew that Joe didn't want to do it, but he also knew that Joe would rather do it than be looked down on by one of his closest friends.

"All right," Casey complied. "Let's give it a shot."

Bobby released a grin that stretched across his entire face, and he turned back to the old man. "Can we all do it at the same time?"

The old man stood up straighter now, and he looked down at the four boys with a victorious smirk. "You definitely can," he stated. "You each pay me for however long you want your experience to last, and then you all pull down the lever together."

Bobby turned back to the group. "Whataya say, guys? How about we each do five minutes on 'extremely scary?'"

"Hell no," Willy retorted immediately. "I don't know how this thing works, but I'm definitely not jumping in full throttle just like that."

"Oh, come on," Bobby groaned.

"One minute each on 'slightly scary,'" Casey demanded. "That's it, or no dice. I don't even want to do this thing; I'm not doing the worst option available."

Bobby rolled his eyes and stomped his foot like a toddler. "It probably won't even be that scary, guys. You said yourself, Willy, that it'll probably just be a bunch of circus freaks parading through here trying to scare us; we might as well get our money's worth!"

The three boys glared back at him with unwavering gazes.

Finally, Bobby gave in, let out a disappointed sigh, and turned back to the man. "Fine," he snapped, "I guess we're just doing a minute each on 'slightly scary.' I didn't realize I was friends with girls." He pulled a dollar out of his pocket and slapped it in the man's open hand.

"Keep talking like that and you won't have any friends at all," Willy snarled back as he handed the man a dollar too.

When the man finally had all of his money, he smiled and motioned towards the machine. "Go ahead, boys. Feel the might of Deimos."

"Who is Deimos?" Joe asked. His face had gone completely white now, and his hands were shaking at his side.

The man said nothing. He simply stood in the same position, holding out a hand at the machine and smiling.

"Probably the freak that runs this place," murmured Willy. "He gave himself a weird name and makes all of his carnies worship him."

Casey put a hand on Joe's shoulder and smiled sympathetically. "It's okay," he whispered. "Just one minute, and then it'll be over. We can do this."

Joe forced a smile and nodded back, and the four boys approached the machine.

Once they each had a hand on the lever, they took a deep breath and pulled it down one notch to "slightly scary." It was harder to pull than Casey had imagined, but once it was finally in place, it emitted a loud "clunk" and the air around them seemed to be hit by a new wave of cold.

His eyes were intently clutched close, but when he finally pried them open, he realized that there was nothing new around. Bobby and Willy were swiveling their heads back and forth with disappointed frowns, and Joe stood with his hand still clamped on the lever, his eyes shut so tightly it looked as if they were glued close.

"What the hell, man?" Bobby asked, looking at the old man. "Nothing's happening."

Willy opened his mouth to offer an insult of his own, but Casey watched as his friend's eyes focused on something before him, and grew wide and unsettled.

Casey turned to see what Willy was looking at, but he didn't see anything. His friend was staring at a blank patch of dirt, but he was backing up and pushing his glasses against his nose with trembling fingers. Casey was suddenly reminded of a time when he and Willy were six-years-old. They had come across a large bull snake in the bushes, and Willy had run away screaming until he reached the house. Casey found him cowering in a corner, two big eyes behind thick-rimmed glasses and a mop of red hair. At thirteen-years-old, he looked as though the only thing that had changed was his height.

"My fucking god," he murmured. "What the hell is that?"

"What?" Casey asked urgently, looking from his friend to the patch of ground confusedly. "What do you see, Willy?"

Suddenly there was a high pitch scream, and Casey and Joe turned to see Bobby swatting the air around him as he jumped and flailed around the tent.

"Jesus fuck!" he wailed, slapping and swiping at the air around his arms. "Get them off! Jesus Christ, get them off!"

"What the hell is going on?!" Casey demanded.

"Casey!" Joe suddenly yelped, looking at the ground around him with wide and terrified eyes. "Casey, help me!"

Casey looked at his friend, but nothing was happening. Joe was simply standing on a patch of dirt, clawing at the air above him as though he were sinking. His eyes, which he usually reserved for looking at the ground, were open wider than Casey had ever seen, and his face was as white as a bedsheet. Though Joe had always been substantially smaller than the other three boys, he looked even smaller at that very moment, and Casey felt as though he were watching the little brother he never had be tortured.

All three of his friends were screaming and praying for mercy, but he didn't see a damned thing.

Casey was reaching forward to offer Joe a sympathetic hand when he felt something crawling on his neck. He reached back to swat at it, expecting it to be just a fly. As he did, though, he felt something much larger. Instinctively, he grabbed it with tense fingers and flung it at the ground, and when he finally saw it, he saw that it was a 10-inch-long, black centipede.

His heart stopped a beat, and all of the noise around him subsided. Suddenly, as if out of nowhere, his entire body was covered in an unsettling, prickly sensation. He looked down at his arms, and all he saw was a sea of squirming black. The beady eyes of thousands of centipedes looked up at him, and he watched in terror as one crawled right up his face and settled on his head.

And just like that, he lost it.

He started screaming and jumping around, just as his other friends where doing. His trembling hands swatted every single centipede off of his body, but no matter how many he forced off, they all seemed to reappear. They weren't just on him anymore, either. Now they were everywhere. With every terrified jump and stomp, he heard a gruesome *crunch* as he stepped on the enemy, and his fingers were soon covered in green and black bile as he squeezed and crushed them before tossing them to the ground.

This was it – this was his childhood nightmare come true. For years he had been plagued by nightmares of being covered in centipedes, but now it was finally happening. With tears of terror flowing down his face, Casey didn't know how much longer he could take.

And, as soon as it had started, it was over. Casey realized that his fingers were no longer covered in bile, and when he looked down at the ground, he no longer saw a deathbed of the centipedes he had stomped on- it was just a patch of dirt. His skin was smooth and unharmed; the only thing wrong with his appearance was his ghost-white face and his disheveled hair.

He looked at his other friends, and they looked back at him with the same expression – terrified and confused.

"What the hell just happened?" Willy asked in a shaky voice.

Bobby opened his mouth to reply, but was interrupted by a choking sound coming from Joe's direction. They looked over, and they saw their friend standing with his hands clasped around his throat. His bloodshot eyes seemed to bulge from their sockets, and his face was so white that it was turning purple.

"Jesus," Casey exclaimed, rushing towards his friend. "Joe, you're alright, buddy. What are you doing?" He grabbed his friends' hands and forced them away from his throat. Doing so was like prying a frozen lock open, but when he finally did it, Joe let out a deep breath and looked at his friend with wide eyes.

"Casey," he gasped.

"What was that?" Willy asked of the old man. "He was practically dying, for God's sake!"

The old man just shrugged. "He wasn't dying. Fear attacks us all in different ways. Your friend thought that he was drowning in quick sand. So, in order to make the apparition as real as it seemed, his body responded by choking himself. He would have passed out before he would have died."

"Oh, and that makes it all right," Willy retorted with an exasperated roll of his eyes.

"I thought that... I thought that I was drowning," Joe stated through heavy breaths.

"Jesus," Casey murmured. "I thought that I was covered in centipedes. Thank God it wasn't as bad as yours, huh?" He smiled and patted his friend on the shoulder, but Joe only replied with a vacant gaze.

"I saw a fucking horde of moths," Willy stated with an angry shake of the head. "God, I haven't been that scared in years. They were all coming at me, you know? It was like the butterfly room from Hell."

"Moths?" Bobby asked with raised eyebrows. "That's what you're afraid of? Are you afraid of butterflies too?"

Willy glared back and him and snapped, "And what were you afraid of, big guy?"

"Spiders," he replied curtly. "I'm afraid of spiders, like a normal person."

"Yeah, well, I wish our fears could have seen each other. Then your stupid spiders could have eaten all of my moths and *I* would at least have been sitting happy."

"Okay, guys, we're leaving," Casey stated bluntly as he grabbed Joe by the elbow and started to lead him out of the tent. "I'm happy that you guys are amused by this, but I think this is sick and I never want to come back here."

"Oh, come on," Bobby urged. "That wasn't even that bad. Besides, it's one hell of a rush, isn't it?"

The three of them glared at Bobby and started leaving the tent without him.

"Good bye, boys," the old man said with a wave of his hand. "See you tomorrow."

"Not a chance in hell," Joe murmured under his breath, still shaking throughout every part of his body.

They all left the carnival and went home on only a soft-spoken "good-bye" to each other, and when they finally crawled into their beds they were met with nothing more than an uneasy restlessness that gave in only to terrible, terrible nightmares.

***

The four boys awoke that Saturday morning in cold sweats. Willy shot up from his bed with a gasp, afraid that he would open his eyes and see nothing but a cloud of moths swarming around his bedroom. Casey woke up with a shrill cry, instinctively scraping at the air around his skin, expecting to find thousands of bugs crawling all over him. The worst was Joe, though. He shot straight up from his bed, screaming at the top of his lungs as rivers of sweat raced down his purple face.

His mother came stumbling into his room with an angry frown. She leaned one hand on his doorframe in order to steady herself, and she glared down at him with narrow, blood-shot eyes.

"What the hell is going on?" she growled.

Joe shrunk back underneath his covers, trying to force the image of drowning out of his mind. Even as he was breathing, though, it felt harder. It felt as though he were still trying to force little grits of sand from his lungs, and it took his strongest effort to keep himself from lapsing into another panic attack.

"Nothing," he murmured. "Sorry. I just had a nightmare."

His mother rolled her eyes and shifted on her feet. "News flash, kiddo, we *all* have nightmares. You're a little too old to be trying to get attention from it. Your father and I have stuff that we're trying to do."

Joe nodded as he pulled the covers further up on his chin. He watched his mother stumble away, and through the thin walls he could hear her complaining to his father in short, concise grumbles.

When he heard nothing but silence, he knew what was happening. It was their "morning coffee," their "wake-up call." He didn't have to see it to know what was happening; he had seen it a million times before. His father would be filling an old needle with that strange, clear liquid, and the two of them would sit there and stab themselves in the arm. Sometimes it was only once, but it could be as many times as three. If he were to come in to see them, they would just look at him with those zoned-eyes, as if they weren't really looking at him.

"Your mother and I are busy," his father would say slowly. "Why don't you run along now, Joe? This doesn't concern you."

And run along he would. As fast as he could, in fact. As fast as he could to any place that wasn't the horror he called "home."

He didn't want to be in the house anymore. He jumped out of bed, threw on the same, raggedy clothes that he wore every other day of the week, and he scurried from the house in the same hurried fashion that he had done every other morning of his life.

Maybe tonight would be the night that he didn't come back to that rickety old trailer house on the outskirts of town. Tonight might be the night that he changed his life and ran away forever. Tonight might just be the night that he was set free.

But, in the depths of his mind, he knew the truth. This was *home*, after all. You can't just forget about *home*.

No matter how hard you try, some nightmares never surrender to morning.

***

Casey left his house that morning to find Joe standing outside the gate that surrounded his front yard. This wasn't the first time, and he knew that it wouldn't be the last. No matter how many times he had told Joe that he was always welcome to come inside, he always found his friend standing courteously on the sidewalk like that – even in the dead of winter.

"Jesus, Joe. How many times do I have to tell you that you can come inside? We were having breakfast, for crying out loud. You could have had some."

Joe shrugged his shoulders and forced a smile. "It's alright, Case; I already had some. I'm not hungry."

Casey wasn't fooled – Joe hadn't eaten a real breakfast in thirteen years, but the two of them partook in this meaningless dance every morning, and neither of them planned on changing it anytime soon.

"I had the worst nightmare last night" Casey started as the two of them walked down the sidewalk. "Centipedes. Centipedes everywhere."

"Yeah, I had a pretty bad one too," Joe said. "It was the quicksand thing again. I don't like it, Case. I don't know how long I'll be able to take something like this."

Casey was alerted by the quiver in his friend's voice, and it hurt him to think about how much pain Joe was in. No matter how hard he pushed, though, he knew that Joe would never cave in and admit that something was hurting him. He had been trained his entire life to keep a face and play in the background; it would take a long time to break an old habit like that.

Just as he was about to push a little bit anyway, his cellphone rang, and he dug it out of his pocket to see that Willy was calling him.

"Hey," he greeted as he pressed it against his ear.

"Hey, Case," Willy stated. "What time are you and Joe going to the carnival today?"

It was the routine question of the second Saturday of September. This was the day that they were generally allowed to stay at the carnival from dusk until dawn, but what usually filled Casey with excitement now filled him with an uneasy sense of trepidation.

"I don't know," he mumbled slowly. "Do you want to go some place else today? We could just hang out at your place and play video games or something."

There was a momentary pause on the other line. "Casey, what the hell are you talking about? This is the carnival, dude. We go all day every day every single year. What's your deal?"

"It's just that... I don't know. Don't you think that the carnival is starting to get a little old? I mean, we've already done everything there. Can't we do something else?"

Willy started to sputter on the other line. "Like playing video games will be something new and exciting? We do that every *other* day of the year. This is the *carnival*, Case. This is the only exciting thing that ever happens around here. Besides, all of my sisters are home today and they'll probably be watching some stupid chick flick on the TV. Nobody wants to be around for that."

Casey let out a sigh and looked over at Joe who reciprocated the stare. "All right. Well, we're walking towards town anyway, so we can meet you at the carnival in about five minutes if you really want to."

"Sounds good to me." Casey could hear a loud thump and a couple of curse words as Willy fumbled to put his clothes on. "I'll meet you guys there. Oh, and don't call Bobby. Please. If he calls and insists on coming that's one thing, but I don't want to be hanging out with that asshole anymore than I'm forced to, okay?"

"Dually noted," Casey murmured with a smirk. "Don't get your hopes up, though. I *never* call him first; remember that."

"Yeah, yeah." Casey heard another loud thump as Willy cursed out his pants, and then he hung up.

"Back the carnival, huh?" Joe whimpered.

Casey looked solemnly at his friend. "Joe, we don't have to go if you don't want to, you know. I don't want to go either; you and me could go do something on our own."

Joe shook his head. "Nah, let's hang out with our friends, okay? I just won't go anywhere near that stupid machine again."

"Rodger that."

They walked for four more minutes before Casey's phone rang again. He looked at Joe with an unhappy frown. "I'll give you three guesses as to who's calling me right now."

Joe just laughed and shook his head.

Casey pulled the phone up to his ear and answered it with a dreary, "Yeah?"

"Hey there, Case." Bobby's familiar and annoying voice came oozing out of the cellphone, and Casey couldn't fight the urge to roll his eyes. "You guys going to the carnival today?"

"Maybe," Casey murmured.

"Well, sounds good to me. I just left my house now and I'll be there in about 10 minutes. Meet you guys there?"

Casey sighed. "Yeah. We'll find you."

"Alright. Catch ya later, loser." There was a click, and then static.

Casey groaned and shoved his phone back in his pocket. Bobby's constant tug-of-war between being the gang's buddy or being the gang's superior was the most annoying thing of all. If he chose one position over the other he might have been able to grow on them, but his flip-flopping nature just pushed them all into the arms of resentment.

"Great," Joe murmured. "Awesome Bob is coming with, huh?"

Casey grunted in affirmation as he stared the carnival that was now only three blocks in front of them. A wave of popcorn, cotton candy, and something fried wafted through the air, and the two boys closed their eyes and absorbed the tantalizing smell with sly smirks.

"All right, I'm glad we came," Joe stated with a smile.

The two boys approached the ticket booth, and when they entered the carnival, they realized that it was practically empty. The Pierz carnival always opened at 8 AM sharp, but very few of the booths ever opened before 10. The boys didn't mind, though. They would walk around aimlessly, eating a bag of popcorn they got from the only food stand open and bullshitting about anything and everything. This year wasn't any different; the only people walking around were eager children and random carnies. It didn't take long before Casey and Joe found Willy walking their way.

"What's up, guys?" Willy greeted, pushing his glasses up on his nose and smiling. "I don't see the Awesome Bob, so that must mean good news, right?"

Casey opened his mouth to reply, but before he could even do that there was a shout coming from behind him.

"Hey, guys!" that annoying voice roared.

Willy let out a groan and his smile was lost. Casey closed his eyes, emitted a deep breath, and turned around to greet the cousin he wished he didn't have.

"Geezus, this place is dead, ain't it?" Bobby grumbled as he approached. "Why the hell do you guys come this early anyway?"

"Tradition," Willy snapped. "We've been doing this every year since we were like 8. And it's always been just the three of us." Willy mumbled the last sentence low enough that Bobby couldn't hear, but Casey elbowed him in the ribs anyway.

"Well, what are we supposed to do at an empty carnival?"

"We usually just walk around," Casey explained. "There's usually at least one food stand open where we can get something to eat, and every once in a while there is a booth or two open too. In a couple of hours, though, more things will start to open up."

Bobby scoffed and placed his hands on his bony hips. "Whatever."

Willy rolled his eyes. "All right, boys, let's get trucking. This carnival ain't going to aimlessly walk itself."

"I want some popcorn," said Joe. "I know they're serving it because Case and I could smell it from two blocks back."

"Rodger that, buddy," said Willy, and the four of them went off in search of food. Not long after they started walking, though, Casey and Willy both felt a hard *thump* on their backs. They turned around to find Bobby pointing eagerly at a small booth tucked away behind the ring-toss.

"Look, guys," he urged. "The scare tent is open. Who woulda guessed? Wanna go check it out?"

Casey scoffed and shook his head. "No way in hell. That was a grade-A shitshow last time, and I'm not going through it again."

"Ah, c'mon," Bobby whined. "Don't be a bunch of pussies on me now. You gotta admit that it was kind of cool last time. Besides, I want to try the next level."

Casey gazed over the ominous tent. It was sitting so complacently, and yet so portentously, acting as though it may not really exist at all. The tent covers were darker than the rest of the tents throughout the carnival, waving gently in the soft breeze of the September morning. He didn't really know why, but just *looking* at the tent made him afraid.

"I wouldn't mind going in there again," murmured Willy.

Casey turned on his friend.

"Don't get me wrong, I don't' want to try the damn thing again," Willy defended. "I just want to ask that old creep how the hell that thing works. I couldn't stop thinking about it all night long. I mean – it was *real*. Wasn't it? I just want some answers."

Casey cast brief glances at the three other boys, and in fear of being perceived as the "pussy" of the bunch, he agreed to go in. Out of the corner of his eye, though, he could see Joe's hands trembling, and he felt a sudden pang of guilt as the four of them entered into the dark tent once more.

The man greeted the four boys with an eerie smile. “Welcome back.”

“Can it, old man,” Willy snapped. “We came for answers.”

“Willy,” Bobby growled, elbowing his friend in the ribs. “Jesus, don’t get us kicked out of here.”

“How’d you do it?” Willy continued. “That freakshow yesterday – how’d it work, huh? What the hell happened to us?”

The man gazed at them blankly for a long second, his beady eyes scanning each of them in a fogged-over haze as he maintained his half-smile. “That would be the might of Deimos.”

“And who would this Deimos freak be?” questioned Willy.

“I looked it up last night,” Joe whimpered, his eyes darting uneasily at his friends. “Deimos is the Greek god of terror.”

The man gazed down at Joe, pleased. “And don’t you forget it, boy.”

There was a moment of silence as the four boys exchanged glances. Willy, exasperated, threw his hands up in the air. "You're not trying to tell me that some ancient Greek god is what happened to us yesterday, are you? Because that's just fucking crazy. We were hallucinating our balls off, and I want to know how you did it."

Seeing that the old man was getting frustrated with Willy's irritated yells, Casey cut in. "Where did this machine come from?"

"It's old," the man explained. "Older than your grandparents and your great-grandparents. The façade is new, but the core is ancient. It comes from a time when sorcery was still a practiced concept."

"So, witches made it!" exclaimed Willy with wide, sarcastic eyes. "Well, why didn't you just say so? That explains everything! Why, who wouldn't believe in witches, boys?"

The man glared down at Willy and continued. "The followers of Deimos created a shrine to help the god live on through times of non-believers. The shrine was destroyed long ago, but the portal that it encompassed survived. It was wounded, but a fragment still exists, and that fragment is in this machine. Though the portal is no longer strong enough to bring Deimos himself into our world, it is still strong enough to convey his strength, and it is my duty to help spread his wrath to all of the people who have forgotten his true power."

The boys looked at the old man with disbelieving stares.

"So, he's crazy," Willy grumbled, turning to his friends and motioning for the door. "How about we scram, kids?"

"Wait," Bobby insisted, grabbing Willy's arm. "He's not serious, you dumbasses. Can't you see? It's just a show. That's what carnivals are. He's been told to say all of this crazy stuff just to keep the illusion alive."

"Guess what?" Willy started. "I don't give a fuck. I wanted answers, and all I got was a bunch of crazy gibberish. I'm outa here."

"C'mon, guys," Bobby whined. "Let's give it just one more go. Whaddaya say? We can each try the 'very scary' and get our socks knocked off. It was fun last time, wasn't it?"

"Fun?" Casey cut in. "You thought that that was *fun*? It was terrifying, Bobby, and I don't want to do it again."

"Aw, c'mon, you pansy-ass bitches." Bobby was doing it again. He was tossing his head back and stomping his foot just like a child, throwing around insults in an attempt to get the boys to go his way. "Are you really so scared that you can't even give it a go?"

"It's not that we're *scared*," Willy emphasized, "it's that we don't *want* to. I don't want to do anything as creepy as this, especially when I don't understand how the damn thing works."

"Why is the 'biggest fear' out of order?" Joe's shaking voice cracked the tension like a block of ice, and the old man turned his sour gaze on him.

"I told you boys already, I don't have time to answer every needless question."

"How about this," Bobby started, putting his forefinger and thumb on his chin as though he were lapsing into a moment of enlightenment. "You tell us why that option is out of order, and then we'll try the next level available."

"Don't speak for us, dumbass," Willy snapped. "How about *you* try the next level of fear if he tells us?"

Bobby looked at all of them angrily for a moment, a quiet dread flashing across his eyes. It dissipated quickly, though, replaced with a false sense of pride, and he turned back to the old man. "All right, that sounds like a deal. You tell us why the 'biggest fear' is out of order, and I'll try the next level."

The man let out a long, haggard breath, and he rolled his eyes. "The last time somebody tried that level, it malfunctioned. These fears are supposed to be just an apparition, but the last woman to try it ended up... injured. The fear became very, very real, and I don't want to risk it happening again."

"You don't want to? Or Deimos doesn't want to?" Willy asked, rolling his eyes.

"What do you mean she was injured?" Casey cut in.

"Her biggest fear involved… magic, I suppose you could say. Have you boys ever seen a show where the magician takes a woman, puts her in box, saws the box in half, seemingly cutting the woman in half too, but the magic is that she is actually just fine?"

The boys nodded.

"Well, her biggest fear was that she was that woman, but that the trick malfunctioned, and that she ended up cut in half instead."

The boys were silent for a moment.

"You mean that instead of just imagining it she was *actually* cut in half?" Willy questioned.

The man nodded solemnly.

"Right here in this tent?"

"Okay, I'm done with this crap," Bobby cut in. "I told you guys already, he's been told to say all of this stuff just to keep the illusion alive. It's probably out of order just to keep up the mystery or something stupid like that. Anyway, let's get to it." He fished through his pocket and pulled out a dollar bill. "I'll show these pussies how to deal with this fake crap. Here," he handed the man the dollar.

The man took the money and held out his hand, motioning to the machine. Bobby flashed the boys a cocky smirk, approached the machine, and pulled the lever down to the "very scary" notch. It clicked into place with a loud *thunk.*

"Have fun, Bobby-boy," Willy growled sarcastically. "Can't wait to watch you squirm."

Bobby rolled his eyes. "Keep talking like a bigshot, Ragmore, but I don't see you trying it out."

Before any more words could be exchanged, Bobby's eyes darted to the corner of the tent right behind his friends. His face contorted into a fearful grimace, but it was quickly transformed to a snide sneer as he looked from the empty corner to the three boys before him. "All right, this is making a lot more sense now. Look, guys, there's carnie standing right behind you. I told you that all of this apparition stuff was a bunch of bullshit."

The boys turned around, but all they saw was a dark, empty corner. When they turned back, they saw that Bobby's sneer had been replaced with a petrified gawk. "All right," he whimpered, taking a step back and staring at some unknown entity before him. "Never mind, I'm done. Make it stop." He turned to look at the old man. "Make him go away."

The man didn't say anything, he just watched Bobby blankly.

Suddenly, in the midst of his pleas, Bobby's neck turned sideways at nearly a right angle, and he let out a high-pitched, terrifying scream. The scream refused to subside, and its intensity only grew as he crumbled to his knees and began to thrash.

Casey felt the urge to help, but he didn't know what was going on. As far as he could see, Bobby was simply lying on the ground, flailing his arms and legs about like child throwing a tantrum. His shrill shrieks, however, conveyed a fear and a pain that was sent from none other than the horrific depths of Hell itself.

"Make it stop," Joe shouted over Bobby's cries.

"There are fifteen seconds left," the old man grumbled.

And those following fifteen seconds seemed to last an eternity. The boys watched as Bobby squalled and thrashed, cries for mercy breaking through in between his heart-wrenching shrieks. His head was tossing viciously from side-to-side, and as his gaze darted around the room, all that could be seen were the whites of his eyes.

Finally, it all came to an end. Bobby lay limply on his back, his eyes rolling back into the right place and staring blankly at the ceiling. If it hadn't been for his heaving chest, Casey would have guessed that he was dead.

"Bobby," Casey murmured. "Are you all right?"

Bobby let out a heavy breath. "Holy shit. Am I still alive?"

Nobody answered, maybe because after a fit like that, they weren't even sure either.

Bobby sat up stiffly and rubbed at his right temple. “That man… he had a drill.” He turned to the boys, and his eyes were bloodshot and wide. “He was drilling holes into my head. Then another guy came, and he started to pull my fingernails out.” He looked down at his hands. “Jesus Christ. The pain just felt so *real*.”

“That was some show you put on,” Willy grumbled, crossing his arms and gazing down at Bobby with an unimpressed frown. “Reminds me of two years ago when you had us all believing that you had a broken arm for two weeks. What now? You gonna try and tell us that all of this ‘illusion’ stuff is real after all?”

For the first time in a long time, Bobby seemed to be looking at his friends with a look of honest sincerity. “What are you talking about, dude? You think I’m messing with you?” He scoffed and stumbled onto his feet. “Listen, you don’t have to believe me if you don’t want to. I’m telling you the truth, though; I felt fucking drills boring into my head and fiddling around with my brain. It hurt like a bitch, and that’s the truth.”

Casey had an idea of what was going to happen next, but he was hoping that he would be proven wrong. This battle of ego between Bobby and Willy had happened before, and it all went the same way. Bobby did something stupid to prove that he was more of a man than the three younger boys, and, even though Willy knew that it was actually nothing more than imbecilic immaturity, he would do it, too. Why did he do it? Case believed that it was partially out of pure spite, but that it was also a way for Willy to prove to himself that he, too, was a daring and stupidly brave idiot.

Willy reaching into his pocket, fished out a dollar, and approached the old man.

“What the hell are you doing?” Bobby snapped.

“Well, if you can do it, I sure as hell can do it, too. Besides, I want to see if I can be the first one to do it without crying.” Willy slapped the dollar in the man’s hand and walked towards the machine.

“Willy, please don’t,” Joe whimpered.

Willy shot a look back at them, and as he did so he pulled the lever of the machine down to "very scary." Casey saw a flash of trepidation pass behind those thick-rimmed glasses, but Willy used his usual silly grin to pass it off as confidence.

As Bobby, Joe, and Casey stood audience, they watched a similar thing unfold all over again. Willy's grin was replaced with a terrified frown as his eyes focused on something that the other boys couldn't see, and his begs for mercy were interrupted as he was forced to the ground-thrashing and screaming just as Bobby had done earlier.

The minute finally ended, and Willy–just as Bobby had done before him-lay on his back, breathing heavily with tears streaking his face. His eyes were clenched shut, though, and when he finally opened them, he let out a sharp gasp and sat up bolt-up-right.

"Sweet Jesus," he whimpered, his chest still heaving as he readjusted his glasses.

"Not so fake, huh?" Bobby inquired.

"What the hell?" Willy questioned, turning to the old man and fumbling to his feet. "I don't get it. I just don't get it. How did you make that happen?"

The man simply stared back vacantly. "I told you boys already; it's the might of Deimos."

"Cut it with this Deimos crap." Willy pushed his sweaty, orange locks out of his face and took a step closer to the man. "Five seconds ago I was being buried alive, and there's no way I could have imagined it because it was too *real*."

The man just shrugged his shoulders. "I've already explained it to you."

"Willy, let's just go," Casey grumbled. "I'm done with this stuff."

"You mumbled a bunch of crazy, witchcraft, gibberish at us," Willy continued, his voice rising and his face flushing with color. "That wasn't explaining it."

Casey reached forward, grabbed Willy's arm, and started yanking him towards the entrance of the tent. "C'mon, Will. We don't need answers; we're done."

"This is a bunch of bullshit," grumbled Willy under his breath, following reluctantly behind the three boys.

The sunlight hit them like a wall when they finally escaped the shroud of icy darkness, and they reentered the carnival with pale, trembling faces.

"I just don't get it," Willy continued to grumble. "I want answers, is all. That scared the living shit out of me, and I want to know how he did it."

"I kind of want to do it again," Bobby stated almost guiltily.

The three friends turned on him. "What the hell are you talking about?" Casey sniped. "We saw you, Bobby. You were crying like a pansy."

"You know..." Willy cut in, pushing the glasses back up on his nose, "I kind of want to do it again too."

Casey rolled his eyes and shook his head in confusion. "Willy, you were just yelling at that man because you said it scared the living shit out of you. You were crying, too, buddy; either you guys are messing with us or you've actually completely lost it this time."

Bobby and Willy looked at each other, and Casey saw something that he didn't like. There was a weird, excited addiction exchanged between the two of them, and he saw their mouths twitch upwards into discreet smirks. Something had happened to the two of them, and Casey couldn't manage to wrap his head around it.

"It's just..." Bobby slapped his hands together as he tried to come up with the words. "There's something addictive about it, man. I mean, it's such a *thrill*." The weird excitement made another parade across his face as he said those words. "Don't get me wrong, it definitely scared me to death, but knowing that it's all just fake makes it almost *exciting*."

"I never thought I'd say this, but I agree with the Lone Ranger on this one," Willy added. "Maybe you ought to try it out one more time, Case. You have to understand where we're coming from; it's the same reason you go on roller coasters. It's terrifying and exciting at the same time, you know? Why do you think people go to horror movies?"

Casey was at a loss for words. "Where is all of this coming from?" he finally blurted. "You guys were just raving about how horrible that was! And what? Now you want to go back and try it again? What the hell is the matter with you guys?"

"I just think that you should give it another go, cousin," Bobby said as he prodded Casey on the shoulder and offered an encouraging smile. "C'mon, we know you're not a pansy. You'll try it, won't you?"

Casey glanced over at Joe who was simply glaring at his friends, and he shook his head as he tried to formulate words. "You guys are crazy, all right? I don't want any more talk about that damn machine for the rest of the day. Understood?"

Willy and Bobby rolled their eyes and dropped their gaze—their form of acquiescence.

"I say we go and see if any of the rides are open," Joe offered quietly.

"Seconded," Casey affirmed, starting off towards the carnival rides without allowing any input from the other two.

The rest of the day went by slowly, though, and the horrors of The Scare Machine were in the back of all their minds.

When they were leaving the carnival that evening they passed by the area where that dark little tent had been. They came to find, however, that it wasn't there anymore. The only thing that sat behind the ring-toss was an empty patch of dirt. So, the four boys went home thinking that the fright and excitement they had endured the last couple of days had came to a complete end.

Little did they know that it was actually just beginning.

***

The next day was Sunday, and it was the last day that the Pierz carnival was in town. Willy and Bobby awoke that morning with the same excitement they had every year during the carnival, but Joe and Casey rose from their beds in shivers of trepidation.

Casey had a bad feeling in the pit of his stomach, and he couldn't quite put his finger on it. He sat at the dining table that morning, moving his spoon around in his bowl of oatmeal, but refusing to eat any of it. His mother sat across from him, her brow furrowed in worry as she anxiously bit at her lip.

"Casey, honey, are you all right?" she finally asked.

Casey sat up in his seat as if startled, and he forced a spoonful of his breakfast into his mouth as he shook his head. "No, Ma, I'm fine. I was just zoning out."

His mother simply grunted in dissatisfaction while continuing watch him. Casey knew that she was thinking about the fight he had gotten into only a year prior, and he also knew that she was considering telling him to not go to the carnival at all that Sunday. Her telling him not to go, however, would be his only motivation to go at all.

"Are you going to carnival today?" she asked.

Casey fought the urge to roll his eyes as he forced another spoonful of oatmeal in his mouth. Here it was. "I was thinking about it."

"Well," she started tentatively, "I'm not sure it's such a good idea. You've been in such an odd funk lately... and we both remember what happened at last year's carnival."

"That's not gonna happen again, Ma," Casey stated irritably. "And I haven't been in a funk; I've just been a little tired."

"Well, then maybe you should stay home today and sleep."

Casey let out a sigh and bit his tongue. If only he would sleep eighteen hours a day like some kind of sloth, his mother would be the happiest woman in the world. Nothing dangerous can happen to you if you're asleep, after all. In fact, he wouldn't have been surprised if she asked him to start wearing diapers; you can't get harmed in the bathroom if you never have to go to one.

"Mom, I'm fine," he stated bluntly. "I'm going to the carnival."

His mother sat there biting her lip, and he knew that she was hating the fact that she was losing control of her son. "You'll be home by 5:30," she grumbled through clenched teeth. "A minute late and you're grounded for a month."

Casey lifted his head to look across the table angrily at his mother, but when his eyes wandered to the window that sat behind her, he noticed the short and slim figure of Joe standing at his picket fence. Casey pushed his chair back and stood up.

"Joe's waiting outside," he mumbled, heading to the door. "I'll be home by 5:30, Ma."

"Be safe," his mother shouted from her seat. "I don't want to hear about any misbehavior!"

At that moment, Casey shut the door, and he walked towards Joe who was standing alone on the sidewalk playing with a stick.

"How ya doing?" Joe greeted, throwing the stick into the bushes.

"Fine," Casey grumbled. "My mom's just giving me trouble again. She might as well slap a diaper on me and give me a binky with the way she treats me. I'm sick of being babied, man."

Joe shrugged. "Could be worse."

Casey looked at his friend and his cheeks flushed red. He was filled with shame when he realized he was complaining about over-protective parents to the kid who was being raised by drug-addicts.

***

They met up with Willy and Bobby around 10, and they spent the rest of their morning having the same old fun that they had remembered having at the Pierz carnival. They rode the Ferris wheel, ate corndogs, and lost money at games they couldn't win. They never wandered over near the Scare Machine tent, though, and that was mostly due to Casey's doing. He continued to suggest activities on the opposite side of the carnival, but his cousin soon caught on to his intentions.

"When are you gonna admit that you're too scared to go over by the Scare Machine again?" Bobby finally groaned.

"Scared?" Casey asked with a glare that was supposed to mask his fear. "What makes you think I'm scared? Maybe I just want to do things that are on this side of the carnival."

"Case, I'm not one for picking Bobby's side, but you aren't being very sly about it," Willy stated plainly.

"All right," Casey sighed in frustration. "I don't want to go back to that tent, plain and simple. I don't want any talk about that tent, and I don't want any talk about going *near* that tent. Is that too much to ask?"

Bobby began laughing in way that made Casey's blood boil. He pointed a long, slender finger at his cousin as he hunched over and slapped his knee. "I didn't know that they raised pussies in our family," he finally said, pretending to wipe a tear from his eye as he slapped Casey on the shoulder. "Must come from your dad's side, huh?"

Casey clenched his teeth and tried his hardest to maintain his composure. He had always been taught not to give into those silly bully-tactics such as name-calling, but it was a damn hard thing to refuse. He was overcome with the agonizing urge to strangle his tall, gangly cousin to death, and it felt like pure torture to resist. "I'm not a pussy, you dumbass," he snarled. "I just think that it's stupid, and I'm tired of us spending all of our time over there."

"Oh, quit with the bullshit," Bobby declared. "You're scared shitless, and you know it. We haven't spent more than 30 minutes in that tent this entire weekend, so that was the lamest argument you could have come up with."

Casey was sure at that moment that he was going to leap forward and reach right for Bobby's throat, but when he felt Joe's small hand grab his wrist, he restrained himself. "I just don't want to," Casey growled, speaking through his teeth like some sort of wild beast. "I'm not scared."

"It's all right, Case, you don't have to justify yourself to us," Willy cut in. "We don't have to go into that tent if you guys don't want to; it's all good."

"No, we don't have to go," Bobby agreed, looking down at his cousin and flashing a mocking grin. "We don't want any of us to pee our pants and have to run home to mommy."

At this Casey reared forth, his hands held out before him like talons ready to rip Bobby's eyes from their sockets. He didn't make it, though, because both Willy and Joe leapt forward right when he did, grabbing Casey by both elbows and holding him back.

"Case, Case..." Willy grumbled as he struggled to restrain his friend.

Casey ignored both of them, and he squirmed any which way he could in order to get free. He glared at Bobby who stood not five feet in front of him, his hands on his bony hips as he grinned down at his cousin mockingly.

"Casey!" Willy shouted.

Casey calmed down and stopped thrashing.

"Do you *really* want to get into another fight?" Willy asked, pushing his glasses up on his nose with one hand while maintaining a sure-fire grip on Casey's elbow with the other. "How do you think your mom would react to that one? Especially if it was your cousin? You'd never be allowed to hang out with us again, man."

Casey thought about it for a long second, and he realized with a burning resentment that his friend was right. As he stared into Bobby's over-confident eyes, though, he knew that he couldn't rest until he firmly asserted his place at the top of the group.

"Fine, I'll do it." Casey growled.

Willy looked from Bobby to Casey with a confused frown. "Do what?"

"Do the Scare Machine," Casey stated. "I'll show you I'm not a fucking pussy. I'll even do it on extreme."

"Casey," Joe started, with a quiver in his voice. "You don't have to do this."

"I *want* to do it," he insisted, pulling his arms free from his friends' grasp as he took a step forward to look up at his cousin. "I think it's time to knock a dumbass down a notch."

So they set off, and before they knew it they were back in that cold and musty tent with nobody there but the old man and the machine itself.

"Good to see you boys again," the old man greeted them with the first smile they had ever seen him give. "Back for one last go, I take it?"

"Just me," Casey stated eagerly, rummaging through his pocket before fishing out a dollar. "I want to do a minute on 'extremely scary'."

The man took Casey's dollar and gazed down at him skeptically. "Are you sure, boy? That's the most intense setting we offer."

"I'm sure," Casey snapped.

The man bowed his head and motioned toward the machine. "Feel the wrath of Deimos."

"Casey, please don't do this," Joe urged uneasily.

"Shut-up," Bobby snarled, still wearing that mocking grin. "Let the big man play the game."

Casey ignored all of them and advanced toward the machine, pulling the large lever down three notches until it hit 'extremely.'

Just like the last time, nothing happened immediately. It wasn't until his friends and the inside of the tent began to fade away that Casey realized he was in for a doozy.

Out of the darkness appeared four men in white coats, all wearing sanitation masks across their face and blue gloves on their hands. He realized with a pang of horror that they were doctors, and his mind raced immediately to his biggest fear about doctor visits.

As if they had read his mind, each of the doctors reached into their pockets and pulled out a syringe with a long needle. They advanced closer to him, and Casey was about to let out a scream when he heard the voice of his father coming from his right.

"Sorry, son," his father stated, waving at Casey with one hand and holding Casey's mother close to him with the other.

His parents looked like they were miles away, but their voices resonated off the darkness with such intensity that they sounded as if they were standing right there with him.

"Dad," Casey yelped with a nervous crack in his voice, looking from his parents to the doctors and back again. "Dad, please help me!"

"Sorry, son," his father repeated. "Your mother and I are leaving now. It's time for you to grow up and start acting like a man."

Casey's eyes fell on the needles as the doctors drew nearer, and it wasn't until he wanted to run that he realized he was physically incapable. Looking down at his feet, he realized that he was strapped upright to gurney, and the only parts of his body that he could move were his neck, his fingers, and his toes.

The doctor closest to him pulled down his mask, revealing the face of an alien. From its mouth sprang rows and rows of razor-sharp teeth, and its tongue was forked into three, separate serpent-like spirals. A strange noise came from the monster as it drew nearer to Casey, and he felt his heart stop as the other doctors revealed their similarly disfigured faces.

"We wish we could say we were proud," he heard his mother say, "but you were always such a disappointment. For ten years we prayed on having a child, and when we were finally granted one we were given *you.*"

Her last words struck Casey with such force that he felt himself catch his breath. He had to fight back tears as he watched his parents stride away into the darkness hand-in-hand, and even though he screamed relentlessly after both of them, they simply continued to walk until they were nothing more.

By the time he finally turned his attention back to the monsters, they were practically on top of him. He watched in horror as they began to raise their needles into the air, and he closed his eyes and started screaming for the whole thing to stop.

"Shut it off!" he howled, shaking his body vigorously in a vain attempt to break free. "Let me go! Get me out of-"

His cries were cut short as the first needle plunged into his skin. His cries turned into wails, and there was nothing he could do as the four monsters stabbed him repeatedly with their needles. Some were in the arms, some were on the legs, but the one that made him vomit was the one that struck him in the stomach. Blood spattered the ground at his feet, and he was forced to watch as his very body was turned into a pegboard.

That moment was the closest he had ever felt to death. The pain had grown to such an intensity that he was beginning to feel numb, and he was overcome with an exhaustion so extreme that his eyelids began to droop despite the fact that the doctors were still stabbing him with the same tenacity as when they had started.

It was right when he thought that his eyelids were going to close for good that the nightmare stopped. He gazed around the dark tent at the old man and his horrified friends, overcome with a queasy feeling in the pit of his stomach and the nauseous smell of death.

"Jesus Christ, dude," Bobby sputtered with a disgusted scowl. "You blew chunks everywhere. That's disgusting."

Casey looked down at his feet and saw the garbled remains of corndog and cola littering the ground around his feet. His cheeks flushed scarlet red, and he pushed past the three boys and out of the tent. His emotions were in such a state of turmoil that he couldn't keep himself from crying, and he turned back to his friends who had followed him into the sunlight with a face streaked with tears.

"I want you guys to promise that we will never go back in there," he told them firmly, glaring at each of them with a serious ferocity.

"Casey, what did you see?" Willy asked tentatively.

"It doesn't matter," Casey retorted, wiping the tears from his cheeks. "I just want you guys to promise me. I never want any of you to feel the way I felt in there. I felt like I was gonna die, for Christ's sake." His last few words broke off as his fierce stance was replaced with that of a broken, crying child.

Joe was the friend who stepped forward and wrapped his arms around Casey. “It’s all right,” he murmured. “We’ll never go back.”

“Promise,” Casey murmured from behind the hands that shielded his face. “I want you guys to promise on each others’ grave.”

“We promise,” they murmured, looking quizzically at each other as if they could find the answers to their terrors in each others’ eyes.

***

Casey tossed and turned in his bed that evening while his dreams replayed the nightmare of that afternoon. The sounds of sobs continuously reverberated throughout his sleep, and it wasn’t until he was awoken from his slumber that he realized the sobs were coming from a figure hulking beside his bed.

Casey jumped upright from where he lay and flicked on his bedside lamp; the figure crying beside him was Joe.

"Joe, what the hell are you doing?" He asked.

Joe was hysterical, crying with such force that his breath was coming and going in vigorously uneven puffs. His head was hanging so that Casey couldn't see his face, but when he finally looked at his friend he realized that Joe's eyes were so bloodshot that they looked about ready to shrivel up and die.

Even though Joe hadn't said a word yet, Casey was overcome with a disheartening fear. He felt that needle stab into his stomach all over again, and he was worried that he was going to be sick.

"Joe," he repeated firmly, reaching out and grabbing his friend by the shoulder. "What the hell is going on?"

Joe's sobs eased slightly, and he shifted around where he kneeled. He looked up at his friend and shook his head. "They made me do it, Casey. I didn't have a say. You weren't there to stick up for me this time."

Casey furrowed his brow. "What are you talking about?"

"Bobby and Willy. They made me do it."

"Do *what*?"

"Play the game."

Casey's heart sank and his fingers fell off of Joe's shoulder. "You guys promised that you wouldn't," he whispered hoarsely.

"We're not children making a fucking promise in a playground anymore, Casey!" Joe's voice came through with more force than Casey had ever heard before, and for the first time in what could be called reality, he was truly terrified. "They didn't give a damn about that stupid promise we made, and they made me go back to that carnival with them after it was closed."

"You guys went in after it was closed?" Casey questioned. "Why? I left at 5:30; if you wanted to do it, why didn't you guys just do after I left?"

"Because," Joe murmured between sobs. "They wanted to try the 'biggest fear' setting."

Casey's face went pale. "Why?"

Joe simply shrugged his shoulders, but they both knew that morbid curiosity was all that could be blamed.

Neither of them knew what to say for a long second. Casey simply sat in bed, trying to make sense of the whole thing, and Joe knelt beside him, sobbing quietly while looking at the floor.

"Well," Casey started uneasily. "Are you all right?"

Joe shot him an angry glare. "All right? I broke into your house and am crying on your floor. Does that sound like I'm *all right*?"

Casey's eyes went wide, and his voice was lost. Joe had never lost control like this, and seeing him in such a frenzy was like seeing a caged beast who had just been let loose.

"It was fucking terrifying," Joe growled. "I've never been more scared in my life."

"It's okay," Casey urged tentatively. "It's just a game, Joe. I know it's scary as hell, but it's just a game. It's all over, and you're all right."

Joe bit his lip and shook his head, his tears falling lightly to the ground. “It’s not that easy,” he muttered, his hands shifting behind his back and returning to the surface to reveal a handgun.

Casey scooted back in his bed until he hit the wall, his eyes nearly popping out of his head in horror. “Joe, what the hell is going on? What are you doing?”

“Don’t you remember why the man told us the ‘biggest fear’ setting was out of order?” Joe stood up from where he knelt and used the hand holding the gun to wipe the tears from his eyes. “It was because that lady’s biggest fear wasn’t just an apparition; it came to life. Remember?”

Casey opened his mouth to reply, but all he could do was nod his head.

“Well, my biggest fear was that I would have to kill the only people I loved.” Joe’s sobs were coming back, and he was licking his lips and staring at the ceiling as if he had gone entirely insane. “But my parents never really loved me, and I never really loved them… not in the way that I loved you guys.”

Casey saw where this was going, and he thrust his hands out in front of his face as his friend began to raise the gun. “Joe,” he screamed. “Joe, it’s just a game! You don’t need to do this, buddy. Please, don’t!”

“It’s not me,” Joe murmured between sobs, pointing the gun at Casey’s head. “It’s Deimos. He talked to me; he told me to. Bobby and Willy are already gone… I’m sorry, but you have to go too.”

They were caught in an agonizing stalemate for about a minute; Casey was crying and sputtering as Joe held him at gunpoint with shaky hands. Despite their wails and their yells, however, nobody came to their aid. They were forced to bear the face of mortality like men, and it had turned them both in blubbering babies. The only thing that could silence their cries was the sound of a gunshot, and it finally came roaring through the room in two momentous *pop*s.

By the time Casey’s parents finally came stumbling downstairs from their bedroom to see what had been happening, they would find that the bodies of two terribly terrified boys had been replaced with the bodies of two peacefully dead ones.

The End

Made in the USA
Middletown, DE
07 November 2018